Mission: Soul Sacrifice

Book Two of the *Escape the New Immortals* Series

William Fietzer

Mission: Soul Sacrifice

Story Copyright@William Fietzer 2022

Book Design Copyright@Cactus Moon Publications, LLC 2022

All rights reserved. No part of this book may be reproduced or transmitted in any form or by any means—electronic or mechanical including photocopying and recording—without written permission of the Publisher, except when permitted by law.

This is a work of fiction, and all characters were created by the author's imagination. Any semblance to persons living or dead is coincidental.

Cactus Moon Publications, LLC
2407 W Nopal Ave; Mesa, AZ 85202
www.cactusmoonpublishing.com

Book Two in the series – *Escape the New Immortals*

ISBN: 978-1-7347865-4-5

This book is dedicated to psychiatrist, philosopher, and Holocaust survivor, *Dr. Viktor Frankl*, whose own search for meaning in life inspires mine.

Acknowledgments

Numerous people helped bring this book to fruition. First, of course, are Kelsey Wiseman, my editor, and Lily Woodmansee, my publisher at Cactus Moon Publishing.

Second are my colleagues at two writing groups of which I've been a member. This novel wouldn't be nearly as realistic without their helpful suggestions and keen criticisms.

Third and last are my wife and extended family without whose emotional support the grind of creating and readying a novel for publication might have overwhelmed me.

Introduction

This introduction includes terminology, word definitions, and concepts particular to the mythologies of the ancient Greeks, Zoroastrians, and Kurgan (later Germanic/Norse) peoples. By no means definitive nor exhaustive, it itemizes in thumbnail fashion the ancient archetypes that legions of authors over the centuries have mined and added to their stories.

Acheron (River of Woe or Misery)—the river which provides entrance to the realm of Hades in Greek mythology.

Adrasteia (The Inescapable)—Greek goddess who taps on her tympanum to accompany Nyx's chanting by which the whole universe moves in ecstatic dance.

Aeacus—a son of Zeus and king of the isle of Aegina, he became one of the three judges in Hades upon his death, specifically concerned with the disposition of European souls in Hades.

Ahura Mazda (Lord of Wisdom)—the beneficent brother in the Zurvanite branch of the Zoroastrian religion.

Alecto (Greek Goddess of Endless Anger)—she is one of the three Erinyes which guard the inmates imprisoned in Tartarus.

Anausavared (Persian name; New Immortals in English)—term that refers to the Sassanid nobility whose warriors never seemed to die in battle.

Angra Mainyu (Ahriman in Persian)—evil brother of Ahura Mazda who Zurvan decrees shall lose dominion over the Earth to his good brother after their battle at the End Time.

Brisingamen—a gold, interlocking ring necklace worn by Freya which focuses her magic powers.

Cerberus—in Greek mythology a three-headed guard dog who blocked the ravine leading to the Fields of Asphodel and prevented unprepared souls from receiving judgment.

Cocytus (circular River of Wailing)—river associated with murderers that flows into the Acheron.

Dakhanavar (Armenian word for vampire)—legendary creature which protected the area around Mt. Ararat from intruders by sucking out their blood through the soles of their feet. In this book, an eponym for the region in the Lower World inhabited by Angra Mainyu/Ahriman and his demons.

Elysian Fields (Elysium)—paradise in the Greek afterlife for the righteous, the heroic, and those chosen by the gods; also known as the Isle of the Blessed,

End Time (Last Days, Final Days, Doomsday)—beliefs about mankind's ultimate destiny; in this book's case, how Ahura Mazda will defeat his evil brother Angra Mainyu/Ahriman after 9000 years and rule Earth for eternity.

Eponym—term taken from the Greek for the name of a thing or place which originates from that of some person (real or fictional) such as Rocky Balboa of the Rocky film series.

Erinyes (Furies)—three daughters of Hades and Nyx—Alecto, Megaera, and **Tisiphone**—which according to Virgil guard the fortress of Tartarus and torment the prisoners held within.

Fields of Asphodel (Asphodel Meadows)—the neutral place in Hades where people who led ordinary lives go after they drink from the river Lethe.

Freya (Norse Freja, The Lady)—goddess of love, beauty, fertility, sex, war, gold, seeing and influencing the future, and ruler of Folkvangr where half of those souls who die in battle go in the afterlife.

Hayastan—name for the ancient kingdom of Armenia derived from Hayk, the first ruler and great-great grandson of Noah; the Persian "stan" was added in the Middle Ages.

Hermes (Mercury in Roman mythology)—Greek trickster and herald of the gods, he protects travelers, thieves, merchants, and orators and also acts as a "soul guide" in the afterlife.

Keres (singular: Ker)—Greek female death spirits which hovered over battlefields and feasted on the blood of the wounded or dying.

Lethe (Greek River of Forgetfulness)—a river in Hades whose name comes from the goddess of oblivion and enables souls sent to Hades to forget their earthly lives.

Megaera (Greek Goddess of Jealous Rage)—one of the three Erinyes which guard the inmates imprisoned in Tartarus.

Minos—another son of Zeus and king of Crete, he became a member of the tribunal of judges in Hades, casting the deciding vote on the disposition of souls in the Greek underworld.

Mount Ararat—mountain in eastern Turkey that is the purported resting place of Noah's ark, symbol on the Armenian national flag, and home of the ancient state of Hayastan.

Nyx (Goddess of the Night)—first principle in Greek mythology who lives in a cave and whose chanting moves the entire universe.

Phlegethon (River of Blazing Blood)—the river in Hades that surrounds the fortress of Tartarus used to imprison mortals who had sinned against the gods.

Psychic vampire—term for a group of beings who feed off the mental energy (particularly negative) of other humans instead of their blood.

Psychopomp (Guider of Souls in Greek)—a spirit or deity which guides newly deceased souls to the afterlife. Hermes is one.

Rhadamanthys (Radamanthus)—the wise king of Crete, upon his death he became another of the "judges of the dead" in Hades, specially deciding the disposition of Asian souls in the afterlife.

Shahanshah (King of Kings in old Persian)—the title given to the ruler of the Sassanid empire which ruled from 224 B.C. to 651 A.D., making it the longest-lived imperial Persian dynasty.

Styx—one of five rivers that flow through Hades, it also is the name of the marsh where the five rivers converge at the entrance to the Underworld.

Sessrúmnir (Seat-room in old Norse)—name of Freya's hall where half of those slain in battle forever feast and tell war stories.

Tartarus—a deep abyss used as a dungeon to torment and punish the Titans; later writers such as Virgil described it as a forbidding fortress with high and impenetrable bronze walls.

Thunraz (Thor in old Norse, Thunder in German)—the god of lightning, thunder, storms, sacred groves and trees, strength, veneration, and the protection of mankind.

Tisiphone (Greek Goddess of Vengeful Destruction")—the fiercest of the three Erinyes which guard and punish the inmates imprisoned in Tartarus.

Vahagn—god of fire, thunder, and war in ancient Armenia and celebrated fighter of dragons; later identified with the Greek hero Herakles (Hercules).

Wodenaz (Proto-Germanic name; Odin in German meaning Lord of Frenzy)—the god associated with wisdom, healing, death, royalty, the gallows, knowledge, war, battle, victory, sorcery, poetry, frenzy, and the runic alphabet.

Zalim—Turkish name which translates to cruel or brutal in English; more generally, blood-thirsty, tyrant or demon to connote the vampirical nature of this group of beings.

Zoroastrianism—one of the world's oldest religions, it has a dualistic cosmology set within a monotheistic framework of good and evil. In the context of this book, the Zurvanite form was practiced by the Sassanids who ruled Eastern Turkey at the time of the Anausavareds.

Zurvan—First Principle or creator deity (Time) in the fatalistic branch of Zoroastrianism which created the equal but opposite twins Ahura Mazda (Good) and Angra Mainyu (Evil).

{1}

As a rule, sacrifice involves surrendering a person, animal or possession in worship of a deity or supernatural being. It should not be done on behalf of the self and never for revenge.

Such spiritual concerns were far from psychologist Victor Furst's mind, but they soon would form the heart of his existence. At the moment, however, he let the thrust from the Blue Air 737 passenger jet push him against the back cushion of his window seat as the plane rumbled down the runway, skipped twice, and lifted into the sky. Bucharest's plowed fields and housing developments surrounding the airport diminished and blended into the late afternoon rain clouds cloaking the mountaintops around the Romanian plain.

Victor's elation rippled through his lanky body. As the plane soared to cruising altitude, he closed his bloodshot brown eyes and savored every bit of the sensation. It didn't match the ecstasy he experienced when entering the alternate reality of another person's psyche, but his buoyant sense of relief at their escape from the Lower World of Hades was undeniable.

My resurrection, perhaps?

He scratched his salt-and-ginger beard and grimaced.

Probably not.

He wanted their freedom to be permanent and everlasting, but not at the expense of his ethics as a psychologist and shaman. Though he vowed never to let his shamanic powers be used for evil purposes, he'd agreed never again to use them against that psychic parasite, Basil Zarkisian, in order to secure the release of his ex-wife's soul. Whatever joy he might derive from making such an agreement, the expressions on the faces of the two women seated beside him showed him it was a false euphoria.

With a feeling of both accomplishment and concern, Victor eyed his ex-wife, Evelyn, dozing between him and her sister, Desdemona, seated on the aisle. Together with Desdemona's help, he had freed Evelyn's conscious self from the alternate reality of Hades and the energy drainer who stranded it there—Basil Zarkisian. Evelyn slumbered like an exhausted child, her honey-blonde tresses encircling her head like a burnt-gold wreath; however, her sweaty forehead, rapid breathing, and sudden twitches suggested her sleep was anything but soothing.

Just as troubling to Victor was Desdemona's apparent lack of concern. She adjusted her seat and fiddled with the head rests to make herself more comfortable, as though securing Evelyn's release had been the simplest thing in the world. Desdemona had aided him in her sister's escape from Hades, to be sure, but she also had helped Zarkisian trap her soul there in the first place. Did her current indifference signal her break from him? Or, was she spying in Zarkisian's behalf? The shield that went up whenever he probed her psyche suggested the latter.

"There," Desdemona said, satisfied with the arrangement of her head rests. She glanced toward her sister and smiled her approval. "Sleeping like a baby." Desdemona's dark gray eyes glinted at Victor like reflections off a gun barrel. "Wouldn't you say?"

"I hope she is," Victor replied, frowning. "How can you be so certain?"

"Why not?" Desdemona folded her puffy, delicate hands in her lap. "We're a hundred miles away from Zarkisian and getting farther all the time. Soon the Atlantic Ocean will separate us from his psychic power."

"Three fugitives," Victor replied with a sour smile. "With no passports. We're not free yet."

"You needn't sound so dire," Desdemona said, settling back in her chair. "There's plenty of time to come up with something before we change planes in Liverpool. Let's enjoy freedom while we can."

Four hours isn't much freedom. Victor scanned the dark clouds clotting the sky over the Carpathian Mountains beneath their plane. He wanted to share Desdemona's optimism, but their fugitive status bothered him.

Evelyn's legs twitched again.

"That doesn't look like restful sleep to me," Victor said, pointing at Evelyn's leg movements. "You know leaving Lower World reality can have lasting consequences—mental and physical."

"I don't see any aftereffects," Desdemona replied, scanning her sleeping sister. "A sweaty face—turn up the air conditioning." She reached up and adjusted the knob. "Sudden movements?" She reached across Evelyn's lap. "Loosen her seatbelt."

She unsnapped Evelyn's belt and watched her sister nestle into her chair. "There," Desdemona said, grinning at Victor. "Accept her sleep for what it is—simple exhaustion."

"Evelyn has never slept on a plane to my knowledge," Victor replied. "Ever."

Desdemona's pale lips pursed into a thin beige line. "Was that before or after you abandoned your family?"

Victor gritted his teeth. *Must she remind him of that, too?* "It seemed at the time the best way to protect her and Miriam from Zarkisian."

"By leaving her?"

"By drawing his attention away from them." Victor folded his wiry arms across his chest in irritation. "How can you still doubt my faithfulness after I've rescued her?"

Evelyn stirred and turned toward her sister, a golden tress cascading into her mouth. She pushed it aside but did not waken.

"You see?" Victor burst out. A dusky, slender flight attendant dealing with another passenger a few rows ahead turned in their direction and knitted her eyebrows. They didn't need to call attention to themselves, Victor realized. Evelyn twitched again, and he lowered his voice. "See that?"

"See what?" Desdemona replied. "Evelyn changed position, that's all."

"She displayed the same symptoms when I examined her at Walter Reed Hospital."

Evelyn stirred again, turning this time toward Victor. Her cheeks flushed and her breathing grew raspy. She wriggled once more, faced straight ahead, and lunged forward.

"Angra Mainyu, Angra Mainyu!" she mumbled and kicked the bottom of the seat in front of her. "ANGRA MAINYU!"

A cadaverous, braceleted hand shot up to the call monitor above the seat in front of them. The flight attendant's signal bonged.

"Evelyn," Desdemona said in a calm, firm voice as she pulled Evelyn back into her seat. "Evelyn, wake up."

Evelyn's sapphire eyes popped open. They scanned Victor and Desdemona, her pupils blazing like diamond needle-points, but she recognized neither of them.

The willowy flight attendant materialized above Desdemona's shoulder. "Is something the matter?"

"No, nothing," Desdemona answered with a yawn and sat back in her seat. "Everything's fine."

Evelyn's pupils dimmed as realization came back to her. She brushed her disheveled hair from her face, rubbed her neck, and beamed a shaky smile at the flight attendant. "Must have been sleeping wrong."

"A bad dream," Victor added, smiling at Evelyn for the attendant's benefit. "Sorry for the disturbance. We'll make sure she stays quiet."

The attendant's ebony eyes scanned all three of them. "OK, then," she said, grimacing. "See that you do."

After the attendant comforted the old woman seated in front of Evelyn, she returned to her station in the rear of the plane. Desdemona grabbed Evelyn's hand. "Are you all right?"

Evelyn cupped her right temple. "I think so."

She's unsure. "Do you remember anything?" Victor asked.

Evelyn hesitated, her eyes flitting back in forth in self-examination. "Not a thing." She shook her head. "I was dreaming, I think, then a curtain came down, and I wasn't there anymore."

Desdemona frowned. "What do mean you weren't there?"

"No presence, no sense of self." Evelyn ran a shaky hand through her hair and flashed Victor a broken smile. "Am I losing my mind, Victor?"

"No, no," Victor replied and squeezed her arm in reassurance. This could be worse than he thought. "Do you remember what you were dreaming before the curtain descended?"

"No. Nothing," Evelyn replied.

"Are you feeling different in any way?" Victor asked.

"I feel fine." Evelyn took more internal inventory and frowned. "A bit tired." Her wispy brows beetled in bewilderment. "I never sleep like this on planes."

"It's not surprising given all you've been through," Victor replied, masking his concern. Nothing felt different about her—or was he unable to sense it? "Just a matter of sleeping too hard."

"Here, dearie." Desdemona pressed the flaps of Evelyn's head rest tight against Evelyn's temples. Once she was sure Evelyn was secure, she stood and reached into the overhead bin to pull down Evelyn's overcoat. "Let's get you comfortable."

"My big sis," Evelyn giggled, wriggled her athletic frame under her overcoat, and closed her eyes. "Always taking care of me." Her left eye popped open and eyed Victor. "Unlike some people I know."

"You're lucky to have her," Victor agreed and pulled the collar under Evelyn's chin. "I'll keep the bogeyman away."

"See that you do." Evelyn smiled, snuggled further under her coat, and yawned. "Remember," she said, enclosing Victor's wrist in a delicate embrace. "I'm counting on you."

She trusts me.

Victor swallowed the lump in his throat and glanced at Desdemona.

More than her sister?

He noted the harsh lines of disapproval punctuating the corners of Desdemona's mouth.

Don't turn Evelyn's affection into a popularity contest.

Victor grimaced, removed Evelyn's fingers from his wrist, and watched as Evelyn fell fast asleep. Desdemona leaned over and studied her slumbering sister for a moment. Smiling her satisfaction, she bobbed her iron gray head in Victor's direction. "How do you think she is now?"

"I'm not sure," Victor replied, stroking his beard. "It looks like a simple case of night terrors—"

"Which she's never had in her life," Desdemona finished.

"Or Zarkisian's not through with her," Victor said.

"I don't believe it." Desdemona shivered. "He promised he wouldn't bother us."

"And you believe him?" Victor replied.

Desdemona shrugged. "I don't have to. A psychic vampire's mind-draining ability doesn't work over this much distance."

"It does seem improbable," Victor replied with a skeptic shake of his head. "He's miles away as you said—probably in another country if he's on the plane we saw him boarding at Orsova airport."

"How can we be sure?" Desdemona's chin quivered, revealing her growing doubt. "Ordinary distance and time have little meaning in the alternate reality of the Lower World."

"True," Victor replied. "And the repetition of Evelyn's previous symptoms signals Zarkisian's renewed power over her, something her conscious self wouldn't recognize. But I'd have to enter Evelyn's mind to know for sure."

"What's stopping you?" Desdemona asked.

"This is neither the time nor the place," Victor replied. "Evelyn's exhaustion reflects the physical strain she endured when we revived her soul from the dead."

"Which is more important?" Desdemona replied. "Our freedom or Evelyn's well-being?"

"The latter, of course." Victor glanced toward the attendant's station where the lithe young woman was loading the snack cart. "We've already alerted the flight attendant to us."

"Humph." Desdemona's jawline hardened. "You decide."

Victor hesitated. Evelyn's welfare was paramount, of course, but entering a person's consciousness without their permission violated the shamanic code of protecting personal privacy. And drawing more attention to them jeopardized their already chancy reentry into the United States. So why was Desdemona ready for him to reenter Evelyn's mind when a moment before she'd dismissed Evelyn's symptoms as over-exhaustion? Would he discover that motivation as well?

"Fine." Victor squared his shoulders. "I'll do it. But without a drum beat to focus on, the results won't be conclusive in a noisy, uncontrolled environment like this."

"I'll slap my hand on top of my thigh," Desdemona suggested. "The sound from that won't draw much attention."

Desdemona began tapping her thigh. When she achieved a regular rhythm, Victor started counting. "Speed it up," he said after a minute. "When we did this last time, I counted four beats per second before reaching the threshold of alternate reality."

He closed his eyes and focused on the rhythm of his heart thrumming in his ears.

"Faster," he ordered.

Desdemona groaned and sped up her tempo.

"Faster," Victor urged.

Desdemona heightened the tempo of her thigh taps.

"There," Victor said when he counted four thigh taps for every beat of his heart. "Maintain that tempo."

With Desdemona's steady staccato as backdrop, Victor spied afterimages of Evelyn and Desdemona float upon the back of his eyelids, coalesce, and fade into a blue-black drapery punctuated by shimmering stars and bars. He slowed his breathing and imagined himself penetrating the energy field surrounding Evelyn's body, flowing up the vertical energy meridians traversing her chest, and heading toward the Ajna chakra between her eyes, the third-eye gateway to the pineal gland and her subconscious.

The *Ganzfeld Effect*, that instant of blindness before the colors and geometrical patterns which mark the euphoria of crossing into another person's energy field, did not occur. The stars and bars glimmered and faded, glimmered and faded, then turned gray rather than evaporating into the subtle blackness Victor was used to encountering.

Sensing no resistance from Evelyn, he leaned closer and tried again—still no moment of crossover. Was it their environment? Was Zarkisian responsible somehow? He reached inside Evelyn's overcoat, enclosed her clammy left hand in his right and tried again. Still no result.

He pressed his forehead against Evelyn's, minimizing the distance between his and her third eye chakras. Still, the blackness did not come.

"It's no use, Desdemona," Victor mumbled. "Sto—"

The star-spangled curtain before his eyes paled and dissolved, replaced by a visual and auditory static like that found on vintage black-and-white television sets. Dim, elongated shapes like giant, fluttering seagulls swooped into a crowd of terrified male and female silhouettes. The figures screamed in terror as they sought refuge from the winged attacks. Cackles of satisfaction soared above the tumult.

BONG!
BONG!
BONG!

{2}

"Wha—wha?" Victor forced open his eyes. The seatbelt sign flashed above his head. The captain's voice crackled over the loudspeaker, first in Romanian, and then repeated in English, "We await turbulence the rest of our way to Liverpool airport. Please return to your seats and fasten your seatbelts."

The plane bucked, plummeted, and stabilized. Evelyn's eyes popped open. She clutched Victor's arm. The plane plummeted again and Victor's stomach slammed violently against his rib cage.

"Angra Mainyu," Evelyn chanted, terrified. "ANGRA MAINYU!"

Victor's cell phone vibrated inside his pants pocket.

Damn! I thought I'd switched it to airplane mode!

He fumbled inside his pants pocket and pried it out on his third attempt. He did not recognize the international phone number it displayed.

Who'd call me up here?

"He-hello?" he answered.

"This is Armenian Consular Section Chief Todd Helsingford," a husky male voice announced on his phone. When Victor did not respond, Todd added, "Miriam's former fiancé?"

Calls from Miriam's jilted suitors were of no concern to Victor when their lives were at stake now. The plane bucked again, and Victor ended the call.

Victor's phone rang a second time; he did not answer. As the phone continued to vibrate, Evelyn's eyes sparkled. "Answer it."

"Now?" Victor asked. "In the middle of this storm?"

"It's about Miriam," Evelyn replied, frowning with concentration. "She's in trouble."

"H-huh?" Victor replied in amazement. "How do you know that?"

The plane rocked again and slammed Victor's phone hand against his seat rest, which sent his phone scuttering under his seat. He leaned forward, his fingers scrabbling for the elusive device. When he retrieved it, a different phone number showed on the display. Reluctantly, Victor again answered his phone.

"This is Ambassador Harrison Gifford calling Dr. Victor Furst," the resonant male voice announced, "on a matter of national security."

Victor enclosed the phone between his thumb and index finger. "I have nothing to say," he replied, heeding his promise to Zarkisian. "To you or the State Department."

"If you've heard about the current developments in the Middle East," Gifford said, "you owe it to your country to hear Mr. Helsingford out."

"I have not," Victor said. "I expect you, Mr. Helsingford, and the rest of the State Department will act in our best interests."

As she watched Victor abruptly end the call, Evelyn knit her brows together. "It WAS about Miriam."

"It had nothing to do with Miriam," Victor replied. How had she reached that conclusion? Evelyn's renewed interest in things happening around her was an encouraging yet puzzling sign. The plane bucked again. "We have more pressing concerns—like our plane crashing."

The floor rumbled beneath their feet. Evelyn ignored it. "Tell the truth, Victor."

He studied his ex-wife's face. Color had returned to her cheeks; her eyes were clear yet concerned. A direct call from the State Department—if something *was* wrong with Miriam, could Evelyn handle it? "It was Todd Helsingford," Victor said. "Calling from the State Department."

"Angra Mainyu." Evelyn clutched her arms against her chest. Her whole body quivered. "Angra Mainyu."

"There, there, Evie." Desdemona patted her sister's shoulder. "Don't excite yourself. He may just be wondering whether Miriam's still in New York."

"Angra Mainyu!" Evelyn wrenched herself away from Desdemona's grip and stood up, quivering all over. "Angra Mainyu."

Something *was* wrong. Evelyn wouldn't continue this behavior otherwise. Victor's phone rang again. He grabbed Evelyn's arm and pulled her back into her seat.

"Don't hang up," Todd said when Victor answered. "It involves Miriam."

"Todd?" Evelyn grabbed Victor's phone. "Is Miriam all right?"

"Miriam is OK, Evelyn," Todd replied. "Please let me speak with Dr. Furst."

Evelyn bit her lip in disappointment. She wanted Todd to supply more details yet handed Victor his phone.

"Please hear me out," Todd said.

The hairs on Victor's hands bristled with fight-or-flight expectancy. Evelyn fidgeted in her seat while Desdemona watched her with dour concern. Given Evelyn's agitated state, this call signaled an involvement in Zarkisian's plans Victor had sworn to avoid. If it involved Miriam, however, he owed it to Evelyn to at least listen. "You have one minute."

"I'm calling from the Khor Virap monastery on the border of Armenia and Turkey," Todd said. "I won't go into details, but I'm here as a result of yesterday's explosion at the American embassy in Yerevan. Our information shows the perpetrators are an Armenian nationalist revolutionary group called the Anausavareds—New Immortals in English—who have seized the area around Mt. Ararat in an attempt to reestablish the ancient kingdom of Hayastan in eastern Turkey."

"Very interesting, Mr. Helsingford," Victor replied. Noting both women's rapt attention to what they could hear of the conversation, he switched his connection to speakerphone but lowered the volume and motioned them to lean closer to the phone.

"What does that have to do with us?" Victor asked in a low voice.

"I believe the leader of the New Immortals is someone you've worked with before—Basil Zarkisian?"

Evelyn gasped; Desdemona bit her lip. "That was a long time ago—twenty-five years," Victor replied, wiping his sweating palms on his trousers. "Anything I could tell you about that gentleman occurred before the American CIA's involvement in Operation Desert Storm."

"That's it, exactly," Todd said. "We need to know the details of your Psy-ops tactics leading up to the invasion of Baghdad."

"Why?" Victor asked. The plane shuddered beneath his feet. Rain pelted the window with sludgy streaks. "That was a long time ago in a war that nobody cares about anymore."

"Well, I do," Todd replied.

"Again, I ask 'why?'"

"Because we have reports that they're using some of the same psychological tactics you and Dr. Zarkisian developed on our troops surrounding Mt. Ararat."

"Hmmm." Victor stroked his ruddy beard. Had Zarkisian learned to apply his mind-draining abilities to more than one person? "That is concerning. But field reports aren't always reliable."

"I know first-hand what the New Immortals' psychic powers can do," Todd replied and lowered his voice to an awestruck whisper. "I saw an Azeri terrorist leader drop dead beside me during a meeting with Zarkisian."

Victor's skin prickled. Zarkisian had upped the stakes—using his mind-draining powers to kill. "Could it be a coincidence?" Victor replied, remembering he agreed not to interfere in Zarkisian's activities. "Or something he was suffering from already?"

"It could be, yes," Todd said. "His colleagues called it zar, a disease of the mind—with fatal consequences in his case. All I know is he displayed none of its symptoms before our meeting with Zarkisian."

"Then I suggest you talk with him again," Victor replied, the plane rumbling beneath his feet. "He's still with the Department of Defense as I recall."

"Not anymore," Todd replied. "He's somewhere outside the United States, perhaps the Middle East—we think Eastern Turkey around Mt. Ararat."

"Get in touch with—Aw—argh!"

The plane plummeted for what seemed an eternity, then suddenly righted itself and stabilized; the unexpected jerking of the plane sent Victor's phone to the floor again.

"Dr. Furst, are you there?" Victor heard Todd asking. He searched under his seat, seized the unruly phone, and plastered it against his ear. "Look, Todd," Victor said after checking whether Evelyn and Desdemona were all right. "Unless you can control the weather over Central Europe or get us through customs when and if we land, I can't help you."

"But—"

"We have our own problems to deal with," Victor said and closed the connection.

Evelyn eyed him like a detention hall monitor. "You weren't very polite to him, Victor."

"This isn't the time for politeness," Victor said, the plane bumping again. "Zarkisian's clout with Romanian officials got us onto this plane without passports." He glanced at Desdemona and she nodded in confirmation. "Even if we make it through this storm, I think he expects American or, in this case, British security officials to arrest us when we enter customs."

Victor rubbed his neck in apprehension. Their legal situation was worse than misplaced passports. If the custom officials discovered Evelyn's fugitive status, Victor and Desdemona's roles in aiding and abetting her made them criminals too.

Evelyn focused on the backs of her hands to quash her uneasiness. "What do we do, Victor?"

The shuddering aircraft bumped and leveled off.

"First, we get our coats," Victor replied, signaling with his thumb for Desdemona to open the overhead storage bin. "Assuming there's no more turbulence, we have an hour before we land," he added after she distributed their wraps. "As soon as our plane lands, we make a run for it."

Fifty minutes later their plane descended beneath the leaden clouds and skittered onto Liverpool's rain-slick tarmac. While it taxied to the gangway, Victor gathered his coat around his shoulders. "Gather your things and follow me."

Muscling his way into the aisle before the plane stopped, he bulldozed into the people between them and first class. If they left ahead of the other passengers in coach, they might blend with those in first class whose random actions leaving the plane British security and immigration agents were less likely to notice. Between the gangway and the immigration check booths they could slip through or under a crowd control tape, find an exit door, and escape. After that, they'd take their chances.

But they didn't reach the check-in station. Three British immigration agents dressed in blue shirts with black epaulets and tiny white lettering waited for them at the head of the jetway. Victor peered over the shoulder of the ground assistant receiving baggage from his partner that couldn't be stored in overhead bins. *Too narrow an opening and too high a jump to the concrete for safety.*

Sighing, he escorted the two women up the jet way.

Mission: Soul Sacrifice

A hulking, middle-aged agent stepped forward. "Are you Dr. Victor Furst?" he asked in a low feathery voice. When Victor nodded, he turned toward Evelyn and Desdemona. "Evelyn and Desdemona Gorovic?"

They nodded and he nodded back. "Fine. Come with us, please."

"Wh—where are we going?" Evelyn asked.

"Airport British Immigration office," the officer replied.

"You're arresting us?" Desdemona declared.

"Detaining you," the officer replied.

"We've done nothing wrong," Desdemona protested.

"That's for your criminal justice system to decide," he replied and motioned his two companions to stand behind Victor and the women. "Come along, please."

He turned on his heel and started up the jetway. His two companion officers edged forward, herding the trio ahead of them.

"This is too much," Victor said, surging to the lead officer's side. "Where are you taking us, Mr., er—"

"Officer Connery," the official replied. "John Connery with a J—no relation," he added, unsmiling. "Liverpool Airport Border Office."

Zarkisian's behind this, Victor decided as they marched through the crowds of people arriving and departing for their destinations. "How'd you learn about us?"

"Your Homeland Security alerted us."

"How did they know we'd be on this plane?" Victor asked.

"You'd have to ask them."

Zarkisian.

Victor and the others descended the escalator under the sign headed Baggage Claim and Ground Transport, passed through a bank of acrylic glass doors, and approached an office door with Border Patrol stenciled in small, Arial type above it. The window beside the door resembled a bank teller's window.

"Stop in front of the window, please," Connery ordered, turning to face them. "All three of you."

"I want to speak to a lawyer," Desdemona demanded.

"As soon as you're processed," Connery replied.

"How long do you plan to keep us?" Victor asked.

"Until we make arrangements to turn you over to your government officials," Connery said.

"I want to speak to a lawyer," Desdemona cried again. "NOW!"

"Angra Mainyu," Evelyn muttered, trembling all over. "ANGRA MAINYU!"

"What's wrong with her?" Connery asked, cocking a cynical brow. "Is she ill?"

"She suffered a difficult experience overseas," Victor explained while Desdemona stroked the back of Evelyn's hand to calm her. "This detainment procedure upsets her."

"It bothers everyone," Connery replied. "It isn't meant to be fun."

Victor glanced at the travelers passing back and forth, too preoccupied with their own problems to notice the disturbance by the office. One or two glanced over their shoulders in their direction once they'd passed. "Is this public exposure necessary?" he asked. "Isn't there someplace more private?"

"In here." Connery guided them inside the door. Behind the small office stood two cramped cells.

"Is that where you're holding us?" Desdemona gasped.

"ANGRA MAINYU!" Evelyn shouted, shaking all over. "ANGRA MAINYU!"

Desdemona turned toward Victor. "Help her, Victor." She turned to Connery. "Can't you get somebody to help her!"

"Cavanaugh, call the rescue unit," Connery ordered. "We need medical assistance."

Mission: Soul Sacrifice

"That's not necessary," Victor said while Connery's second in command pressed a quick dial button on his phone. He turned toward Desdemona. "Calm down. You know Evelyn reacts to the mood of her surroundings." He turned to Connery. "Don't you have something a little less intimidating?"

"We're not running a hotel," Connery retorted.

"I'm not asking that," Victor replied. "Something less institutional to settle her down."

Evelyn began dancing from one foot to the other. She shimmied around Connery twice like a belly dancer.

Cavanaugh looked up from his cell phone and frowned. "Bad news, Cap'n," he said, eying Evelyn shimmying around his commanding officer. "Air control grounded all planes until tomorrow morning due to the weather."

"OK," Connery sighed and turned back to Victor. "Make her stop, please."

Victor seized Evelyn's wrists, but she continued hopping from one foot to the other like an anxious child in a game of musical chairs waiting for the music to stop. "Time for rest, Evelyn."

"Yes, rest," she murmured. "Need rest."

What does she mean? When Evelyn's hops diminished to trembling, Victor signaled with the shrug of his shoulder toward Desdemona to pick up Evelyn's overcoat.

Desdemona hesitated, frowning.

"Pick up Evelyn's coat and wrap it around her shoulders," Victor ordered.

Desdemona did not move.

"Wrap her coat around her shoulders, and draw her to you," Victor ordered, releasing Evelyn's wrists.

"What will that accomplish?" Desdemona asked.

"To comfort her," Victor replied, exasperated by her obstinacy. "Just do it!"

"NO REST!" Evelyn protested when Desdemona opened the coat and approached her. "NOT NOW! NOT EVER!"

Eluding Desdemona's grasp, she shimmied around Connery once more.

"Make her stop," Connery ordered through gritted teeth. "This is the last time I'll be nice about it."

Evelyn raised her arms above her head and shimmied around Connery a third time. Victor grabbed her right wrist and pulled her toward him, but Evelyn wrenched herself free. She dodged Desdemona and headed for the doorway, but Officer Jones cut off her escape.

"Angra Mainyu!" Evelyn chanted, her eyes darting from one to the other of her would-be captors, as they encircled her in front of the desk. "No rest. EVER!"

Connery flicked his eyes in Cavanaugh's direction. The security officer plunged between Victor and Desdemona and grabbed Evelyn's left wrist. Evelyn plunged and twisted like a calf being branded while Cavanaugh clamped a manacle around Evelyn's wrist.

"You're hurting her!" Desdemona cried.

"Do your job, Cavanaugh!" Connery exclaimed and motioned toward Cavanaugh's partner. "Jones, keep her still."

"Handcuffs won't make her shimmying stop," Victor said, pushing the officers apart.

"They'll sure slow her down!" Jones replied, wrestling with the squirming Evelyn. "Get her other wrist, Cavanaugh."

B-r-r-r-ring!!

The noise blared from the black desk phone on top of the counter.

B-r-r-r-ring!!

Evelyn stopped struggling. Cavanaugh seized her other wrist and pulled it behind her back. Jones snapped the other cuff around it.

Evelyn did not notice. Instead, she stopped moving, and the pupils of her eyes focused on the desk phone like diamond pinpoints.

Something's up. Evelyn knows it. But how?

Victor scanned her body—no auras or obvious signs of psychic possession. Victor wheeled toward Connery as. the phone kept ringing. "Aren't you going to answer it?"

"Certainly," Connery harrumphed. "Keep her still," he said with a stiff nod toward his colleagues and picked up the receiver. "Connery here."

He said nothing for a minute, intent upon the communication from the other end. "You have their passports?" he asked and listened again. "Understood."

Connery handed the receiver to Victor. "He wants to speak to you."

"Who does?" Victor asked, bringing the receiver to his ear.

"I do, Dr. Furst." Todd Helsingford's voice crackled over the faulty connection. "Your emergency passports are ready—assuming you cooperate."

"And if I don't?"

"The system runs its course, and the FBI brings you home."

{3}

Victor glanced at the faces surrounding him— Evelyn's showed anxiety and Desdemona's disdain while professional detachment etched the countenances of Connery and his men.

Evelyn clutched Victor's coat sleeve. "Hear him out, Victor."

Tears welled up over the diamond pinpoints in her eyes, yet she seemed more herself again.

"It's about Miriam," Evelyn pleaded. "Please, Victor."

What choice do I have?

"OK," Victor sighed in acceptance and spoke into the phone. "What do you want to know?"

"Not there. Not now," Todd answered. "Give the phone back to Connery."

Victor did as Todd requested. Connery held the receiver against his ear, nodding every so often before hanging up.

"All right, then," Connery said, rubbing his hands together. He whirled toward Jones. "Take them to the airport guest house. Don't lock it; stand guard outside." He turned toward Victor. "No phones and no communication with anyone until your State Department calls us."

Cavanaugh and Jones shepherded Victor, Evelyn, and Desdemona through the bottom floor of the terminal to the airport shuttle. From there the shuttle took them through several interchanges to a three-story brick building at the end of one of the runways. After securing a room key, they took an elevator to the second floor where the agents deposited them inside a small hotel room with a double bed, desk, chair, and sofa, the sole concession to luxury its fireplace in the wall opposite the bed.

Victor side-stepped around the wiry Cavanaugh standing inside the doorway and helped Evelyn remove her overcoat. After draping it over the lone wire hanger in the closet, he helped Desdemona guide her sister to a seat beside her on the brown, pullout sofa. Victor pulled out the metal frame chair under the desk across from the women, plopped onto its worn cushion, and peered at Cavanaugh. "When do you figure we'll get to leave?"

"Assuming your paperwork arrives overnight," Cavanaugh said, scanning the room while thinking out loud, "the earliest available flight leaves seven a.m., sharp."

"Less than twelve hours from now," Victor replied.

"Do we get anything to eat in the meantime?" Desdemona asked.

"I'll order you some sandwiches," Cavanaugh replied. "OK?"

"It will have to do," Desdemona said.

A half hour later Cavanaugh entered the room and placed a box of vending machine sandwiches on the desk.

"Get some sleep after you're done," he advised. "You're in for a long day tomorrow."

Cavanaugh closed the hallway door with a click, and the shadows from his dress shoes peeped under the door jamb. Evelyn picked through the sandwiches in the box, then sat straight up on the edge of the sofa with her hands resting on her knees.

"Better eat something," Victor coaxed, grabbing an egg salad that looked OK.

"I'm not hungry," Evelyn replied.

"Try and get some sleep then," Victor said, placing a hand over hers.

"Not yet." Evelyn pulled her knee away. "Not until Todd calls again."

"It could be a while," Victor replied, offering her a baloney sandwich. "This isn't much, but you need to maintain your strength."

"I don't care." Evelyn's jawline hardened. "How can I eat when Miriam's out there all alone?"

"How do you know she is all alone?" Victor asked. "Todd said she was OK."

Evelyn's eyes flitted back and forth in self-examination, then leveled on Victor's. "I don't care what Todd said, I know what I know!"

Victor shrugged. What other answer did he expect? He glanced up at Desdemona eating a cheese sandwich and pointed at the bed. "All yours, if you want it."

"No, thanks." Desdemona's jawline mimicked Evelyn's as she ate beside her sister. "I'll wait with my sister."

"Fine," Victor replied. *No surprise there—what is she waiting for?* "We'll all wait."

He scooched his buttocks against the chair's hard back and gulped his sandwich in four bites, its spicy flavor reminding him how hungry he was. "Maybe there's enough time to make sense of all that's happened."

"If that's possible," Desdemona said in derision, putting half her sandwich back in the box. She turned toward Evelyn and tucked throw pillows behind her sister's back to make her comfortable. Evelyn leaned back against the pillows, shuddered, and closed her eyes.

Was Evelyn's shaking a reaction to England's damp, Victor wondered, or left over from their exchanges with the border control agents?

Victor frowned. Evelyn's emotional sensitivity raised a third possibility. After witnessing Desdemona's indignant behavior towards him and the Border Patrol officers, he mistrusted her motives more than ever. Him he could understand, but the officers? Why antagonize them? What could she gain? How could he know for certain without penetrating her mind?

Evelyn trembled again. Victor glanced at the fireplace. "Let's get some heat in here," he said, rising to his feet. But when he approached its glass doors, he found a coat of dust on the floor under the twin gas pipes, indicating the insert hadn't held a fire in some time.

He whirled about, scanned the room, spotted a wall grate beside the bed and a thermostat by the door. After a brief examination of the thermostat, Victor flipped the switch along the side of the tiny box, heard a gentle pop in the wall behind the bed, and felt a thin stream of heat emerging from the grate.

Evelyn sat up, leaned forward, and rubbed her forearms in the warm draft. Her facial features softened; the gas-fed warmth welled up in the azure depths of her eyes. Sighing, she leaned back against the pillows and closed her eyes again.

"Comfortable?" Victor asked. When Evelyn nodded, he wedged himself between the two women on the sofa until Desdemona scooted away. "I've always wanted a vacation in England."

"Yes," Evelyn replied with a dreamy smile. "Under different circumstances, I could stay here forever."

"As you wish." Victor waved his hand in an expansive swoop and took her hand in his. "I'd like that, too."

"Are you sure?" Evelyn frowned. "I'm not."

"Sure, I'm sure." Victor patted the back of her hand. "At least Zarkisian's not—"

"Zarkisian, Zarkisian!" Evelyn's eyes popped open, and she pulled her hand away. "That's all you ever think about."

"That's not what I meant."

"I told you it was over." She stood up, massaging the back of her hand as if to remove the memory of his touch. "Forget him."

"How can I?" Victor surged to his feet. "He put us in this spot."

"Shh!" Desdemona warned with a nod toward the shadows of the guard's feet under the hallway door. "Don't we have more important things to worry about?"

"Like what?" Victor said, turning toward Desdemona. "Tell me."

"Like our daughter," Evelyn answered.

"What *about* Miriam?" Victor asked, clenching his fists.

Mission: Soul Sacrifice

"Oh, Victor!" Evelyn sobbed, her eyes searching his face. "It's not about us anymore. Don't you know that by now?"

Victor gazed back at her with repressed jealousy and rage.

I DO know.

"I know very well," Victor replied through gritted teeth, "but I choose not to."

Evelyn covered her face with her hands, dashed into the tiny bathroom, and locked the door.

Both hands felt sore when Victor relaxed his grip. Red quarter moons marked where his nails had burrowed into his palms. He shook off the soreness and approached the bathroom door. He'd done everything in his power to protect Evelyn. Why couldn't she see that? "Come on out. Let's talk this over."

No answer. He tried again. Same result. The shadows of the guard's feet shifted under the door once more.

Desdemona stirred on the sofa. Victor whirled toward her.

"That didn't go well," Desdemona said, folding her hands in her lap, a sneer curling her mouth. "Did it?"

"Look, I restored her soul to consciousness, didn't I?" Victor replied, nettled by the truth of the observation. "And I took her away from the psychic vampire who created the need for me to do so. What more does she want?"

"She wants protection for her family."

"Miriam, you mean." Victor flushed.

Desdemona's eyes narrowed to slits. "Of course, Miriam."

His mind flashed back to Kuwait City before Miriam was conceived. "You know Zarkisian's power better than anyone. What more can I do?"

"Finish what you started," Desdemona replied.

"Someone to die for you and more, is that it?" Victor slapped his fist into his opposite hand. "Well, it ain't me," he growled, his knuckles grinding flesh, "Babe."

Desdemona glanced at the shadows showing under the locked hallway door behind Victor. "You have no choice."

The door clicked open, and Connery entered the room. He opened his right hand and extended Victor's cell phone to him. "Helsingford's on the line."

Victor took the phone from Connery's hand. After the Border agent left the room, the bathroom lock clicked, and Evelyn stepped out.

Victor studied Evelyn's face. Color had returned to her cheeks; her eyes were now clear yet concerned. Another direct call from the State Department—if something *was* wrong with Miriam, could Evelyn handle it?

He had to trust her spiritual strength. In exchange for her freedom, Victor's agreement with Zarkisian forbid him from interfering with anything Zarkisian did that involved Evelyn's mental or physical health. If he didn't keep his vow, he sacrificed all his integrity as a psychologist, shaman, and human being.

Helsingford could talk his head off, it didn't matter.

"Are you there?" Todd's voice asked.

"Yes, I'm here," Victor answered. Noting the intensity on the women's faces as they leaned toward him, he clicked the speaker phone icon. "We're all here."

"Fine. Fine," Todd responded. "And your accommodations are acceptable?"

"They're fine, too," Victor said, gritting his teeth at Todd's obedience to social decorum. "You said you had emergency passports for us. What is it you want to know in exchange for them?"

"OK, down to business," Todd chuckled. "I thought your knowledge of Zarkisian's Moonstruck program could be useful. You remember it?"

Victor said nothing.

"Well?"

"Ye-es," Victor replied. "My psy-ops work for the CIA. Not a time I'm proud of."

"Why not?"

"Because they're still killing each other over there!" Victor retreated to the desk chair, shaken at the memory of a program gone out of control. "We started out hoping to shorten the war and reduce the bloodshed. So many people killed—for what? Oil? Money? Power?"

He frowned. "What gives you the right to pry into my personal history?"

"The Second Gulf War is when you and Zarkisian split ways, right?" Todd asked.

"Our partnership broke up over the direction Moonstruck took between Operation Desert Storm and the Second Gulf War." Victor winced at the memory. "What does that have to do with the three of us?"

"Nothing, everything—I don't know yet," Todd replied. "He's the leader of the New Immortals, and you're the one person still alive who worked with him."

"What of it?"

"You're the only one who has any clue about who and what we're dealing with."

Victor grimaced. *Acknowledgement at last.*

"Why now?" Victor asked. "Nobody wanted to deal with my whistle-blowing at the time; now the government's admitting it made a mistake?"

"Mistake?"

"I went through all the proper channels with Special Activities Division and warned them about Zarkisian's operations. He used Moonstruck's mission statement as a psychological operations unit and turned it into an attack force dedicated to him body and soul to punish and eliminate his enemies inside and outside the Agency."

"Did you end the program?" Todd asked.

"I didn't have that authority," Victor replied. "My testimony at my SAD hearing ended with the same result as if I hadn't testified—nothing."

"You were a whistleblower, at least," Todd said. "That's commendable."

"Don't patronize me," Victor replied. "I told my superiors at the CIA that Zarkisian was dangerous, but they ignored me." Victor's neck prickled with resentment at the memory. "It sounds like professional jealousy, but Zarkisian's practices endangered a whole lot of people inside and outside the Agency."

"How do you know this?" Todd asked.

"I was one of them," Victor replied. "His agents tried to kill me—twice—but I couldn't prove it. I wasn't going to give Zarkisian a third chance."

"That's when you left your family?" Todd asked. "To hide out?"

"Yes," Victor replied. "Why else would anyone spend ten years in the Amazon unless they had to?"

"Why did you come back?" Todd wondered.

"WHY?" Victor retorted. "I thought ten years in the rain forest was long enough for Zarkisian to forget about me and my family. I'd learned enough shamanic techniques over that time to protect us in a face-to-face confrontation if I needed to."

He flushed when he glanced at Evelyn's anxious face. "I hoped that," he added and rubbed the back of his neck in chagrin. "It didn't work out like I planned."

"Ten years," Todd whistled his commiseration. "All the more reason for us to stop him now."

"That's easy to say," Victor replied, rubbing his neck in dismay at his self-imposed impotence. *Zarkisian anticipated my every move.* "But there's nothing I can do about him now."

Todd said nothing for a moment. "You ever hear of CECOM, Dr. Furst?"

"U. S. Communications-Electronics Command?" Victor replied. Psy-ops coordinated directly with that communications branch of the military during the war, but he saw no reason to divulge that information to this bureaucratic functionary. "What about it?"

"I spoke to Miriam on one of their linkups ten hours ago. She said she was at a government hospital installation. I don't know where it was, but I'll bet you do."

So that's what Zarkisian had done with her—used his medical connections to confine her as well. Victor rubbed his neck and ransacked his memory. Two military hospital installations, Fort Ticonderoga and Fort Somerset, had CECOM links in the immediate New York City area. "Fort Ticonderoga and Fort Somerset are closest to New York City," he replied and noted Evelyn and Desdemona leaning closer toward him. "Fort Ticonderoga's too far away if they abducted her last night." Victor lowered his voice. "Fort Somerset's the better bet. What of it?"

"The military's not in the habit of facilitating conversations with civilians in psychiatric hospitals," Todd answered. "Yet somebody manipulated the army's health and communication networks to let me talk to your daughter. The only person with that much pull seems to be Basil Zarkisian."

"Of course." Zarkisian had wormed himself so deeply into the gut of the government bureaucracy over the years that his power put him beyond conventional oversight. "But I don't see how anything from my past can help you now."

"You tell me," Todd responded. "What would Zarkisian want with Miriam?"

"He must think holding her in a psychiatric hospital ensures my noninvolvement in Turkey," Victor replied. "She's his trump card in case I back out of our agreement."

Helsingford did not respond, and Victor added. "Sounds fantastic and self-centered, doesn't it?"

"It does if you think Zarkisian's plans stop with you."

Zarkisian planned this—their release, their detention, Miriam's abduction—for what?

"Evelyn was right," Victor murmured. "Zarkisian never loved her. Or considered me a rival."

He stroked his beard and frowned. But if that was true, why did Zarkisian need Victor's promise to stay out of his affairs? It must center around his hero role as Vahagn in Evelyn's subconscious. Vahagn defeated Ahriman's plan to conquer Hades in the spirit realm, which explained why Zarkisian felt he needed another ace up his sleeve—Miriam.

If Zarkisian and the New Immortals had control of Mt. Ararat, how did Miriam figure into their plans if she was still in New York? Victor clenched his fist. "What did you say Zarkisian's demands were?"

"He wants to reestablish the kingdom of Hayastan around Mt. Ararat," Todd replied.

"Turkey and the other powers in the area won't let *that* happen," Victor said.

"The news blackout in eastern Turkey suggests otherwise."

"And the U.S. is doing nothing to stop this from happening?"

"Sure, they are—they're bombing Mt. Ararat in less than fourteen hours, noon in Eastern Turkey time, nine a.m. Liverpool time. But that won't stop them." Todd's voice dropped to a whisper. "I told you earlier I saw an Azeri rebel leader die from the madness his people called zar. I think the New Immortals caused his illness."

"Zarkisian's using people's anxieties against them," Victor said, jumping to his feet in anger at the realization. "Just like our psy-ops group did during Operation Desert Storm."

"That's what it looks like," Todd agreed.

"That's what psychic parasites do." Victor rubbed a hand through his hair. "Feed off people's negative energy."

"You have any idea why they're doing it now?" Todd asked.

"They're like tapeworms. Starve their host body and the stench of a dead carcass draws them into the open—a carcass like their old country of Hayastan."

"But if they had such power before, why did they wait until now?" Todd asked.

"A guy doesn't become head of EDIC overnight," Victor replied. "Zarkisian had to secure his authority within DOD first. That takes time."

"Damn!" Todd replied and blew the air out of his cheeks. "Have you ever heard of the Last Days, Dr. Furst?"

"It's a term people use to describe the end of life on Earth—Judgment Day in Christian theology." Victor's palms grew sweaty. "Many religions have versions of the concept. Why?"

"Arkadian, the head cleric of the monastery overlooking Mt. Ararat, referred to it as a time in the ancient Zoroastrian religion when two brothers, Ahura Mazda and Angra Mainyu, fight for control over the Earth. Could that time be now?"

"It could if either of them feels he has enough power," Victor replied, glancing at Evelyn. Her cheeks glowed. "Zarkisian and the New Immortals could provide that power."

"Hmmm," Todd mused out loud. "Arkadian said the Last Days would be when Ahura Mazda, the force of goodness and light, takes his rightful place from his brother, Angra Mainyu, the destructive force, to rule earth for all eternity."

Angra Mainyu!

"But not without a fight you said," Victor declared, getting to his feet. He beamed at his ex-wife. "As Evelyn warned us all along."

"But Angra Mainyu is destined to lose," Todd replied. "That's what Arkadian told me."

"For control of the universe, wouldn't Angra Mainyu use every weapon he has to defy Fate?" Victor asked. "Zarkisian and the New Immortals' feeding off and controlling people's psyches could be a decisive weapon to overturn such prophecy."

"Maybe in the spiritual realm," Todd agreed. "But how can they transfer the mental energy they absorb from the spiritual realm to the physical world on earth?"

Victor pondered. "They would need biological batteries or physical beings of some kind to store the mental energy they drain from others," he said at last. "Through them Angra Mainyu could project that energy over a distance."

"Yes, I've witnessed that," Todd said. "How is it possible?"

"I'm not sure," Victor replied. "Perhaps through spirit animals, which is what shamans call them, familiars in western culture."

"Spirit animals?"

"Something through which shamans, witches, wizards, and other so-called 'magic beings' use to project their powers," Victor replied.

"I don't understand," Todd said.

"You know," Victor said with a shrug of frustration, glancing at the two women who listened to the conversation with rapt attention. "a household animal, like a dog or cat."

"Snakes, too?" Todd asked. "A snake wound around the rebel leader's boot just before he demonstrated zar symptoms. Could that have been a spirit animal?"

"Possibly," Victor added. "Depends on the individual—spirit animals can act like alter egos—appropriate in this case because a snake is an animal nobody would notice that is associated with dark energy and emotions."

"Hmm, interesting," Todd said. "For Angra Mainyu's purposes, though, wouldn't Zarkisian's familiars have to be bigger or more numerous to be effective?"

"It's not a matter of size or number so much," Victor replied, "but the familiar's ability to store and project the mental energy these psychic vampires absorb—that, along with the strength of the emotion."

"Such as passion or hate, you mean," Todd said.

"Whatever's strong enough to make their victims mad and lose control of their faculties," Victor added. "Like the Alzheimer's-like symptoms my ex-wife experienced."

"Or the zar that possessed the Azeri leader I saw," Todd added. *Strong enough to kill.*

"Ye-es," Victor agreed, eying Evelyn with renewed concern. He turned sideways and lowered his voice. "Certain types of empathic personalities with blurred senses of self would make familiars powerful enough to project the full force of such destructive energies—like biological transistors."

"That's what killed the Azeri leader," Todd said. "I'm sure of it."

"That's Zarkisian's plan," Victor declared. "Absorb the emotional energy of others and redirect it toward the enemies of the New Immortals."

"But he'd need an army of people for the mental energy his Immortals require to fight our troops," Todd protested. "Where could he get so much psychic energy? Who'd supply it?"

"Zar and Alzheimer's patients, for starters," Victor replied, rubbing his neck in thought. "Anybody with a diagnosis of a long-term mental illness like catatonia would be a candidate."

Someone like the Wailers, perhaps? Is that why they remain along Hades' shore?

"Zarkisian's stockpiled his energy source along the shores of the Lethe," Victor declared. "That would give him an eternal and unlimited supply."

"Where?" Todd asked.

"In Hades," Victor replied. "The souls of spirits abandoned along the banks of the Lethe in the spiritual Lower World."

"All right," Todd said, incredulity creeping into voice. "If that's so, I need you to destroy Zarkisian's energy source there."

"I already said I can't," Victor replied. "I promised not to interfere with Zarkisian's activities for the well-being of my family."

"What family?" Todd asked in exasperation. "You abandoned them years ago."

They're still family!

"To protect them," Victor countered. "Everything I did was to save them from Zarkisian. I always considered them my family."

"Didn't you end that relationship when you divorced Evelyn?" Todd asked. "They aren't your legal family anymore."

"I suppose so," Victor replied, wringing the back of his neck in anguish. "That's enough of a loophole to break our agreement."

"So, what's the problem then, Doc?" Todd asked. "Zarkisian broke his end of the bargain when he alerted British Immigration about your lack of passports. And if Miriam's no longer your legal daughter, you have every right to save her without breaking your promise."

Use the loophole!

"That's true in a legal sense," Victor admitted, searching Evelyn's anxious face. "But she's not my biological daughter, either," he added in a bitter voice. "How much do I owe her?"

"How much do you owe anyone?" Todd retorted. "If you abandoned your family for their well-being, the person you thought was your daughter now is held in a hospital facility against her will."

"I know, but—"

"Geez, Victor!" Todd exclaimed. "How much worse does her well-being have to get? Why won't you help her?"

Victor clenched his jaw. Miriam never forgave him for abandoning her and her mother. If he gave into his bitterness over her paternity, Zarkisian won.

He eyed Evelyn and forced a smile. When she smiled back, a lump formed in Victor's throat. He always respected her mental privacy. When they returned to the States after the press leaked stories about psychological warfare against Iraqi citizens, he never asked why she returned with him. They argued, fought, made up. The lovemaking afterward was steamy, wanton—terrific. Miriam's birth was a premature delivery, Evelyn said. And he believed her.

How could anyone be so blind?

Latent fury flared inside his throat like magma inside a volcano.

"Well?" Todd asked.

Victor stared at his hand gripping the phone, its knuckles drained of color. Bitterness was getting the better of him—no way for anyone to act, let alone a shaman. He relaxed his grip.

"What do you want me to do?"

{4}

"Whatever you think best," Todd replied. "Miriam, for starters. She's a patient in a military psychiatric ward. Could you secure her release?"

"Not within the next fourteen hours." Victor frowned. "Or the next fourteen days, for that matter."

"Why not?"

"A close relative or parent can petition for a release or a transfer to a civilian hospital, but Evelyn is in no condition to pursue that undertaking." Despite Zarkisian being a soul-sucking parasite, Victor had to keep his word for Evelyn's safety. Zarkisian had ensured that. "And, as the divorced parent of an adult child, my trying to gain her release would be iffy."

"Is she in any danger at Fort Somerset?"

"I doubt it." Victor scratched his beard. To detain Miriam at Fort Somerset, Zarkisian needed some kind of cover story to justify her confinement. Could he have stolen Miriam's soul? The resulting Alzheimer's symptoms would justify her hospitalization just as they had Evelyn's. He explained his misgiving to Todd. "I'm almost certain of it, given what he did to Evelyn. But it depends on what Zarkisian's intentions are."

"Any way to find out?"

"Yes, if I examined Miriam myself," Victor replied. "But there's no time for that and Zarkisian's eliminated that possibility even if there was."

"Darn it!"

"Wait a minute," Victor advised, scanned his speed-dial numbers, and spotted Walter Reed's number. "Call back in fifteen minutes. I think I know someone who has a contact at Fort Somerset."

Victor dialed the Walter Reed Hospital number and Charles Kincaid's extension. He answered on the second ring.

"Victor, listen," Kincaid said. "Turn yourself and Evelyn in to the authorities."

"Listen a moment, Charles," Victor replied. He quickly described Todd's requests, Miriam's detention, and Evelyn's current condition. "She still experiences dementia episodes."

"All the more reason to bring her in for treatment."

"Have you heard nothing I've said?" Victor replied. "I'll bring her to you after the crisis in Turkey is over."

"You expect me to risk Evelyn's life over a communication blackout on another continent? What kind of doctor are you?"

"Call the Somerset psych unit and check if Miriam Gorovic is a patient there. If she isn't, I'll surrender Evelyn to you upon our return to the States."

"Fine. I'll call back."

Ten minutes later, Victor's phone buzzed. Kincaid said, "Fort Somerset's chief neurologist, Dr. Runnholme, told me he hospitalized a Jane Doe fitting Miriam's description last night."

"Did he say what the woman had done to merit hospitalization?" Victor asked.

"Said a story she wrote caused war to break out in Turkey."

"Sounds like Miriam," Victor replied. "Who hospitalized her?"

"Dr. Basil Zarkisian."

Like Zarkisian did to Evelyn.

"She's not military personnel," Victor replied. "On what basis this time?"

"National security." Kincaid cleared his throat. "That's not all. Runnholme said the woman became so agitated he had to sedate her several times."

"Why?"

"Enough of what she said checked out that the military wanted Runnholme to hold her for further questioning," Kincaid replied. "But her dementia is so aggressive that every time she comes to, Runnholme fears she'll take her life. Or someone else's."

"Restraints aren't enough?"

Kincaid sighed. "She broke out of them twice. She's so disoriented she doesn't recognize she's in a hospital."

"Where does she think she is?"

"Prison."

Victor groaned. "Miriam's perception isn't far wrong."

"Not at Fort Somerset," Kinkaid said. "That's what's so disturbing."

Victor's palms sweated. Kincaid seldom used that word to describe a patient's condition. "What do you mean?"

"She says she's in Tartarus."

"Where?" Victor responded in disbelief.

"A prison in Hades."

"Oh-h-kay," Victor replied, noting the anxiety on the women's faces. "Thanks."

He ended the call and redialed Todd's number. Without a doubt, Zarkisian had trapped Miriam's soul in the Lower World. It didn't matter where. What new horror did this scheming parasite have in store for her?

"What'd you find out?" Todd asked.

"Nothing good." Victor turned away from Evelyn and whispered, "Miriam couldn't be in a worse spot. Her body's confined to a military mental hospital and her soul's in the Hellenic version of Hell."

Todd whistled. "Then what Catholicos Arkadian told me about Zurvan and the End Time must be true."

"It looks that way." Victor fidgeted. End Times and psychic parasites—more than the breakup of his family was at stake. "Zarkisian IS playing a bigger game than I thought."

"What do we do?" Todd asked.

"You delay the bombing until I retrieve Miriam's soul."

"How?"

"That's your department, Helsingford. Negotiate. Lie. Whatever. Just handle that end until I tell you we've got her back."

Victor ended the call and turned toward Evelyn. Despite her uncertain mental state, he needed her to guide him back to Hades to counter whatever plan Zarkisian had devised. Access to the Lower World meant going through the individual's subconscious but entering a particular realm like Hades was a product of the person's cultural inheritance. Evelyn's Balkan/Hellenic heritage supplied a direct route; Victor's Nordic background meant wasted time and energy reaching Hades by himself through his own subconscious.

He studied Evelyn up and down. She seemed all right, but her haggard eyes and lined face showed her exhaustion. Who wouldn't be after returning from the dead in the Lower World? More important: was she strong enough to endure another spiritual descent so soon?

"Is everything all right?" Evelyn asked. Desdemona's hands grasped the back of the sofa with the same anxious intensity. "You look upset."

"Everything's fine." Victor pinched the bridge of his nose. He didn't want to upset Evelyn before their return to Hades. "Just strain from answering all these phone calls."

"No, it's not," Evelyn retorted. "We heard your conversation with Todd. You're upset—I see it, I feel it. You agreed to something with him you didn't want to do, something about a bombing which involves Miriam somehow. I know it. Why won't you tell me?"

You asked for it!

"You're right," Victor admitted. "I *am* upset. I'm upset we're stuck in Liverpool airport. I'm upset the American air force is bombing people in Turkey. I'm upset Miriam's stuck in a military hospital and can't get out. And I'm upset I can't do anything about any of it."

The stunned Evelyn said nothing. Victor kneeled in front of her and clasped her hands between his.

"Most of all, I'm upset you're involved in any of this," he added. "You've been through an ordeal that would exhaust anyone. You need to rest."

He released her hands and stood up. "All of us do," he said, eying Desdemona for assistance, "if we're to get on that flight tomorrow morning."

"I'm not tired and I'm not made of porcelain," Evelyn declared and surged to her feet. "I promise I won't break," she added, eying both of them with tears in her eyes. "If it involves Miriam, I want to help."

"We know you do, Evie." Desdemona agreed and squeezed her sister's shoulder in reassurance. Easing her sister onto the bed, she fluffed the pillows, and sat on the edge beside her. "But we can do nothing for her here. We can help Miriam most by going back to the States rested and ready to go when we get there."

"All right," Evelyn agreed unconvinced. She stifled a yawn and patted the bedspread beside her. "If you do." She cocked an eye at Victor. "You, too."

"Okay," Victor agreed, scowling at Desdemona. "All of us."

He sat in the corner of the sofa, folded his arms, and waited for Evelyn to fall asleep. It didn't take long. When her breathing turned into gentle snores, he got up, rounded the bed, and jiggled Desdemona's shoulder.

"Wha—?"

Victor placed a hand over her mouth and gestured toward the bathroom. Following him into the cramped room, the vexed Desdemona glanced in the mirror and straightened a runaway tress. "What do you want?"

Victor peered over his shoulder at Evelyn sleeping on the bed and closed the bathroom door. "I need more specific information about Hades before I decide whether to return there again."

"Okay," Desdemona growled and sat on the toilet seat. "Shoot." *Where to begin?*

"All right then," Victor declared and rubbed his hand through his hair. "First off, what do you know about Tartarus?"

Desdemona's eyes widened with fear. "It's the dungeon of Hell in Greek mythology. The worst spirits are confined there."

Victor clenched and unclenched his hands. Miriam's fate was worse than he thought. "What could Miriam have done to Zarkisian to consign her soul there?"

"I-I don't know," Desdemona said in a low voice. "Maybe it's punishment for Evelyn rejecting him. The infernal goddesses called Erinyes or Furies are assigned to afflict the spirits they guard there with endless torments. It might be his form of psychological retribution."

Or revenge.

"Is there any way to get her out?" Victor asked.

"Perhaps." Desdemona's steely eyes flitted about the cramped room as if the answer lay in one of its corners. "Like Evelyn, Miriam's soul was sent to Hades before its time. Standard procedure for disposing of Miriam and Evelyn's souls would be to send them to the Meadows of Asphodel. Unlike Evelyn, however, Miriam's soul isn't drained of its psychic energy, but trapped in Hades against her will."

"Does that make a difference?" Victor asked.

Mission: Soul Sacrifice

"Miriam's not dead," Desdemona replied. "Her body and soul are in a state of limbo—perpetual suspended animation, if you will."

"She's not hurt, then," Victor replied in relief. "But she's at Zarkisian's mercy now whenever he wants something more from her—or us."

"You're right, of course," Desdemona agreed and shook her head in dismay. "But freeing Miriam's soul from Tartarus would be more than a matter of finding the right Lower World judge and explaining the circumstances for them to release it."

"What do you mean?"

"There's no protocol for her situation I know of," Desdemona replied. "Even if we got permission from the three judges who decide the fate of the souls sent before them to release Miriam, the guards of Tartarus don't have to honor it."

"Why not?" Victor asked, rubbing his neck in dismay. "You're an expert in Hellenic culture, but—"

"Miriam's soul is in Hell, Victor," Desdemona declared. "Forever. Believe me."

"That can't be," Victor declared. "I got Evelyn's soul out—just as Orpheus did with Eurydice's."

"The situations aren't the same," Desdemona replied. "Evelyn died, but you restored her soul before it went through the judgment process. Miriam's assignment to Tartarus is the Hellenic equivalent of eternal damnation. Exile there means her soul can never leave."

Damn! Victor clenched his hands in frustration. *Or be damned!*

Zarkisian figured it out, so they had no options. Make Victor promise no further interference to save Evelyn's soul, then exile Miriam's to safeguard Victor's compliance and his family's.

Wait a minute!

To save Evelyn's soul he promised never to meddle in Zarkisian's affairs. Miriam's well-being was never part of that agreement.

A sly grin spread over Victor's face. Zarkisian violated the spirit of their contract when he imprisoned Miriam's soul in Tartarus. Therefore, restoring Miriam's soul did not violate Victor's side of their verbal contract.

Payback.

"OK, let's get ready," Victor said. "We're going back to the Lower World."

{5}

Desdemona flushed. "Did you hear nothing I just said?"

"Difficult journey, arcane protocol, a prison breakout if we're unlucky—mission impossible," Victor replied. "I get that."

"But you were the one who said Evelyn needed rest."

"That was before," Victor said. "I need her to retrieve Miriam's soul from Hades."

Desdemona's eyes widened. "Evelyn's not up for that, yet."

"We have less than ten hours before our air force bombs Mt. Ararat," Victor replied. "Not enough time for me to reach Hades on my own and retrieve Miriam's soul."

"Is that it—time?" Desdemona asked. "Or are you afraid Miriam would rather be rescued by anyone other than you?"

Does Miriam hate me that much?

"That's ridiculous!" Victor spat, stung by the underlying truth of her insinuation. "Miriam may resent me, but Zarkisian exiled her soul in Hades. By rights, she should hate him more."

"That's true," Desdemona agreed, her jawline hardening. "But you risk Evelyn's health again if you ask her help to rescue a soul you cannot save yourself."

"Would you rather I do nothing?" Victor retorted, throwing up his hands. "With Miriam's and who knows how many other lives on the line, that's what you want?"

"Of course not," Desdemona replied, looking away. "But who knows what will happen if Zarkisian finds out you're rescuing Miriam?"

"He'll never know unless somebody warns him." Victor eyed her and grimaced. *Somebody like you, perhaps?* "We won't let that happen, will we?"

"No—" Desdemona glanced toward the hallway door. "What about the guard outside?"

"We'll keep it quiet like we did on the plane—just get a mirror." Victor glanced about the room, flipped open the cabinet mirror over the sink, and pulled the knobs of its hinge rods. "Pull the rods out," he said, turning back to Desdemona. "And bring the mirror into the bedroom. I'll do the rest."

While Desdemona removed the hinge rods, Victor reentered the bedroom and knelt at Evelyn's bedside. "Evelyn," he said in a loud whisper. "Wake up."

He repeated his request with no response. On his third attempt, Evelyn awoke with a start.

"Shush," he whispered before she could protest. "We need to make another visit to the Lower World."

"Are you sure?" Evelyn asked in a groggy voice. Her red-rimmed, sapphire eyes searched Victor's face. "After you just got me out of that horrible place?"

"We need to return to Hades as soon as possible," Victor replied, studying her anxious gaze. The rigors of retrieving Miriam's soul could undo the gains Evelyn made—dare he risk her health again on a venture even more difficult? "I need you to help me return to where we entered it the last time—Charon's pier."

But you're not coming with me to Tartarus.

Evelyn clutched his arm. "What aren't you telling me?"

"Todd and I decided I can help him most if I release the Wailers before the bombing starts," Victor said. "Desdemona can watch us."

"Victor." Evelyn's voice carried the peremptory tone she used whenever he tried to hide something from her. "Tell me."

Charon's pier is as far as you go.

"All right," Victor sighed and looked away. "Miriam's soul is stuck in the Lower World, and we need to retrieve it."

Mission: Soul Sacrifice

Evelyn paled. Her hands trembled. She folded them across her lap. "Angra M—" she whispered and cleared her throat. "Mainyu."

"How'd her soul get there?" she asked with a tight smile.

"Government agents took her to a psychiatric facility by mistake," he replied, omitting Zarkisian's involvement in ordering her detention. "The psychiatrist there reported Miriam thinks she's stranded in Hades. I think her soul's there to keep us from interfering with the New Immortals' rebellion in Turkey. That's what Todd's call was about."

"Oh, Victor!" Evelyn cried. "We can't leave her there!"

"We won't," Victor replied. He took Evelyn's hands and laid her face upward on the bed. Turning to Desdemona who brought the bathroom mirror along with two hand mirrors from their purses, he directed her to prop the big mirror against the headboard and prop the smaller ones against pillows placed on either side of Evelyn's head. After Desdemona placed the mirrors as directed, Victor knelt beside Evelyn. "The mirrors will enable Desdemona to monitor our progress," he explained in a comforting voice. "I'll use every trick I learned in the Amazon to get Miriam's soul back. Just relax and fold your arms over your chest."

Evelyn crossed her arms and smiled up at him. "All set."

Is that smile for me? Or for my retrieving her daughter? Victor felt his lungs constrict at the possibility she still cared. He coughed and held his breath.

"Are you all right?" Evelyn asked.

"It's nothing." *Why her fake concern? Miriam's all she cares about.* Victor gritted his teeth and smiled. "Make yourself comfortable and we'll get started."

Evelyn squared her shoulders and settled into the pillows. Victor grimaced. Zarkisian's scheme amounted to blackmail; retrieving Miriam's soul was Victor's payback.

Todd could negotiate with Zarkisian and the New Immortals in the corporeal world. Meanwhile, he'd retrieve Miriam and the souls of the New Immortals' other victims from the Lower World. That would undermine the Anausavareds' psychic power while Todd blunted their political and military strength.

Victor dragged the desk chair beside Evelyn's head and turned to Desdemona. "Start slapping your knee." Then he turned toward Evelyn. "Focus on Desdemona's knee slaps."

After Evelyn drifted into a trance, Victor stared at the cabinet mirror behind Evelyn's head. Black diamonds blinked in the corners of his consciousness. The warm, familiar bliss spread throughout his body.

Without altering her rhythm, Desdemona slipped two coins into Victor's palm and wrapped his fingers around them. "Charon always wants his toll."

"Take my cell phone in case Todd calls again," Victor said, grabbing her wrist. "Promise me you'll keep an eye on us. That's what the mirrors are for. I'll signal if we need help."

"How—?"

"You'll see it," Victor murmured. "I'll be obvious about it."

His soul drifted through the floorboards of their hotel room and penetrated the Earth underneath the building. Evelyn's shimmering silhouette preceded him down the smooth floor of a winding cave, like a fissure vent of a volcano. Instead of ending upon a pool of magma, however, this one opened onto the bank of the River Acheron across from Hades.

He caught her at the head of Charon's pier. "You've completed your part in our Lower World journey. I needed you to return here, but I won't jeopardize your health to rescue Miriam from prison."

"Prison?" Evelyn's eyes sparkled. She grabbed Victor's arm. "Why didn't you tell me?"

Fire surged in Victor's throat. *Why didn't you tell me Miriam wasn't my daughter?* "I didn't want to upset you."

"Upset me?" Evelyn asked. "Being in prison in Hades isn't something you hide from—"

Victor pressed a finger against Evelyn's lips. "You're right. Todd told me that Zarkisian is holding Miriam's soul hostage in a prison in Hades called Tartarus while his corporeal forces secure the area around Mt. Ararat. He wants to resurrect the kingdom of Hayastan. Why he needs Miriam's soul for that purpose I have eight corporeal hours to find out and retrieve it before the deadline."

"Let me go with—"

"Zarkisian already has one soul," Victor said. "We can't afford to lose yours to him again."

"I know." Evelyn's eyes teared up. She grabbed Victor's forearm. "I *am* grateful for what you've done."

She sounded as if she was complementing a pet dog. "Why didn't you tell me about you and Zarkisian?"

Evelyn's brows knitted. "I-I don't know."

"Were you afraid? Ashamed? Did he threaten you?"

"Basil *can* be charming," Evelyn replied in pouting defiance. "Sophisticated. Considerate. Kind, even."

"Everything I'm not," Victor retorted, remorse creeping into his voice. "Or wasn't, I suppose."

"He was around, Victor." Evelyn's fingers pressed into the flesh of his arm. "After you left us the second time, I had no one else to turn to. He cared or seemed to."

"And I didn't?"

"The flight-or-fight impulse, isn't it?" Evelyn released her grip. "When we returned to Washington, Zarkisian followed."

She cocked a derisive eyebrow. "He stayed around. You ran off to the Amazon."

Victor's jaw dropped.

"You saw him *after* I left?" he exclaimed. "He was nice to you in Kuwait, so you allowed him to be nice to you again in D.C.—even after his second attempt on my life?"

He shook his head in disbelief. "How long did this second affair last?"

"I saw him a couple of times," Evelyn said. "The last was maybe six months after you went to the Amazon."

Zarkisian abandoned you, too.

"That was it?" Victor asked. "You ended it?"

"No one *ended* it," Evelyn replied. "He stopped calling."

"After you told him where I was," Victor said.

"Oh, Victor," Evelyn sighed in exasperation. "It isn't always about you—he never asked."

"He already knew," Victor retorted.

"Maybe. I don't know!" Evelyn's jaw hardened. "Maybe I didn't believe him or you. Or any of it."

She still doesn't believe me.

Victor groaned. Evelyn never understood his shaman's commitment was like a mainstream physician's to do no harm. "Let me explain the difference to you. To heal our patients, shamans never enter the psyches of their patients to control them or feed off their energy like the Anausavareds do. Instead, shamans use positive, curative approaches like reiki, journeying, and soul retrieval to remove hostile spirits like Angra Mainyu and restore the body's energy balance. Got it?"

"I think so," Evelyn replied, biting her lip.

"Zarkisian's exiling Miriam's and your soul in Hades violates every principle a shaman stands for," Victor said, squaring his shoulders. "That's the anxiety and fear energy they feed upon."

"I see," Evelyn said.

Mission: Soul Sacrifice

"Okay," Victor said, noting her uncertainty. "So, you have no idea why he wants Miriam's soul."

"I can guess," Miriam replied. "Basil mentioned Hayastan several times as his ultimate goal. He said his destiny was to unite all the ancient Armenians under one flag."

"Could that be what the gold helmet was for we saw at the airport?" Victor wondered out loud. "Part of a coronation?"

"Angra—" Evelyn replied, hands trembling. She clapped them against her thighs. "As his daughter, Miriam would be a part of that, I suppose. What role she'd have is unclear."

"Not if Miriam is Anausavared," Victor said. "Is she?"

Evelyn gazed toward the mists shrouding the opposite shore. "I hope not. She's shown no sign up to now." Her eyes teared up. "I was always grateful for that." She turned toward Victor. "And you."

You should have told me.

Victor clenched and unclenched his fingers. *Dammit all!* Despite everything he still loved her.

A bell tolled. The last of those who had money for passage boarded the ferry. Charon barred the others from boarding by stretching his oar across the gangplank.

Without a word, Victor left Evelyn and headed toward the dock and strong-armed his way through the restive crowd. When he reached the gangplank, he blew her a kiss.

"Why won't you let me go with you?" Evelyn shouted.

"Can't." Victor relished the intractability of that single word. "I promised."

"A promise to the devil," Evelyn said, frowning.

"That's the difference between him and me," Victor replied. "I keep mine."

"So has he."

Victor scowled. What she said was true. Zarkisian hadn't hindered their return from Orsova, but he hadn't helped, either.

He pointed to the line of ferryboat passengers that snaked down the pier and across the beach to the cave entrance. "Of the thousands of souls in this line, hundreds are in it wrongfully because Zarkisian sent their souls here, including Miriam's. The only way to save her and them is to find out how he does it and free their souls from the Lower World."

"Miriam's my daughter." Evelyn's jaw set like the determined woman Victor remembered. "That should be enough for me to go with you."

Victor hesitated. Zarkisian had manipulated Evelyn into the psychic morass they were in. He would do so again if the need arose. But, given the rigors of her spiritual journey, hadn't Evelyn earned the right to retrieve her daughter's soul?

Given Miriam's resentment toward me, can I rescue her soul without Evelyn's help?

He relented and beckoned Evelyn toward the dock who shoved her way through the crowd to the end of the pier. Heeding the cries from the mob, Charon dropped his oar, but continued to block their way. Victor deposited two coins into the oarsman's gnarled hand. Charon's eyes blazed with recognition from their previous trip to Hades, but Desdemona's passage tokens barred any further dispute.

Charon pulled the gangplank into the ferry boat and shoved it away from the pier. Evelyn and Victor settled onto their plank seat and watched Hades' infernal mists shroud the other souls still waiting onshore as the ferry pulled away.

"What's your plan of action?" Evelyn asked.

Do I have one?

"All we know is Miriam's imprisonment is tied somehow to the Anausavareds' takeover of Hayastan's ancient territories," Victor replied, wriggling his hips in discomfort on the wooden plank. "Zarkisian has sent hundreds of souls like hers to Hades. Unlike them her soul went through the judgment process on the Meadows of Asphodel and was sent to Tartarus."

"So?"

"So, if we learn why her soul was sent on for judgment while the Wailers remain along the banks of the Lethe, we might figure out what distinguishes her soul from theirs."

Evelyn scrunched her mouth. "How do you plan to do that?"

"They all took the same ferry across the Lethe to the opposite bank which forms the border of Hades," Victor replied. "Some Wailers must have noticed her. If we find them, we might learn what that distinguishing quality is so we can free them and her."

"How are you going to find them?"

"I'm not sure yet." Victor shrugged. "I can call upon Shalah and my other spirit animals to screen out and interrogate those Wailers who noticed her."

"Is there enough time for that?" Evelyn wondered.

"It'll be close," Victor replied. "Last I checked, twelve hours of corporeal time remained. Given the two-hour time difference between Turkey and England, we have less than ten hours."

The packed ferry boat lumbered through the foggy marsh, then whisked across the Lethe toward the opposite shore, buoyed by the water sloshing high against the river bank. The ferry slammed twice against the pier before Charon lashed the boat to one of the support posts, a docking more perilous than Victor recalled from his earlier crossing.

Is the river higher than last time we came?

He turned and scanned the shallows nearby. Wailers hugged the shoreline despite the rising water line. In the water beyond the pier purple and indigo lights glimmered like fireflies darting in the dusk of a summer evening.

What are those?

"Look up there!" Evelyn cried, pointing to the sky.

Lightning crackled through the volcanic fires bathing the mountains to the northwest. Sulfurous sparks spouted into the sky and reflected off the river as if all of Hades was celebrating an infernal holiday.

Reflections? There are no stars and the lights in the water aren't the same color as the sparks.

Evelyn and the rest of the passengers cringed. One turned toward Charon. "What do those fires on the horizon mean?"

Charon struggled to keep the gangplank steady over the unruly current. "My task is to bring you here," he huffed as he ushered his passengers out of the boat. "What happens after that is your problem."

The odor of brimstone grew stronger as the last passenger left the ferry. Charon struggled against the current to keep the boat headed back to the opposite shore for another load of passengers.

A bolide streaked across the sky toward the opposite shore, then another. Their afterglow revealed a bat-like Ker hovering in the sky. Unlike during Victor's first visit, these female death spirits merely patrolled the skies and did not swoop upon the souls below.

Victor scanned the souls crowding around the pier. The Wailers' numbers had increased since their last visit. Thousands, perhaps tens of thousands, eyed him with the distress that characterized Evelyn's behavior. Victor tried to question them, but they skittered away like land crabs. One lamented in English, "The intensity of the volcanic displays has increased."

Are these events connected? How?

Mission: Soul Sacrifice

Victor summoned three of his power animals, Shalah, Altaira, and Shakira, to search among the clusters of despairing souls. "We need to learn if any of these Wailers saw Miriam come through here."

"Did anybody see a tall girl named Miriam pass through here?" Victor called to the retreating Wailers. "Reddish-brown hair and hazel eyes. Anybody?"

He stepped off the pier and called out her name while heading up the beach. "Miriam-m!" he cried, cupping his hands around his mouth. "Has anyone seen a woman named Miriam?"

Victor directed Evelyn to do the same thing in the opposite direction while Shalah and the two mares split up and shadowed their movements along the top of the sand berm underneath the cliffs. They made two dragnet sweeps up and down the beach without success.

"That's enough," Victor said after he, Evelyn, and the horses met at the pier the second time. "Miriam must have passed through here but everyone's afraid to admit it."

"Too afraid and too exhausted," Evelyn corrected.

"That might be the distinction between them right there," Victor suggested. "Assuming Zarkisian hasn't absorbed Miriam's mental energy, too."

"Not without a fight he wouldn't," Evelyn replied, grinning.

"I can't imagine it, either," Victor laughed, sharing her levity. "She wouldn't let him."

"That's for sure," Evelyn chuckled, then her face sobered. "So, what do we do now?"

"Follow the trail to the Plain of Asphodel, I guess," Victor replied, scratching his neck. "Miriam had to go there for judgment before being sent to Tartarus."

He scanned the chalky cliffs for a cave or path to access the interior. "Too bad Akvan's not here—we could trick him into revealing

Ahriman's plans for Miriam and the Wailers. But I don't see him or his pals around here, just Keres. They're not doing a thing."

"I wonder why," Evelyn mused aloud, peering into the sky.

Another bolide streaked across the sky and crashed into the water beside the opposite shore. Its afterglow outlined Charon's skiff approaching the dock with another load of passengers. A giant wave thrust its stern into the sky, and the ferry plunged sideways into the trough. The Wailers scrambled up the bank. The wave surged toward shore, crashed against the bank, and retreated in a slurry of mud and foam.

Charon righted the ferry and headed toward the pier. Another bolide streaked across the sky and plunged into the water a hundred yards away. The resulting swell rippled across the marsh and slammed his boat against the dock. Gasping voyagers stumbled onto shore. Charon and the wreckage flowed downriver.

A fourth meteor plummeted into the murky river. Victor grabbed Evelyn's shoulder and steered her toward the base of the cliffs. "Now I get it."

"Get what?" Evelyn asked.

"Those meteors are not random explosions from erupting volcanos, they're missiles," Victor exclaimed. "Warnings targeted at every Wailer along the banks of the Lethe."

Gomez, the ship's purser of the Angela Negre, emerged from under the dock, more wild-eyed and emaciated than during their first meeting. "You again!" he cried and scrambled to the top of the sand berm. "Stop asking us about your infernal Miriam and leave us alone."

"Why?" Evelyn shouted at him. "Why don't you help us?"

"He's afraid," Victor said. "They're all afraid. Afraid to answer questions about Miriam."

Mission: Soul Sacrifice

"Tell them nothing!" Gomez cried to the Wailers cowering behind him. "Drive these people away. That's the only way to stop the fire from raining on our beach."

Nearby Wailers turned toward each other and shrugged. Some picked up sticks, pebbles, even sand and hurled the debris at Victor and Evelyn. Soon, a hail storm of debris dropped upon them, the smallest impact stinging like a flea bite.

Gomez retreated to the shelter of Charon's pier. Victor and Evelyn retreated with the horses to the safety of the cliffs. The other new arrivals scattered along the beach.

The Keres suddenly swooped into action and began plummeting towards the Wailers on the shore. They strafed the stragglers with their razor-sharp claws, isolated them from their companions, and feasted upon the entrails of their victims. When the next barrage lit the sky, they soared above the bluffs from the explosions then renewed the process.

Gaping craters now littered the berm. Foul, fiery slag splattered across the sand and oozed into the river. Broken bodies and mangled limbs sprinkled the beach like treats from a piñata. The survivors' pain was excruciating and everlasting. Those that had escaped the bombing ran in circles; others sought shelter by digging foxholes. A few pulled their hair and waited for the end. Their lamentations pierced the air like the dark whine from a hundred buzz saws.

Victor helped Evelyn comfort the few Wailers nearby willing to receive their aid. He felt so helpless. Helpless and impotent.

That's how Ahriman wants everyone to feel.

More projectiles lit the sky. Gomez slid out from under the devastated pier again. "Now do you see?" he shouted, pointing at Victor and Evelyn. "They're the ones responsible for the Keres attacking us. Destroy them and the dive-bombing stops. Do it and save yourselves."

The uninjured Wailers didn't hesitate this time. A score approached Victor and Evelyn from all sides. Victor scoured the formidable rock face for some place to hide. Spotting a fissure in the cliff face, he, Evelyn, and the horses retreated toward an enormous boulder which hid a sandy stream bed leading to the top of the limestone bluffs. The floor of an ancient riverbed, the path grew rockier the further they climbed. Halfway up, a flaming boulder crashed and knocked them to the ground. Stones, rocks, and debris rained down from both sides.

Victor staggered to his feet and dusted himself off. One of the Keres swooped down from their lookout above the bluffs and strafed them with its claws. One talon nicked Victor's side. Milky blood spurted from the razor cut.

The Keres circled for another attack. Victor stanched the flow of blood with one hand and shoved Evelyn into the ditch with the other. "The Keres can't target us if we separate."

Another barrage of flaming projectiles cratered the path all the way back to the riverbank. Victor regained his feet, shook off the dust, and checked the progress of their pursuers. The other three Keres strafed the terrified Wailers fifty yards behind them. Screaming and waving their arms, the Wailers hid among the rocky outcroppings.

"Evelyn!" Victor cried. "You and the horses head to the top of the ridge before the Wailers reorganize."

They did not budge. He turned toward the top of the ravine and the reason became clear. Cerberus, the giant ravenous, three-headed guard dog of Hades, blocked the ravine. All three of its heads slobbered at the meals Evelyn and the horses would provide.

{6}

The dog's two outside heads lunged at the three horses. The middle head snapped at Victor. He dodged its gnashing teeth and slid behind a rock outcropping where Evelyn lay hidden. A long, jagged cut trailed down his left calf; in the chaos he wasn't sure whether the Keres or Cerberus inflicted it. Didn't matter; either way it hurt like hell. "We can't stay here long."

Victor peered around the rock. Shalah and the mares darted back and forth across the trail, their forays confusing and irritating the blood-thirsty dog's heads. Cerberus prevented the horses from escaping up the ravine though chained to a pole in the center of the path. Victor turned toward Evelyn and pointed toward the top of the gulley. "When I step out, run up there as fast as you can."

Evelyn frowned and grabbed his arm. "What about you?"

"Shalah and the mares will protect me." Victor grimaced. "Long enough for you to make it, I hope."

"And if I don't?"

"Make sure you do." Victor's lips brushed hers. *For the last time?* He hoped not. "One of us has to, or Miriam doesn't stand a chance."

He popped up beside the rock and wriggled his fingers beside his ears. The dog's middle head snapped toward him, and Victor leaped to the side. "Go!" he shouted, waggling his fingers at the dog again. "Go, now!"

The dog's middle head lunged at Victor's face. Again, he dodged. Viscous white liquid spurted all over him. Victor checked his shoulders. It wasn't blood—dog slobber? Didn't matter. He couldn't keep this up for long.

Evelyn darted up the path. One of the outside heads lunged toward her, but Shalah wheeled, pivoted on his front legs, and landed a blow to the hinge joint behind the dog's jaw. The head shook and snapped to and fro in a blind rage.

The other outside head cut off Evelyn's escape. She doubled back, but it cut off that route, too. Trapping her against the rocky wall, its eyes narrowed, and its dripping jaws gaped open.

Evelyn squatted, grabbed a handful of grit and sand, and hurled it at the ravenous red eyes looming before her.

The head roared, its neck rearing up to its full thirty-foot height, while shaking with fury and surprise. Evelyn dove into the ditch beside the path and scuttled behind a jagged boulder.

Shalah and the two mares formed a semi-circle around Evelyn's hiding spot. They wheeled and kicked every time any of the dog's slavering heads attacked. Deep, bleeding cuts soon lined their legs and flanks.

The Keres and the Wailers kept their distance further down the path. Some Wailers cheered and shouted while others jeered and screamed. The dog's snapping jaws, the Keres' screaming swoops, and the unrelenting lava bombardment kept the Wailers' animosity at frenzied pitch.

"Won't any of you help us?" Victor called after he rolled under another of the middle head's lunges. "Just distract them long enough to give us a chance!"

"Don't let them retreat this way," Gomez shouted at the others. "Keep your distance and let Cerberus do his job."

Shalah and Altaira split from the cordon, circled away from Victor, and clambered up the slope on the dog's hind side. They reared and plunged, feinted, and dashed away.

The horses' attacks on one side and Victor's feints on the other flustered Cerberus. The ravenous dog returned to the center of the ravine and regrouped. The center head focused on the Wailers and any

Ker that flew too close; the two outside heads concentrated on Victor, Evelyn, and Shakira.

Victor felt a sting in his right side. A pointed rock bounced off a boulder beside him and nicked his knee. A larger stone slammed against his back. He staggered in pain while a handful of smaller stones pelted his cheek and neck. Gomez and the other Wailers bombarded Victor and Evelyn from behind with rubble taken from the ravine walls.

Two errant stones hit the snout of the dog's middle head. Cerberus wheeled and all three heads attacked the Wailers. Two of them grabbed a Wailer straying from the group, ripped him in two, and gobbled the innards. Gomez ducked among the fallen boulders; the others backed down the trail toward the river.

Cerberus' middle head swung back toward Victor and Evelyn. The other two heads broke off from their feast and joined the middle one. Crouching like a three-headed wolf ready to spring, six eyes followed Victor and Evelyn's every move, alert to any sudden action.

What can we do? Victor scanned the area. The dog blocked the route to the top of the ravine; Gomez and the angry Wailers blocked the other. The ravine walls plummeted down to the chasm floor.

Victor curled his index finger toward Shalah, indicating for him and the mares to rejoin the cordon around the rock concealing Evelyn. Their leg wounds showed the lunges of the three heads had taken a toll. They couldn't fend off Cerberus much longer.

Victor eyed Cerberus. Why was the dog waiting? Had they surprised him enough to be wary of this particular prey?

The outside heads shook, snarled, and snapped at each other; the middle head stayed focused on him and Evelyn. Victor understood the psychology of the wolf pack. If this beast's psychology was similar, perhaps he could reason with the dominant head.

Victor stretched his arms above his head and stepped forward. The middle head slanted to the right, intrigued by Victor's movements.

He took another step forward. No reaction. Another step placed him inside the periphery of the middle head's snapping jaws.

Still no movement. What now?

Music to soothe the savage beast?

With no other recourse, Victor began singing, "Oh, angry dog, curb your fire," Victor crooned, making up lyrics fit for the situation. "Cast hatred aside and let us be friends."

The outside heads stopped their snapping. Three sets of canine ears flicked forward. The center head remained cocked at an inquisitive angle, but the beast's four legs were poised to spring. The outside heads growled but kept their distance.

"Feast upon what's already flesh and bone," Victor continued, singing with all his might. *How long can I keep this up?* "And we will be gone before you're done."

The center head leaned forward until its gory, dripping muzzle hovered inches away from Victor's face. It sniffed his hair, clothes, and crotch before snorting and retreating to its companions.

Ugh! Victor struggled not to move despite the overpowering stench from half-eaten flesh and bone stuck in the dog's teeth and gums.

Had music soothed the beast? Victor wiped one of his palms on his pants as a test. The dog did not move—stalemate. Cerberus remained uncertain and they uneaten, yet Victor was not a friend to the animal, either.

Another brimstone volley lit the sky. The first salvo exploded down the path in the middle of the Wailers. Two more ripped the earth in front of the blood-thirsty hound. The earth erupted; giant rocks tumbled down the ravine into the chasm. A giant fissure yawned and zigzagged down the path toward the river.

Mission: Soul Sacrifice

Victor jumped behind the boulder shielding Evelyn. The tremors kept coming, sulfurous gas ballooned into the air from the fissure. The terrified Cerberus retreated and cowered against the ravine wall on the other side of the trail.

This is our chance!

Victor covered his mouth, grabbed Evelyn's shoulder, and pointed toward the top of the trail. "As soon as the quakes stop, sprint as fast as you can for the top."

One Ker, dazed by the gas billowing from the fissure, dipped near the ravenous dog. Cerberus' middle head shot into the sky, its nature overcoming its terror, snapped the demon in two, and feasted on the gray pulp inside each half. The remaining Keres darted like agitated dragonflies above the carnage.

"Now!" Victor said in a loud whisper and shoved Evelyn past the feasting dog heads. "Go! Fast as you can!"

He watched Evelyn bustle up the rocky trail, his vision suddenly blurring when something warm trickled into his eyes—blood. He touched his forehead, winced at the stinging pain, and tore off a piece of his shirt. Pressing the cloth against his bleeding forehead, he staunched the wound and examined the horses surrounding him. The jagged gash on Shalah's hindquarters he cleaned with another strip from his shirt. Altaira's injuries were deep but not serious.

Shakira was not so lucky, however. She kicked and rolled at the bottom of the impact crater, her back broken by a boulder dislodged from the explosions. Cerberus' left outside head extended toward the struggling mare and grasped her neck between its jaws.

Crunch!

Monstrous jaws snapped the mare's neck in two. The other outside head sparred with its brother to devour her entrails.

Concealed among the rocks, Gomez took this opportunity to sneak past the dog's feasting heads. Dashing toward the open Plain of

Asphodel with a screaming Ker in pursuit, he raced past Evelyn and reached the top of the ridge before the jaws of one of Cerberus' outside heads clamped around the purser's waist. The other outside head shot up and plucked the Ker out of the sky.

Evelyn sidestepped the latest carnage and reached the top of the ravine. After catching her breath, she waved for Victor and the horses to come. Despite her entreaties, Victor, Shalah and Altaira waited among the rocks for another chance. Cerberus was already sniffing around searching for its next victim; the dog's appetite seemed unending.

Another barrage of magma bombs exploded around Victor and the horses, but Cerberus wasn't so lucky. Dazed and bleeding from the impacts, Cerberus fell to the side of the path. A handful of Wailers dashed toward the top of the gorge, but the insatiable dog, spotting new prey, rallied and climbed to its feet. Despite his wounds he ripped apart every would-be escapee.

The eruption subsided and the tremors stopped. With no more Wailers left to devour, Cerberus scanned the trail, yawned, and finally settled into a satiated sleep. Victor, Evelyn, and the horses crept from their hiding spots. All three of the dog's heads snored and slobbered in semi-conscious satiety. Victor, Shalah, and Altaira joined Evelyn at the top of the gorge. Once together, Victor and Evelyn mounted the two horses and scrambled up the remainder of the path toward the open plain.

After they reached the relative safety of the Plain, Evelyn leaned over and wrapped her arms around Victor's neck. "I thought you weren't going to make it!"

"Me, either." They were lucky. Victor surveyed the carnage around them, taking in the scores of souls destroyed or maimed for all eternity. The impact on their corporeal selves was difficult to predict—catatonia for some, schizophrenia for others, deeper stages of psychosis for all. He sighed, dismounted, and reexamined Shalah's wounds. Aside from a deep cut on his right flank, his wounds amounted to nicks and bruises.

"You don't sound very happy," Evelyn said.

"I am. I'm amazed we got this far," Victor replied, tearing another strip from the bottom of his shirt. "But it's not over," he said, cleaning Shalah's cut. "The dog still blocks our way home."

"How?" Evelyn asked.

"The ravine is the sole route from the Asphodel Meadows to the River Acheron."

"There's no other way?" Evelyn asked.

"Acheron's the sole river to the Asphodel Meadows and Charon's ferry the sole means to cross it."

Evelyn's mouth twisted in thought as she dismounted from Altaira and followed Victor's lead, ripping pieces of her blouse into bandages and treating the horses' injuries. Thankfully, their wounds, while numerous, were not as severe as Victor had feared. Turning to Victor, she examined the cut on his forehead, tore off another strip from her blouse, and directed Shalah to dip the cloth in the creek flowing at the bottom of the nearby olive grove.

When the stallion returned, she daubed the dry blood from Victor's wound. "Let me get this straight," she said, wiping off a sticky blood clot. "You're saying we're stuck here?"

"Ouch!" Victor cried, not wanting to upset her. "Not so hard."

"You didn't squirm like this facing the three-headed dog." Evelyn finished wiping and examined her handiwork. "There! Good as new."

"Hardly." Victor winced. "What I'm saying is that we'll have to face Cerberus again on our return journey."

"Why?" Evelyn asked.

"I already explained that," Victor replied.

Evelyn placed her hands on her hips. "After we rescue Miriam, why can't we just wake up? Or have Desdemona wake us?"

"It's not that easy," Victor replied. "This isn't a dream."

"Why not?"

Victor scanned the nearby area. What would make her understand? Spotting nothing useful, he grabbed the fleshy inside of her upper right arm and pinched it—hard.

"Ouch!" Evelyn slapped his hand away and massaged the reddened area. "Did I rub so hard you needed to get back at me?"

"I needed to make a point."

Evelyn pouted. "Which is?"

"That our actions here have consequences," Victor replied. "Just like in the reality of the ordinary world."

"You didn't have to pinch so hard."

"Perhaps not." Victor smiled. "But did you ever feel pain like that in a dream?"

Evelyn reflected and shook her head.

"Neither have I," Victor said. "But everything we do here has the same impact as in the ordinary world. The Wailers confined here suffer pain like in ordinary reality. The minds of souls that die here expire and die in ordinary reality as well."

"You mean they become brain-dead in ordinary reality?" Evelyn asked.

"The physical link isn't that direct," Victor replied. "More like they become demented or catatonic—complete divorce from reality."

Evelyn's mouth twisted in thought. "But everyone's soul isn't trapped in Hades." Her face brightened. "Many people don't believe in the soul or an afterlife at all."

"That's true," Victor replied. "But it's part of your and Miriam's cultural heritage. And why Zarkisian put your soul here the first time and placed Miriam's in Tartarus now."

"Why?" Evelyn asked in dismay.

"To keep Miriam and you under his control."

Evelyn frowned. "Then Miriam truly is stuck here."

"Possibly." He cupped his hand under Evelyn's chin, guided her towards Altaira's right flank, and boosted her onto the mare's back. "But we're here of our own volition, like Orpheus and Hercules," he said, scrambling onto Shalah's back. "I don't know how much difference that makes, but if we're to have any chance at all, we have to find Miriam first, then take our chances with Cerberus again if we're to return to ordinary reality."

{7}

Victor scanned the plain: a semi-arid vista of low, sage-covered hills with small, gray-green olive groves dotting the valleys all the way to the horizon. Where was Tartarus amongst this desolation?

The volcanoes along the northwest horizon remained inflamed, but the barrage had ceased, the Keres killed or eaten. Without them serving as range finders, Angra Mainyu/Lord Ahriman, the ruler of Dakhanavar, and Akvan, his primary subordinate, had no means to monitor Victor's party. How long would the demon lord let this ceasefire last?

Without precise knowledge of where Tartarus was located, Victor followed the path hoping to find someone or something that could help them. Bouncing along on top of Shalah's back, he marveled again they had made it this far. Was it luck? Or the inaccuracy inherent in using lava bombs as guided missiles?

A solitary Ker appeared and watched their movements from the sky. Whatever the reason for their escape, Victor knew Ahriman and Akvan would devise more effective measures for their next air strike. He jabbed his heels into Shalah's ribs. "Pick up the pace!"

After several miles, the serrated turret of a bronze tower loomed above the western horizon. At the top of the next grassy hillock the air reeked of sulfur.

Descending toward the bottom of the hill, Victor spotted flames leaping from the water and lapping at the walls of a rugged fortress. A dark, beautiful woman wrapped in a blood-stained robe prowled the top of its battlements. Terrible oaths and screams emanated from inside.

"Who's that?" Evelyn asked, pointing at the menacing deity.

"No idea," Victor replied. "Desdemona never mentioned her."

"It is Tisiphone," Shalah answered. "She is chief among the Furies which guard the prison."

Evelyn shivered. "How awful."

"Yes," Shalah agreed. "Her duties are simple and two-fold: prisoners stay in; visitors stay out."

At the bottom of the hill the path forked in two directions. One must lead toward foul-smelling Tartarus, Victor decided, because he smelled brimstone from that direction. The other path, marked by a conical heap of stones, headed toward the daffodil-laced hillock opposite.

"Where does the fragrant path go?" Evelyn asked.

A green puff of smoke sprouted beside the stone pile. Out of it stepped a handsome blond boy sporting a red cloak, a round winged hat, and winged sandals. Two snakes coiled around the bronze staff nestled in his left arm.

"The Palace of Hades," the boy said with a roguish grin. "Where the souls of heroes and the just enjoy Hades' eternal delights."

The boy zoomed up beside Shalah. "You and your band have done well, Dr. Furst. Eluding the terrible guard dog of Hades is seldom accomplished."

Evelyn's eyes widened. Her hands shook. "Wh—who is this creature, Victor?"

"Hermes, the god who first guided me to Acheron's shore," Victor replied.

"Yes, Hermes, messenger of the gods," the boy said, doffing his hat. "Patron of travelers, athletes, and herdsmen, as well as official guide to the Underworld."

"Oh, I've heard of you, all right." Evelyn's nose wrinkled in disapproval. "Thieves count you as their patron, too."

Victor flashed a reassuring smile at Hermes. "Let him take your hand, Evelyn. Show that you trust him."

Evelyn's brows knitted, but she let Hermes clasp his sinewy hands around hers. "Where did you say that fragrance came from?"

"Let me show you." Hermes led them down the right-hand path and up the shallow knoll. At the top, he pointed toward the splendid palace whose marble walls shimmered like fresh milk under Hades' tepid sun. "There you are—the palace of Hades."

"Magnificent!" Evelyn exclaimed. "Who lives there?"

"The good and the just," Hermes replied. "And the ruler of this realm—Hades."

Victor knitted his brows as he studied the palace. "I thought Hades was the name of this grim place."

"They're identical," Hermes replied with a mordant chuckle. "Grim is the right word for it, in keeping with a ruler for the domain of the dead, don't you think?"

"It's appropriate," Victor agreed. "But you don't sound happy about it."

"Why should I for a reputation that's undeserved?" Hermes retorted. "'The unseen one' mortals call him—Humph! They fear mentioning his name because he rules the dead, but since he never leaves his castle, why worry what he might do?"

"Not everyone can be as sanguine about the afterlife as you are," Victor replied drily, reminded of his own mortality. "Not if Tartarus awaits them."

"Who are all those people down there?" Evelyn asked, pointing toward the marble dais at the bottom of the hill. Surrounding the platform, crowds of people sought the attention of three men seated on gilded thrones.

"That's the Court of Eternal Judgment," Hermes replied.

"What does it do?" Evelyn asked.

"See those three men seated on the dais?" Hermes said, pointing with his staff. "They are the judges—Aeacus, Rhadamanthys, and

Minos—who decide whether the souls of the dead spend eternity in Tartarus or the Palace of Hades."

"Miriam's not dead!" Evelyn's face flushed with outrage. "A spirit-sucking vampire sent her soul to Tartarus."

"Nobody is sent to either place without the three kings passing judgment on their worthiness," Hermes replied and wrapped his cloak tighter across his chest. "That's the protocol every soul sent here must follow."

"Then the kings made a mistake," Evelyn replied.

"They never make mistakes," Hermes said. "No one can leave Hades' domain once their soul enters it, so their judgment is final."

"They—he did this time," Evelyn huffed.

"Hades may be stern and cold and distant—like his kingdom," Hermes replied, gazing at the tumult. "But never unfair."

"I don't care," Evelyn cried and tapped the left side of Altaira's neck. "I know where Miriam is and I'm going to get her out."

"Hold on!" Shalah cried, blocking Altaira from pivoting. Evelyn's jaw dropped in amazement. "As Victor's spirit guide, I advise you to follow procedure and obtain the judges' permission to secure your daughter's release."

"Listen to him, Evelyn," Victor added. "We have no plan and no weapons to enter the prison, much less defeat the Furies guarding it."

Evelyn stared at Victor and Shalah, then spun around. "Hermes, what do you—?"

She looked about. "Where'd Hermes go?"

"He comes and goes." Victor cleared his throat. Hermes' abrupt appearances and departures troubled him, too, appearing when least wanted, departing when most needed. "Like a messenger."

"Ohhh!" Evelyn wailed, covering her face with her hands. "We can't just leave her there."

"We won't," Victor said, placing his right hand over hers in consolation. They had gone too far to quit now. "I promise."

Mollified for the moment, Evelyn and Altaira followed Victor and Shalah down the hillside toward the Court of Judgment. The three solemn, majestic men seated on the three golden thrones listened with varying degrees of concern to each plaintiff before them. Seated on the left, the tallest and lankiest of the three men joined his fingertips in the shape of an arch while he listened to every detail of the petitioner's presentation. His jeweled crown held an embossed representation of an ant and a goat.

"Who's that?" Evelyn asked.

"Aeacus," Shalah said. "He is the decider of the fate of men from the West."

"And the other two?"

"I'm not sure which is which," the stallion replied.

Not as tall, but as wiry, the other two judges resembled many people from the modern Near East. Victor and Evelyn watched both men listen to the petitioners' arguments. The decisions given by the judge seated in the right-hand throne seemed more deliberate and eventempered. His verdicts often contradicted the more aggressive pronouncements of the judge seated in the middle. "Based on what I recall from an introductory freshman history class, the right-hand judge must be Rhadamanthys," Victor decided. "The judge in the center would be his older brother, Minos."

Victor's troop approached the court. Victor dismounted and maneuvered through the mob until he reached the dais. "Noble ones, I come with a petition of the utmost importance," he declared, pushing back against the mob. But as one against many, the other petitioners shoved him back where he began. "It is imperative I speak to you now!"

"Let us handle this," Shalah said. He and Altaira formed a wedge in front of Victor. Plunging and rearing, they conducted the human couple through the crowd. When they reached the judges' stand, the three magistrates rose to their feet in unison:

"You have breached our judicial procedures," Aeacus cried.

"Who are you?" Rhadamanthys asked.

Minos eyed the Ker hovering above the crowd and shook his head. "You caused the recent barrage of flaming rocks, did you not?"

"You saw that?" Victor asked.

"They were hard to miss, even at this distance," Minos replied. "And you are the only ones who have approached the court since then."

"Ahriman directed them at us, yes," Victor said, deciding directness was the best approach.

"The demon king of the North?" Rhadamanthys replied. "That does not justify your disruption of this court."

"They're the reason we are in Hades at all," Victor said. "The gods who inhabit the fiery mountains to the northwest abducted our daughter. We came here to get her back. The flaming rocks were one of Ahriman's ways to stop us."

"The Persian gods of Zoroaster who rule Dakhanavar never bothered us before your arrival," Aeacus said, frowning. "Why should this court's proceedings and all of Hades be disrupted when your conflict is with them?"

"Since you know Ahriman's name, you know he and his followers are not the adherents of Ahura Mazda but of Mazda's evil brother." Victor pointed toward the northwest horizon. "If those mountains never belched fire before, they do so now because of the threat we represent to Ahriman."

The crowd's grumblings grew louder. Minos raised his arms and cried, "Hear him out." He turned toward Victor. "If what you say is

Mission: Soul Sacrifice

true, what does this court have to do with their abduction of your daughter?"

"Her soul was taken before its time," Victor replied.

"So was mine," a supplicant cried.

"So were all of ours," said another.

Minos stood up and waved his arms to quiet the crowd. "How many of you believe your sentencing to Hades is unjust?" When most of the crowd clamored their innocence, Minos turned back to Victor with a wry smile. "It seems the Field of Asphodel is overflowing with souls taken before their time."

You're losing the argument. Do something fast!

Victor turned and addressed the throng in front of the dais. "How many of you died in the corporeal world before arriving here? Raise your hands."

Hundreds of hands shot into the air including several souls who had derided Victor earlier. "Is that everyone?" he asked to appear inclusive. A few more raised their hands. "You're standing before the triumvirate of judges who determines your fate for all eternity. Your honesty on this issue will speak on your behalf."

Victor turned toward the judges for confirmation. Aeacus and Minos nodded their agreement; Rhadamanthys remained noncommittal. Victor turned back to the mob. "Heed me now, how many?"

Two-thirds of the crowd acknowledged their physical deaths. "Lower your hands," Victor scanned the crowd. "How many did not?"

Scores of supplicants raised their hands. "How many of you were diagnosed with Alzheimer's disease?"

Fewer supplicants raised their hands. Many hands dropped. "How many are dangerous to yourselves or others?"

More hands shot up.

"Delusional or hallucinatory?"

A few more hands rose.

"How many among those whose hands are raised have died?" Most of the hands dropped.

"What does this mean?" Rhadamanthys asked.

"It means Miriam and thousands like her are not dead," Victor replied. "Their energy is being used by Ahriman's avatars in the corporeal world to restore the old kingdom of Hayastan to be ruled by zalim—psychic parasites."

A murmur of recognition rippled through the crowd. Many of them spoke Arabic or were clothed in Eastern Mediterranean garb. "What does that have to do with us?" one asked in English.

"Your family, your relatives, your friends all may become as you are, their souls trapped in the Lower World while their zar-infested bodies serve as obedient reservoirs of energy for the zalim in the corporeal world."

The crowd buzzed. Minos stretched out his arms again to quiet it. "What does that have to do with this court?"

"Our daughter along with these many others did not deserve being sent to Hades," Victor answered. "Has a young woman named Miriam appeared before you?"

All three judges looked at one another in bewilderment. After Victor described Miriam to them, the judges huddled together, then summoned the record keeper to bring a list of recent petitioners. More discussion and consultation followed before Aeacus addressed Victor and the throng. "We have no evidence such a young woman has appeared before our tribunal."

"Which judge would have passed sentence?" Victor asked.

"As a member of a western race, such a young woman would have appeared before Aeacus," Minos replied.

Victor turned toward Aeacus. "Noble one, I beseech you to wrack your memory. Do you recall a feisty young woman, mid-twenties, with rusty red hair like mine? She is curious about everything, wanting to know how and why it all works."

"No one like that," Aeacus said. He unclasped his palms and scanned the record keeper's roll of parchment. "No one of that name appears here."

Evelyn stepped forward. "You're certain no one could have gotten past you?"

"Everyone who enters Hades is judged here," Minos replied. "No exceptions."

Victor hesitated. What other action could they take?

Three petitioners from the front row pulled Victor and Evelyn off the dais. The others elbowed him out of the way. Evelyn placed a hand on Victor's shoulder. "What about an assumed name?"

Which one? The record keeper's scroll listed thousands. If Miriam appeared as someone else, they had little means to discover her identity.

Victor waved his arms and bulled his way to the front of the petitioners again. "Were any of the female petitioners redheads who acted dopey or withdrawn?"

Aeacus stood up. "Repeat the question."

"Has anyone who appeared before you acted dopey or withdrawn?"

Aeacus turned toward his fellow judges. "Let us confer on this matter one more time—in the name of justice."

They summoned the record keeper once more. Aeacus made several emphatic gestures toward the scroll during their protracted discussion, then turned back to Victor. "Three women of such description have appeared before the court. One claimed to have been from Sardis, another from Liverpool."

"And the third?" Evelyn asked.

"Said nothing at all," Minos replied.

"Except Ahura Mazda." Rhadamanthys cocked his brow. "Mazdaism?"

"That's her!" Victor cried.

"Then Ahriman has already won," Aeacus declared. "Since she provided no defense in her behalf, the judges sent her to Tartarus."

"From which there is no escape," Victor said.

"For any of us," Evelyn groaned.

{8}

Victor guided Evelyn away from the dais. She staggered once, sobbing with sorrow and frustration. He placed his hand under her armpit, propping her up while Shalah and Altaira steered them through the crush of petitioners.

Let her cry. Get all her grief out.

Victor felt nothing. What should he feel? What could he do? The right words weren't there—if there were any. What could he say when he felt nothing except shame for returning Evelyn's soul to this awful place? Now their fate was worse than ever.

Shalah and Altaira escorted them from the melee to a flat rocky outcropping at the bottom of the hill and formed a protective barrier between the pair and the angry petitioners.

"It's OK, Victor," Evelyn said, sniffling and wiping her eyes. "You couldn't have foreseen this happening."

"Yes, I could," Victor retorted. "If Desdemona had warned me about the three kings and the difficulties in dealing with them the first time I was here, I could have prepared better rather than jumping right back into Hades."

"We didn't have the time," Evelyn replied, the corners of her lips trembling as if she would cry again. "You said we had less than ten hours."

"Yes, I did," Victor said, acknowledging his misjudgment wasn't the right thing to say, either. How could he make her feel better? He curved his index finger, cupped it under her chin, and pulled it toward him. "I knew I shouldn't have brought you back to the Lower World so soon."

"I had to come," Evelyn countered, her jaw muscles tensing with defiance. "It's what a mother does." She peered into Victor's eyes. "How do we help Miriam now?"

Whatever a father does—I'm not her father. But if I were?

Victor dropped his hand. He hadn't thought of Miriam's welfare until this moment. "If Miriam had just defended herself before the judges—

"Do you suppose Zarkisian's influence has grown so strong over Miriam that her soul no longer resists him?"

"No—" Miriam replied, her features caving with fear. "That *can't* be."

"Master Furst," Shalah interrupted. "Look at the petitioners."

Petitioners from other parts of the corporeal world shoved the Middle-Easterners aside, insisting they wait their turn. The Middle-Easterners stood their ground and pushed back. Fists started flying from both sides and in all directions.

"Tisiphone, come!" Rhadamanthys shouted above the melee. "Bring your sisters, Alecto and Megaera, and restore order to these deliberations."

The three Erinyes soared above the mountaintops in the western sky. Dropping like three fighter planes on an attack run, they strafed and lashed the howling litigants with brass-studded whips. They wheeled back into the sky and arced over the petitioners once more.

Instead of quelling the supplicants' furor, however, the Erinyes' ferocity stoked their anger. With their renewed rage, petitioners from every ethnicity attacked the dais, overturned the thrones, and broke through the knot of clerks and bodyguards surrounding the horrified judges. Aeacus, Rhadamanthys, and Minos ran off in three different directions.

Evelyn scanned the horizon and pointed toward the northwest. "Look! Something's happening in the mountains." The snow-capped peaks had regained their blood-red glow. Sulfur jets spewed hundreds of feet into the air. "Does that signal Ahriman's next barrage?" Evelyn wondered aloud. "Would he try to reach us here?"

Victor gazed upward. "I don't think so," he said with a shrug of uncertainty. "The Ker that has been following us hasn't left her position above us. She would move away to monitor the barrage from a safe distance if one was forthcoming."

Rhadamanthys and his retinue of clerks and servants regrouped and, surrounded by bodyguards with raised lances, parted the crowd of battling petitioners and marched toward Victor and his band.

Shalah nodded at Victor who signaled the stallion to let Rhadamanthys through. When the two horses opened their protective phalanx, Rhadamanthys strode up to Victor and declared, "See what you have done?"

"What I've done?" Victor replied in surprise.

"You must have noticed the sentinel above you," Rhadamanthys said, pointing toward the Ker hovering a safe height above their heads. Then he pointed toward the northern horizon. "And the fires on the horizon. As the creator of this discord, it is your responsibility to restore order to the operations of this court."

Victor sensed an opening. "Is that a threat?"

"You say that your journey here was to recover your daughter," Rhadamanthys replied. "Be assured you shall join her in Tartarus, if you do not heed our request to restore order."

"And if I refuse?"

"Tisiphone has even more refined torments at her disposal than you have yet witnessed."

"Hmm." Victor stroked his beard and glanced at the three Erinyes struggling to keep the perverse petitioners under control. Rhadamanthys was not making an idle threat. The screams coming from Tartarus could be heard even at this distance. But he needed to secure Miriam's release—time for brinkmanship. "That's not much better than the deal the Zoroastrian devil Akvan offered me to leave Hades."

Rhadamanthys drew himself to his full height. "You dare compare me with Ahriman's sycophant?"

"Your tactics seem much the same as those that operate in Dakhanavar."

"There is no comparison," Rhadamanthys protested. "We fulfill our promises. The Persian devil doesn't."

"Then, you'll release Miriam if I agree?" Victor countered.

Rhadamanthys frowned. "Tartarus is outside my jurisdiction."

Victor grimaced. He had expected as much. He crossed his arms and turned away. "Do your worst."

A rumble shook the ground. Even in this timeless place it seemed to last forever. When it stopped, lava again poured down the distant mountain sides like steaming raspberry syrup.

"There is an alternative," Rhadamanthys said. "But you must bring the fight between the warring factions to a stop."

"How can I curtail hostilities in a place where three kings and three deities cannot?" Victor asked.

"How can a mortal come to place himself in such a position?" Rhadamanthys replied. "Restoring order is a fair request for revealing the secret of restoring your daughter to you."

So, there is a way. Has Rhadamanthys known it all along?

Victor spun toward the Cretan king and noted the firm set of his jaw. He couldn't push this man too far.

He rubbed his hand across his chin while considering the best way to negotiate. "My band of two horses is much too small for the task as it stands," he declared. "The deities assigned to quell the groups' outbursts seem to feed off the feuding factions' animosities. Before I do anything, you call off the Erinyes."

Mission: Soul Sacrifice

"Im—impossible," Rhadamanthys spluttered. "Once released upon a target, their attacks are relentless."

Victor pointed above his head at the Ker that shadowed their activities, a safe distance above the commotion. "Have the Erinyes redirect their vengeance toward the Ker that Ahriman has spying on us."

Rhadamanthys signaled Tisiphone and pointed toward the hovering Ker. She and her screeching sisters zeroed in on their new target. The startled Ker fought back, but, overwhelmed by the ferocity of its attackers, retreated toward the cliffs overlooking the River Lethe. The Erinyes whipped the beleaguered demon back and forth until her frenzied escape attempts brought her to the head of Cerberus' ravine.

Waiting in bloodthirsty anticipation, the dog's three heads rose out of the ravine and snapped at the fleeing demon. The three horrible sisters prevented the Ker's attempts at soaring to safety. First, Magara obstructed the Ker's path towards the Field of Judgment as it swerved and avoided Cerberus' jaws. Then, Tisiphone and Alecto intercepted it and forced the Ker lower and back towards the ravine. The Ker flitted and dodged the Erinyes' stinging whips and the dog's snapping jaws, frantically trying to maneuver away from the dangers that surrounded it until it misjudged a dive by the dog's middle head. Cerberus seized its opportunity and snapped its jaws around the demon, ripping it in two.

The distant eruptions subsided.

"Well?" Rhadamanthys said, turning toward Victor. "We've done as you requested."

"Thank you, your eminence," Victor replied. "Our turn."

Stationing Evelyn behind him, Victor flanked a horse on either side of her. With Victor leading the way, the four of them marched toward the squabbling petitioners.

"Look!" Victor ordered and pointed toward the mountains still rumbling and smoking on the horizon. "The strength of those eruptions depends upon the discord generated by the factions appearing before the judges here."

Victor turned back toward the judges with a sweep of his arm. "Let these fair men give your petition an honest hearing."

"How can we count on that?" one petitioner shouted.

"You have my word on it," Victor replied. "If anyone complains about the fairness of the proceedings," he added, "I shall stand judgment in their stead."

He turned toward Rhadamanthys for confirmation and saw him respond with a curt nod. Evelyn grabbed Victor's arm. "Don't do this!"

"It's the only way," Victor replied in a low voice. "If we fail, our souls are stuck in Hades for eternity anyway."

He turned back to the petitioners. "Is that arrangement satisfactory?"

A mixture of unwilling agreement, dissatisfaction, and resentment rumbled from the throng. Nonetheless, the warring factions formed three ragged lines in front of the marble dais. Aeacus and Minos resumed their seats and waited for Rhadamanthys to join them.

Victor marched up to the dais and addressed Rhadamanthys. "You must now keep your side of the bargain."

"The only way for souls to escape the wrath of Tartarus is to prove the gods of war sent them there by mistake," the Cretan king replied. "Exceptions do exist, such as for those souls who fall in battle."

Victor furrowed his brows. "Miriam did not participate in any kind of battle."

"Hasn't she?" Rhadamanthys sneered. "Didn't she participate in defeating the corporeal agents of Ahriman?"

"I suspect not," Victor replied. "Otherwise, she wouldn't be confined to a mental hospital."

"Her success or failure is not in question here," Rhadamanthys replied. "She did, however, engage in war-related activities with the purpose of defeating your enemies."

"She does not comprehend her role in defeating Ahriman's agents," Victor replied. "Given her level of awareness, I would consider her an unwitting combatant at best."

"That is of no consequence," Rhadamanthys replied.

"Is it legal for us to obtain a certain status for a person on their behalf without asking their permission first?" Victor asked. "Is it ethical for us to do so without informing them first?"

"Adults do so for their children all the time," the king replied.

"But she's not—"

"For goodness sake, Victor," Evelyn said, pushing him aside. "There isn't time for dealing with legal niceties. Or your wounded male vanity."

She turned toward Rhadamanthys. "How does such an exception help Miriam?"

"You must beseech the god or goddess who takes in such heroes on their behalf. As your daughter is of Indo-European origin, you must approach the proper god of the Kurgan races to intercede with Tisiphone in your daughter's favor."

Rhadamanthys tapped Aeacus's shoulder. "What is the name of the Kurgan god who determines the Lower World outcome of warriors fallen in battle?"

Aeacus turned to his assistant. "Hand me the scroll that lists the appropriate intercessors for each ethnic group."

His assistant produced and unrolled a short piece of parchment for Aeacus to read. Aeacus perused the scroll, consulted with the other judges, and turned to Victor. "The Germanic goddess, Frigg, often called Freya, is the one whom you must seek."

Evelyn's knees buckled. Victor grabbed under her armpit, steadied her, and leaned her shoulder against Shalah's right flank for support. "The task you assign us is enormous," he said, readdressing the king. "And we have little time as it is for us to accomplish it."

"You asked the conditions to secure your daughter's release," Aeacus said. "How you accomplish the task or the time frame in which you do it is not our concern."

Evelyn rallied, stepped around Victor, and approached the judges.

"Where can Freya be reached?" she asked, her voice quavering with indignation and renewed determination.

"In Valhalla," Rhadamanthys replied. "On the other side of the mountains that belch fire."

{9}

"We'll do it," Evelyn declared to the surprised king. "Just have your release papers or whatever is needed to release us from this place ready when we return!"

She wheeled on her heel, climbed onto Altaira's back, and peered down at Victor who remained unmoving. "Are you coming, or must I handle this on my own?"

The implied "Again" remained hanging in the air between them.

"It's not that I don't want to come with you," Victor replied, scratching his beard with a frown. "It's the time frame. It's too short."

"You said before we entered the Lower World, we had ten hours."

"Do we really?" Victor replied, cocking an eyebrow.

"Don't play games with me, Victor," Evelyn replied in annoyance. "All I know is we have to hurry."

"Sure, we do," Victor agreed, calculating in his head. "But it's more complicated than simply meeting a time schedule."

Evelyn's face scrunched up with mistrust. "What do you mean?"

"I mean our efforts to reach the Three Kings took—how long would you say in ordinary reality? It took three, maybe four hours to leave the dock and elude Cerberus? Another couple of hours to locate and deal with the Kings?"

"I guess," Evelyn replied, wary of where their conversation was headed. "So?"

"So, how do those estimated four to six hours translate into the corporeal world?"

"I don't understand," Evelyn said, her mouth puckered in confusion. "Shouldn't it be the same?"

"We have no way of knowing whether the time that elapsed here equates to six hours or a blink of an eye in the corporeal world," Victor said, scanning the horizon. "I'm guessing the renewed volcanic activity in the mountains of Dakhanavar indicates the remaining time before the bombing deadline in the physical world is waning fast."

"So?" Evelyn asked. "Why does that matter so long as we rescue Miriam?"

"Her fate and the Air Force bombing seem intertwined. Every time we progress in our rescue attempt, the volcanoes spew lava missiles to prevent us," Victor replied. "Now the volcanoes are erupting again, louder than ever, but they're not shooting fireballs at us."

"Our good luck," Evelyn said. "Ahriman realizes they're ineffective."

"Or he's redirecting them," Victor replied. "We've barely survived his attacks as it is, so why not continue them and finish the job?"

"Unless he has a more important target," Evelyn said, her face brightening with comprehension. "Like End Time?" she suggested. "He'd want his big guns ready for that one."

"Exactly," Victor agreed. "If preventing End Time and rescuing Miriam are interdependent, we can't stop the one unless we save the other."

"All the more reason to get to Valhalla as soon as we can," Evelyn retorted, digging her heels into Altaira's sides. "Let's go!"

"Hold it!" Victor grabbed Evelyn's arm. "We need to contact Todd."

"What for?"

"If Helsingford and his allies can delay the bombing, it would delay End Time and give us more time to reach Freya's court and rescue Miriam."

"Are you sure of that, Victor?" Evelyn asked, shaking free of his grip. "How much time would we gain?"

"I don't know," Victor admitted, looking away. "But more than we have now."

"OK, say you're right," Evelyn said, placing her hands on her hips. "Here's another question: how?"

Victor smiled. Evelyn did listen to him—once in a while.

"Desdemona is monitoring our progress on the psychomanteum we improvised, remember," he said. "She could relay a message to Helsingford to gain us more time."

"I don't see how Desde—"

"There isn't time for debate," Victor declared and strode between the horses. He raised his arms and waved them like a railway brakeman flagging a train. Would Desdemona recognize that he was about to transmit a message?

He had to take that chance. Since their connection through his improvised psychomanteum was visual rather than auditory, he pantomimed his message by cupping his hand beside his ear and pretending to speak into a telephone. Then, he grabbed a nearby fig branch and scraped Todd's name and a clock face in the earth. The longer hand he set at midnight and the shorter at ten p.m., the approximate time he and Evelyn departed into the Lower World. He ended his communication by scoring a question mark in the dirt alongside his watch image.

Evelyn's brows knitted with disapproval. "Are you certain Desdemona will understand your hieroglyphs?"

Victor grimaced. "Who knows if she received my message at all?"

He eyed the judges handing out their eternal judgments. "See if any of the judges know of a faster means of transportation to Freya's court than our horses."

The corners of Evelyn's mouth drooped. "This is just to give me something to do, isn't it? If we can't get there in time, why don't you say so?"

"No, not at all." Victor placed one hand on her shoulder and cupped her chin with the other. "Shalah and Altaira can get us there in time. But finding out if there's a faster alternative never hurts, does it?"

"No, I suppose not." Evelyn sighed, squared her shoulders, and headed for the judgment stand.

Victor signaled Shalah to join him. "If Evelyn's spiritual reserves were stronger, I could enlist one of her own power animals to protect her. But since she's not—"

"She needs our protection." Shalah nodded at Altaira. "Altaira will go with her."

Reassured for the moment, Victor sat on the flat rock and waited for Evelyn's return. A huge, brown house spider crawled from under the outcropping and climbed on his hip.

Victor flinched. He hated spiders. "Get it off, Shalah."

"It won't bite," Shalah replied. "Nor is it poisonous."

"Are you sure?"

"Be still!" The splendid stallion snorted.

The hairy spider hesitated, then hopped onto Victor's shoulder. It turned its spinnerets towards his face, spewed four streams of gauzy silk into a pile, wrapped them into a ball, and deposited it in Victor's hand. Then the spider crawled down his arm and disappeared behind the stone.

"How did you know it wouldn't bite?" Victor asked. "Nothing else here has been friendly."

"A spider is one of a good witch's power animals," Shalah replied. "The discharge signifies Desdemona's receipt of your message."

"Because a spider is a good power animal," Victor replied, "you figured Desdemona must have sent it."

Victor stroked his beard to disguise his mistrusting Desdemona's dependability. "So, what does the spider's appearance mean?"

"Eight of your corporeal hours are left before your deadline, I think. Assuming the number of strands is intentional, no other explanation seems likely."

Victor smeared the sticky remains on the jagged outcropping and did a mental computation. If they entered the Lower World with ten hours of ordinary time and six hours had elapsed, that meant they had four hours of ordinary time left. And if Evelyn's estimate of their Lower World exploits time elapse was accurate, that meant each hour of ordinary time amounted to two hours in the Lower World.

He gazed up at the pallid, unending sun and frowned. Seven, perhaps eight hours at most in the Lower World, left little time to reach Valhalla, return, and free Miriam from Tartarus if Keres still patrolled the skies above Dakhanavar.

Victor got to his feet as Evelyn bustled toward him, her face gleaming with excitement. "Wonderful news! My spirit animals can fly us all the way to Valhalla."

Victor's stomach fluttered with increased anxiety. "Wh—what animals are those?"

"Butterflies." Evelyn beamed. "You're not the only power source in the Lower World."

"How did you find out?" Victor asked, skeptical of her self-discovery. *It took me months to find mine.* "You've never done this before, have you?"

"Uh-uh," Evelyn replied with a shake of her head. "I sat down and concentrated like you do," she added, wiping a sweaty hair strand from her face. "And after a moment, they materialized."

Victor looked about. "Where are they now?"

"They flew away," Evelyn replied and shrugged.

"What?" Victor asked. "Can you bring them back?"

"I think so," Evelyn replied, wincing. She touched her forehead. "It's all so new to me!"

"There isn't time for uncertainty!" Victor grabbed her shoulders, sat her on the rock beside him, and explained the meaning and implications of the spider's message. Evelyn stared at the ground when he finished.

"Your butterflies' flying abilities would save time," he concluded, acknowledging the value of her idea, "if they were strong enough to transport two human beings in the Lower World. But they're as weak and delicate as their ordinary world counterparts."

Evelyn's jawline hardened.

"And it's unsafe," Victor added, searching for another reason to soothe her frustration. "Exposure in the air signals to Ahriman our destination isn't nearby. Given the number of Keres at his disposal, it's better he thinks he needs just one to track us."

Evelyn said nothing.

She knows I'm right.

Victor tried to wrap her in his arms, but she pulled away. "I don't need your sympathy, or your affection—just a workable alternative."

Victor recoiled. Was this outburst part of her hatred toward him? "You don't understand the difficulty of our predicament."

"Yes, I do," Evelyn replied. "Better than you think."

"I know you want to help, but—"

"You think you alone have spiritual powers," Evelyn responded through gritted teeth. "Who got you here in the first place? Who distracted Cerberus? Stop patronizing and let me think."

She paced back and forth in a tight circle. Then her eyes lit up. "Do all of a person's power animals come in pairs?"

Victor nodded. She was more perceptive than he'd given her credit for. "They originate from complementary environments. Like sky and sea or earth and fire."

"If yours are land and sea, is there any way to find out what my combinations are?"

"Either sea or land, given your first spirit animals were sky creatures," Victor replied, upset by her persistence. "But we don't have the time to identify your other power spirits."

"Why not?" Evelyn pouted as she scanned the throng beseeching the judges and the distant mountains belching fire. "What else is there to do? What's the alternative?"

She's right.

Victor relented and sighed his acknowledgement. "Close your eyes and concentrate as you did when you summoned the butterflies. If your other spirit animal is willing, it will appear if you summon it."

Evelyn sat on the rock and directed her focus inward. Energy radiated from her body with an intensity Victor never encountered from her in the corporeal world. She seemed so weak on the plane and at the airport. As an empath he always regarded Evelyn as a passive receptacle which absorbed and transferred energy from more dominant personalities. No wonder Zarkisian wanted Evelyn out of the way if she can supplement such power with her own, even amplify it.

Was I too protective of her before?

Victor winced in remorse and with admiration at her powers of concentration.

Did I dismiss her butterfly option before as a bad idea or out of my need for control? He flushed at his self-deception. *The latter.*

A flutter of flapping wings coincided with dust swirling about their feet. A pair of mated blue herons landed and strutted twenty yards away. Evelyn approached them, but the birds did not startle. The male wrapped its azure wings about Evelyn's shoulders; the female cooed in Evelyn's ear.

"This is perfect!" Evelyn clapped her hands and stroked the female bird's long, slender neck. "Herons can fly, and they can stay under water for long periods of time. We can swim beneath the surface of

Acheron until we circle the mountains, and then fly the rest of the way to Valhalla."

Victor rubbed the back of his neck. Evelyn's spirit animals' affection for their human counterpart seemed suspicious. "Doesn't their appearance seem a little convenient?" he asked. "We're stymied about how to reach Valhalla, and, Voila! The very spirit animals we need appear right beside us."

Evelyn patted the two adoring birds. "Must you rain on everything I do? You can't stand it when anybody else tries to help themselves."

"It's not that," Victor replied, irked at how she mistrusted his motives. "My dealings with the demon Akvan show how cautious you need to be with spirits in the Lower World."

"Not every spirit is a demon. Hermes has helped us."

"So far." Victor shook his head in skepticism. "Gaining the trust of my spirit animals took weeks, not minutes. A working relationship takes even longer."

"You're just jealous," Evelyn replied, stroking the female heron's neck. The male embraced Evelyn with his wing. "We can do it alone."

Shalah and Altaira stood aside to let the trio leave. Evelyn's accusations were unfair and untrue. *How could he prove it?*

"Tell me this," Victor said suddenly. "Would your power animals be as affectionate if you had rejected them and stayed with me?"

Evelyn said nothing while the herons led her away from the circle of horses.

"Show me I'm wrong," Victor said. "Tell them you're taking the land route with me."

Evelyn glared, patted the herons' necks, and headed toward the horses' protective flanks. Both herons squawked and flapped their wings. When she pushed the male heron aside, he nipped her cheek. Both birds blocked her path and buffeted her with their wings.

Mission: Soul Sacrifice

The two horse spirits galloped to Evelyn's rescue. They plunged and reared and kicked up dust until the air surrounding them became a cyclone of blue feathers and swirling motes. The herons buffeted the heads of their attackers and snapped at their faces. Shalah kicked the male bird in the neck; Altaira's blow bent the female bird's right leg, allowing the horses to separate Evelyn from her attackers and reform a protective guard around her.

Both herons flapped into the air. The male heron strafed Evelyn's protective circle; the female dived toward Victor.

Covering his head with his arms, Victor zigzagged toward Evelyn crouching between the horses' protective bodies. When he reached safety, the female heron transformed into the hoary blue demon Akvan, the male into frog-faced Lord Ahriman.

"Vahagn," Ahriman rasped in a dark voice, his black forked tongue fluttering. "Neither you nor your cohorts shall escape."

He pointed a webbed finger toward the mountains belching fire and turned toward the petitioners surrounding Hades' judges. "The fires of Dakhanavar soon will begin their cleansing work of the Plains of Hades. Those who join forces with me shall be spared my wrath; those who do not shall be entombed in torments they cannot imagine."

"We're not afraid of you!" Victor spat.

"So be it," Ahriman replied. Turning toward the judgment stand, his bulging green eyes scanned the petitioners. "No one shall be spared."

The two demons soared into the air toward the fiery mountains. Spotting the demons' departure, the petitioners stormed the judges' stand and demanded protection.

Evelyn trembled beside Victor. "He called you Vahagn. Why?"

"Mistaken identity," Victor fibbed. *Do we really need to go into that now?* "Even gods make mistakes sometimes."

Evelyn cocked a doubting eyebrow. "That's all it is—mistaken identity?"

"Comparative mythology is full of such mistakes in every culture," Victor replied.

"What's the mistake here?" she asked.

"Ahriman thinks I'm Vahagn."

"So?"

"He's the Armenian equivalent of Hercules," Victor replied and noted the twitch playing at the corners of Evelyn's mouth. *A repressed smile, perhaps?* "Ridiculous, right?"

Evelyn cocked her eyebrow again. "Why?"

"Do I look like a Hercules to you?"

"No." Evelyn frowned in chagrin. "But you're the one I need."

To Victor's surprise, Evelyn sidled into the crook of his arm, took his wrist, and wrapped his arm around her. "And still do, regardless of my connection with Zarkisian. That makes you Vahagn to me."

The honesty of her gaze melted Victor's distress. He wanted to believe it meant he could restore her love for him as well.

Don't be a fool.

Victor removed his arm from her waist. "You can't be serious."

"Why not?" Evelyn bit her lower lip. "Why can't you accept that role in my life?" She gazed about the leaden landscape in desperation. "You're in my psyche. What more do you need?"

"I can't play that role." Victor blew his cheeks out. "It doesn't feel right."

Evelyn's brows knitted. "Because of Zarkisian?"

He threw up his hands. "And everything else."

"Like Miriam, you mean."

Of course, Miriam.

Victor flushed with resentment. "Yes, her."

"And?" Evelyn's eyes pierced him like daggers.

Mission: Soul Sacrifice

"I feel betrayed." He turned away. *Does Evelyn's betrayal or my lack of professional detachment disturb me more?* "If you must know."

"As does Miriam." Evelyn touched his shoulder. "This retrieval is as much about you as it is about her. If you feel this way, why are you rescuing her?"

"Because it's a good idea." He whirled toward her. "Because it will help us gain our passports and get into the U. S. Because more than our puny lives are involved."

"Whole nations are at stake, I get it." Evelyn's lower lip trembled. "But Miriam means nothing to you? Or her happiness?"

Victor clenched his jaw. Miriam embodied the emotional chasm between him and his ex-wife. "You're asking too much right now."

Evelyn sighed. "So, what do we do now?"

"We take the land route around Dakhanavar to Valhalla."

"The air route is out, you said," Evelyn replied. "What about going by water?"

"Too indirect given our limited time frame," Victor answered and boosted Evelyn onto Altaira's back. "With horses the land route is shorter and safer."

He climbed onto Shalah's back. "I just hope Helsingford negotiates enough of a delay in the corporeal world for us to get there and return in time."

{10}

Todd shifted the banana-yellow, flatbed truck into second gear, pulled out of the monastery driveway, and headed down the rocky lane toward Highway Five, eastern Turkey's main highway. The clutch in the Russian-built truck was workable but sticky. However, the act of shifting gears required him to use the hand of his broken arm, so he confined shifting only to climbing larger hills or when the road was smooth. He could ignore pain and inconvenience, but wished he was driving a less conspicuous vehicle.

Desdemona's relayed message from Victor could not have come at a worse time. Ambassador Gifford had placed Todd in charge of coordinating communication between the American Air Force and the American Embassy in Tehran. Victor's request to delay the bombing arrived after the air group's attack squadron had departed from their base in Kirkuk.

"Can you delay the attack, General Patterson?" Todd had asked over the phone. "My agents need more time."

"Enemy forces on the ground take priority over spirit forces in the air," Patterson replied.

"Thousands of innocent Armenian and Azeri nationals will be killed."

"Assaults on American embassies that result in loss of life cannot go unanswered," Patterson said. "Without mitigating circumstances, they must be responded to in kind."

"Our air attack can't wait beyond four hours?" Todd asked.

Patterson sighed. "Zero hour's less than that—*if* you can't get the Hayastanis to stand down. If the leaders of this outlaw government will discuss their grievances with others in the region, I guarantee U.S. planes will not attack."

He cleared his throat. "If they continue to fortify the mountain and strengthen their authority in the region, however, the first bombing run will occur as scheduled—with many more, for however long it takes."

Todd had commandeered the monastery's pickup truck for those reasons. Following Metropolitan Arkadian's directions, he drove the lumbering vehicle along a smuggler's route north of the one he had taken to the Khor Virap monastery. This route connected Highway 5 with the village of Yenidogan where Seraphina with her squad of New Immortals had captured Mt. Ararat.

He hoped the New Immortals would regard his solo effort as an olive branch rather than another example of American lone wolf diplomacy. Whatever influence he had with Seraphina and she over Zarkisian, he had to trust it would prevent the massacres anticipated with the End Time.

He passed two mud huts at the village outskirts. Five gunshots strafed the front passenger-side door. Two more blew off the driver's side-view mirror. His rearview mirror showed three of Dubromov's rebels rushing out into the street behind Todd's truck. He floored the accelerator and swerved into a side street. Two bullets whizzed past his head, two more embedded themselves in the tailgate.

Yenidogan's backstreets resembled those of most Turkish villages—a peasant-farm labyrinth of alleys and dead-ends. Todd rammed the truck through a backyard chicken coop and two barbed wire fences to get back to the main road. Behind him, he saw an angry rooster pecking the face of Todd's nearest pursuer while frightened hens flapped about his companions in a flurry of squawks and feathers.

Todd steered the truck back onto the paved road and headed toward the town square. Distant gunfire rattled Mt. Ararat's foothills to the north; a second spatter erupted from the Turkish army's checkpoint on the main road to the southwest, then stilled.

Nausea washed over him. The road conditions and the truck's balky steering had taken their toll on his endurance. He pulled another of Arkadian's pain pills from inside his shirt. Two tablets made the throbbing in his arm manageable. Three would—

Don't think about that!

He popped one in his mouth, stuck the bottle inside his shirt to keep his faculties as intact as possible, and headed up the mountain route he and Seraphina had taken out of the city to the public park at the base of the mountain. Ararat's frosty peak shone like the copper dome of a minaret in the morning sun.

When Todd reached the park, he stopped the truck at the picnic area entrance where Cramer had chased Seraphina's troops into the woods. No Anausavared troops stationed there, not even a sentry. No Turkish forces either.

Where is everybody?

He stepped out of the truck and trod the remaining quarter mile to the overlook point. Again, he found the site deserted. Where were Seraphina and her Anausavared troops? Or their opposition?

Striding to the overlook's coin-operated telescope, he popped in a coin and surveyed the mountain's snow-capped summit. The gravel deposit from Ararat's Abich glacier began where the vegetation ended. The craggy outcropping that formed the outline of what some people claimed was Noah's ark appeared another thousand feet above that. If Seraphina's squad was on the mountain, they must have hidden in the caves and ravines located below the boat-shaped ridge in the Ahora gorge.

Todd clambered down the hillside until he reached the gentle stream of stones and gravel that formed the glacier's flood plain. Tramping up the gravel slope, the plain turned into a narrow, steep path with a bubbling stream running through the litter of lichen-covered rocks and boulders.

Higher up, the incline grew steeper, the stream splashing over stony outcrops jutting from the rubble. He leaped from one outcrop to another. The jostling increased the pain in his arm, but he ignored it with a wry smile, thinking that next time he'd bring along hiking boots and a walking stick.

Three rifle bullets zinged the rocks ten yards in front of him. Todd stood erect and raised his good arm to show his surrender. A guttural voice barked an order in a language Todd didn't understand. Another shot ricocheted off the boulder to his right followed by a repeat of the command.

Todd shrugged, shook his head, and pointed at his forehead, hoping his mime conveyed his lack of understanding.

"Keep your arm up and keep moving," Seraphina said. "As you can see, my colleagues are trigger-happy."

Todd cautiously leaped from boulder to boulder until he reached the pebble-strewn delta that extended from under the glacier. Rock caves on either side formed natural guard posts. Two uniformed guards, whose bulletproof vests sparkled like brass spittoons, emerged from the entrance on Todd's right with their Kalashnikovs trained on his stomach. Outfitted in the same chainmail, copper plate, Seraphina watched the guards pat him down for weapons. "Where are the others?" she asked.

Her reserve disappointed him, though he wasn't much surprised. *Dammit!* Her tailored brass fatigues and cap clung to her like she was a superheroine in a fanboy's wet dream. "Glad to see you, too."

"Where *are* the others?" Seraphina repeated with annoyance.

Keep her off guard. Annoy her.

Todd surveyed his surroundings and grinned. "Nice digs."

"Don't waste our time with your American attempts at levity. Where are the other ambassadors?"

Mission: Soul Sacrifice

"I'm here to speak on behalf of the other concerned parties," Todd answered. "Whatever you say I can relay to them."

"Is that so?" Seraphina cocked her left eyebrow. "You come here without weapons or communicating devices of any kind, yet you are equipped to relay our demands to your American and Turkish overlords?"

"We're prepared to negotiate," Todd replied and nodded toward the entrance. "Is Zarkisian in there?"

"You shall see." Seraphina directed the guards to fall in behind them. She led Todd past the two-inch thick steel plate door down an excavated entry to a large chamber cut out of the rock which he recognized as the Anausavareds' site for the CECOM teleconferences. Seated at the head of the conference table were the two other members of the Hayastan triumvirate.

"This is the lone representative the six belligerents have sent us, Shahanshah," Seraphina announced and assumed a seat at the table near Zarkisian's left hand.

"Shahanshah?" Todd murmured, taking a seat beside her.

"Shah of shahs in Persian," Seraphina whispered back. "King of kings is the literal translation in English."

Across from her sat the dapper blond playboy, Rupert Albrecht, that Todd remembered. Albrecht conferred with a dark, handsome woman also dressed in form-fitting battle fatigues. "The American flight squadron has left Kirkuk headed in this direction," the woman announced.

"Seventy-five minutes at most before they're here," Zarkisian said, turning toward Seraphina. "You're certain our troops are prepared?"

Seraphina nodded. Albrecht glanced up from his secretary's iPad at Zarkisian. "The price of gold has never been higher on the Turkish exchange," he announced. "We should sell now."

"You're doing this for money?" Todd exclaimed.

"Hayastan's cash reserves are small," Zarkisian replied, his dark eyes sparking with indignation. "Hard currency is necessary to maintain its defenses and build up our infrastructure."

"Do we sell or not?" Albrecht asked.

"The gold market will go higher because this boy's masters will not allow him to come to harm," Zarkisian replied and patted Albrecht's forearm in reassurance. "Let us hear what he has to say."

"With American jets soon entering Turkish air space," Albrecht exclaimed, "we should sell now before they get here."

"Ararat is impregnable," Zarkisian declared, folding his arms across his chest. He turned to Todd. "What are your terms?"

Todd explained the armistice plan offered by the American Embassy in Tehran and the Turkish-Armenian Reconciliation Commission. The plan provided a non-intervention pact while giving the tentative government of Hayastan a month's time to air its grievances before a regional tribunal that included Russia and Turkey with the United States playing an advisory role. "This is an altogether fair, even generous offer to your band of usurpers."

Zarkisian chuckled. "No doubt you think the offer generous, but it does not seem so to those whose national claims upon this area go back millennia." He stood up. "Your terms are unacceptable."

"With all due respect, Shahanshah," Albrecht said. "A month's time is more than enough to secure our gains on the stock exchanges and establish an official currency."

"Yes, Great Leader," Seraphina added. "A month would help us solidify our defenses and increase our nation's army."

"Enough!" Zarkisian ended further debate with an imperious wave of his arm. "You know the timing of the bombing is crucial. Ahriman's order regarding it is absolute." His implacable gaze reduced Albrecht to silence. "You must do what you can with our finances in the time that is left."

He spun toward to Seraphina. "Are we not entrenched?" he asked her. "Is this mountain not impregnable? Are you not the major general of the New Immortals—the Eran-spahbed?"

Seraphina nodded her agreement. "Bunkered as we are, though, even immortals cannot long withstand continual bombardment," she replied. "Non-negotiation may trigger a more forceful response by the Americans." She turned to Todd. "Something atomic?"

Todd nodded. "I was told all options are on the table."

Time to trot out the big guns. "Though the social and political blowback might be terrible," Todd added, "prolonged and willful belligerence on your part could tempt American intelligence to play the nuclear trump card."

"Not to worry," Zarkisian replied. He grabbed Seraphina's shoulders and spun her towards him. "Prophecy states that this conflict was fated from eternity. Now the End Time has come when all are judged. The forces of Ahriman shall triumph over whatever fires our enemies use to destroy us."

Seraphina's eyes widened. "You *want* this attack to happen?"

"It is our destiny."

{11}

"Do whatever is necessary for Mr. Helsingford to relay our message," Zarkisian ordered before he stood up and left the chamber.

Todd spun toward Seraphina. "You *trust* that guy?"

"He is the Shahanshah of the Anausavared," Seraphina replied. "As the oldest and wisest among us, he must be obeyed."

"And you're at his command," Todd said in despair, resting his aching arm on the table. The hierarchical age structure dominated the decision-making of many Middle Eastern clans. As one of the oldest clans, the New Immortals appeared to apply this thinking to all their decisions. "The prophecy of Zoroaster predicts Ahriman's downfall," Todd said. "If Zarkisian's tying the future of Hayastan to the overthrow of Ahura Mazda, it's a battle neither side can win."

"Come." Seraphina beckoned toward the passage that led to the cave entrance. "Our communications area is available if you need help. Otherwise, you may go outside where the cell phone reception is better—under guard."

Todd rose and halted inside the doorway. *What will make her change her mind?* "Zarkisian's rejection of the allies' terms means there's no way the American fighter squad won't attack." Seraphina's expression did not change. Her disregard infuriated him. "Every possibility is on the table in these circumstances. You know that."

"I *am* aware," Seraphina retorted.

Two guards standing at the hallway intersection snapped to attention at their approach. Seraphina turned into an annex filled with radio and telecommunication equipment and Todd followed. Two Kurd communications officers watched separate monitors. One monitor contained four separate views of the glacial field outside the caves and the surrounding area. The other contained news stations from four separate TV channels: The Turkish and Armenian government stations, Al Jazeera, and CNN.

The senior officer, a corporal, stood up and snapped to attention. His partner, a private, continued monitoring the TV screens. "The glacier valley and periphery around the mountain remain clear," he reported in Turkish.

"What are the news reports?" Seraphina asked.

Todd didn't grasp everything the corporal reported, but understood Al Jazeera reported several rumors of secret negotiation among representatives of Turkish, Armenian, and Azerbaijani governments. The Armenian Irredentist movement disclaimed knowledge or involvement of those secret transactions. The Turkey and Armenian government stations maintained their information blackouts as did Azerbaijan, according to CNN.

Seraphina gestured toward Todd and told the corporal that Todd was a representative of the U.S. government sent here to report the Shahanshah's response to the Triad's peace proposal. "Give him whatever help he needs to contact his government—within reason," she said in English, "If he says or does anything else, shoot him."

Todd did not move. If Seraphina would not listen to reason, he did not want to take his chances surviving an all-out bombing assault on the mountain. If she wasn't receptive to the dictates of physical reality, he had to appeal to her cultural sensibilities. "The prophet claimed Ahura Mazda would gain his rightful place at the end of nine thousand years." He racked his brain. What other lore had Khor Virap's Metropolitan, Arkadian, supplied him? "If that is so, and this is the End Time, how can Ahriman and his disciples, as Zarkisian and the others claim to be, succeed?"

"You know the outlines of our sacred texts well," Seraphina replied. She pulled Todd into the passageway to prevent her subordinates from overhearing their discussion. "But whoever instructed you failed to inform you of their proper meaning."

"Which is?"

"The followers of Ahriman had nine thousand years from time's beginning to convince humans that material existence is all there is. If they stayed unconvinced, Ahura Mazda would free them from their material bodies to a spiritual life everlasting."

"So?"

"So, if the New Immortals can show immortality can be achieved in the ordinary world, then humans will welcome Ahriman and his representatives as their rightful rulers on this earth." Seraphina scanned Todd's face and frowned. "Don't you see? Reestablishing the ancient kingdom of Hayastan is the first step in your ultimate acceptance of our role."

"If zar is your example of bliss here on earth—no thanks," Todd replied. "Nobody will exchange their free will for an eternal life of mindless submission."

Seraphina smiled. "Isn't that the same bargain other religions offer? With ours there is no waiting, no shedding of this 'mortal coil' as your British writer, Shakespeare, put it."

It was Todd's turn to frown. Much of what Seraphina said was true. Most humans sought immortality whether they believed in it or not. Most people preferred having it in the here and now rather than in some vague paradise regardless of the truth or the consequences of achieving it. "If this is as inevitable as you claim, why must Zarkisian re-conquer this land? Wouldn't the benefits speak for themselves?"

Seraphina's pretty face clouded, and Todd pounced on the opportunity. "Is that why he refuses to negotiate—because the benefits are not as certain and rosy as you claim? Maybe just the opposite, given what happened to the Azeri rebel leader, Dubromov."

"That was a mistake," Seraphina said. She grabbed Todd's good arm and pulled him further away from the annex opening. "Dubromov resisted so much, he—"

"Had to be made an example?" Todd pointed toward the communication officers who continued scrutinizing their respective monitors. "Are they members of your new elite? Are they New Immortals, too?"

Seraphina's caramel complexion turned ashen. "N-not everyone can be a leader. Even in your hallowed democracy there are those who lead and those who follow. What we offer them more than makes up for any loss of authority or self-determination."

"Yes, I saw what it did for Dubromov." Todd grimaced. *At least she's on the defensive for once.* "Since then, I've wondered: why me? Why didn't the same fate happen to me?"

"You are my chosen one." Seraphina reached up and caressed Todd's face with the back of her hand. "The one destiny chose for me."

Todd cringed at her touch. Yet, the wistful rapture in her eyes softened the reproach nestling on the tip of his tongue. A gentle glow basked his body in familiar, suppliant radiance. "Our fate, I suppose."

Their fate? Or was this just another deception?

"Of all potential mates, you chose me," Todd said with a catch in his voice. He cupped her chin in his hand and fought to keep sarcasm out of his voice. "Could any mortal be more fortunate?"

"Yes, Todd, you," Seraphina whispered, nibbling his ear lobe. "Above all others—you. As consort, as equal, as father of my—"

"Brood?" Todd pushed Seraphina away. Her purpose was all too clear. "You need me to propagate. Like a ringworm infests a human stomach to lay its eggs."

Seraphina's dark eyes hurled daggers at him. Todd headed toward the communication alcove, pleased he had flummoxed her at last, even if it was with her own pretense of affection.

Mission: Soul Sacrifice

She grabbed Todd's bad arm and spun him around. "If you had any feeling, you'd see it's not that way at all."

Todd winced. "What do you know of feeling?" Her fingers felt as strong and sharp as the claws of a leopard. "You know it as the energy that keeps you and your parasite pals alive."

"You want feelings? Energy?" Seraphina retorted. Her bearing grew regal and erect. "These are the feelings the control of my energy has kept from you."

Todd doubled over. The pain from his injured arm riddled his body in wave after wave of agony. He grabbed the vial inside his shirt, popped two pills into his mouth, and gritted his teeth. "You're causing this."

Seraphina nodded in affirmation and summoned the guard stationed at the cave entrance. "Throw this one out onto the debris field. Prepare for aerial bombardment."

The guard lugged Todd to the cave entrance and flung him toward the debris field. Todd stumbled, slipped on the slippery rocks, and fell. He sat among the stones and pebbles, too exhausted and in too much pain to get up. Warm, buoyant air surged from the plain below. Lightning crackled above the glacier. A thunderstorm appeared imminent which often happened as Arkadian had warned him before Todd left the monastery. And his arm hurt like hell.

"No woman should have to ask twice!" Seraphina shouted above the gale. "The Eran-spahbed of Hayastan does not beg."

She slammed the entrance's steel door. Twin lightning bolts crashed into the ridge above. Fine black dust drizzled through the ionized air. Moments later, icy pellets of black rain hammered the gorge.

{12}

She might have given me a sling to wrap my arm in.
   Todd gritted his teeth and scanned the opposite ridge for shelter. Seraphina's message was clear: *You won't live long enough to need one.*
   The nearest cave was half a mile away, his truck even further away in the park at the base of the mountain—both too far to reach before the deluge from the glacier destroyed everything lying in its flood plain.
   He stumbled down the gorge towards the flatter ground at the foot of the glacial plain where flood water surges scattered and dissipated. Black sleet stung his face and hands like wasps defending their hive. Beside him, the gurgling stream swelled beyond its gravel-strewn banks and turned into a seething cataract.
   Clutching his aching arm against his chest, Todd scrambled through the furious torrent lapping at his heels toward a jagged boulder. He squeezed behind a protruding rock slab and watched the raging water swoosh by. Away from the storm's onslaught, he fumbled with his shirt pocket and popped yet another painkiller into his mouth.
   With his good arm, Todd clutched his knees against his chest to make himself as small as possible within his rocky niche. Inches beyond his toes, silt, sand, and boulders the size of Volkswagens tumbled down the gorge. Ice slabs the size of houses crashed into the flood and bounded down the mountainside. The glacier's front face seemed about to give way when the cloudburst dissipated, and the sun appeared.
   Todd shivered, pulled himself up to his feet, and stretched, grateful to have survived the corroding glacier's onslaught. In the smoke and mist further down the plain he spied what looked like two rows of

stone slabs buried in the earth. Their orderliness resembled grave markers in a cemetery, but who would locate a village this close to the mountain?

Picking his way amongst the debris, he headed toward the markers. Maybe they signaled a herder's settlement where he could find medical help and a way back to his vehicle. Better yet, he might find some means to call off the American air attack since he had been thrown out of the cave before he'd been able to establish a connection with his superiors.

It wasn't a grave site, however. A cross with four curved arms of equal length topped each of the granite slabs exposed in the silt and mud. Worn smooth as bed sheets, the markers surrounded a cracked stone tub shaped like the votive candle holders he saw at the Khor Virap monastery. The tub's submerged portion abutted an oblong chest fashioned out of mummified sandalwood.

It looks ancient. Could it be tied to myths about Noah?

Todd fingered the ivory insets in the lid. The dovetail joints of the exposed half showed fine craftmanship. *Even if it is valuable, I don't have time to dig it out, do I?*

He cupped his hand over his eyes and checked the sun's position—about forty-five minutes left before the Air Force made its bombing run—then studied the menacing clouds around the peak. Another mudslide might roar down the valley at any moment.

He scanned the valley wall opposite the Anausavared side. *Is that another cave in the rock face? I'm no Indiana Jones, but I can't leave this chest buried here another thousand years. If I drag it over there, I could hide in there too until after the Air Force makes its bombing runs.*

Clutching his shirt lapel to secure his sore arm against his chest, Todd scraped away with his right foot the three to four inches of silt and mud covering the submerged end of the box. With his left arm to buttress his body, he kneeled into the shallow ditch he created and wiped the muck and grime from the beveled edge along the top of the box. He ran his thumb under the edge of the lid, found where the metal prong sank into the latch, and lifted. On his fourth attempt, the prong sprang free from the corroded latch, and the lid popped open like a pillbox.

A dozen parchment scrolls lay inside. He undid the string around one. *Oh, oh!* The scroll disintegrated. Scrutinizing the fragments, he noted faint check marks next to crude representations of sheep, horses, and other domestic animals—a tally sheet?

What felt like the business end of a pistol jabbed the space between Todd's fourth and fifth ribs. "Wha—?"

"Look, Consuela," Rupert Albrecht said, leaning on the pistol to keep Todd's face in the dirt. "It's the reliquary of St. Jacob of Nisibis."

Albrecht, his slinky secretary, and two massive Kurdish guards surrounded Todd's find. Albrecht gestured with his free hand for his guards to climb into the shallow pit Todd had created. "Lift the box out."

The two guards raised the box out of its oblong resting place, placed it alongside the pit, and climbed out. After they lifted Consuela next to them, Albrecht handed her his Glock. "Aim for the middle of his chest," he directed, scrambling to his feet beside her. "Keep it there."

"How do you know it's the reliquary?" Todd asked, his nose squashed against the sour dirt. He glanced around the shallow pit. If they shot and buried him, it might take another thousand years to uncover his corpse. "Are you an expert?"

"Hardly," Albrecht replied. "But it pays to know one's origins. In this case, the markings and location make it a good guess the scrolls belonged to the monastery founded by the legendary saint who received a sliver of the Ark from an angel." He grinned. "Thanks to you our excursion here may still be a profitable one."

Todd grimaced. *Keep Albrecht talking.* "Is finding this box that big a deal?"

"To Armenians," Albrecht replied. "St. Jacob is the country's patron saint."

"You'd give it to them then?" Todd asked, raising his head. "To put in their national museum?"

"Face in the mud," Albrecht ordered, shoving the back of Todd's head down. "If they were the highest bidder, sure. But you won't have time to worry about that."

"I take it, then," Todd groaned, struggling for air, "that you're not staying for the U.S. Air Force's welcome?"

"Pass," Albrecht replied, brushing off his pants.

"Weren't you supposed to marry Miriam?" Todd chided as Albrecht's guards scuffed the dirt with their feet. "I would have thought staying through marriage thick and thin was expected for the Hayastani Officer of the Exchequer."

"I'm the Hayastanis' Chief Financial Officer, not a saint. Nor pawn in a state-arranged marriage." Albrecht grinned. "Take heart. Your discovery proves Ararat was the resting place of the Christian Ark, not the Zurvanite."

"What difference does that make?" Todd replied, incredulous that religious distinctions should matter at a time like this. Albrecht already had billions of dollars, but psychic parasites appeared to succumb to the same desire as their human hosts to accumulate more. He had to use Albrecht's avarice as a weapon if he could. "Do museums pay more for Christian artifacts?"

"Depends on the museum." Albrecht signaled his Kurd helpers to raise the box onto their shoulders. He took the Glock from his secretary and refocused it on Todd's chest. "You wouldn't believe me if I told you."

"Try me," Todd replied, eyeing the hole in the gun muzzle. It was all he could see from ground level. "Take all the time you need."

Albrecht chuckled and pecked his secretary on the cheek. "Which would be more godlike, Liebchen? To let Mr. Helsingford ponder the vagaries of chance while we leave? Or to give him the quick and merciful death he hasn't earned?"

Todd shivered. Consuela's lemon eyes studied him like a snake's following the movements of a charmer's flute. Her thumb popped out of her fist and rotated downward.

Closing his eyes and gritting his teeth, Todd awaited his painful end. His worst fear had come true: dying in some forsaken part of the desert on his first assignment. Would anyone care? Would Miriam?

Three shots zinged on the rocks around him.

"Bandits!" one of Albrecht's guards cried. "Yazidis!" said the other.

Todd flattened out. He wasn't dead—yet. He peeped open one eye. Albrecht sprayed bullets at the shooter hiding in the rocks along the ridge. Consuela cowered at his knees. His guards crouched behind him, the reliquary chest on their shoulders serving as a shield.

Albrecht fired again. A faint cry of despair signaled his bullet had met its mark.

"Fall back," Albrecht ordered, pointing between shots toward the shadowy opening below the ridge. "Use the box for protection. They won't damage religious relics."

But it was too late to retreat. Knives gleamed; Consuela screamed. The relic chest crashed to the ground. Albrecht's guards stumbled forward and collapsed, their slashed throats gushing blood. Two black-robed bandits grabbed Consuela. Seven more attacked Albrecht and knocked the Glock from his hand. Albrecht snapped the neck of one bandit and hurled the one directing the others against a nearby boulder, laying him out in a daze.

Todd crawled behind the fallen chest and stretched his body along the length of it. His protection wouldn't last long, whatever the outcome. His arm throbbed. He couldn't run. They'd catch him anyway. He glanced around and saw a cave fifty yards away. In all the fighting, maybe they'd forget about him if he crawled over there. It was his only hope.

He peered over the chest top. Seven bandits remained. One held the Glock against Consuela's forehead; the leader lay unconscious beside a boulder. The other five circled Albrecht like panthers waiting for an opening. Albrecht eyed his attackers like a trapped badger deciding which to attack first.

Then he smiled. The two Yazidis wielding knives dropped to their knees, grabbed their heads, and screamed in agony. The other three leaped on Albrecht and pummeled his face, chest, and neck, dropping him to his knees.

The three bandits hovered over Albrecht to finish the job, pounding and kicking him without letup. Somehow, Albrecht staggered to his feet. Like an enraged grizzly bear, he grabbed his largest attacker by the neck and slammed his head against a rock. Grabbing the wrists of the other two, he slammed them together three times and hurled their inert bodies into the debris field like crash-test dummies flung from a car.

Their heads cleared, the two knife-wielding outlaws regained their fallen knives and attacked Albrecht from behind, hacking at his back and arms. Despite the blood spurting from his wounds, Albrecht spun around, grabbed his two assailants, and slammed their heads together, knocking them unconscious.

With five of his companions dispatched, the revived bandit leader grabbed a discarded knife, got to his feet, and rushed Albrecht headlong, wielding his blade back and forth before him like a scythe. He forced Albrecht to jump back, his blade drawing blood before he grabbed his head and fell to his knees, wailing in agony at Albrecht's feet.

The bandit holding Consuela slammed the butt of the Glock against her right temple and emptied the five remaining rounds into Albrecht's chest. Albrecht staggered forward, grabbed his assassin by the neck with both arms, and squeezed.

The bandit leader staggered to his feet. Pulling a scimitar from his belt, he hacked at the back of Albrecht's neck like a lumberjack felling a tree. His first blow dropped the financier to his knees, the second drew blood, and the third severed his neck. Albrecht's lifeless torso slumped to the ground while his glassy-eyed head tumbled into the pit and halted beside Todd's outstretched feet.

Exhausted and bleeding, the leader revived six of his comrades still breathing and helped them stand up. After applying field dressings to their wounds, two of the robbers hoisted the chest onto their shoulders while two more each hoisted the body of a fallen partner on their shoulders and headed down the gorge.

Todd, his protection gone, stayed where he was and closed his eyes as the two bandits toting the chest passed alongside him. His executioners' ethnicity didn't matter; the result would be the same.

Todd felt the prickle of a knife point running along his chest. Another prickle, harder and focused, prompted him to open his eyes.

The fine point of the bandit leader's scimitar hovered before his face. With an upward toss of the blade, the bandit leader signaled Todd to climb out of the shallow pit.

Confused, Todd worked his way clumsily out of the ditch and waited to see what the bandits would do to him now.

Instead of attacking him, the bandit leader rolled Albrecht's secretary and his torso into the pit and directed his remaining man to bury the bodies with mud and silt from the stream. "*Ehsan,*" he murmured, Arabic for perfection. "*Al-ḥamdu lillāh.*"

After praising Allah for his protection, he picked up Albrecht's head and grinned at his companion. "Trophy," he said in English and shoved it into Todd's stomach. He pointed down the mountainside with his scimitar. "Go."

How can this be happening?

"Why are you sparing me?" Todd asked in amazement.

"St. Jacob's box," the Yazidi leader replied, grinning. then added in Turkish. "You find. We save."

Todd grimaced. His small role in the box's recovery had saved him for the moment. But, as he had seen, the bandits' gratitude could turn murderous at any time.

The New Immortal's glassy eyes stared at Todd, etched in death forever like a startled mannequin. Todd retched, and a thin stream of vomit dripped from the side of his mouth. His fingers trembled. He wanted to toss the grisly prize into the bushes, but he didn't dare. Albrecht had fought well, but his superior mental and physical powers were no match for the bandits' numbers and ferocity.

Save your pity.

Todd directed Albrecht's unseeing gaze toward the ridge line along the horizon. The double-dealing energy sucker abandoned his own kind. All in all, he deserved what he got.

Nestling the trophy in the crook of his good arm, Todd preceded the bandits down the glacier's alluvial plain. At its base twenty goat-hide tents surrounded the dozen children kicking a tattered soccer ball beside the communal noonday fire. The bandit leader grabbed Albrecht's head and pointed down the valley. "*Gitmek!*"

Ignored for the moment, Todd continued down the slope in a haze of pain and self-loathing, grateful he hadn't received the same fate as Albrecht—for now. After stumbling around a boulder the size of a small house, he halted, stomach churning. The unmistakable odor of burning flesh assailed his nostrils. Behind him Yazidi adults clapped and whistled at the children's soccer exploits.

The fire blazed higher. At its center, Todd spotted Albrecht's head, sizzling like ham loaf in an oven. Holding back the gorge rising in his throat, Todd stole back to the camp, grabbed a wooden stake leaning against a corral post, and waited behind a nearby tent. While everyone cheered and whistled at a boy's crossover move for a score, he crept to the fire, worried the charred head out of the flames, and sneaked away from the cheering crowd.

Todd crossed the stream with the reclaimed head, knelt in the muck, set the head beside him, and gagged. When his stomach churned up no more bile, he scooped out a shallow pit with his good hand, closed Albrecht's eyes, and buried his head. Despicable and double-dealing though Albrecht was, any human being deserved this much respect.

The scimitar blade flashed and plunged into the ground between Todd's outstretched arms. The bandit leader gazed down at him with a mixture of anger, surprise, and perplexity. *"Neden?"*

The leader was in no mood for explanations. Todd leapt up and ran, the ring of the bandit leader's sword echoing on the rocks behind him. The leader ululated and footfalls of a dozen or more men sloshed through the soft mud of the bank. A moment later, Todd heard the leader's shout directives and the splashes of men scrambling through the stream to catch him.

Despite his head start, the boulder-strewn alluvial plain was difficult to navigate in the harsh sunlight. Todd stumbled over the uneven ground toward the rocks on the opposite side of the gorge where he might hide long enough to discourage pursuit.

A gray, oblong blot materialized in the canyon wall a hundred yards away. Was it a boulder? Another cave?

The surrounding rocks in the stream bed quivered, and a subsonic rumble emanated from the top of the gorge. Behind him the bandits asked their chief to stop the pursuit. Was it going to rain again?

The emergent blot transformed into a small cave. Todd scrambled inside and shrank into its shadows.

A second, deeper roar rumbled down the gorge. Up in the sky three jets throttled down their afterburners in preparation for their final approach runs.

{13}

The three jet planes soared over Ararat's main peak like migrating silver birds. They glided through plumes of scattered anti-aircraft fire from the village, wheeled about in a graceful arc, and returned toward the mouth of the gorge.

The bandit chieftain barked new orders. His men scattered to retrieve their women and children already fleeing toward them in the direction of the canyon wall.

Todd backed away from the sunlight streaming through the cave entrance. As he crept further inside, the cave roof lowered until the ceiling shrank to half his height fifty yards in. Squeezing inside a small crevice, he hid out of sight as the Yazidi men, women, and children poured through the sun-filled opening.

Todd clutched his injured arm close to his chest. Escape during a bombing run would be suicide, but he couldn't stay hidden for long in such a confined space. He thought of Albrecht's head roasting in the fire. He didn't want his to be next.

The drone from the jet engines grew louder. Men crowded around the entrance and peered outside. Todd edged around the fringes of the crowd. If he reached the entrance, he'd run for it, bombs or no bombs.

Two men pointed toward the sky. The jets descended to the mouth of the gorge. With their outstretched wings and dark pointed noses, they resembled silvery cooper's hawks zeroing in on their prey.

One plane yawed at a crazy angle and crashed into the bottom of the gorge. Its partners zoomed into the canyon mouth. The first bomb crashed at the foot of the glacier gravel bed, its shock wave churning the mud and gravel beneath Todd's feet like they were water.

The second bomb ripped the north wall of the gorge and slammed everyone to the ground. While Todd and the others scrambled to their feet, third and fourth bombs exploded at the base of the glacier, ripping away pillars of ice and snow. Boulders, mud, and ice chunks the size of houses rumbled down the valley.

A moment later, a roaring avalanche of snow and rubble streamed down the gorge and flowed into the cave in a slow-motion cascade. The bandits and their families retreated further into the darkness as the advancing wave of debris outside the entrance became ankle-high, waist-high, and finally chest-high before sealing the entrance entirely.

The bandit leader told everyone to wait until the two planes made their second runs. Digging out would be useless until the planes expended their bomb loads. Todd had no idea how many that might be.

He cocked his ears, listening for the planes' next pass. The muffled drones from the planes seemed shorter than their first run. Inside their sealed-off cave, the bomb explosions sounded like chocolate chips plopping into a bowl of cookie batter.

Once the explosions stopped and the sound of the planes died away, the bandit leader lit a length of driftwood and handed it to the women and children crouched at the back of the cave. "Ah—ee!" he cried, finding Todd hidden in the shadows. He grabbed him by his jacket collar, flung him toward the front of the cave, and pointed at the debris pile blocking the entrance. "*Kazmak!*"

Despite the language barrier, Todd knew what the Yazidi leader's gesture meant: dig.

The leader lit another piece of wood and handed it to the nearest woman. Then he climbed to the top of the ice pile and shoved aside the top stone. At the bottom of the debris pile, his men scooped away the mountain of rocks, pebbles, and black powder with their hands.

Todd shoveled what he could with his good arm. The jets had targeted the north side of the gorge where the Anausavared were dug in. A warning strike rather than full-scale bombardment, the Air Force's bombing run achieved collateral damage by burying the cave entrance where he and the Yazidis took shelter. If the Yazidi men didn't dig too

Mission: Soul Sacrifice

fast and consume their air supply, they might free themselves. He held his breath, let it out, and focused on keeping a steady pace. If the avalanche extended to the bottom of the gorge, this cave might be everyone's tomb.

After an hour assisting his men, the bandit leader leaned back against the base of a flat, upright stone. Todd kept digging. Rest breaks didn't apply to him.

The leader grabbed Todd's shoulder and pulled him away from the rubble. "*Mnats'atsy.*" The leader opened the top three buttons of his tunic. "Rest."

"*Shnorhakalut'yun,*" Todd replied in Turkish. "Thanks." Could he reason with this man? He ransacked his elementary-school level knowledge of the Kurd language. The Yazidis spoke a dialect few westerners understood. Sign language and his high school Turkish would have to do. He clasped his palms together, opened them, and pointed at the men resting around them. "Thanks to them."

The wrinkles around the leader's face deepened. He pointed toward his men. "*Yazidi,*" then at his chest. "*Mir.*"

Todd frowned. Many ethnic and tribal groups in the region had adopted the medieval Muslim term for a wise or spiritual leader. But unlike other tribal groups, the Yazidi were considered outcasts among the Kurds and Armenians for their reputations as devil worshipers. Neither group was likely to rescue them from their entombment.

The Mir's obsidian eyes glinted. He pointed at Todd's chest. "American."

Todd nodded, his neck flushed. Ambassador Holbrook's first lecture had involved encouraging local support of American interests. The Ambassador identified the Yazidi as one of the few minorities that had welcomed American involvement in the region. Could they connect? Wasn't that why the Americans were in this part of the world in the first place?

He pointed at his chest. "Todd." Then he raised his eyebrows and pointed at the Yazidi leader. "Name?"

"Amar." His eyes flashed. "Amar al-Ararat."

Adopting the mountain for his last name showed how much he identified with it. Todd eyed the rock pile blocking the entrance and Amar's men struggling to remove it. How much did that identification extend to protecting the relics he'd found?

"*Kalinti*?" Todd asked. Amar's brows beetled. Perhaps he didn't understand the word "relic." Treasure might be more accurate. "*Hazine*?"

A slow grin enveloped Amar's face. "Yes."

He nodded and Todd grinned back. Despite being in a cave from which they might not escape, he had to ask what Amar had done with scrolls that hadn't seen the light of day for thousands of years.

"*Nerede*?" Amar's stare showed that word wasn't right. Todd made shoveling movements with his arms. What was the Turkish word? "*Digi*?"

"Ah, no underground." Amar's thick brows beetled again. "Noah mausoleum. Cizre."

Todd grimaced. According to Holbrook, that was the city where Alexander the Great once crossed the Tigris. Transporting the relics of Saint Jacob to a Muslim museum was good politics from the Mir's standpoint. But, transferring them there was sure to anger many Christians in the region—and elsewhere—if the Yazidis ever got out of the cave.

Before Todd could ask if the Yazidis had already transferred the relic, one of Amar's men rushed up and pointed toward the rock wall. The torch his men used for digging flickered. The flame at the rear of the cave guttered, too. Their oxygen was running out.

Amar ordered the women and children to the rear of the cave. Two huge boulders still blocked the entrance. He ordered his strongest men to gather along the top of the rock pile. They braced their backs against the cave wall and pushed against the two keystone boulders with their legs, but they wouldn't budge.

He gave them five minutes' rest, and they tried again. Neither rock moved.

Todd climbed up the pile and squeezed among the six men pushing against the smaller boulder. Hugging his arm against his chest, he braced his back against the stone wall and thought of the tree stumps he'd help move on the family farm. The boulder quivered. He motioned for more men to join them. Amar's men did not move.

"*Yardim etmek onu!*" Amar motioned the men on the larger stone to join Todd and the others. Eight of Amar's men joined the seven others around the stone. The boulder shivered and slid down the pile.

The fifteen men encircled the larger stone and pushed. When it didn't move, Amar squeezed beside Todd and pushed. Nothing happened. They pushed again. The boulder trembled and rumbled down the pile. A slow-motion wave of black ice and sand slid through the opening and engulfed the children's feet, their knees, and their waists.

Todd tumbled head over heels down the pile and slammed against the cave's back wall. Dazed by the impact and flood of pain, he sat on his haunches and wheezed. Sulfur gas and black grit clogged his lungs.

A second slurry engulfed him. The rock floor collapsed. Tossed into darkness like a pebble, Todd plunged and plunged into the depths of the cave system.

"Ooofff!"

The right side of Todd's body slammed against rock. Stars flashed through the sky and winked out. When he woke, he was on his back. Grit clogged his eyes, ears, and nose. His chest ached, but at least he was breathing. He removed the grit, rolled over, and peered into the darkness. Where was he?

He lay on a long slab of basalt. Mud bubbled and churned in the pool beside him. Black snow sprinkled down like soot from the pale light of the small, jagged opening in the ceiling far above. Phosphorescent stalactites glowed in the dark beside it.

Renewed pain stabbed Todd's right arm. Another break? His left ankle ached, too.

He rolled onto his left side. Two children whimpered against the cave wall. Two men, three women, and a teenaged boy brushed themselves off and scoured the rubble.

He pulled himself to a sitting position and popped several of his remaining painkillers into his mouth. While waiting for them to take effect, he studied his surroundings. It became apparent that the weight of the debris had collapsed the thin floor of the cave they had been in and dropped them into this limestone cavern below.

More survivors became visible in the dusky light. Amar hobbled across the floor of the smoldering pit and urged his men to exhume and attend to the others.

The cavern seemed brighter than what could be supplied by the stalactites. Todd cupped the hand of his good arm around his eyes and scanned the ceiling. Thirty feet up dull red gas vented through the fissure where the cave had been.

He struggled to his feet and approached Amar kneeling beside a groaning man lying in the rubble. A wizened man in a teal and blue speckled robe chanted beside Amar on one side of the injured man while a woman in a black chador chanted on his other side.

Where did the old man come from? Todd stood beside Amar as the injured man's groans increased and the old man raised his arms in a gesture of entreaty.

"Amar," Todd said, edging into the Mir's field of vision. Tapping Amar's shoulder, he pointed toward the light source. "A way out."

Amar nodded, intent on the groaning man and the old man's attentions to him.

Doesn't Amar understand? Todd scanned the limestone walls and noted the giant crack zigzagging up the rock face. He tapped Amar's shoulder again, then his own chest, and pointed toward the crack. "*Kacma.*"

Amar tossed Todd's hand away.

"Don't you see?" Todd cried in English. "It's a way out."

Amar stood up and unsheathed his scimitar. "*Gitmek.*" He swung his sword in a broad arc. "Go!"

A Mir's people came first, Todd realized. That's what any good leader would do. He watched Amar squat down beside the peacock-robed man again who grew very still, his chants dwindling to murmurs as if entering a trance.

Is he some kind of doctor?

Undeterred by Amar's rejection, Todd set out toward the other side of the pit. While the Yazidis recovered their dead and injured, he'd assess the fissure as a possible avenue of escape.

As wide as the width of Todd's shoe, the fracture ascended the rock face as far up as he could see. To determine whether it extended to the original cave entrance, he had to climb it.

Using his good leg as a fulcrum and favoring his uninjured left arm, he crawled up the cliff face one laborious sideways step at a time. Sweat beaded on his forehead. Thirty feet above the cavern floor, the lurid light from the escaping gas showed an outcropping in the rock face ten feet above his head, almost to the opening in the cave floor.

Was the gas poisonous? One way to find out.

By the time he reached the outcropping, his right arm throbbed, and his left ankle ached—more like a sprain than a break—pain that was manageable not excruciating. He hauled himself onto the ledge, let his legs dangle into space, and focused on the order of what he needed to do next. Catch your breath. Let the pain subside. Then make the final climb.

The rotten egg odor became overpowering when he reached the ledge. He covered his nose and mouth with his bad arm, pulled out another pill, ground it to powder, and swallowed it.

Purple dots swirled across his vision. Todd shook his head and ignored them. *No time to pass out. Do it later.*

He sat upright, fished out his handkerchief, wrapped it around the lower half of his face, and waited until his breathing returned to normal. Then, he slid back and upwards against the cliff face until he reached a standing position.

The crevice above his head seemed almost as far away as when he started. Below him Amar and the other Yazidis milled about the cavern floor like ants around a platter of steaming gumbo. The rock wall he faced looked sheer and unforgiving. His leg and arm trembled with pain, reluctance, and fear. Who wouldn't be afraid?

One person: Miriam.

He sidled toward the vent like a fiddler crab and pivoted his right foot across his body until it met the rock face. His left foot screamed until he shifted his weight onto his good leg. Then he repeated the action in the opposite direction, his strength ebbing with every step.

At long last he reached the opening.

Todd turned away, closed his eyes, inhaled three times, and stuck his face through the gas and into the hole. Opening his eyes to slits to protect against the stinging gas, he peered inside. A single shaft of sunlight illuminated the rubble pile outside the cave entrance where they had been trapped.

Todd shifted his head back and forth, searching for a better angle in hopes of seeing beyond the light shaft. Finally, by pressing the right side of his head against the rock face, he was able to see through the crack and out into the gorge. He saw that huge potholes dented the

Mission: Soul Sacrifice

rubble-filled valley and only a few twisted sticks smoldered where the Yazidi corral had been.

Without warning, the rumbles of more jets filled the foul air. Todd turned away, gasping for breath.

The ledge beneath his feet trembled . . . and gave way with the shock from a titanic explosion.

Todd plummeted head first toward the mud pit. Warm and enfolding, the bubbling chocolate mud embraced him like a mother welcoming her willful baby to her breast . . .

{14}

A baggy-eyed charge nurse laid Miriam's head on the cool, harsh, hospital bed and wiped her matted auburn bangs away from her closed eyes. "This is her third time in the treatment room," she mused in a gravelly voice. "She's exhausted, poor thing."

The needle prick in Miriam's shoulder signaled another dose of phenobarbital; the knowledge of what that meant slammed Miriam back into the corporeal world. She popped open her blue-green eyes, desperate to speak, to communicate the horror she had seen, but words stuck in her throat, her utterances sounding like water trickling through a clogged pipe.

"I-I'm a-awake," she croaked at last, flailing her leaden arm back and forth across the bed stand like a walrus stranded on an ice floe. Her mouth and throat felt stuffed full of cotton wads. "Awa-ake, awaaake, awaaakke . . ."

She never wanted to sleep again. Sleep was where the demons lived. Her protests rang inside her head, "I'M AWAKE. I'M AWAKE! I'M AWAKE!"

The physical world closed before her eyes like the final curtain in a stage play, plunging her into the whirlpool that deposited her into the dank courtyard of Tartarus. Agonized groans and cries of despair rattled the bars of the noisome cells on either side of her.

Miriam wandered the castle corridors and arcades without restraint or apparent punishment, unlike some of the prison's other inhabitants. She had seen the legendary Greek, King Ixion, forever bound to the spinning, fiery wheel and Tantalus, the father punished here for cutting up and serving his son to the gods, who could never reach the life-restoring food above his head or water at his feet no matter how hard he tried.

Unlike them, Miriam's anguish derived from no fault or misdeed she could see. The injustice in her detainment made her torment all the more intolerable.

Tisiphone and her sister Hadean guardians of Tantalus, Alecto, and Megaera took turns monitoring her movements. Why, Miriam wondered. Why was she different?

"Won't anybody listen?" she cried, throwing up her hands in despair. "There's been a mistake. I don't belong here."

Several inmates lamented in return how their punishments, too, were unjust or political. One, a fat, middle-aged man covered to the waist in oily white clown makeup sat beside a jagged hole in a wooden fence. Chained to the ground by both a neck collar and arm chains, he nodded in agreement with Miriam. "I don't belong here, either," he said, gazing at the other inmates in the grassless prison courtyard. "None of us do."

"Why are you here?" Miriam asked, relieved to find a sympathetic soul who would listen to her.

"Social bias," the dismal clown replied without emotion. "Same as you."

What does he mean by that? The clown's empty stare prompted Miriam to shiver despite his shared sympathy at their plights. She had never met the man, but felt she recognized him somehow. Was it his sad clown makeup? What had he done? "Do I know you?"

"I doubt it," the dismal clown replied. "Before your time."

"You down there!" Tisiphone cracked her whip across the clown's back. "Back to work!"

The unhappy clown quivered with rage, but a second lash from Tisiphone's whip prompted him to reinsert his head into the jagged hole cut into the wood wall. On the other side, three blue, snub-nosed imps threw balloons filled with excrement at his exposed head.

Mission: Soul Sacrifice

Tisiphone vented her ire on the backs of all the inmates this way—except Miriam. She only lashed at Miriam when Miriam tried to communicate with Tartarus' other inmates. Then, the prison's bloodthirsty enforcer whipped her harder than the others. Every stroke from her lash burned like the sting from a thousand paper cuts.

Miriam's actual escape attempts were just as frustrating and demoralizing as her cries to be let out. Razor wire extended along the tops of the prison's three bronze walls. Phlegethon, the flaming moat of blood that surrounded the castle, scalded those souls desperate or foolish enough to swim, climb, or tunnel under it. After her third or fourth reconnaissance of the jail's defenses, Miriam abandoned all thought of escape. If she did manage to escape, where could she go? Her soul would be trapped in Hades while her body languished in the military psychiatric hospital to be drugged again and again for as long as Zarkisian willed it.

Why had he done this? She'd met him several times when she was little, always when Victor was away, the last time after Victor deserted her mother to live in the Amazon. She remembered little from Zarkisian's visits except that the haughtiness of his presence always made her glad when he was gone. Evelyn always changed the subject when Miriam asked why he visited them. Was he the reason Todd warned her not to get more involved with the New Immortals?

She repressed a mordant chuckle. How uninvolved could she be when her body and soul resided in separate prisons?

That was what Zarkisian wanted.

He'd wanted her out of the way all along. If he was responsible for stranding her soul here, why? What had she done to deserve such confinement? Aside from schlepping after Albrecht, her connection to the New Immortals or their rebel activities in eastern Turkey was nonexistent.

Distant thunder rattled the prison's dank brass walls. Miriam waited until Tisiphone relieved her anger by lashing another unhappy prisoner, edged up the slippery bronze steps beside the watch tower, and peered through an opening in the castle's crenelated fence.

Off to the northwest, lightning bolts stabbed the black smoke erupting from the fiery mountaintops. Brimstone jets spurted through those clouds. The bronze walls of Tartarus trembled in unison with each eruption. And trembled again.

Miriam struggled to regain her balance on the bronze steps. When another temblor shook the walls, she bustled down the steps to the courtyard. Behind her the prisoners confined to their cells cried in terror, those chained in the courtyard screaming loudest of all.

Tisiphone shrieked at them from her tower atop the prison battlements. With renewed venom, she and her sisters pummeled the terrified inmates until the din from their lamentations rivaled the volume of the eruptions.

Like an unrelenting tsunami, wave after wave of earthquakes pulverized Hades' parched hills. Tartarus' bronze walls buckled. The fiery waters of the River Phlegethon spewed through the splits and cracks in the metal, setting scattered patches of desert grass on fire. Inside the castle or out, nothing and no one seemed safe.

Tisiphone and her sisters exchanged worried glances and pummeled their charges harder, as if their heightened cries might appease their master, Hades, to intervene with Poseidon, the god of the sea and earthquakes, to call off this assault.

With upraised arms, Miriam fended off debris falling from the ramparts and scanned the vicinity for a place of refuge. Staying in the open was out—the quakes had reduced the castle's earthen quadrangle to a soupy mass. But hiding inside was worse. The confined inmates' screams heightened her fears amid the bedlam.

Tisiphone's tower stood firm despite the quakes. Miriam hid in its shadow to minimize the debris falling on her and to avoid Tisiphone's wrath while remaining outside in case the castle walls collapsed.

What caused these sudden eruptions? Never in her short time here were they this intense or prolonged. The blue imps pelting the sad clown ceased harassing him and ran about the courtyard seeking shelter.

Miriam pulled one aside. "Why is this happening?"

"Dakhanavar!" the imp replied, squirming in her grasp.

"What about it?" Miriam asked.

"Disciples of Ahriman," the imp said and bit his lip. "Whenever he or his archangels return to the land of Zoroaster, their mountains breathe fire and our lives become more miserable."

The imp snapped at Miriam's face and wriggled from her grasp. Startled by the ferocity of his attack, she let him go and watched him flee from one cell to another in search of shelter. She recalled some of the inmates whispering about the demons that inhabited Dakhanavar. She remembered years ago when Victor had warned her about attacks by powerful demons. Was he right then? Could his seemingly unwarranted fear of Zarkisian in ordinary reality be right as well? She was beginning to believe it.

Victor can't be right twice.

Miriam frowned in anger. Did being right once justify Victor abandoning his wife? Or leaving his daughter to grow up without a father?

No!

Zarkisian's command of psychic energy in the corporeal world, however, seemed to translate into power in the Lower World, too. She bit her lip in bewilderment. Did her confinement in Tartarus somehow play a role in that power?

A fiery meteor blazed across the sky, showering sparks everywhere before it plunged into the prison quadrangle. The shockwave rocked the castle walls to their foundations. When the tremors stopped, a trim, blond man wearing a black Italian suit emerged from the crater unharmed, although he carried his own charred head in the crook of his right arm.

The head's vacant blue eyes blinked, surveyed their surroundings, and the par-boiled face fashioned a bloodied, broken smile. "Ah, Ms. Gorovic," the head said while his torso clumsily brushed itself off with its left arm. "You're here?"

He expected her to be here?

"Rupert Albrecht, Chief of Exchequer for the Kingdom of Hayastan, at your service once again," he said, bowing from the waist. "I feel so disoriented. Do you know where Lord Ahriman is?"

Was this playboy connected with Ahriman? And Zarkisian? How?

Miriam's pained expression prompted Albrecht to ask another question. "Perhaps you know him by his other name, Angra Mainyu?"

"Right demon, wrong hell," Miriam replied. *Why be formal with this man?* She glanced at his neck stump and sniggered, "Not worth losing your head over."

"Yes." Albrecht's mouth pursed in chagrin at her joke. "But not amusing."

"How did this happen?" Miriam asked, pointing at his neck stump.

"Some would-be shareholders carried sharp swords." Albrecht grimaced. "Do you know where Ahriman is or not?"

"Uh-huh." Miriam's smile broadened. Albrecht's punishment fit his crimes. The Azeri rebel, Dubromov, Albrecht bilked must have gotten him somehow and severed his head. She stepped out into the courtyard and pointed at the rumbling mountains whose fiery tips appeared between the castle's battered battlements. "You want Dakhanavar, the hell that belches smoke and fire."

Mission: Soul Sacrifice

Albrecht's hands raised his head high above his shoulders while his body pivoted in a clockwise circle until it faced northwest. "Oh, no!"

Tisiphone screeched and swooped down from her tower, flailing Albrecht's neck and shoulders like a drover beating an ornery mule toward the corral. In this case, the corral consisted of alternating rows of stocks and pillories staffed by hook-nosed, blue demons.

"Wait! This isn't fair or equitable treatment," Albrecht protested and pointed at Miriam between blows. "She deserves to be punished as much as I do. She's why I'm here."

Miriam covered her head from Tisiphone's painful lash. "I know nothing about this man," she cried. "Or why he's here."

Tisiphone ignored Miriam's objections and scourged her too. She and her sisters herded them together and clamped the couple in adjoining leg stocks while two hook-nosed trolls and a blue gremlin produced sacks filled with rotten fruit and vegetables from a granary box. From the bowels of the castle another blue gremlin rolled out a pot of flaming excrement. The four demons positioned their fetid containers in a row ten feet in front of Albrecht and Miriam's leg stocks and hurled the malodorous missiles at them.

"Why are they doing this?" Miriam asked after dodging a rotten tomato. "I can understand it happening to you. You're a terrible person who deserves this. But why me?"

"Come off it," Albrecht replied, lunging away from a rotten banana missile. "Your Little Miss Innocent act doesn't work in this place."

"Wha-what do you mean?" Miriam spluttered.

"You think I'm here just because I short-sold some eastern stocks?" Albrecht asked. "Think again."

"Our relationship was nothing more than a means to publicize stocks you short-sold to the Azeris," Miriam declared as she ducked another flaming plate of excrement. A third flaming bag of excrement splattered beside her on the wooden seat. She tamped out the foul spatter on her jeans. "Didn't that transaction make enough to satisfy your master, Dr. Zarkisian?"

"The profit-taking was sufficient for Hayastan to meet all its short-term financial obligations as a nation-state," Albrecht replied. "The allies in the region and the United States were more than happy to let us continue our economic model."

"As vassal states run by psychic parasites?" Miriam said. "I don't believe it."

"Whatever," Albrecht replied and shrugged off the rotten tomato splash on his shoulder. "That's what their envoy told us."

"Envoy?"

"Some junior-grade officer from the U.S.-Armenian embassy," Albrecht replied with a sneer. A bag of excrement splattered across his expensive black suit. "Helsingboard, I think his name was."

Todd.

A pang of remorse shot through Miriam's chest. And admiration, too. Todd would never sacrifice the Turkish locals to the demands of these energy-sucking parasites. "I hope the U.S. Air Force bombed the hell out of you."

"I imagine they did," Albrecht replied.

"You don't know?" Miriam asked in surprise. "How do you know for sure it happened then?"

"Zarkisian insisted on it. I pointed out to him we'd already won, but he demanded the American planes bomb us. That's when we parted company."

Miriam eyed him up and down to check whether he was lying. "You ran off, you mean."

"Have it your way." Albrecht crossed his arms in vexation, and his head plopped onto the ground. He bent and retrieved it before his head tumbled out of its reach. "Heads of state," Albrecht's head replied, spitting out dust, "shouldn't have to endure an aerial bombardment without good reason."

Miriam giggled. "Decapitated heads of state shouldn't have to either." To her delight, Albrecht frowned in response. Taunting him further, she asked, "There wasn't one? A reason, I mean."

"No. Not enough for me." Albrecht's crystal blue eyes scanned Miriam up and down as if weighing her readiness for market. "You're not it."

"Me?" Miriam dodged another overripe tomato. "What have I got to do with your problems?"

"Political succession is always a problem even in the most stable countries." Albrecht's head blew the air out of its cheeks. "Zarkisian addressed the problem right away. Hayastan has always been a hereditary monarchy. Marriage between the Chief Officer of the Exchequer and an heir to the throne eliminated the problem of legitimacy and any counter-claims."

Impossible!

Miriam stared at Albrecht in disbelief. "That's why I'm in Tartarus?"

Albrecht nodded. "You're my intended, my bride-to-be."

"That's impossible," Miriam repeated, flushing with outrage and—
Ohmigod!

Miriam trembled all over at the implication of his statement. How would Albrecht respond to her next question?

"Why me?"

"Isn't it obvious after what I've told you? You're one of us."

{15}

A pair of grease-stained tennis shoes bounced off Miriam's chest, but she disregarded their impact and inhaled twice while processing what Albrecht said. If she was a New Immortal and their leadership succession was hereditary, she must be the progeny of—

Miriam exhaled hard, shaking her head in revulsion at Albrecht's revelation. *Has my worst nightmare come true? Haven't I suspected this all along?* She grasped the right side of her head and tried to remember her recent dreams.

But this was no fantasy. Having a parasite like Zarkisian for a father was inconceivable. That he sucked energy from people's souls was fantastic. Even if he wasn't a vampire in the classic sense, what "father" condemned the soul of his offspring to an eternity of torture only releasing them to further his own ends?

Her neck flushed. She felt—what? Shame. Regret. Humiliation. All three—and more.

Victor must have known. Why else would he warn her about Zarkisian? It explained why he abandoned her and Evelyn, ashamed to raise a daughter that wasn't his own, much less one that was a psychic vampire.

But why wait until now to warn her when it was too late?

Miriam dodged another tomato and massaged the throbbing right side of her head.

How could Evelyn have let this happen? Why hadn't she told her this before?

Albrecht wiped more tomato-splatter from his forehead. "You're taking this new information well," he said. "Most non-orgonics would have gone into hysterics."

"I'm raging inside, believe me," Miriam replied, her mouth twisting in disgust. She hated the name. "Inorganics—is that what energy suckers call us?"

"Non-orgonics. All life forms have it. Psychic parasites," The corners of Albrecht's mouth curled. "Such a distasteful term." His shoulders shrugged and his mouth sighed. "Better than energy suckers, I suppose. We're able to tap into it, that's all."

"If the name fits . . ." Miriam smiled wryly. Albrecht wanted his behavior to seem normal, but she wouldn't let him get away with it. Still, she was curious now that she learned she might be one.

"Which do you do first?" Miriam asked, dodging a ripe tomato with a toss of her head. Tormenting Albrecht was more fun than considering the implications of what he'd told her. "Suck the life out of people or frame them for a trap you devised?"

"Whatever works." Albrecht shrugged. "We're pragmatists. Like most 'terrorist groups' I could name."

"What is your terrorist group called?" Miriam asked.

"Anausavareds." When Miriam made a face, Albrecht added, "That's the Persian word for New Immortals."

Miriam ducked a puss-ridden cat carcass. Albrecht's term sounded as grandiose as their aspirations, but appropriate if they lived as long as their blood-sucking cousins. "Why are you telling me this?"

Albrecht's head made a wry face. His shoulders shrugged toward their refuse-pelting trolls. "You are my betrothed, my intended—my destiny, if you will, though I never wanted it that way."

Miriam squared her shoulders, nettled by his rejection yet determined not to show it. "What do you mean?"

"Avoiding one's fate results in what you see before you. Everyone is destined for a purpose. To refuse it is unacceptable in Zurvan's plan."

"I didn't ask for any of this," Miriam replied. "Most of all any part in the plan of some god I've never heard of."

"He's not a god, more a first impulse—like time." Albrecht braced himself as another temblor rocked the ground. He gazed toward the rumbling mountains. "Those volcanoes erupt as part of the End Time Zurvan set in motion."

"For what purpose?"

"To cleanse the world and restore it to Ahura Mazda, silly." Albrecht turned back to face Miriam, his face wearing a concerned smile. "It's close now."

Miriam shook her head in amazement. "We—our souls—are locked up here in Tartarus—in Hades." She pointed at their leg stocks. "Remember?"

"Hades, Dakhanavar, Sheol, Hell—it's all the same, depending on your belief system." Albrecht set his head in his lap and leaned back on his arms, the fear-filled devils halting their fruit barrage as another eruption rocked the ground. "Ahriman plans to defeat Zurvan's intentions, but he won't succeed, even with Zarkisian's help. Fate won't allow it."

"Why not?"

"Because Ahriman is *fated* to be defeated by his twin brother, Ahura Mazda. Even Zurvan can't prevent that."

"Fated or not," Miriam replied, pursing her mouth, "you should try to save yourself; whatever Ahriman's plan is."

"Can't." Albrecht's head flashed a wan smile. "That's why I'm here."

Miriam grimaced. Was this another of Albrecht's tricks? "Use your psychic powers, then. Like you did before when we were in the alley in New York."

"I'm dead." Albrecht grinned when Miriam frowned. "I'm immortal, not indestructible. When the Yazidi bandits decapitated me, they buried my head apart from my body." His arms flipped his head upside down and righted it. Albrecht's head grinned. "Without it, I stay dead, like all good vampires."

Miriam smiled with chagrin. "Does your physical demise mean your psychic powers are dead, too?" Another of Albrecht's sardonic smiles confirmed her worst fears. "So much for getting out of this."

"Some consort," Albrecht replied.

"What do you mean by *that*?"

Albrecht's smile turned crafty. "If I tell you, promise you'll get me out of these cursed stocks?"

Miriam hesitated. So, it was a trick. If Albrecht knew anything, he would have used his knowledge to save himself. Aside from his severed head, nothing else corroborated his story. What else was he hiding from her? "Go ahead, tell me."

"You're a princess," Albrecht said. "A princess of the Anausavareds, imbued with their psychic powers. You must have suspected it by now."

"Perhaps," Miriam conceded as the barrage of rotten fruit resumed. She realized those powers enabled her to get in and out of Albrecht's Morningside complex, but she also felt detached from them—as alien from her now as the Alzheimer's patients she discovered in that same complex seemed to her then.

Albrecht would say anything about her heritage at this point. Freeing him would accomplish little if her soul remained trapped in Tartarus. Whatever he told her would be what she wanted to hear in this frightful place. "How much have those supposed psychic abilities done for you?"

"I'm dead, you're not," Albrecht replied. "Your corporeal world beliefs keep you from realizing your abilities."

"I haven't any," Miriam replied.

"Remember the police raid?" Albrecht asked. "Explain that." When Miriam shook her head, he added, "They drove right by us. Remember?"

"That was just dumb luck."

Albrecht turned his head toward the gnomes. "Try your dumb luck on those guys. Focus on their energy and imagine yourself invisible."

His suggestion was ridiculous, but what else did she have to do? Miriam hunched her shoulders and focused on the lead gnome. Nothing happened. She grinned at Albrecht. "See?"

"Stay focused," Albrecht replied.

Miriam tried again. The shoulders of the lead gnome sagged. Two more sprites gazed at their pals in confusion, dropped their ammunition, and walked away.

Crazy as it seemed, Miriam's thought directive seemed to be working as though she was invisible to them. The rest of the gnomes refocused their barrage on Albrecht, but without their original intensity.

"Do you think they can't see me?" she whispered.

"Yes," Albrecht's head replied, grinning. "Keep it up." The trolls continued bombarding him. "Wrap your arm around my shoulders."

Miriam stretched her arm across Albrecht's chest, and he tucked his head under the crook of her arm. The torrent of refuse directed at him stopped. The bewildered demons looked at each other and shrugged.

"Tisiphone and her spells," groused one gnome with a nose broken in two places. "She never tells us anything."

"Or lets us have any fun," said another.

After they dispersed, Albrecht said, "Release your grip on my shoulders." He extended his head above his shoulders and surveyed Tisiphone's guard post. "We haven't much time."

"For what?" Miriam asked.

"Escape." Albrecht pointed at the wooden trusses that stretched across their ankles. "Pull those off."

"I haven't the strength for that," Miriam said.

The right corner of Albrecht's mouth twisted with impatience. "Even in the depths of Hell, you refuse to accept the truth of your firsthand experience."

I'll firsthand you.

Shrugging her shoulders in exasperation, Miriam pushed against the beam with all her strength. Nothing happened.

"Push harder," Albrecht urged.

Miriam focused on each individual wood fiber, imagining them rupturing like pulled shreds of cotton candy. The wood surrounding her braces shuddered, groaned, and split in two. Albrecht pointed at the crack formed around the metal clamp that locked their legs in place. "Use the crack as a focal point."

Miriam pushed harder. The pine beam splintered along the length of the clamp.

"It worked!" she crowed, lowered her voice, and pointed at the result. "It worked."

"Fine, fine," Albrecht replied. "Get me out of this."

Miriam shoved the broken bar aside, removed the clamp, and released Albrecht from his stocks.

Albrecht tucked his head in the crook of his right arm and wrapped his free arm around her shoulders. "Head towards the front gate."

"Are you serious?" Miriam retorted, glancing at the walkway above the gate. "Alecto and Megaera are still up there. We should take a less conspicuous route."

"The shortest distance between two points is a straight line," Albrecht's head replied. "You want out of here or not?"

He steered her under Tisiphone's watch tower, slid the twin iron bolts back, and pushed open the massive iron gate. Tisiphone's sisters,

Megaera and Alecto, patrolled the fortress perimeter from the air, timing their routes so each observed half of the castle and the surrounding area at any given time. When Alecto flew past the entrance, Albrecht tucked his head in the crook of his right arm, wrapped his left around Miriam's shoulder, and kept it there while she strode out the front gate. Once they rounded the curve in the path that led toward the Plain of Asphodel, he released his grip.

A pair of blue herons appeared overhead when the castle was out of sight. Albrecht clasped the neck stump under his head with both hands and waved his head back and forth like a signaling lantern.

Miriam's stomach knotted. It *was* a trick all along.

"What are you doing?" she cried.

"Joining my tribe," Albrecht answered. The herons swooped down, each clasping one of Albrecht's shoulders in its beak, and hoisted the decapitated financier from the ground.

Panic replaced fear in Miriam's belly. "You're leaving me here?"

"The End Time could happen any moment," Albrecht replied, as the birds soared higher.

"And you're just going?" Miriam said, aghast. "After I helped free you?"

"Zero-sum game," Albrecht replied. The herons toted him toward the lava-spewing mountains. "I showed you what you're capable of. Use it to survive if you can. It's up to you."

Miriam trailed the trio on the ground. *Why expect anything else from this—this creature?* She focused her budding energy-draining ability on the birds, but they flew on undisturbed. Either she'd depleted her new-found powers, or they were too far away.

The herons sheered away from Tartarus while the three Furies dipped and strafed the prisoners to quell the havoc within. Disconsolate and disillusioned, Miriam returned to the spot in the trail where Albrecht abandoned and betrayed her. Again.

A dust cloud blotted the sky to the southwest. Miriam shielded her eyes and scanned the horizon. A man and woman astride two white horses raced across the plain toward the rugged frontier hills beyond. The gray auburn hair of the lead rider resembled Victor's.

"Hey, you guys!" Miriam shouted, waving her hands above her head. "Victor and Evelyn."

The riders didn't hear her. Miriam cupped her hands around her mouth and tried again, louder. The two riders brought their steeds to a plunging halt. Evelyn spotted Miriam, wheeled her mare about, and raced toward her daughter.

A warm glow rose inside Miriam's chest. She felt lighter, as if someone had lifted a giant burden from her shoulders. She bounded toward them, buoyant as a feather. Reuniting with someone from the corporeal world who was still alive made her feel giddy. She sprinted toward them, closing the gap to fifty yards after twenty steps. Evelyn's outstretched fingertips brushed Miriam's with her penultimate step when Miriam abruptly catapulted toward the sun.

"No!" Miriam screamed, clenching her teeth with dawning awareness. "Not more analysis. Not more doctors!"

{16}

Groggy and disoriented, Miriam identified the light source mimicking the Hadean sun. She slapped the penlight from Dr. Runnholme's fingers, heaved herself to the other side of the bed, and tottered onto her feet.

But her labored attempt at freedom was momentary. A muscular ward assistant grabbed her arms, spun her around, and pinned her against the bed, her protests muffled by the pillow. Miriam thrashed and kicked, hoping her foot might hit a vulnerable spot. Another assistant grabbed her ankles, swung her lower half back onto the bed, and pinned her legs onto the mattress.

"Cooperate, and the ward assistants will let you go," Dr. Runnholme advised, his freckled face remaining boyish despite the sternness of his warning. "If you won't allow me to complete the examination voluntarily, they'll reinstitute the restraints and I'll do it anyway—your call."

Miriam ceased struggling. She was helpless anyway. The orderlies released her limbs, and Runnholme completed his examination of her eyes. "Response to light stimulation—normal."

She noted the gold oak leaf insignia on his lapel, indicating his rank as major, while Runnholme recorded the information into his iPad with the comment, "No apparent physical damage to the optic nerve or retina."

"What did you *expect* to find?" Miriam asked. *Maybe I can reason with him.*

"The secret to your soul," Runnholme replied with a grin. "Isn't that what the poets say?" His expression sobered. "In place of that, a physical reason for your hallucinations."

"Ha. Ha." Miriam laughed without mirth. Zarkisian had chosen her corporeal prison well. Runnholme and his staff searched for physical explanations alone for her behavior not psychic or supernatural. Escape was her sole option. To do that, she needed to determine the exact nature of her confinement.

She flashed Runnholme an innocent smile and asked in a sweet voice, "Are you a member of EDIC?"

Runnholme pursed his mouth but not did not answer.

"Well? Are you or not?" Miriam asked.

"The question is irrelevant," Runnholme replied.

"That's an evasion," Miriam said.

"Do you want me to be?" Runnholme asked. "Does it fit in with your preconceived notion of reality?" He knitted his brows in consternation as he tried to figure out what Miriam was after. "Or do you want to know the truth?"

Keeping a cautious eye on the ward assistants to determine their reactions to her movements, Miriam sat up and folded her arms around her legs. At last, somebody was listening to her rather than just drugging her into unconsciousness. If this *was* consciousness—she still felt groggy and uncertain on that point. "It would help me trust you more if you answered it."

"OK, then." Runnholme shrugged. "I'm not."

"Why was I put under, then?" Miriam asked. "Three times—that I remember."

"You fought so hard, we had to restrain you," Runnholme replied. "I seldom prescribe sedatives in these cases, but the depth of your agitation was sufficient for me to agree to it."

Miriam's eyes widened. "Agree with whom?"

"Colonel Zarkisian, the doctor who referred you."

"Aha!" Miriam exclaimed triumphantly. "You *are* a member of EDIC."

"He is." Runnholme's ice blue eyes scanned his iPad. "He wrote in his notes you might say something like that."

"Like what?" Miriam pointed at Runnholme's iPad. "What does he say about me in there?"

"Just so it doesn't become an issue later," Runnholme said after a moment's hesitation, "I assumed your implied consent to read Dr. Zarkisian's medical notes about you while you are hospitalized here."

He turned the screen in her direction and ran his finger down the government form to Zarkisian's concluding assessment: Manifests delusional behavior with alternate fits of grandeur and paranoid aggression.

Miriam readopted her defensive position. Clever guy, that Zarkisian—no matter what she said about Hades or her tormenters, they would be regarded as the ravings of a mad woman. "Do *you* think I'm delusional?"

"Depends on what you tell me." Runnholme folded his arms across his chest. "If you tell me about your actions as a freelance journalist, I would say not. But all that psychic parasite stuff you said in your drug-induced state, well . . ."

Miriam sighed. If this compassionate doctor believed Zarkisian's diagnosis, what chance did she have convincing anyone that her episodes in Hades were anything other than narcotic-induced hallucinations? She wracked her brain for any way to get Runnholme to reassess her so called delusions. She had an idea: maybe if he concluded himself that Zarkisian was lying to him he would believe her. "Where's Zarkisian now?"

"The Caucasus," Runnholme replied. "The exact location is top secret."

"That doesn't tell you anything?" Miriam hinted.

Runnholme shrugged. "You tell me."

Miriam related her investigations of Zarkisian's and Albrecht's travel itineraries along with Todd's communication through the Army Communications-Electronics Command. She made no reference to psychic parasites or the Lower World. When she finished, Runnholme deliberated for a moment, raised a flattened palm, and rocked it back and forth. "Persuasive but circumstantial."

Miriam groaned. What other information would persuade him? "Have you heard any news from Mt. Ararat?"

"The United States conducted a strategic air strike in that area during the past twenty-four hours," Runnholme replied. "Other than that, there's been a total news blackout."

"And how long has it been since you heard from Dr. Zarkisian?" Miriam asked.

"Less than forty-eight hours." Runnholme shifted uneasily in his seat beside the bed. "Still circumstantial."

Miriam noted Runnholme's fidget—his confidence was cracking. "And how long since Zarkisian committed me here?"

"About the same length of time. Dr. Zarkisian said you'd tie the two events together."

Miriam smiled. Zarkisian's preparations were too perfect. "Did he give you a specific reason why he anticipated I would say that?"

Runnholme reexamined his notes and frowned.

He doubts Zarkisian's honesty, too.

Would he accept her story about the Anausavareds and the Lower World now? If she could convince Runnholme about the dangers they both faced, together they could stop the government's linkage with whatever Zarkisian had planned. She related the gist of her dreams and the explanation Albrecht had given her to Runnholme.

"You're tying the news blackout around Mt. Ararat to the Zoroastrian version of End Time?" Runnholme replied when she finished. "And our government's tactical bombing to a group of psychic

Mission: Soul Sacrifice

parasites?" He keyed her statement onto his iPad and flashed Miriam a skeptical smile. "How does that work?"

"Who knows?" Miriam replied, throwing her hands into the air. "Zarkisian has coordinated American airstrikes to coincide with the volcanic eruptions in the Lower World."

"To what end?"

"You said it yourself—End Time."

Runnholme finished typing into his iPad. He shook his head again. "You've given me a lot to think about. Let's say I believe that you believe it."

"Isn't that enough?" Miriam asked.

"Not enough to call the Pentagon." Runnholme's icy blue gaze penetrated to the back of Miriam's skull. "That's what you want, isn't it—to call off the bombing?" When Miriam nodded, he asked, "Why haven't you contacted them already? Or better yet, stopped these creatures yourself if you have such powers."

"I just found out."

"During one of your visits to the Lower World while in our psychiatric clinic." Runnholme's gaze softened. "Forgive me, Ms. Gorovic, but if you wanted to stop them, why not become invisible, walk to the nearest phone, and call them yourself?"

"They'd dismiss it as another crackpot call," Miriam answered.

"Can you blame them?" Runnholme asked and slipped his iPad into his lab coat. "You get a good night's sleep without sedatives, and we'll discuss your problem further in the morning."

He shepherded his orderlies out the door and paused in the doorway. "I'll be the first to admit that portions of your story are disturbing—and convincing."

Miriam noted that Runnholme didn't close the door behind him as he exited—an oversight? Or a sign of trust?

She heard his baritone voice filter in from the discussion in the hallway, slipped out of bed, and crept closer toward the door, staying out of Runnholme's line of vision. Another medical officer engaged Runnholme in agitated conversation. His face drained of color by the time they finished, Runnholme turned back toward her room.

Miriam jumped back onto her bed before Runnholme reentered her room, his face still ashen. "NOAA reports seismic activity in Anatolia," he mumbled in disbelief, staring at her. "If you can make yourself invisible. . ."

Runnholme's anguish was palpable, and Miriam absorbed it like an alcoholic relishing her first drink of the day. Like a double dose of amphetamines, the infusion of his psychic energy made her feel focused, powerful, invincible.

Focusing on Runnholme's solar plexus, Miriam psychically backed him toward the wall opposite the doorway and drained every drop of his mental energy. Runnholme tottered back against the wall and slid into a dazed, seated position on the floor. Miriam slipped out of bed and quietly hummed to herself while she removed Runnholme's lab coat, shoes, wallet, and keys.

Once she had divested him of pertinent items, she helped the depleted neurologist to his feet, guided him into her bed, and pulled the bedsheets over him. After his eyes closed, Miriam tiptoed to the doorway, made sure the corridor was empty, closed the door, and rummaged through the nightstand and closet.

Finding neither her clothes nor her identification, she removed Runnholme's pants and donned them with his lab coat. She then wadded up her lab charts, stuffed them into the toes of his shoes, and put them on, too. Even stuffed and tied as tightly as they could go, they still didn't fit well and clunked awkwardly as Miriam made her final preparations to escape.

Mission: Soul Sacrifice

Miriam crept to the doorway and peered down the empty hallway heading away from the nurse's station. Going that way, she had less chance of encountering people who'd question a major whose lab coat hung below his knees and whose shoes flopped with every step.

She took a deep breath and began walking the hallways with as much confidence as she could. The hallway led to another hallway which intersected with another on the other side of the ward which she discovered led right back to the nurses' station. The plate glass door behind the station provided the only exit to the twin elevators beyond.

Stymied, Miriam leaned against the wall and pondered. How long until Runnholme woke up? How many security men guarded the ward? Who knew? And who knew what she'd do if she escaped the ward?

She bit her lip.

Do something!

Anything was preferable to staying here and forcibly returning to the Lower World. Goose bumps formed on her forearms at the thought.

Miriam brushed back her hair in the military's button-down style and marched past the nurse's station, head held high. Neither nurse bothered to look up. If not invisible, she at least did not appear unusual.

The elevators were located a few steps beyond the plate glass door. She fumbled Runnholme's pass card out of his lab coat and dropped it on the floor.

Slow down, stop breathing so hard. You'll give yourself away.

Miriam inhaled and exhaled twice to center herself, knelt to retrieve the card, reached up, and pressed the coded end against the sensor.

Click!

The heavy door nudged backward.

"Doctor?" The charge nurse hailed behind her. "Can you spare a minute?"

"I'm late for an appointment," Miriam blustered in the deepest voice she could marshal. "Talk to you later."

She barged through the doorway, shoving the key card into her pocket while she heard the nurse calling out the alarm behind her. A warning siren screeched, and three white-uniformed sentries materialized in front of the elevators ahead of her.

Miriam groaned and assumed a battle-crouch stance. So much for escaping unnoticed.

{17}

The three sentries advanced toward Miriam in chevron formation. She focused on absorbing energy from the lead sentry, a wiry, broken-nosed sergeant who carried a stun gun in his holster. No response. The emotions of the other two sentries were as opaque. If her power accrued from the anxieties of others, how could she tap their energies when those emotions didn't exist?

"There will be no trouble if you return without incident," the sergeant said.

Miriam shook her head.

What now? Think of something!

She pulled Runnholme's penlight from his pants pocket, grabbed the handle with both hands, and brandished it like a light saber. A smile flickered on the baby-faced soldier to her left. The minute dip she felt in the group's resolve tantalized her energy cravings.

Don't go down without a fight!

Miriam slashed the air in broad strokes with her miniature light sword. The sentries encircled her but kept their distance. She felt their intensity dwindling, but their resolve remained intact.

The sergeant reached for her with both hands. Miriam dived under his outstretched arms and rolled to the other side of the hallway. Babyface grabbed her left wrist, but she pulled free before he could tighten his grip. Feinting toward the nurses' station, she ducked under him again and stumbled toward the stairwell at the other end of the hallway.

"No escape that way, Missy," the sergeant said, cutting her off. "All locked up. Better you should deal with us."

He turned toward his less-agile colleagues.

"We're not so bad, are we?" he asked while backing her toward them.

"We're great!" Babyface replied.

"Yeah," the third one muttered, his leaden eyes unblinking.

Miriam veered away from him until she felt the wall against her back. She'd exhausted all the defensive tricks she could think of. Which one should she attack first? Who looked the weakest?

The three men surrounded her again, and the sergeant stepped forward. "We promise to treat you like gentlemen should."

"I don't believe you," Miriam replied, swiping her penlight again.

"That's too bad," the sergeant replied, pulling out his stun gun. "I don't like to use this unless I have to. But you give me no choice."

Miriam glanced at the blunt, pistol-shaped instrument. Two vice-like pincers protruded from the barrel. Two black wires ran out the bottom of the handle to the battery pack belted around the sergeant's waist. It was no toy.

"Fifty thousand volts," the sergeant said, patting the battery pack. "Sure you won't change your mind?"

Miriam shook her head. She saw Babyface wince in anticipation of the gun's firing. The sergeant's resolution also lowered. His reluctance was genuine.

Miriam concentrated. Babyface looked tired, flustered, but the guards' combined resistance remained too strong. The sergeant jabbed the gun toward her shoulder, but Miriam ducked beneath his thrust and slid between his legs, scrambling to her feet against the opposite wall. From the strained faces of the sergeant's comrades, she could tell they were tiring of the chase. And felt it, too, she didn't know how.

The sentries surrounded her again, but their chevron formation was ragged, sloppy. Babyface stood aside from the others, his face twisted with anguish.

Mission: Soul Sacrifice

"Had enough fun now?" the sergeant asked, revolving the Taser in a small loop before Miriam's face. "We haven't got all day."

"I'm not going anywhere with you three," Miriam replied. She felt their energy draining, but not enough for her to overpower one guard, let alone three.

I can't play cat-and-mouse with them forever.

Miriam dodged left, feinted right, and dove for the elevator. Two of the guards missed grabbing her by inches, but the one-syllable sentry recovered in time to block her escape.

The three men closed in. Miriam hesitated. She felt their energy reserves draining away, but time was running short. By the time they gave out, reinforcements would arrive. Or the sergeant would tire of the standoff and apply his weapon.

She noted the stairwell beyond Babyface's left shoulder and felt the bulge of the plastic card key in her pocket. Pointing at the stun gun, Miriam declared, "You'll have to use that if you want to catch me."

"Are you aware how much damage fifty thousand volts can do?" the sergeant asked. "It could be perman—"

"Go ahead, shoot," Miriam replied, staring directly into his eyes.

"Neither of us wants this," the sergeant answered, his face twisting.

"It's the only way." Miriam felt the sergeant's resolve dwindling. "Do it."

"No," he replied. "Even if you insist."

"Do it!"

The ward sergeant sighed and glanced at his men. "Get ready, boys." He turned back to Miriam and patted the handle. "This will hurt, I promise you that."

Miriam licked her lips. The sergeant's indecision intoxicated her, his dwindling energy flowing through her. She thrust her right arm forward in her best Errol Flynn imitation. The sergeant did the same. The prongs of his Taser skimmed her shoulder . . .

She whirled left, dodged past the out-stretched sergeant, whipped out the keycard, and locked the elevator panel.

. . . and stuck in the wall behind her.

Miriam dashed past the stupefied sentries as if they were mannequins, unlocked the stairwell door, and fled down the steps. The thuds of a dozen military boots thundered down the cement steps above her head. Four stories down, she opened the metal fire door at the bottom of the stairwell. A warning alarm blared, and the sound engulfed her as she rushed outside to freedom.

Calling up her psychic reserves, Miriam barricaded the fire exit with a nearby dumpster and scanned the parking lot for a car with a running engine or an open driver's door. Finding neither, she fished Runnholme's keys from his lab coat and pressed the alarm and unlock logos again and again as she raced towards the lot in the gathering dusk, zeroing in on a gray Mazda 3 beeping and blinking three rows in front of her. It was no sports car, but it was fast enough to escape the horde of security men who had just burst through the fire exit behind her.

Runnholme's Mazda GPS system flashed its location in a map on the dashboard. It also showed all of the entrances and exits to the complex. She headed west toward the main gate, then doubled back to one of the smaller gateposts on the east side of the grounds.

This is fun! Exhilarating. May it last forever!

She tightened her grip on the wheel and headed toward the camp's northeast entrance. Criss-crossed cement slabs blocked the gateway. Twin steel bollards protected the guard station.

Miriam spotted two military policemen inside the guard station following her movements on their security system. Sirens blared from every direction. It wouldn't be long before she was surrounded again—too late for her to head for another exit.

Aiming for the space between the guard station and the bollards, Miriam unlocked the driver's door, revved the engine, and popped the clutch. The Mazda burned rubber and leaped forward. Fifty feet from the guard station, she jumped out and rolled to the curb.

Runnholme's car slammed into the space between the wood enclosure and bounced onto the bollards. Metal fragments, fiery splinters, and chunks of cement showered and scattered everywhere. Miriam got to her feet and dashed toward the gap between the dented bollards.

A fusillade of warning shots ricocheted off the cement slab in front of her. Skirting the cement slabs, she turned left on the sidewalk, crossed the median strip on the road before her, and headed for the nearest back street.

Miriam's heart hammered in her ears. She felt so alive! But she had to dump Runnholme's clothes and iPad before the MPs tracked her movements and found her.

She scanned the street. A La Quinta Inn logo loomed in the darkness above the neighboring housetops. Using it as a guidepost, she zigzagged through the alleys and side streets of the city until she reached the motel's service entrance.

The entrance's metal door stood ajar. Miriam peered inside—nobody in the hallway. She entered, closed the door, locked it, and rummaged through the lockers in the maintenance room.

All the lockers were secure, but Miriam found an extra housekeeper's uniform in the storage closet beside the wash basin. She ditched Runnholme's lab coat in a nearby garbage can, buttoned the uniform over her hospital gown, and tucked her hair under a hair net. Grabbing one of the unused cleaning carts, she double-checked the hallway, pushed the cart into the service elevator, and rode it to the second floor where she tried each doorway until she found an unlocked room.

Miriam stationed the cart in front of the doorway and slid inside. After locking the door, she sat on the bed and hugged her knees against her chest. Where could she go? Who would believe her story?

Flicking on the room's TV, she scanned the local channels. Nothing about her escape. She used Runnholme's iPad to call her editor; it went to voice mail. Her calls to her friends and other associates went unanswered, too. If Todd had been available, she'd have called him, as well. Miriam smiled, hoping he was too busy protecting the government's interests to worry about her.

What next?

She took Runnholme's wallet from her pocket and searched through it for anything useful. She only found the usual cards, cash, and receipts. The small denomination bills she kept. The rest she dumped dejectedly into the cleaning cart's refuse basket; the iPad followed quickly behind.

Now what?

Runnholme's iPad pinged inside the basket. Miriam rummaged through the soiled tissue papers and discarded newspapers until she retrieved his tablet. The desktop showed he had received one message. She clicked the notification and read the following:

Monitoring Furst's progress toward Valhalla. Contact me as soon as your interrogation provides meaningful results.

The message came from an unknown number, but that number had a D.C. area code. The only person she knew who lived in downtown D.C. was her mother, but the number wasn't hers. Who else would contact Runnholme about her?

Her curiosity piqued, she clicked into the message thread and revealed a dozen messages to and from the same source. They began two days earlier, about the time of her admission to the psych ward. Runnholme had supplied someone with regular reports throughout her confinement. Zarkisian?

Mission: Soul Sacrifice

The previous text message had arrived an hour earlier. If Runnholme was still incapacitated in her hospital room, he wouldn't have been able to update this mystery texter on her escape. She could use this to discover their identity and maybe that information could help her.

She texted: Miriam's answers to my interrogations have been encouraging, but the process has hit a snag.

Miriam waited and, in a few minutes, received a response: Continue treatment regimen. Will contact you as soon as they reach Valhalla and Freya grants an audience.

Was Valhalla her parents' destination when she spotted them in the Lower World? How did that relate to her current situation? How could Freya help? If anything, she was more confused than ever now.

If Runnholme or the military was monitoring his account, she had one or two texts left before she had to dispose of his iPad.

She typed the message: What is the purpose of Victor and Evelyn meeting with Freya?

The response was instantaneous: To liberate Miriam's soul from Tartarus. You must keep her under your protective care until we exhaust all attempts to free her soul.

Miriam scratched her head in confusion. Why must Runnholme have her under protective care if Mom and Victor freed her? That made no sense unless Zarkisian and the New Immortals stood to gain by her incarceration. Did they know she was a New Immortal?

They knew all along.

Miriam dropped the iPad and rolled back on the bed, sick to her stomach. Why didn't they tell her? Victor she could understand, but Mom?

She gritted her teeth, grabbed the iPad, and texted back: Escaped from the psych ward at Fort Somerset hospital but need to find my mother. Identify yourself if you can help me.

The response was swift: Thank Demeter for your escape. Evelyn and Victor are in GREAT danger. Text me for instructions if you wish to save them. Desdemona.

{18}

Miriam stepped off the Amtrak commuter train and headed down the tunnel marked Metro Area per Desdemona's directions. Despite her apprehensions, buying a train ticket to D.C. proved fairly easy.

At her aunt's instruction, she'd sold Runnholme's iPad at a pawn shop several blocks away from the motel and netted a hundred dollars, no questions asked. After purchasing an outfit at the consignment shop next door, she'd used the rest of the iPad money to buy a train ticket to Washington, D.C.

Taking a seat on the mid-afternoon commuter train, she stared straight ahead, then out the window, her heart racing with every passer-by.

Could the old man with the bowler hat be a plain-clothes officer?

She grimaced and shook her head.

Too obvious.

After no one came up and arrested her, Miriam eased back against the foam padding of her seat and tried to make sense of her brief but chilling phone conversation with her aunt.

Desdemona, her mother, and Victor were locked in an airport hotel room waiting for emergency passports Todd Helsingford promised to deliver to them in exchange for Victor's help defeating Zarkisian and the New Immortals who were dug in around Mt. Ararat. Reluctant at first, despite the U.S. air force's threats to bomb the area, Victor agreed to help Todd by rescuing Miriam's soul after learning from his colleague, Dr. Kincaid, she was confined to Tartarus prison in Hades.

"But I'm not there anymore," Miriam had protested to her aunt. "I escaped."

"I know that dearie," Desdemona replied, hesitating. "I'm glad."

"Can't you waken them and tell them I'm all right?" Miriam asked.

"Your mother and Victor are in a very deep and difficult part of their journey," Desdemona explained. "Waking them abruptly would cause tremendous harm to them physically and mentally."

What did she mean by that?

"I could come there," Miriam suggested. "That would give you time for them to prepare to leave the Lower World."

"Not enough time," Desdemona replied and cleared her throat. "If everything works as Todd said it would, our passports should be here first thing in the morning."

"When's that?" Miriam asked.

"Less than two hours from now, Liverpool time," Desdemona replied.

"Well, I can't stay at this La Quinta," Miriam said. "They're bound to trace this call and find me."

Silence on the other end.

"Aunt Dezzie?" Miriam asked.

"Sorry, just thinking," Desdemona replied. "I suggest you wait for us in D.C."

"How do I get there?" Miriam asked without hesitation. "Where should I meet you? My mother's house?"

"No, no!" Desdemona exclaimed. "That's the first place they'd look."

"Who's 'they'?" Miriam asked. This sounded conspiratorial. "Won't you be free if you receive passports?"

"To enter the U.S.," Desdemona replied. "The FBI still wants Victor and your mother for the death of a security guard at Walter Reed Hospital."

Her mother faced murder charges? Miriam scrunched her face in surprise before relaxing just as quickly as the memory returned.

Mission: Soul Sacrifice

"I'd forgotten," Miriam responded. "Where then?"

"Victor's place," Desdemona replied.

Miriam shivered. The prospect of meeting him at his place distressed and intrigued her. "Why there?"

"No one will expect your being there," Desdemona replied. "After ten years without contact, I doubt anyone suspects he even has a daughter."

Or cares. Except me.

"How do I get in?" Miriam asked. "Is there a key?"

"I'll alert the concierge to let you in," Desdemona replied. "Let me know the moment you arrive."

Miriam sighed. Her aunt's arrangements made everything seem so cloak and dagger. But they'd worked so far; she was grateful for that.

She scanned the commuters surrounding her in the passenger car. This might be a good opportunity to experiment with her new-found orgonic powers.

Most of the passengers were ordinary people, but at a certain angle a flickering glow surrounded some of them as if shrouded in colored cellophane. Some, like businessmen and government officials, glowed bright red—stress from their jobs?

Or did the shrouding color relate somehow to sexual potency? The shrouds surrounding male adolescents and housewives glowed various shades of blue.

Blue also aligned with tension and anxiety. A navy chaplain, in particular, appeared wrapped in a thick swath of ultramarine. Whatever their color, the shrouds exposed their owners as dynamos of repressed energy.

Miriam consumed the energy from this random sample of strangers like a sommelier at a wine tasting. Each color possessed its own psychic flavor and she sipped (that's what the energy exchange felt like) from each passenger in turn. The ones with red auras jolted her nervous system like a caffeinated drink. Those with blue auras infused her with a warm, comfy feeling as if wrapping her in a down blanket. The green and yellow auras tasted diluted and milder, like drinking herbal tea from a reused bag.

Then she combined flavors, diluting the jalapeno rush from a red aura with the chamomile blandness of a yellow aura or complementing the cozy contentment from a green aura with the sweat-inducing warmth from a blue aura. The other time she felt as exhilarated was during the car chase. Neither time had she felt so dissolute or so reckless. Or so alive.

By the time Miriam reached her stop, she felt powerful, confident, in full command of her energy-absorbing ability. She stepped off the bus and headed down the street toward the address Desdemona had given her.

Abutting the south end of the National Zoological Park, Victor's apartment building was a tawny, rectangular, four-story brick edifice. The eight-unit complex possessed neither a distinguishing style nor architectural embellishment—totally undistinguished. The square oak desk she spotted in the cove off the entryway could serve as the concierge station, but it was empty, and judging from the dust in the corners of the desktop, seldom-used. Miriam sniffed, rubbed her nose, and grinned—like Victor.

But when she rang the bell, a blond, muscular man with a military-style crewcut emerged from a door behind the desk. "Can I help you?"

"I'm here to see Dr. Victor Furst," Miriam replied, troubled at the smile creeping along the man's lips. "On a health-related matter."

"Of course," the man responded. "Fourth floor, Room 4E."

Didn't he know Victor wasn't there, Miriam wondered. "Are you going to give me a key?" she asked, holding out her hand. "Or ring him I'm here?"

"No. Go right in," the man responded with a stiff smile. "You're expected."

Miriam's new-found energy sensors did not register a reading regarding the man's psychic energy levels. "Who's ex—"

Without waiting for her to finish speaking, the military man exited through the door behind the counter and clicked it shut.

Miriam dawdled toward the elevator, wondering if someone waited for her in Victor's apartment.

Stop being so paranoid.

She shook her head in annoyance. Of course, no one was in his apartment waiting to pounce. The concierge must have been referring to Desdemona's notification of Miriam's arrival. Within the family, Desdemona had a reputation for the unusual and unexpected. This incident seemed in character.

Miriam pressed the panel button, rode the elevator to the fourth floor, and paused in front of Room 4E. Everything looked OK so far. She took a deep breath, squared her shoulders, and tapped on the mahogany door. No answer. She tried again. Still no answer. She slowly tried the handle. Finding it unlocked, she turned the handle, and stuck her head inside the doorway. "Hello?"

When nobody answered, she stepped inside and gazed around her father's spare, one-bedroom apartment. The glass-covered fireplace was the lone luxury in Victor's spartan apartment. Textbooks on Freud, Jung, and Frankl filled the small mahogany bookcase inside the doorway. Those she expected; the books by Burton, Assagioli, Harner, and the Vedas she did not.

She opened drawers in the galley kitchen and bathroom, searching for any sign of personality or clue as to who Victor might really be. Unsure what to expect, she searched cabinets and drawers in his bedroom and the living area where the fireplace stood. She knew little about the man who left her mother when Miriam was a teenager, even less about psychology or shamanism.

In her wildest flings of imagination Miriam pictured bookcases filled with elixir vials and racks of enchantment flasks lining the walls of Victor's apartment. She found instead, a single black laptop computer lying on top of a battered coffee table in front of the thread-bare, tan sofa facing the fireplace.

The hairs on the back of Miriam's neck stood on end. This seemed as fortuitous as the military man at the vacant concierge station. If the laptop was Victor's, why did he leave it?

The laptop beeped in a high and low circular loop that Miriam recognized as Skype's incoming call alert. Should she answer it? The call must be for Victor. Who else would call here?

The beeping stopped and started again, sounding louder, more insistent than before. Could it be her aunt?

Miriam opened the laptop and pressed the Enter key. The laptop woke up and a blank page popped onto the desktop followed by a sky-blue Skype screen with a white popup announcing a call. When Miriam pressed the Enter key again, the shadowy image of her aunt's face filled the screen.

"Miriam?" Desdemona's image asked in an uncertain voice. "Is that you?"

"I'm so glad to hear you, Aunt Dez," Miriam replied, relieved to hear a familiar voice. She shook her head to gather her thoughts. *Don't bother with small talk.* "Whose laptop am I using?"

"Victor's, I imagine, that's who I called," her aunt replied, her eyes widening with surprise.

"That's strange," Miriam replied, the hairs on the back of her neck tingling again. "Wouldn't he take his laptop with him?"

"It's been a wild ride, dearie, all the way to Liverpool," Desdemona answered. "I can't tell you all about it now, but Victor didn't mention bringing his laptop with him."

Miriam rubbed under her nose, pondering. That sounded like Victor. Still—

"He just left it here?" she asked. "Without password protection?"

Desdemona's silvery brows knitted in irritation. "I don't know. I guess he thought it was safe inside his apartment. You'd have to ask him."

Miriam fidgeted, unsure whether to believe Desdemona or not. Her explanation was weak but plausible under the circumstances. "Where is he? And my mother? May I talk to her?"

"They're journeying," Desdemona responded. "They had almost reached their destination in the Lower World last time I checked."

"Which is?" Miriam asked.

"Valhalla," Desdemona answered.

"Wha—?"

"Shh," Desdemona said, glancing over her shoulder. "They're almost there." A moment later she added, "They've arrived at Freya's castle."

Miriam pouted in frustration. "How are you seeing this?"

"Through a psychomanteum," Desdemona replied. "It's a mirror that helps me connect to alternate realities like in the Lower World.

"Here," she added. "Let me show you.'

The Skype image pivoted from Desdemona's face to the dusty bathroom mirror propped against the hotel bed. A man and woman lay stretched out on the carpet before it—Victor and Evelyn. Dusky silhouettes of two people dismounting from their horses appeared in the mirror in front of their heads.

Miriam gritted her teeth in perplexity. "The image is so dark. What's happening?"

"The room needs to be dark for us to see their images," Desdemona replied and moved the smartphone closer to the fireplace. "Look closer."

Miriam pressed her nose against the computer screen. Evelyn and Victor leading two white horses approached a magnificent castle. In the distance, jagged peaks towered over a glistening multi-turreted fortress. A golden tree blazed in the courtyard.

"Where are they?" Miriam whispered, captivated by the scene.

"The tree in the courtyard could be the Tree of Life," Desdemona answered. "If so, the castle is Valhalla, home of all the Norse gods and heroes."

"Why there?"

"Shhh. I'll explain later."

Victor and Miriam pulled their mounts to a halt before the castle's rainbow drawbridge. A rugged, raven-haired giantess wearing a brass shield and helmet stood guard duty on the parapet over the entrance. After a testy exchange with the would-be petitioners, the woman rolled up the portcullis, lowered the drawbridge, and escorted Victor and Evelyn to the main gate.

Their arrival and entrance seemed to throw the warrior women who served as castle staff into a tizzy. After much discussion, they unlocked the massive oak gate that opened onto a sumptuous banquet table ringed with rows and rows of carved aspen chairs. Golden shields stuck in the ceiling set the hall ablaze from the fires in the roasting pits at either end of the hall.

"Who are those women?" Miriam whispered, fascinated by the other-world display.

"Valkyries," Desdemona replied.

A glowering, senior Valkyrie directed the trolls and gnomes setting the table. She scowled in displeasure when Victor interrupted her preparations.

Mission: Soul Sacrifice

"What is she saying?" Miriam asked. "There should be subtitles running along the bottom, like for foreign language movies."

"The Valkyrie's name is Rotomir," Desdemona explained, lip-reading and summarizing out loud. "She is in charge of running the castle and is telling your parents that the first guests are not expected for another two hours, the major deities and heroes not for another three, at least."

"Why is Victor waving his hands like a crazy person?" Miriam asked.

"He's explaining to her the urgent need behind their request," Desdemona replied. "His animated gestures are for effect to show how agitated and important their mission is."

Miriam watched Rotomir guide Victor and Evelyn to the front steps. The goddess pointed toward a second, smaller castle standing in the middle of a broad meadow.

"She is saying Freya's castle Sessrumnir is where you will find Freya," Desdemona said. "But I doubt whether the goddess is holding audiences today."

More discussion from Victor prompted Rotomir to point toward the southern sky. Three pale-faced Valkyries directed an unending string of white swans descending toward the castle. Each swan bore an inert warrior dressed in modern military fatigues. After further discussion, Victor and Evelyn returned through the portcullis, mounted their horses, and headed toward Freya's castle.

The image dipped, bounced upward, and focused on a green carpet. "Our eyes need rest from peering at these dim images," Desdemona explained.

Miriam rubbed her eyes. "Why isn't Freya in Valhalla?"

"A major battle in the corporeal world has led to the judgment and disposition of many souls to the Lower World. That is the reason for dinner's delay, and why Wodanaz and Freya are judging souls at Sessrumnir."

"Who's Wodanaz?" Miriam asked, raising an eyebrow.

"The Kurgan king of the gods," Desdemona explained. "In Norse mythology he's called Odin, Wotan in German."

"What battle?"

"Ah!" Desdemona smiled. "For Mount Ararat."

The one for which Todd sought Victor's assistance. Miriam nodded. Much of Runnholme's interrogation had focused on her knowledge of that conflict. She shivered at the recollection. "Why are they delayed?"

Desdemona pointed toward the lower-left corner of the image where distant mountains belched fire and smoke. "The magic fires of the mountains of Dakhanavar are holding up the decision-making process."

Miriam knitted her brows. "What process do you mean?"

"Wodanaz and Freya divvy up dead warriors' souls. Freya sends those who defend the homeland to the Plain of Folkvangr—Asphodel, in classic Greek mythology. Evil warriors went to Tartarus."

Like Rupert Albrecht, damn him.

"Where I was," Miriam said.

"But now you're safe in D.C.," Desdemona replied, her mouth curling with curiosity. "How *did* you escape?"

"Luck, mostly," Miriam answered. Why did Desdemona sound so surprised? Her neck hairs tingled again. Better not to reveal her newfound powers to her aunt just yet. "And Rupert Albrecht."

"Ah." Desdemona pursed her lips as if Miriam's answer explained everything. "How did he help you?"

"Like the evil warriors you mentioned, his soul was sent to Tartarus, decapitated by angry investors—he said. His hands held his severed head while he told me this," Miriam said, quivering at the memory. "Echhh. Weird."

"That doesn't explain how you escaped," Desdemona replied.

"The eruptions of Dakhanavar you mentioned shook the foundations of Tartarus," Miriam answered. "Tisiphone and her sisters whipped everyone there trying to maintain order. We escaped in the confusion."

"That got you out of prison," Desdemona replied. "But how did your soul return to ordinary reality?"

"The doctors brought it back," Miriam said in a flat voice. "But I managed to escape from their prison, too." She looked up. "And here I am."

"Yes, you are," Desdemona replied, smiling. "What happened to Mr. Albrecht's soul?"

"Two blue herons carried it over the mountains," Miriam retorted, her resentment at his rejecting her resurfacing. "He's in Dakhanavar for all I know. Or care."

"I see," Desdemona said, pondering.

Ask her. You have to confide in somebody.

"Aunt Dez?" Miriam asked, welling up her courage. "Do you know anything about prearranged marriages with New Immortals?"

Desdemona snapped to attention. "Who told you about that?"

"Albrecht," Miriam replied. "He told me I was his intended bride before the herons took him away."

"That egomaniac," Desdemona said under her breath. "You know he'd say anything to get what he wanted."

"But am I?" Miriam persisted despite fearing the answer. "Don't I have to be a New Immortal to marry one?"

"Yes, that's true," Desdemona replied. "Do you think you are?"

"No, yes." Miriam shook her head, her mind in a whirl. The separation of mind and body was too complicated to comprehend. She knew it was true despite her reluctance. "I don't want to be."

"You have no choice," Desdemona replied and pointed at Victor and Evelyn's bodies lying on the floor. "They returned to the Lower World to rescue your soul and prevent your marriage from happening."

Then it's true. To marry one of them, I must be one—Zalim.

Miriam shuddered and grabbed the tabletop for support. Everything around her in Victor's tiny living room looked dim, strange—alien.

She shook her head to clear it and peered at the two bodies reclining before the headboard on the laptop monitor. Mother should have told her. And despite her dislike of Victor, she felt sorry for sending him and her mother on this goose-chase. "Can't you waken them now that I'm here?"

"Like I told you," Desdemona retorted, "abrupt rupture from the Lower World often results in harmful consequences."

"It didn't happen to me," Miriam responded with a shudder. *Another part of my heritage?*

"Someone must inform them that their mission is no longer necessary," Desdemona declared.

"But if they saw me leave Hades, wouldn't they stop their journey?" Miriam asked.

"Maybe, maybe not," Desdemona replied. "Who knows what they saw? Perhaps they thought you were a vision of some kind. All we know for certain is that they continued on."

Desdemona eyed Miriam with expectation. "Once we bring their souls back to the corporeal world, we'll find out."

Miriam hesitated. "I spent the last thirty-six hours escaping from the terror of the Lower World," she replied, detecting Desdemona's intent behind her reply. "Now you want me to return?"

"Their passage to the corporeal world will be easier if you inform them their task is unnecessary since you escaped Fort Somerset's psych ward," Desdemona answered. "Then you can signal me you're all ready to rejoin your material bodies."

Miriam nodded. Given the trauma she'd experienced the past thirty-six hours, she couldn't deny her mother an easier return. Regarding Victor, she wasn't as sure. Leaving his soul in Hades seemed fitting punishment for the hell he'd put her mother through.

Another squadron of white swans streamed down to Freya's castle. Each carried the soul of a dead soldier. Miriam shivered at the thought of so many souls receiving judgment. "Did all of those souls die during the assault on Mt. Ararat?"

"Yes," Desdemona said. "So many young men and women. Dead. And for what?"

"All over a country that hasn't existed for centuries," Miriam mumbled in agreement. "What a waste."

Desdemona peered straight into the phone camera. "Your return will make sacrificing additional lives unnecessary."

"You think my return can make that much difference?" Miriam asked.

"Retrieving your parents can end a war that might otherwise grind on forever."

Miriam drummed her fingers on the corner of the table. "Albrecht told me not to get involved," she said with trepidation. "Wouldn't my return to the Lower World renew my involvement?"

"Consider the source," Desdemona replied and pointed at Victor and Evelyn. "Aren't you already involved? Their souls may never come back again."

Miriam stopped drumming her fingers. For once, her actions could save others. "All right. Let's do it."

{19}

Under Desdemona's direction Miriam's descent to the Lower World proved less difficult than her drug-induced passages under Dr. Runnholme. Converting Victor's fireplace cover into a psychomanteum, Miriam lay prone in front of it and positioned the laptop beside her head. Her aunt's hypnotic slaps against her thigh through the Skype connection did the rest, lulling Miriam into a state of enchantment. Her body seemed to dissolve and melt through the floorboards, and floating in the warm updraft from Hades' leaden clouds, her psyche descended in front of the portcullis that protected the entrance to Sessrumnir.

The swans continued their airlift of dead soldiers' souls, landing beside the fountain in the courtyard where they transferred their human cargos to the castle staff. Some flapped their wings and re-ascended into the sky to retrieve more soldiers. Others transformed into their female human shapes and helped the fortress staff tend to their new charges.

The soldiers brushed ash and soot off their uniforms, hefted the flagons of beer served to them, and entered the fortress' great hall. The variety of their insignias showed the fallen soldiers came from half a dozen countries, including Turkey and the United States.

Hooves rattled the bridge beneath Miriam's feet. She turned and stepped aside as Victor and Evelyn halted their steeds and dismounted.

Evelyn's eyes popped upon seeing Miriam. "What are you doing here?" she exclaimed, wrapping her arms around her daughter's neck. "It's wonderful to see you after you vanished in front of us. We wondered whether you were recaptured or had disappeared somewhere."

"My soul returned to the corporeal world," Miriam said as she hugged her mother long and hard. "Long story, but now I'm here."

She turned toward Victor. His shaggy auburn hair and Van Dyke beard were peppered with silver, but his piercing blue eyes revealed the same contrary, dynamic, feckless man who abandoned them years ago. Resentment smoldered inside her like a hot coal, ready to flame at the smallest provocation. She'd never forgive him for his betrayal, but she'd be polite—for now. "Hello, Victor."

"Hello, yourself," Victor said, dusting himself off. "If you're not in Tartarus, how'd you get here?"

"Will power," Miriam replied. *Forget small talk or social niceties. What did Mother ever see in him?*

Miriam gritted her teeth and recounted her confinements and escapes from Tartarus and the Fort Somerset psychiatric ward in a few sentences. "Thanks to Aunt Desdemona, there's no need to rescue me. I'm free."

"But then why is your soul still in Hades?" Evelyn said, pointing at Miriam.

"To rescue you." Miriam's parents exchanged bewildered glances instead of the gratitude she expected. "Now that you know there's no need to save me, I can signal Desdemona and she can summon all of our souls from the Lower World."

Victor frowned and pointed toward the souls of the dead soldiers and airmen streaming onto the palace grounds. "What about them?"

"It's too bad about them," Miriam agreed with a lack of conviction. *Rescuing Mother is my first priority.* "Their plight is terrible."

Evelyn frowned. "Why do you suppose they're here?"

"They died in battle around Mt. Ararat," Miriam answered. Uncertainty gnawed her conscience. What dreadful detail had she overlooked? "They're here to be judged, Aunt Dezzie said."

"The dead ones," Victor replied. "Hundreds, maybe thousands more lie along the shore of the River Lethe."

"What does that have to do with us?" Miriam asked.

"With you, to be specific." Victor's jaw hardened. "They're here because of you."

"Wha—?" Miriam doubled over as if punched in her solar plexus. "I-I don't understand." She grabbed a portcullis bar and pointed at the soldiers descending onto the palace grounds. "What do they have to do with me? Or my coming here?"

"Those soldiers died fighting Zarkisian and his New Immortals," Evelyn said. "The souls of thousands of others are stranded along the Lethe. The physical bodies of those along the Lethe serve as batteries for psychic parasites like Zarkisian to feed off."

Like me.

"Are you serious?" Miriam asked, covering her mouth in surprise and dismay. Hundreds had died while a nation struggled to be reborn. "Get outta town!"

And just as quickly she was ashamed. Albrecht was half right—she was Anausavared, a New Immortal, with inconceivable powers. But she was a parasite too, a being whose powers derived from consuming the psychic energy of others, condemning their souls to an eternal purgatory with no hope of judgment, damnation, or salvation.

The revolving door of her emotions spun again as she realized she was no longer struggling blogger, Miriam Gorovic, but Princess Miriam, heir to the ancient throne of Hayastan.

What a rush! Miriam beamed despite her misgivings. The terrible knowledge didn't diminish the thrill surging through her—it enhanced it. Todd had warned her not to get more involved—he didn't know what that meant.

"What happened to Todd?" Miriam asked, tamping down her euphoria. If he was all right, these crazy circumstances couldn't be as bad and conflicted as they made her feel. "Do you know?"

Evelyn shook her head; Victor did, too. "He told me he would try to negotiate a truce among all interested parties," he said. "Judging by the size of the Valkyrie airlift, his effort didn't succeed. I hope he hasn't become another of the New Immortals' victims."

Not Todd, too! Not safe, stalwart, steadfast Todd.

Miriam shuddered. Todd's affection for her always was a given; the possibility of his death made her own situation too immediate, and her careless disregard for his affection too real. "What do you want me to do?"

"Proceed as planned," Victor replied. "Signal Desdemona that we're ready to return to the corporeal world. Our efforts to limit the conflict will be more effective if our souls occupy our material bodies."

Miriam stepped away from the portcullis, turned toward the sun, and waved her arms back and forth above her head. Nothing happened. After two more attempts she dropped her arms.

"Why'd you stop?" Victor asked.

"I-I feel nothing, no warmth, no elation, no euphoria—nothing." Miriam's eyes narrowed. "Something's wrong. All the things I felt while she transported me here are gone, absent."

"All of us should try to gain Desdemona's attention," Evelyn said, noting Victor's grimace, "That includes you, Victor."

Standing on either side of Miriam, Victor and Evelyn joined her in waving their arms back and forth like football fans at a pep rally.

"Save your energy," Victor said after a minute of frantic signaling. "I was afraid of this."

"The psychomanteum must not be working," Evelyn said.

"It's not that." Victor spun toward Miriam. "Is there something you might have forgotten to tell us about your escape?"

What did he mean?

"N-no, nothing," Miriam replied.

"Desdemona would never abandon us," Evelyn said.

"That time in North Carolina notwithstanding," Victor replied with a scowl. "Don't you see? Stranding our souls in Folkvangr would get her back in Zarkisian's good graces."

Evelyn grabbed Miriam to steady herself. "I don't believe it."

"Just because she's your sister doesn't mean she can't be deceitful; she's betrayed you before," Victor replied.

Miriam balled her hands. "Leave Mother alone." The fight with her father she had waited for all her adult life was here at last. With her newfound powers she was ready for it. "Desdemona's not to blame."

"Her allegiance to Zarkisian got us into this mess," Victor said, eyeing Miriam as if weighing her for market. "How *did* you escape from Fort Somerset?"

"I told you already," Miriam retorted. "I escaped from their psych ward and took the train to Washington D.C."

Victor beetled his brows. "You were sedated, yet you escaped from a high security area unnoticed?"

"I-it wasn't as easy as that." Panic gnawed Miriam's conscience. "The charge nurse caught me before I reached the exit."

"You said you got beyond the nurses' station before anyone noticed. *And* eluded three trained security MPs to get outside." Victor stroked his beard as if strumming a violin. "How does it feel when you're invisible?"

"What do you mean?" Miriam replied.

"Were you invisible or did you look like someone else?"

"I wasn't invisible. I moved faster than—"

"And no one suspected you until the charge nurse spotted you fumbling with your pass card," Victor said and whirled toward Evelyn. "You said she didn't have the New Immortals' powers."

Evelyn blanched. "She never displayed them, so I never suspected it."

"All those years—eluding Zarkisian, learning how to defeat the demons in the Lower World . . ." Victor emitted a mordant chuckle. "I thought Zarkisian was after me, but in reality, he was reclaiming one of his own for Ahriman. You and he must have enjoyed playing me for the fool."

"Don't be ridiculous," Evelyn said. "It wasn't that way at all."

"What way was it?" Victor's mouth stretched into a downward broken scar. "She was never my daughter, and you knew it."

"You think I wanted Zarkisian to be Miriam's father?" Evelyn threw up her hands and gazed about the castle wall and moat. "You think I wanted all this to happen?"

Miriam backed against Shalah's flank, her resolve ebbing in the face of Victor and Evelyn's animosity. "Stop it," she cried, waving her hand in surrender. "Please, stop it!"

Victor and Evelyn turned toward Miriam in alarm.

Get a grip. You're not a child anymore.

Miriam shook her head to clear her thoughts. "Hadn't we better drop the recriminations," she asked, stepping between them. "And find a way back to the corporeal world?"

"What's the point?" Victor replied and pointed toward the distant volcanoes. Dark lava now spilled down their sides. "Sticking your spirit in the Lower World gives Zarkisian all the time he needs to conquer the Ararat area and secure his power—either getting you to capitulate or by impregnating another human female."

"We can't just sit here," Miriam exclaimed. "Can't we return to ordinary reality without Desdemona's help?"

"It's not as simple as that," Victor declared.

"Why not?" Miriam asked. "We've got the time, like you said." *So much arrogance.* "So, tell me," she added, screwing up her mouth. "Keep it simple so I'll understand."

"It's not your intelligence or lack of it," Victor retorted, ignoring Miriam's sarcasm. "It's our condition."

"What condition?" Miriam replied.

"Our unconscious condition," Victor replied. "It's like the permanent sleep of fairy tales. Or the state of a surgical patient during anesthesia."

"I don't believe you," Miriam declared.

"We can no more return to our conscious state in ordinary reality—" Victor replied with a sad shake of his head, "—than a stage-4 Alzheimer's patient can recall his or her own name."

Impossible. This can't be!

"Can't?" Miriam asked through gritted teeth. "Or won't?"

She turned to her mother who sat on a rock ledge holding her head in her hands. "Mother? Are you OK?"

Evelyn shook her head. "Please stop bick—"

"It's your mother's empathic ability," Shalah said, stepping between them. "The negative energy upsets her."

Miriam backed away, overwhelmed by her accidental role in unleashing forces beyond her control. She turned back to Victor. "There must be something we can do."

"Our souls are stuck here," Victor said, turning away. He crossed his arms upon Shalah's right flank. "With Desdemona's help, Zarkisian has made Hades our final destiny."

{20}

Victor sank his forehead into his arms until his face brushed the smooth, bristly hairs of Shalah's flank. He never intended for his reunion with Miriam to play out like this. But what should he have expected? *Professionals don't act like this, especially those who call themselves psychologists.* He saw that now and he knew how he should behave intellectually. Miriam was the injured party in their relationship. He had to take the first step, yet he couldn't.

Make an effort, Victor. Take that first step.

He raised his head as Evelyn wrapped an arm around Miriam's shoulders and assured her, "It's all right, Miri."

"Leave me alone," Miriam replied, pouting. "I've ruined everything. Ask Victor."

"All right," Evelyn said with a benevolent smile. "I'll do that." She turned, wrapped her arm around Victor's neck, and asked in a sarcastic voice, "Has she ruined *everything*?"

That's what it feels like.

When he didn't respond, Evelyn added, "I know you've done all you could, Victor."

"Thanks," Victor retorted with sarcasm though he appreciated her vote of confidence. "It's not that," he added and drew himself up. "Miriam's outrage is natural under these circumstances. But I also should have handled my emotions better than I did."

He pulled out of Evelyn's grasp. "I've seen how people behave in moments of stress. But I still feel hollow." He grabbed Evelyn's shoulders. "She's alien. A soul-sucker. Zalim. What other terms are there?"

"Something kinder, I hope," Evelyn answered. "She *did* try to rescue us, after all. That must count for something."

Anger flared inside Victor's chest. "Desdemona tricked her, but that doesn't atone for her jeopardizing our return," he replied. "Or—"

"Or what?"

Victor turned away in frustration. By hiding Miriam's true parentage from him, Evelyn had facilitated their endangerment, too, but assigning blame only made matters worse.

"Or what, Victor?" Evelyn asked, cupping his elbow. "Don't abandon us again. We need you now."

Victor flinched and backed away. Resentment sizzled like a rifle slug in his side.

Shalah nickered. His muzzle prodded between Victor's shoulder blades, but Victor refused to budge. The stallion's nudges grew more insistent.

Victor stepped further away but Shalah shepherded him back. "What is it you want?" he asked.

"This is no time for your personal squabbles," Shalah said, nodding toward Evelyn. When Victor turned toward her, Evelyn pointed toward the southern horizon where the souls which the Valkyries transported were choking on the sulfurous updrafts from the volcanic explosions. More of Freya's assistants soared into the air to escort the choking victims into the palace. "The Valkyries' airlift has increased."

"Their uniforms look American," Victor said with a shrug. "They and their allies have committed more soldiers to the battle. What of it?"

"If the battle has intensified in the corporeal world," Miriam replied, "it means Zarkisian and Ahriman have yet to win."

"'Yet' is the operative word," Victor said. "Your observation's sound, but Zarkisian has the resources and the determination to achieve his ends."

Mission: Soul Sacrifice

"You think he's *that* strong?"

"For the soul of every fallen soldier the Valkyries transport to Sessrumnir, Zarkisian will siphon the psychic energies off of four, five, or more Armenians, Azeris, and Turks into the waters of the Lethe."

"All right," Evelyn replied. "That may be true, given Zarkisian's numerical advantage in psychic power. But something must be interfering with fulfilling Ahriman's takeover for it not to have happened already."

"You're right," Victor acknowledged and turned toward Miriam. "Did Albrecht reveal anything about Ahriman to you during your time together in Tartarus?"

Miriam's nose crinkled with concentration like when she had recited the multiplication tables to him as a child. "All he mentioned was that the End Time was coming soon."

"After which you and he expected to reign as scions of Hayastan with Zarkisian as regent," Victor replied. "Despite all signs, that hasn't happened."

"Albrecht's death was unplanned," Miriam said. "As was his ultimate unwillingness to fulfill Zarkisian's plans for our arranged marriage."

The prophecy is not unalterable!

Victor turned toward the castle. "C'mon! There still might be a chance."

"Of what?" Miriam asked.

"To prevent Ahriman's takeover," Victor replied as he pounded on the portcullis bars.

Miriam did not move. "How can this help?"

"Our only way to find out is through the goddess, Freya," Victor said. "Aeacus said she was a seiðr who possessed the powers of divination."

"How does that help us?" Evelyn asked.

Victor pounded the bars until the portcullis rattled from his blows. "We might not save ourselves, but with Freya's help, we might learn whether the New Immortals takeover of the corporeal world is preventable."

A lance pierced the earth between Victor's legs. He peered up towards where the lance handle pointed. The Norn giantess leaned over the parapet of the watch tower and bellowed, "Be still or I'll run you through."

"Help me," Victor beseeched the giantess. He beckoned Miriam and Evelyn to add to the clamor. "I and my retinue have new information about the Battle for Mt. Ararat," he cried. "We seek to speak to Freya."

The Norn descended from the tower; her heavy footfalls caused the bridge to quiver under Victor's feet.

Victor heard behind him a slap of reins against an animal's flank. A striking woman in full leather battle armor pulled up behind them in a chariot led by two enormous black Norwegian forest cats. Even in the pallid sunlight her shoulder-length ringlets glistened like claret waves on a wind-tossed sea.

"Stand aside for Lady Freya," the Norn ordered, pushing aside the three mortals with her battle lance.

Freya swept past them into the courtyard. The court retinue streamed out of the palace headed by an imposing; raven-haired woman dressed in leather armor. Freya scanned the line of stricken warriors entering the hall and turned to her. "Rotomir, give me the most recent news on the battle for Mt. Ararat."

"The battlefield situation is grave, my lady," Rotomir replied. "The number of casualties mounts into the tens of thousands."

Freya's amber eyes flashed. "I never expected it, but Sessrumnir has not the resources for so many slain."

Mission: Soul Sacrifice

"The trio standing outside the castle entrance claims to have new information on the battle," the Norn said. "They wish an audience."

"Bring more meat and pitchers of beer for our fallen heroes and do your utmost to make them comfortable," Freya ordered. She cast a haughty eye on the three petitioners Rotomir had ushered into her feasting hall. "These mortals are neither fallen heroes nor subjects of mine."

"We are inhabitants of the corporeal world whose souls were tricked into remaining here against our wills," Victor said. "That deception is part of a plot to establish a new kingdom on earth and a new ruler of Hades in the Lower World."

"Who?"

"The demon, Lord Ahriman," Victor replied.

"The ruler of Dakhanavar?" Freya laughed, her eyes dancing with merriment. "A poor, tiny kingdom whose ruler shall lose sovereignty to his brother?"

"In your wisdom you see the futility of his task," Victor said. Her disregard for a demon of Ahriman's stature was disturbing if not reckless. He pointed toward the cloud that enveloped the southwest horizon. "His missiles of fire reign destruction on Hades, and the stream of fallen warriors entering your palace is unending."

"Ragnarök alone is unending." Freya shook her head. "The battle for Ararat shall not differ in outcome from other material world conflicts."

"Your statement rings with truth, but the number of fallen warriors suggests the battle has gone on far too long to be dismissed as another contest among mortals," Victor said. "Its length implies the onset of the Zoroastrian End Time when all souls shall be cleansed and judged according to their merits."

"The adherents of Zurvan have no dominion over us Kurgan gods," Freya declared. "Regardless, his prophecy predicts Ahura Mazda will win."

"Are you certain?" Victor asked. "The evidence shows otherwise."

"Wodanaz has said nothing of this." Freya's eyes blazed as she scanned all three of them. "None of you are volur—seers."

Freya's a woman of action. Time for a bold move. "I'm a shaman—a seer from a far continent," Victor said and grasped the goddess' hands. "State your divinations through me."

"Such impertinence," Freya declared and shook her hands free of Victor's grasp. Four guards rushed forward, and four spear points surrounded Victor's throat. "Show him our dungeon."

"You—*we* haven't time for this," Victor said while two Valkyries pulled his arms behind his back. "Miriam! Evelyn! Tell her what you told me."

"Victor is right," Evelyn said and pointed toward the seething volcanoes. "They mark the End Time when the forces of Ahura Mazda triumph and cleanse the world. Something is holding up its onset."

"We think Zarkisian is draining souls of their psychic energy in Ahriman's behalf," Miriam added.

"To what end?" Freya asked.

"That's what Victor wants you to find out," Evelyn replied.

Freya bit her lower lip, trying to decide. "Release the male mortal," she declared. She grasped Victor's hands, closed her eyes, and quaked like a struck bell. His arms quivered in rhythm with her trembling.

A white light scoured Victor's mind and shoved his consciousness into a corner. "Ahura Mazda will triumph over his brother, Lord Ahriman," Victor said in Freya's voice. "His reign will usher in a new era of tranquility throughout the Lower and corporeal worlds. All people past and present shall be cleansed and judged by walking through the fires of torment and purification. Those who survive shall live in harmony and tranquility forever."

Victor felt Freya's grip on his consciousness diminish, yet his hands remained locked in her vice-like grasp. "This prophecy is true," he said in a voice closer to his own. "However, the cleansing powers of the fires of torment may be diminished. The coolness of the rivers of Lethe and Oblivion can quench the torment of all who walk through them."

Freya's hands stopped trembling. When she released his hands, the light blinding Victor's mind faded. He felt queasy as if he had landed at the bottom of a carousel ride in a fun house. He turned to Evelyn and Miriam. "C-can the g-goddess' words be true?"

"We know the energy of the souls Zarkisian drained has swollen the rivers of Lethe and Styx," Evelyn replied. "We saw it when we crossed the rivers on Charon's ferry."

"Wait a minute," Miriam interrupted. "I don't see the connection between those two rivers and draining energy from the soldiers."

"Every soul that enters Hades must have the memories of their corporeal existence erased before they can reside here for eternity," Victor said, his senses still reeling. "Those who are dead have drunk from Lethe, the river of forgetfulness. Those along the banks have not."

"That energy must be what Ahriman plans to use against the cleansing fires of Dakhanavar's lava," Evelyn said.

"How is that possible?" Victor asked, his mind clearing. "Even if what you say is accurate, I saw no evidence of energy transferring from people's souls to the river."

"That's the sixty-four dollar question," Evelyn replied, then her face lit up. "You removed the demons that paralyzed my spirit. How was that possible?"

Victor placed two fingers against his temple and concentrated. The memory of his battle with the eel demons inside Evelyn's endocrine system resembled a faulty video screen in his consciousness. "The eels tore away slabs of energy from her weakened spiritual organs. They fed upon the energy generated by your solar plexus."

"And what did they do with it?" Evelyn asked.

"I don't—I destroyed most of them," Victor replied, caught up in the recollection. "I tricked them into attacking themselves, then threw their depleted husks into the bloodstream for your white blood cells to gobble up and destroy."

Victor smiled with renewed satisfaction at the outcome. "That's why you're here with us now."

"But what if some got away?" Miriam said. "What happened to them?"

"Everything happened so fast," Victor said, thrumming his fingers against his temple. "Once Ahriman's demon eels were full, they coasted down the stream of Evelyn's spiritual energy meridians. Pizca and I didn't have time to follow them because your mother was rousing to consciousness."

"They must be the source of the energy transference that fuels Zarkisian's power," Evelyn declared.

"Maybe. The eels ingested much more energy than they needed to survive," Victor said in an uncertain voice. Why hadn't this occurred to him before? "But where would such a transfer occur?"

"That's what you need to find out," Evelyn said.

How?

The ground quaked. Goblets and knives crashed to the floor around them. Victor grabbed the table edge nearest him and held on until the trembling stopped. "We don't have the time. If the Zoroastrian prophecy is true, neither Zurvan nor the Erinyes can stop this eruption."

Mission: Soul Sacrifice

"It can be postponed," Freya said, her defiant gaze encompassing all three of them. "For Ahriman's uprising to succeed, his rebellion must coincide with events in the material world. The bombardment I saw so far has failed to trigger the eruption that synchronizes with Ahriman's revolt in the Lower World. Once that resonance is achieved, both revolutions must play out to their inevitable conclusions."

"Resonance?" Evelyn asked, puzzled.

"A congruence, an overlap," Freya replied.

"What do you mean?" Victor asked. "Explain so we mortals can understand."

"Westerners call it the Psychic chord; musicians, the Promethean," Freya explained. "By either name, when the vibrations of the material and Lower World coincide at that frequency, those worlds intersect. Fate in one becomes destiny in the other."

"Predestination," Miriam murmured.

Freya nodded. Victor sank into an empty warrior chair in dismay. "Then all our efforts here and in the ordinary world were destined to fail from the beginning."

Evelyn squeezed Victor's shoulder in commiseration and stepped forward. "You said it could be postponed?"

"The chants of my mother, Nyx, control the vibrations of the universe," Freya answered. "If she can be convinced to change the tempo of her song, the Psychic Chord would also change."

"And the intersection of the two worlds prevented," Miriam added.

"Where is Nyx located?" Evelyn asked.

"On the other side of the great ocean," Freya replied.

"Where's that?" Miriam asked.

Victor groaned. "At the edge of the Lower World."

{21}

A second temblor rocked the castle. The psyches of the valiant soldiers who sacrificed their lives to protect their homelands in the corporeal world quaked and wailed.

Victor stumbled to the feasting hall entrance and scanned the northern horizon. Thick lava poured from the vents of Dakhanavar's volcanoes. Fire and ash spewed into the sky. The Valkyries' airlift stopped. Zurvan's prediction of Hades fate was reaching fruition and neither god nor mortal could do anything about it.

Freya tapped his shoulder and handed him a plain cloak comprised of brown feathers. "Fly to Nyx's cave."

"With this?" Victor asked, holding the cloak into the light to examine it. "How can it help?"

"It's a cloak of falcon feathers," Freya explained, repressing her annoyance. "They enable the wearer to change to the shape of a falcon." She flashed Victor a haughty yet encouraging smile. "Change the frequency of her chants, if you can."

Victor frowned despite her encouragement. If the truth of their predictions required the imminent threat of Hades' destruction to convince Freya, what would convince Nyx to alter the eternal rhythm of the cosmos? "If a mortal like me materializes before Nyx's cave, she'll think I stole this," Victor said, fingering the cloak feathers. "You need to give me some kind of token to convince her you gave this to me."

Freya hesitated before removing Brisingaman, the spangled necklace that hung around her neck, its interlocking rings glinting and dancing like golden flames. "She'll recognize you by this token. By Brisingamen's shining brilliance she will accept you as my emissary."

Victor raised his hand in objection. "My unworthiness does not merit this honor. Wouldn't Nyx be more convinced if you made the request?"

"Gods, like stars, are eternal and unchanging." Freya sighed. "Extraordinary times require extraordinary individuals—heroes—to change them."

"I'm no hero," Victor replied.

"The ordeals of Hercules and Vahagn made them who they are," Freya replied. "Mortals alone can change their destinies; heroes are measured by their willingness to do so."

She believes in me. Why don't I?

Victor took Freya's weighty necklace, draped it twice around his neck, and tucked the pendant inside his shirt. The rumbles beneath their feet demanded haste, but he turned toward Evelyn for reassurance. "Am I the man for this job?"

"Who else?" Evelyn smiled. "We've come this far because of you, but now it's up to you whether your destiny shall be fulfilled."

Her statement wasn't the ringing endorsement Victor sought. He turned towards Miriam, but the bleak look on her face showed she wouldn't be a font of support either.

"You want encouragement—I can't give it," Miriam said, and her jawline hardened. "I should, but part of me wants you to fail." She wrapped her face in her hands. "Isn't that horrible?"

"It's understandable," Victor said, thinking of their contentious relationship. She had grown apart from him, farther than he ever realized.

Wrap her in your arms, you fool. Comfort her.

Miriam pulled away when he reached for her. She was no longer the child Victor remembered. And, given her parentage, her reluctance to support him was unsurprising.

Mission: Soul Sacrifice

He placed a comforting hand on her shoulder instead. Miriam's mouth curled downward when she raised her eyes and met his gaze.

"Our emotional separation may have resulted from our old roles," Victor said, leaning close to her. "If they were pre-destined, so might their reconciliation."

Miriam knit her brows and watched as Victor climbed upon Shalah's back. *Is she considering what I said? Or scorning it?*

He tossed Freya's cape over his shoulders. It landed like a feather and clung to his back like Velcro. He stretched the feathery fabric across Shalah's flanks and leaned against the stallion's neck until his cheek brushed the silken mane, covering as much of him as possible.

The stallion soared into the air and zoomed past the Valkyries taxiing the last of their fallen warriors into Sessrumnir's courtyard. Aside from a light breeze, neither the Valkyries nor the soldiers noticed Victor and Shalah passing them.

Looking around him, Victor saw that off to the distant northwest, Ahriman's demons had sealed off that portal of entry to Freya's palace. Below him he spotted the outline of a square wooden structure, a dozen broad poles, and numerous large wooden disks. Chariots? Was Ahriman building up his cavalry as part of an End Time attack?

He checked the position of the wan Hadean sun, forever motionless in the leaden sky.

If I knew how much time I had . . .

He dismissed that thought as he and Shalah soared over a broad blue river and across a vast sea. The former he guessed was Tethys, the mother of rivers, while the latter must be the Sea of Thalassa.

On the opposite shore Shalah touched down at the base of the mountain range Freya said was the location of her mother's cave. The cliff above them trembled in unison to Nyx's chanting and the beat of her drum. Even at this distance outside her cave, Nyx's chords thrummed against Victor's skin like waves upon a shore.

How do I reason with a deity synonymous with divine retribution? Victor shook his head and climbed the steep rocky slope. Upon reaching the rock shelf overlooking the sea, he spotted the source of the drumming—a lovely blonde nymph thumped upon a simple goatskin stretched over a bronze ring about twelve inches in diameter.

Victor paused. "Are you Nyx?" he asked in confusion. He knew obtaining an audience with Nyx wouldn't be easy, but he'd counted on coping with the quirks of just one goddess. "Who are you?"

"I am called Adrasteia," the nymph replied. Stars danced about her white-mantled shoulders in time to the rise and fall of her drumbeat. "The implacable one."

Victor's shoulders sagged. "Freya didn't mention Nyx had a companion."

"She is my sister," Adrasteia replied, holding up her tympanum while maintaining the beat. "We work together, as you can see."

"You do not look like one of the vengeful goddesses," Victor said, trying to be tactful. Did the ancient Kurgans worship any gods that weren't about the inevitability of vengeance? "Implacable about what?"

"Divine justice," the nymph replied, a smile creasing her face. "I am also known as Nemesis to some mortals and Ananke, or inevitability, to others."

Great. Retribution double-down.

"So few come here," Adrasteia said. "Why have you?"

"I am here to ask a great favor of your sister," Victor replied, noting the echo of Nyx's chant from the cave behind the nymph. Soft and slow, then loud and furious, her chant ascended in the half-tones associated with the Promethean chord and plummeted to their bass under chords. Word-like phrases appeared now and then, but her chant was primordial, more hummed lullaby than lyrical song. "Perhaps you would be willing to speak with her on my behalf?"

"That depends," Adrasteia replied with a bemused smile. "What would you ask of her?"

"That she change the pitch of her chant," Victor replied.

"For what purpose?" Adrasteia asked.

"To prevent the Zurvan prophesy of End Time," Victor replied, noting the nymph's hesitation. "And save the lives of many mortals in the process."

Adrasteia's shoulders heaved.

"Only she can make that decision," she declared, scowling. "I cannot help you."

"Cannot?" Victor asked, drawing his cloak about his shoulders in case he had to fly into the cave. "Or will not?"

"I serve as Nyx's musical accompaniment," Adrasteia replied, shaking her tympanum. "My role is to support her will and ensure punishment comes to those who fail to carry it out."

"You would prevent me from seeing her?" Victor asked, tightening his grip.

The nymph shook her head. "Others inside the cave will assure my sister's repose remains tranquil and undisturbed." She shook her head and the stars danced about her golden tresses. "I beat my drum to whatever tempo she deems appropriate."

Adrasteia returned to her drumming, and Victor relaxed his grip on his cloak. One less goddess to deal with—for now.

He circled behind the drumming goddess and stole to the cave entrance. In its shadows a muscular, wizened man wrapped in chains dozed in a drunken stupor amongst the rocks, boulders, and broken shards of clay.

This is Nyx's bodyguard?

Victor chuckled with relieved disbelief and glanced about until his eyesight grew accustomed to the darkness. An eerie glow from deep inside the cavern emanated from the rock walls. He stepped out from behind the boulders, headed toward the unearthly light, and tripped over a pottery shard.

"Who goes there?" the chained man bellowed.

Victor froze. If he made no sound, the drunken man might think the sound was imaginary.

"Who goes there?" the man repeated in a drunken rasp, squinting in the dark. "Make your presence known. Chronos, the god of time, wills you identify yourself."

Victor held his breath.

"Another phantasm," Chronos said, squinting in every direction and rattled his chains in anger. "No one ever comes here to relieve my suffering—so be it."

Snoring and grumbling angry prophecies, he turned over, scattering his mead cups, and plunged into a deeper stupor.

Victor let out his breath and crept through the broken mead jugs strewn about the dirt floor. Sidestepping a mound of shale and soft mud, he rounded a corner, and the glow brightened against the moss-covered walls.

Seated atop a flattened granite slab overlooking the sea, Nyx chanted and swayed in unison to Adrasteia's accompaniment below. A violet aureole that resembled radiation seeping from a black hole surrounded the goddess' head. Bathed in its dark reflection, her face smoldered with beautiful concentration.

Victor's hands trembled. Dare he interrupt a song whose frequency maintained the stability of the Lower World and beyond? What consequences would it have? What would be the consequences if he didn't?

He approached the goddess and cleared his throat. Nyx did not respond. He tapped her right shoulder. Sparks flew from her dusky eyes at the interruption. When she recognized her disturber as mortal, the volume of her chanting increased.

Mission: Soul Sacrifice

Victor covered his ears, but the power of her chant continued to surge through him like a tidal wave. Fluid seeped between his fingers. He fell to the floor in agony, unable to bear even the sound of his own thoughts.

He fumbled and pulled Freya's golden necklace from under his shirt and dangled it before the pitiless goddess. Nyx glowered at his token and lowered the volume of her crooning. Weaving her enquiry into her song, she addressed Victor. "Why have you dared interrupt my recital?"

Struggling to his feet, Victor summarized the recent events that had occurred in both the material and Lower Worlds. "In the name of your daughter Freya, please change the rhythm and frequency of your song."

The goddess curled her dusky brows and asked in the same rhythm and pitch, "To what rhythm would you have me change it?"

The unexpected question.

"One moment," Victor replied. His mind raced. The pitch and frequency of Nyx's tune resembled the clock speed of a computer applied to the operations of the universe. If she altered either the frequency or the rhythm of her song, the change affected the causal workings of both the Lower and corporeal worlds. The consequences could be disastrous if the wrong frequency was applied. If it could be changed, to what frequency could it be changed so that Ahriman and Zarkisian would not discover the alteration?

"I am waiting," Nyx chanted.

"Continue while I contemplate a safe alternative." Victor calculated the possible deviations. "Immortal goddess, please change the pitch and frequency of your song at irregular intervals. In that way, if Ahriman and Akvan discover the frequency, it will change before they can adapt to it."

"That is not possible," Nyx crooned. "The stars are unchanging in their courses which makes mutable life predictable. Atoms and galaxies alike must dance to the immutable rhythm of my song."

"Even you, dear goddess," Victor replied, "must sometimes wish to vary its pitch and tempo."

"At the end of time, yes," Nyx said. "Once the deeds of men and gods are judged, then the rhythm of worlds can be set anew."

Victor groaned. "That time is already here." No wonder Ahriman and Zarkisian were so confident. "The disciples of Zurvan have made it so."

"If that is true," Nyx crooned with a resigned shake of her head, "I must wait until events play out to their final end before any change is made."

Victor clenched his fists in frustration. "Can you not make an attempt?"

"Even gods are subject to the fate decreed by time and space," Nyx replied.

Victor tucked Brisingamen back into his shirt and retraced his steps through the darkness. If what Nyx said was true, and he had no reason to doubt her, the prophecy of Zurvan would be fulfilled. Ahriman had won.

{22}

"Change is not an option," Victor declared upon re-entering Sessrumnir's opulent dining hall. He gazed at the startled faces of the military men and women sitting along both sides of the feasting table. What did their sacrifice matter if Ahriman gained the End Time he wanted? "Your mother said so."

He felt reckless. Frustrated. Impotent. Spotting Freya at the head of the table, he removed her feathered cape from his back and flung it across the smooth oak surface in her direction as another quake rattled the castle. "Any more wise suggestions?"

"Not even a hero addresses me that way!" Freya rose from where she helped two Valkyries minister to a fallen Iranian soldier. "Turning you into a pig shall teach you respect."

Stepping out from the table, she pushed back the sleeves of her tunic as if readying for a clear shot. Victor advanced toward her as if to guarantee she couldn't miss. *What do I have to lose?*

Watching the confrontation in horror and disgust beside her mother, Miriam stepped between the two hotheads and addressed the goddess. "Change everyone, if you have that power," she said and cast her hand about the hall. "Make us all pigs. No matter how many mortals you transform, such actions merely reveal how powerless you are to change the things that matter."

Evelyn rushed forward to address Freya, "Please forgive my daughter's lack of respect."

She turned toward Victor. "You wanted an alternative and Freya offered you one."

"To send me on a fool's errand?" Victor replied, sickened by Evelyn's deference to Freya. "When it was never possible to begin with?"

"It was up to you to change Nyx's mind," Evelyn declared. "With that door closed, it is up to us to find a workable alternative." She faced their hostess, wrapped her arms around Miriam and Victor's necks, and pulled them toward the main entrance. "Thank you again for your indulgence."

The baleful goddess raised her arms and pointed her fingertips at the retreating trio.

"Help me," a soldier called from the far end of the hall.

"Water," another croaked from the opposite end.

Freya hesitated. The three petitioners turned and scrambled into the courtyard. Victor perceived motion out of the corner of his eye. *Hermes?*

A stronger earthquake rocked the castle. The mercurial god darted between his horse and Altaira, then disappeared.

Dirt and loose mortar sifted down onto the entryway. The castle swayed from another aftershock.

Victor turned toward Evelyn. "Did you see Her—?"

"Mount your horse," Evelyn replied, buttoning her blouse. She climbed onto Altaira and reached toward her daughter. "Miriam, get on behind me."

As Victor mounted Shalah, Miriam hopped onto the fountain ledge, grabbed Evelyn's hand, and jumped onto the mare's back. The two horses wheeled around and headed for the main gate. Behind him, Victor heard Freya's Norn guards hale the watchmen stationed on the parapet above the main gate to lower the portcullis.

In front of him, he saw the watchmen releasing the guard and cranking the winch that that lowered the massive grating to the ground. The castle quaked to its foundation stones. Shalah stumbled to his knees, hurling Victor forward onto the stallion's neck.

Dazed by the impact, Victor clung to Shalah's neck while the stallion righted himself. Despite the haze, Victor spotted the left side of

Mission: Soul Sacrifice

the spiked door sliding sideways in its groove. With the horrible screech of metal against metal, the right side of the door descended in stop-action like the uneven edge of a guillotine, a few inches at a time. With a double burden on her back, Altaira lowered her head and hopped under the slow-moving blade. Shalah ducked down and followed his sister, the bottom of the grate skimming Victor's back. Another temblor rocked the castle, loosening the paralyzed portcullis which dropped the final three feet and crashed to the ground, clipping several inches off the end of Shalah's feathery tail.

Lightning crackled the brimstone-laced clouds huddling over the northwest horizon as the threesome raced past Valhalla. Heading toward the safety of the open plain, Shalah galloped up a gentle ridge and halted.

"What's the matter?" Evelyn asked, gazing behind her as Altaira came alongside. "Freya's Norns are pulling up."

Victor extended his arm to the southwest. "Look."

Lava oozed across the Plain of Asphodel like a slow-motion tsunami, the rolling landscape funneling it toward the ravine that opened onto the River Lethe. A small dot hovered above the river halfway between the pallid sun and the eastern horizon.

"That can't be a star or planet, can it, Victor?" Evelyn asked, pointing into the sky.

"I doubt it," Victor replied, fascinated as the dot divided in two and became a line, then a curved slit. "There's only the sun in Hades."

The slit expanded to the width of a crescent moon. Hazy light filtered through the dusky opening, pearl lights blinking around the edges. "Some kind of eclipse, perhaps?" Victor suggested.

The sky brightened until the shrubs and scrubby trees cast sharp-edged shadows upon the arid ground. The ragged outline of a white triangle inside the opening appeared. The fissure broadened to the size of a half moon and the rugged ridges of a snow-capped mountain became visible.

"Mt. Ararat," Miriam whispered, awestruck. "The interdimensional portal Ahriman was waiting for."

Noting the smile creeping at the corners of Miriam's face, Victor pressed his knees against Shalah's flanks. The stallion pivoted toward his sister, Altaira.

"What now, Evelyn?" Victor asked, patting Shalah's neck for reassurance. They were defeated, done. At least his jittery power animal had sense enough to be wary of forces greater than him. "What course of action should we heroes take?"

"I don't know." Evelyn stroked the neck of her frightened mount. "You said earlier Zurvan's prophecy declares that Ahura Mazda becomes the new ruler—if this is the End Time."

"Doesn't it look that way?" Miriam asked.

"Shush," Evelyn replied in annoyance. "Be quiet for once."

Miriam's face flushed as if she'd been slapped.

"It's OK," Victor said, patting Miriam's knee in sympathy. "We're all on edge."

Miriam snapped her knee away as if stung by a hot poker.

"Look," he said to both women while patting Shalah's neck in an attempt to calm him. "I know I didn't handle Freya very well back at the castle." He flashed a sheepish smile at Evelyn. "Not the way a hero or a psychologist is supposed to act."

Victor glanced at Miriam and rubbed the back of his neck. "I'm just being grateful for your help back there." He turned back toward Evelyn. "And yours, too."

"We're grateful," Miriam replied with muted sarcasm. "But tell me this: if the portal signals Zurvan's prophecy has come true as Mother says, doesn't that mean Ahura Mazda now will rule the universe?"

"That's the prediction," Victor replied. "Ahriman is destined to lose his dominion over Earth at the End Time."

"So, isn't that a good thing?" Miriam asked. "How does Ahriman benefit from opening this portal? If that's what it is."

"Look below," Victor replied and pointed at the lava flowing like raspberry jam across Asphodel's Plain. "Cerberus' ravine provides the only way to the River Lethe."

"Which Zarkisian swelled to overflowing," Evelyn said, her eyes brightening with comprehension.

"How?" Miriam asked.

"By draining the psychic energies of all the souls stranded along the River Lethe," Evelyn replied.

"I don't understand," Miriam said with a shake of her head. "How does Ahriman do this?"

Don't or won't understand?

"He doesn't. Zarkisian does it for him," Victor replied, wondering if her string of questions were as innocent as they sounded. He double-checked whether Miriam was absorbing energy from either of them now. She wasn't. "You know by now the Anausavareds feed off human emotion, particularly pain and suffering. By maintaining a steady supply of souls along the River Lethe who haven't drunk its waters, he builds up a reservoir of energy for the New Immortals and swells the Lethe, the river of forgetfulness."

Miriam's eyes widened in amazement. "But how does a river wipe away people's memories?"

She really doesn't know.

"While it feels and acts like a river of water to us in the alternate reality of the Lower World, it also is a stream of negative energy composed of the memories, emotions, and dreams of those who drink of it," Victor said, smiling. "A psychic current, if you will."

"O-kay-y," Miriam responded, unconvinced. "Even if it does work as you claim, you said you and Evelyn haven't figured out how Zarkisian transfers the stranded people's energy into the river."

"Unfortunately," Victor agreed, shaking his head in dismay. "But whether we discover how or not, it won't help us counteract Zarkisian's preparations for what's going to happen."

"Which is?" Miriam asked.

"If what Freya said is true, and it seems to be," Victor replied, "the waters of the Lethe will cool the lava coming down from the Nakhanavar mountains. During the purification ritual by fire," Victor added, stroking Shalah's mane, "which would maim or destroy Ahriman and his demons, the Lethe's waters will protect them during their walk through the fire. Once purified, Ahriman will defy prophecy by defeating his brother and reign throughout eternity."

"Unless those rivers are diverted," Miriam suggested.

"Or their water levels lowered," Evelyn added. "If you removed all the souls stolen by Zarkisian, wouldn't that lower the river levels?"

"And eliminate Ahriman being purified," Victor added, grinning. A line from his college literature class popped into his head:

A man alone ain't got no bloody chance.

Why hadn't he thought of this before? Their camaraderie had fostered this insight by working together. "But so many souls are stranded along the riverbanks," he said, sobering. "One shaman couldn't do it alone."

"How many would it take?" Evelyn asked.

"Maybe a hundred, given the number of souls just along the banks of the Rivers Lethe and Acheron." Victor's hands trembled. "No one has ever tried soul retrieval on that scale—and certainly never under these circumstances."

"When will there ever be a better time?" Evelyn wheeled Altaira toward the roiling clouds. "Let's go."

Mission: Soul Sacrifice

Evelyn and Miriam galloped away. Victor cut them off before Altaira reached the fork leading toward Valhalla. "You're forgetting one thing," he said and grabbed Altaira's mane, slowing her to a trot. "Returning to corporeal reality."

"Does that matter?" Evelyn asked.

"We can't summon shamans while we're in the Lower World," Victor said and patted Shalah's flank. The stallion quivered. "Desdemona has cut off our communication with the people who could help us. Unless they're here for some other reason we cannot summon them."

Evelyn slowed Altaira to a walk and contemplated. "What do you suggest?"

"A workable plan," Victor replied. "I learned that much dealing with Nyx. Without one, who knows what the consequences might be?"

"Whatever we decide, we need to warn the inhabitants of Hades as soon as possible," Evelyn said.

Victor glowered. Time was the crucial factor, but they needed to coordinate their actions. "Warning them of their doom will worsen the chaos."

"Can chaos be any worse for someone already in Hell?" Miriam's mouth curled with derision. "The souls here are already condemned; they're simply exchanging one form of oppression for another."

*She **doesn't** understand.*

"This isn't a case of replacing bad elected officials with better ones," Victor replied. "The souls of all men and women, alive and dead, shall be judged during the End Time. Zarkisian gimmicked the prediction so Ahriman can rule both the Lower and corporeal worlds forever."

"All I've seen and heard is the possibility of Ahriman ruling the Lower World," Miriam said.

"You've seen the portal," Victor said, pointing toward the sky.

"I've seen it," Miriam answered. "But not a way for him to use it." She shielded her eyes and gazed upward. "Nor does it look wide enough to pass through."

"The other shoe will drop in that regard," Victor said. "Be certain of that."

"Maybe," Miriam replied, her brows kitting in uncertainty. "Could a reign by the Anausavreds be any worse than what the world has already?"

"You can't be serious." Victor probed Miriam's soul this time. Her inner self remained in turmoil, her mind as restless and impenetrable as her mother's. The anguish on her face revealed her suffering was more serious than he thought. "You ask me that after being trapped in the worst part of the Lower World?"

Miriam nodded and wiped her eyes with the heels of her hands. "But I escaped."

"Fate intended it to happen," Evelyn said. "You weren't meant to remain captive."

"How can you know that?" Miriam replied. "I don't believe in fate. I had the power; I feel it now. And I used it—simple as that."

"The souls we're attempting to save have none," Victor said. "Like you, Zarkisian stranded them here. Unlike you, thousands, even millions of people stand to become psychic slaves in the corporeal world or have their souls obliterated in the Lower World."

"I know," Miriam said in a small voice. "But I can't help feeling detached from them. I suffered and survived. So can they—if they try."

"That's your fath—"

"Victor!" Evelyn interrupted in a warning tone. "Didn't you say just now that Zarkisian stranded a million souls on the bank of the Lethe?"

"Ye-es," he replied, irritated by her interruption. Where was Evelyn going with this? Miriam's biological father would want her to believe her actions were of her own choosing. As the daughter of a psychic vampire, why would she think otherwise? "I suppose that's true."

Evelyn squinted. "Given the backgrounds of many of them, wouldn't the shamans of some of those people already have contacted them, even administered to them?"

He nodded. "From what I saw, most were from Anatolia or the Caucasus."

Evelyn beamed. "Then do what you said earlier—contact the shamans you need through those who are already here for some other reason."

Victor pulled Shalah to a halt. The logistics of finding shamans among the legions of stolen souls were staggering. Yet even one connected to the corporeal world could communicate with scores more through the shamanic network. One might even contact Kincaid, find Desdemona, and release their souls from their imprisonment in Hades—if they reached Lethe before the portal widened far enough to intersect the two worlds.

He gazed upward. The Ark-like rock outcropping of Ararat's snow-capped northern peak showed through the narrow opening. "We need more time!"

"You need more than that," Miriam said and pointed toward the northwestern sky. A phalanx of Keres and demons soared out of the valleys of Dakhanavar toward the gorge leading to the River Lethe. Akvan led a dozen legions of demonic infantrymen in the same direction.

"You and Evelyn head back to Sessrumnir and explain the situation to Freya," Victor ordered and swung Shalah toward the mountains. "Have her recruit every available warrior to defend Hades against Ahriman's attack. I'll take the direct route across Dakhanavar and find shamans to airlift stranded souls from Lethe's Riverbanks and prepare the rest for the upcoming battle."

"Listen!" Miriam said and cupped her right ear. "Sounds like jet planes."

Victor gazed upward. Ahriman's demon air squadron surrounded the portal through which he spotted American bomber planes circling Ararat's snow-capped peak. A gigantic explosion obliterated the Ark-shaped outcropping. Ice slabs and lava streamed down Ararat's gulley. A mushroom fireball ascended into the sky and slammed through the portal like a mighty fist, scattering Ahriman's demon air squadron like chaff in a hurricane.

"Shock and awe courtesy of the U.S. Air Force," Miriam said. "No time for more planning."

{23}

Shalah bucked and heaved, frightened by the deafening explosion. Victor grabbed his mane and patted his neck until Shalah settled down. *Zarkisian did it. The portal's wide open. No time left now.*

Altaira stood motionless beside them. On her back Miriam peered with rapture at the mushroom cloud billowing upward and blotting out the ordinary world's sun. Evelyn watched too, more fascinated than awestruck, as scattered ice chunks and debris plummeted into the river.

"Why are you smiling?" Victor asked.

"The mystic chord," Evelyn replied. "Zarkisian's explosion triggered a tonic resonance with who knows how many triads up the scale."

"You're happy about that?" Victor cried, aghast.

"Not at all," Evelyn replied. "It's terrible. But it's an innovative application of acoustic resonance I must admit." She reached inside her blouse, pulled out Freya's feathered cloak, and handed it to him. "Here."

"How'd you get this?" Victor asked in amazement.

"Hermes swiped it before we left Freya's castle. I thought you saw him hand it to me." Evelyn wheeled Altaira around. "You beat the lava to the Fields of Asphodel and find as many shamans as you can. Miriam and I will bring the fallen soldiers from Valhalla and Sessrumnir."

Another fool's errand.

"You think Freya will help us after my outburst over Nyx?" he asked.

"She has to," Evelyn replied. "If she wants to survive."

She leaned forward, pressed two fingers against Victor's lips, and pecked him on the cheek. Then Evelyn and Miriam galloped back toward the Sessrumnir fortress.

The warmth of her kiss lingered on Victor's cheek. Was it for good luck? Or farewell? He hoped the former. If so, he had his part to do. But did they have enough time?

Victor wrapped Freya's stolen mantle about his shoulders, spread it across Shalah's flanks, and they soared into the sky.

Below them on the Asphodel Plain Victor saw Keres and demons reassembling into formation. Zarkisian had counted on a nuclear bomb opening a dimensional rift between the two worlds. What he didn't foresee was the explosion's resonant impact upon the Lower World.

A demon with a detached human head rallied Akvan's ground troops. Ahriman shouted orders to the maimed and fallen Keres scattered about the plain. What once appeared during his flight to Nyx's cave like chassis for a legion of chariots, Victor now realized Ahriman's demons had assembled into a giant wooden pyramid on wheels lumbering alongside the lava river behind his blue-skinned minions.

Whatever that rolling monstrosity is for it isn't anything friendly.

Victor lowered his chin onto Shalah's mane to increase their speed. Restoring Ahriman's forces would take time; he hoped long enough for Evelyn and Miriam to retrieve Wodanaz and Freya's warriors.

His immediate concern was the lava flowing out of Dakhanavar's mountains. The explosion had transformed the viscous lava into a fiery, churning torrent that surged across the Plain of Asphodel toward the canyon leading to Acheron and Lethe.

Anticipating possible attack, Tisiphone and her Erinyes massed along the northern walls of Tartarus, flaying the prisoners without letup to prepare against Ahriman's potential onslaught. Gnome wardens buttressed its bronze walls with sandbags to ward off the advancing lava. Sisyphus rolled his boulder in front of the gate to block it from attack.

Cerberus lunged and yanked at the stake that chained him to his post halfway up the gulch. As the sole passage between the Asphodel Plain and the rivers, any attempt Ahriman made to reach the River Lethe had to pass through the guard dog's canyon. The lava would funnel that way, too, and roast him in the process.

Legions of stranded souls cowered along the near shore of the swollen Lethe. Thousands huddled in foxholes dug with their hands. Thousands more too enervated to dig wailed in apprehension at the upcoming End Time.

Victor shielded his eyes and scanned the riverbank. Someone among them must have a spirit animal, healing stick, or divination rod revealing they were a shaman. But his search proved fruitless. Despite his aerial vantage point, he failed to spot anyone with those telltale characteristics.

He swept up and down the length of the river five times. Each time he soared higher to gain a wider vantage point. Few of the stranded refugees paid any attention to their passes.

Victor spotted one of Charon's prospective passengers ministering to a man writhing and thrashing in the sand on the opposite shore. He swooped across the dark, roiling water for a closer view. The right sleeve of the injured man's Russian field jacket was empty. A Kurd woman dabbed the burns on the invalid's face while a wizened man draped in a speckled robe of lapis and teal chanted at his side.

Shalah landed on the shore and cleared away gawkers with several judicious kicks. Victor dismounted and approached the female assistant kneeling beside the peacock-robed man. "Does your master require any help?"

The peacock-man's assistant shook her head, pointed at her gnarled master, and pressed a finger against her lips. When the peacock-man kneeled beside the invalid, Victor edged closer for a better look. Burns covered half the invalid's body, making his race or ethnicity impossible to determine. What distinguished him from thousands of others prostrate on the sand was the ferocity of his soul's struggle between spirit life and corporeal death.

The invalid's blue eyes flickered. He craned his neck and glanced about. "Hell?" The peacock-robed man did not answer. "Sheol? Purgatory?"

"Hades," Victor replied. When the injured man cracked a painful smile, Victor added, "On the near bank of the River Lethe."

"Whatever," the invalid groaned. His head fell back onto the sand. "Just a matter of time."

The man in the peacock robe rose to his feet and thumped his chest. "Eylo. Pizişk."

When Victor shook his head in ignorance, the old man frowned for a moment, then his face brightened. "Eylo," he said, thumping his chest again. "Doktor."

Victor suspected the robed man was some kind of healer, but beyond that and his name, failed to communicate with him. After trying a number of hand gestures and searching for one-word synonyms in a language he did not know, he gave up with a shrug and studied the surrounding onlookers. If a shaman was here, perhaps an English-speaking one might be here as well. "Are any of you shamans? Or speak English?"

"Just Ya-Yazidi," the invalid man gasped. "Protectors of Mou-Mount Ararat."

"You're from there?" Victor asked.

"Uh-uh," the man croaked. "Vi-vice co-consul from the American em-embassy in Yerevan. Ar-Armenia."

Mission: Soul Sacrifice

"Todd?" Victor gasped in amazement. Asking how his soul got here was pointless. Todd was too weak for explanations. That he lay on Lethe's shore instead of the heart of Hades showed his body retained life. Victor pointed at the healer and asked Todd, "You understand what this man says?"

Another spasm wracked Todd's chest. "A lit-tle. What do you want him t-to know?"

"That can wait." He scanned Todd's injuries. In some places around his abdomen, his jacket fabric had fused to his skin.

Victor pointed at his chest. "Doktor." When his Yazidi counterpart nodded in understanding, he pointed at his chest again. "Victor. Doktor."

The Yazidi shaman grinned. "Eylo. Doktor," he replied, mimicking Victor's action.

Victor returned the grin and knelt beside Todd to examine his chest. A folded black chador served as a sling to protect his right arm. "Where'd you get that?"

"H-her," Todd replied, pointing at the mir's female assistant. "Put it on me here."

"Anything else broken?" Victor asked.

Todd grimaced and shook his head. "Falling into bubbling mud is like pl-plunging into a hot bowl of c-cream soup," he replied and held his breath in a painful grimace. When the spasm passed, he added, "The impact doesn't h-hurt so much as the mud b-broth—it burns li-like h-hell."

I'll bet!

Victor grinned at Todd in admiration. His soul needed retrieval and months of rehab, his body a doctor and several skin grafts—at least. That he hadn't died already testified to the powers of whoever was treating him in the corporeal would.

223

"I can't treat your physical wounds," Victor said and pointed at the man in the peacock robe. "But I can draw out your spiritual pain with this man's help."

"Are you strong enough to relay my intentions?"

Todd nodded.

"Explain to Eylo that I want us to join hands."

Todd conveyed Victor's instruction. However, when Victor reached for the robed man's hands, Eylo backed off. Despite Todd's repeated insistence, cultural taboos dictated that Eylo would not join hands with Victor.

Victor kneeled on the ground, focused on Todd's abdomen, and chanted a shamanic tune to enter Todd's soul.

"Give to me the opportunity to help a fellow being," Victor crooned. "And I will make his soul one with mine."

But the energies battling beneath the surface of Todd's psyche kept Victor at bay. The forces striving to keep his soul in the corporeal world clashed with those pulling his soul into the Lower World. Rather than stream across the precise grid of meridians that mirrored his physical body, Todd's life and death energies collided, exploded, reformed, and collided again, like ions stripped inside the sun.

"His life struggle is too intense," Victor panted to his colleagues after leaving Todd's soul. "A shaman alone isn't enough. I can't ease Todd's pain without Eylo's help."

The river's surface splashed fifty yards away. A beaver waddled onto shore, shook itself dry, and approached the group. It barged between the healers, sniffed up and down Todd's abdomen, and stood on its hind legs. "As Mr. Helsingford's power animal," the beaver spirit said, "I will convince Eylo of the need to lay his hands on Todd's wounds to remove the pain."

"I understand," Victor replied. The beaver explained their intentions to Eylo in the Yazidi language. Despite the shaman's initial reluctance, Todd's power animal's insistence convinced him to do as Victor instructed. With the beaver's direction, the two healers laid their hands on either side of Todd's abdomen and focused on his blistered skin. Eylo closed his eyes and chanted in Kurdish.

Victor hesitated, watching Eylo center his focus on Todd.

My earlier chant didn't work. But Eylo's does!

The pitch of Eylo's chant matched a lower register in Nyx's mystic chord. When Victor hummed the same chord an octave higher, his palms grew warm, then hot. A pleased smile crossed Eylo's face showing he felt the same reaction.

Victor focused on the interface of skin and cloth. Heat vented up his arms from Todd's wound, down Victor's torso and out his feet. Moments later, the cloth puckered and rose off the pink flesh of Todd's stomach.

Eylo's assistant removed the cloth and dabbed the area with cold cloths from the river. Their intervention and the cloth's soothing effect allowed Todd to sit up and relate the events that had landed his soul on the Lethe's further shore. "The explosion outside the cave dislodged me from the cavern face and tossed me into the mud," he concluded and glanced at Eylo's assistant. "Where the Yazidis still must be."

Victor pointed toward the mushroom cloud billowing through the sky fissure. "The explosion on Mt. Ararat triggered lava flows on this side of the portal. Zarkisian must have planned on them all along. If Ahriman and his followers ford the lava when it hits the river, they fulfill the cleansing requirement and defy Zurvan's prophecy for the End Time. Then Ahriman will enter ordinary reality and become ruler of both the Lower and corporal worlds."

"Is th-there any way to st-stop them?" Todd asked.

"If you feel well enough to return to the corporeal world with your colleague, you and he can recruit enough shamans to perform soul retrievals on Zarkisian's victims," Victor replied, pointing at the opposite shore. "If enough of them can be recruited, we can reduce the level of the Lethe to the point where it cannot cool the lava for Ahriman and his cohorts to traverse it."

"So long as it's nothing difficult." Todd's cracked lips formed a pained smile. "Anything else?"

"Do that—no more End Time." Victor grinned back. The young man retained his humor despite the crisis and pain. Why had Miriam rejected him?

You weren't around—remember?

Victor sobered. "Convince our government to stop dropping bombs."

"I'm all for that," Todd replied as Eylo, and his female assistant helped Todd to his feet. He turned to his beaver spirit. "Thank you for helping to ease my suffering."

The beaver spirit saluted him and waddled back to the river. Todd tugged the hem of Eylo's cloak and turned back to Victor. "One more thing—is your daughter, OK?"

She's not my daughter.

"Miriam's soul is trapped here with ours," Victor replied. Explaining their strained relationship to Todd accomplished nothing. "You'll save her and the rest of us if you can get other shamans to help."

Fireballs scorched the cliff tops across the river. In their afterglow, Victor spotted two muscular men attacking Ahriman's advancing forces. An older, one-eyed man riding an eight-legged horse hurled lightning bolts at Ahriman's air squadron. The other, a fierce, red-haired man, plunged his goat-pulled chariot into Akvan's infantry and crushed scores of demon skulls with his golden hammer. Together, the combined legions of Kurgan warriors and modern infantry spanned the rim of cliffs that marked the Asphodel Plain.

Akvan's artillery retaliated with barrage after barrage of arrows. What was left of Ahriman's air demons rained fireballs on the beleaguered Kurgan forces. Huge fireballs from Dakhanavar's volcanoes rained acid death up and down the riverbanks. Bit by bit the Kurgan army retreated down the ravine to the beach below.

Freya's chariot hurtled down the ravine with two Valkyries in tow. The giant, black cats pulling it halted beside Charon's dock. "Bring me the man who stole my cloak of falcon feathers," she ordered, scanning the souls surrounding her.

"Where is that red-haired thief?" she cried and steered her chariot into their midst. "Show yourself!"

"Flee before Freya sees me," Victor said to Todd.

"Why?" Todd asked.

"I'm not on her favorites list right now," Victor replied. "And I doubt anybody I associate with is on it either." He pointed toward the cave opening beyond the embarkation dock. "I'll distract her until your soul returns to ordinary reality."

Eylo and his assistant helped Todd limp toward the cave entrance leading toward ordinary reality. Victor draped the feather cape over Shalah, soared across the Lethe, and alighted beside Freya's chariot. "Spare us, your mightiness," Victor pleaded. "These poor souls here know nothing about the theft."

Freya flinched. "More treachery?" she bellowed and scanned the opposite shore where Todd and his Doktor headed toward the caves of consciousness.

"Aha," she crowed. "You stole my cape before, but no mortal deceives me twice."

She hailed Wodenaz and pointed toward the men scurrying along the base of the bluff on the opposite shore. Wodenaz strafed the riverbank with lightning bolts. Once the dust settled, Victor saw nothing moving.

"I have reclaimed what is mine," Freya said, plucking her falcon cloak from Victor's neck and hoisting it above her head for everyone to see. "Your deceitfulness shall not go unpunished."

"How does that matter?" Victor asked. How dare she obliterate these souls, including Todd's, and ruin everyone's chances of escape? Perhaps Ahriman deserved to win, as Miriam suggested. "With doom all around, you're worried about avenging a garment Hermes took from you?"

"Insolence and treachery cannot go unpunished," Freya declared. "Martial law in the Lower World demands justice be upheld."

"Then punish Hermes," Victor replied. "He's the one who stole it."

"Irrelevant," Freya declared. "Seize him."

Her Valkyries seized Victor's arms, manacled his wrists, and chained him by the neck to the back of her chariot. She wheeled it around and headed towards the base of the cliffs. Victor dog-trotted behind her, the rocky terrain demanding all his attention just to stay erect.

{24}

Sweat and grit clogged Todd's eyelids; the odor of rotten eggs filled his mouth and nostrils. He opened his mouth to reduce the stink and struggled to open his eyes. When that failed, he tried to wipe off the grit obstructing his vision. Pain cascaded down the left side of his body. No matter which world he was in, agony appeared to be a constant in both.

Rolling onto his right side, he pried open his eyelids with his good arm and saw fountains of chocolate sludge bubbling all around him. Then he realized his conscious self had returned to the rock slab inside Mt. Ararat. The mud pot beside him belched and bubbled, its lava crust cracking and oozing like the cooling skin on top of a raspberry pudding.

Todd took a mental inventory of his body. Every place on his torso felt blistered like the mud bubbling around him. His face in particular felt hot, cracked, and dry. His mental anguish in the Lower World may have abated; his physical pain in ordinary reality was just beginning.

He blinked once, twice, three times to clear his vision. Every time he closed his eyes, afterimages of Victor, the shaman, the river of lava, and Wodenaz's thunderbolts played against the back of his eyelids like a recycling montage from a horror movie.

Todd opened his eyes and shuddered.

Never go there again.

He propped himself up on his good right elbow and scanned his body. His jacket was in tatters, but the skin of his abdomen was no longer fused to it.

Impossible.

Dr. Furst and the diplomatic beaver must have been a fever dream.

Weren't they?

Eylo and Amar beamed at Todd. The woman wrapping bandages beside him, however, was not the aide who had assisted him earlier.

"What happened?" Todd asked Amar in Kurdish and pointed at Eylo's assistant.

"Dead." Amar extended his hands above his head, spread them apart, dropped them at his sides, and blew air through his lips that sounded like "Whoosh!"

This is too much. Todd pointed at his forehead and asked Eylo, "Remember my spirit animal?"

Eylo stared back at him, uncomprehending.

Too much English. Todd searched for the Kurdish equivalent. "Heywanek giyani—remember?"

"Oxirê avê," Eylo replied with an emphatic nod. "Lucky."

Water ox? Todd nodded in puzzled agreement while sorting out the logic of Eylo's response. None of the souls in the Lower World or the Yazidis possessed oxen of any kind. People living on the hillsides of Anatolia would not know an animal common to the streams and lakes of North America. Eylo's reference must be to the nearest equivalent he could think of in the Middle East.

Amar and Eylo gazed at Todd in anticipation of his next question while Todd fumbled for an equivalent word for community in Kurdish. He hoped Furst's directive to find shamans wasn't a missing part of the Yazidi experience. "Civati?"

The expression on Eylo's lined face resembled that of a puzzled walnut. Todd searched for a synonym. "Torê?"

"Ah!" Eylo turned and pointed at Amar. "Mir." He spread his arms to encompass the cavern walls, then pointed toward the cave entrance. "Gelek."

Outside?

Todd smiled in appreciation, shifted his weight, and winced at the pain. Having many mir outside wasn't much help unless they could be contacted. Todd pulled out Arkadian's cell phone and mimicked making a call. "C-call mir?"

Amar pointed to the pair of ruptured homemade drums lying at the foot of the cavern wall and shook his head.

A drill-like whine squealed above their heads. The Yazidi women and children gathered in fear behind the men. The whirr of metal against rock intensified until a six-inch light beam penetrated the haze. Two more holes of the same size appeared followed by the methodical clang of a crowbar against rock.

A three-foot chunk of granite plopped into the mud pool beside Todd. Eylo's assistant and two other women jumped out of the way as two more boulders plugged a fumarole twenty feet away to Todd's left. Inside the excavated hole above him popped the olive field helmet of a Turkish army officer. The man wearing it peered around the cavern, spotted the refugees on the floor of the cavern, shouted *"Merhaba,"* and disappeared.

Unbelievable!

Todd's heart leapt.

Four nylon ropes uncoiled from the gaping cave entrance to the foot of the cavern wall. Two American and two Turkish Special Forces officers wearing camouflage hazardous material fatigues and rubberized hoods began rappelling down the limestone face.

I must be dreaming.

He closed his eyes and reopened them. The Special Forces team continued to descend. He wanted to cry in joy and relief, but his eyes felt too parched for tears. A crooked smile was all he could manage.

When the quartet reached the cavern floor, the two lieutenants remained at the base of the cliff and directed the descending rescue harness and medical stretcher; the two captains approached Amar. The Turkish captain took Amar aside and explained their rescue procedure while Eylo tottered toward the medical team. The American officer strode up to Todd and announced, "Hi, I'm Captain Johnson."

Johnson's field patch contained a drab silhouette of a turreted castle. He scanned Todd up and down and signaled the two lieutenants to make Todd their next stretcher passenger. "Yah look like you could use some TLC," he said, smiling. "Though your face seems happy enough."

I must look a fool.

"Never mind that," Todd said, sobering. He grabbed Johnson's sleeve. "Have you got communication to the outside?"

"Anothah bombing run could occur any moment," Johnson replied in a Cape Cod accent and pulled his arm away. "You can contact your family once everyone's out of harm's way."

"That's not what I mean," Todd replied and slumped back against the ground, exhausted. His trip to the Lower World had weakened him more than he thought. Johnson attempted to raise him to his feet, but he pushed the captain away. Any show of weakness hindered his attempts to contact the State Department.

"L-isten to m-me," Todd huffed after pulling himself to an upright position by using a boulder for support. "I need to t-talk to Am-ambassador Gifford. He has to st-stop the bombing."

Johnson's smile revealed Todd had just said the dumbest thing in the world. "You needn't worry about that. Intel says we accomplished what we needed with our bunkah bustah nukes. Our forces have the mountain surrounded, so it's just a matter of rootin' those devils out."

Two medical corpsmen slithered down the ropes and secured a boy with a head wound and a girl with a broken leg into the harness and stretcher. The lieutenants pushed their battle packs to the base of the cavern wall, opened the top flaps, and unwrapped coils of wire and foot-long blocks of plastic explosives.

Mission: Soul Sacrifice

"That's what landed us here in the first place!" Todd cried. Would telling his experience in the Lower World convince Johnson? He decided not. "More bombs will trigger another eruption."

"We're hopin'."

"Call Ambassador Gifford."

Johnson shrugged. "Couldn't if I wanted to." He held up his two-way hand phone. "No range inside a mountain. We get you out first, then you can talk to the ambassador after your debriefing."

"You must listen to me!" Todd cried and pleaded his case until the stretcher returned and Johnson strapped him onto the frame. Todd tried to undo his restraints and fell back onto the stretcher halfway up the cliff face.

Rest. Give them an earful at the debriefing.

When the stretcher reached the top of the hoist, medics squeezed him through the opening the army engineers created and transferred him to a bed inside the ambulance of a mobile medical unit. One corpsman started an IV; the other stripped away the remains of Todd's jacket. Despite the fuss around him, Todd managed to spread his feet apart wide enough to spy out the open back door.

The rift on the corporeal side of the portal descended from a point just below the sky's zenith to the bottom of the Ahora gorge. Its edges shimmered like haze on a summer day. The remains of the craggy outcropping that had once been the source of legends lay strewn about the snow field of the Abich glacier. The flattened mountain top had become the Anausavareds' sarcophagus.

Small arms fire rattled down the valley. Todd spread his feet as far apart as the rolling bed allowed. White smoke popped up from a dozen points in the glacier field.

He squinted and spotted two Turkish soldiers climbing up the glacier field. They advanced within a few meters of Zarkisian's bunker and stood erect, spinning in circles like crazed marionettes, firing their

233

rifles in all directions, and shouting "Angra Mainyu" at the top of their lungs. After two more squads achieved similar results, the ground attacks stopped, and the mountain grew quiet.

Todd peered into the sky. The ragged aperture revealed the chaos that consumed the Lower World. At the head of the gorge, Cerberus' three heads snapped at the demons darting about. Wodenaz and Thunraz hurled thunderbolt after thunderbolt at swarm after swarm of Ahriman's attacking demons. Freya's defensive warriors maintained a standoff with Ahriman's ground and aerial forces, but Akvan's cavalry threatened to outflank them. The relentless push of the lava down the gorge combined with Ahriman's fiery artillery and volcanic bombardment forced Freya's troops to retreat toward the marshy river.

Todd craned his head higher. On the riverbank across from Charon's landing dock, Ahriman's blue-skinned minions sank two rows of caissons which pointed towards the aperture in the sky. Directed by a headless demon, a squad of Ahriman's demons hammered together planking while others flitted back and forth across the river with equipment and supplies.

Gunfire rattled both sides of the ambulance on the corporeal side of the aperture, but Todd's medics stayed on task. One put an IV into his left arm; the other cleaned and bandaged his burns.

"Hadn't we better get out of here?" Todd asked, sinking back onto the cot while the medic connected a bag of saline solution to the IV tube.

"First things first," the medic replied.

Todd peered between his feet and glimpsed a dozen Turkish soldiers charging to within ten yards of the bunker entrance, stop, turn, and fire at each other. When the last soldier collapsed in his death throes, the bunker's plate iron gate opened and an armed squad of a hundred New Immortals dressed in bronze battle uniforms charged down the glacier field. Nimble as scat backs, they evaded the Allies'

Mission: Soul Sacrifice

fire, overran their frontlines, and seized the weapons from the few who hadn't fled.

Todd squirmed in revulsion. *Such a waste. If they'd listened to me or if I'd tried harder—* Zarkisian's men regrouped. A dozen of them planted bazookas and anti-tank weapons onto their shoulders. The rest advanced down the canyon in a column of twos.

"They're coming this way!" Todd yelled. "Hurry up!"

The medic assisting Todd spotted the squad advancing toward the ambulance and closed the rear ambulance door. His partner scrambled into the driver's seat as a cluster of bazooka and anti-tank rounds exploded around the vehicle.

"Gun it!" Todd screamed.

The ambulance pulled away. A splatter of rifle fire sprayed the back window. The medic huddling inside the ambulance door shuddered twice and fell to the floor. Twin red geysers spouted from his chest just before two bazooka shells spun the vehicle around and toppled it onto its side.

Todd removed his IV tube and scooped up the dead medic's two-way radio.

"This is Specialist Farnsworth," he announced, glancing at the dead man's nametag. "Allied troops overrun in the canyon. Request everyone fall back to base camp. Repeat: Request fall back to base camp and regroup."

Todd scrambled the dials and shouted into the transmitter. "Let me speak to the operations commander."

"This is Captain Rourke," a husky voice declared. "Clear the air space."

"Patch me through to the joint forces command center," Todd replied.

"Command Center is not communicating," Rourke replied. "Stay off the airwaves."

"There isn't time for arguing," Todd replied, thinking fast. What options did he have? "Then connect me to Ambassador Gifford."

"Who is this?" Rourke asked.

"The man Gifford sent here to prevent this fuck-up—Vice Consul Todd Helsingford."

Small-arms fire peppered the upturned vehicle and ripped a hole through the roof. Todd unstrapped himself from the bunk and dropped beside the dead medic on the floor as the military and state department channels redirected his call.

Don't let me die here too.

Fingers trembling, Todd clutched the radio against his chest and crawled under the metal-frame wall cot for protection.

"Gifford here," the radio announced.

At last!

"This is Hel-Helsingford," Todd replied. "Stop the attack. Ha-have your forces fall back."

"Why?" Gifford asked.

"Their attack failed," Todd replied. "We're overrun."

"You get out of there," Gifford said. "Our troops know their options."

"Bombs and troo-troops—" Todd coughed until the spasm subsided, "won't work."

Silence. *What else can I say to convince Gifford?*

"I glimpsed a bridge through a rift in the sky," Todd said. "Thousands of troops looked ready to cross it."

"That's why our troops are there to fight them," Gifford replied.

"They're not mortal men," Todd said.

"What do you mean?" Gifford asked, losing patience.

"They're demons from Hades!" Todd said.

"What?"

"Hades," Todd explained. "The Hellenic version of hell."

"I don't care where they're from," Gifford retorted. "Our troops can handle 'em."

"You don't unders—" Todd coughed as rifle fire strafed the top of the cot. There wasn't time for more arguments or explanations. "Contact Captain John C-connery, British Immigration, L-liverpool Airport."

"What for?"

"To bring back the souls of everyone in custody there to this world."

"Souls?" Gifford replied. "What're you talking about?"

The back door of the ambulance cranked open and flipped upward. Three bursts of semi-automatic fire ripped through the interior. Todd rolled under the cot, grabbed the medic's pistol lying on the floor, and emptied it at the door.

More bullets rattled the interior. Todd rolled under the opposite cot, hoping to find another weapon in the jumble of first aid equipment and IV tubes on the floor. Finding nothing, he rolled back but the sling around his injured arm caught in the tangle of plastic IV tubes lying on the metal floor.

When no return fire occurred, a dusky head wearing a bronze beret peeped inside the doorway.

Seraphina.

Todd's heart seized as she climbed inside and surveyed the wreckage. Spotting Todd hiding under the cot, Seraphina's mouth curled into a tight smile. "Such a mess," she said, noting the extent of Todd's injuries.

"Ye-es," Todd moaned. "You c-caused most of it."

Seraphina pulled out her Russian army field knife from her belt. "Let someone ease your misery who knows how."

William Fietzer

Todd groaned in anguish and despair.
End Time for me.

{25}

A cloying odor tickled Todd's nostrils.

Lemon Pledge? This is how heaven smells?

He cracked open his right eye, then his left. The rock-walled chamber possessed a sunny ambience though it had no windows or visible light fixtures. Aside from a sink, mirror, and the cot he lay in, the room contained nothing else.

Todd stretched his legs, wrinkled his toes, and extended his arms. For the first time in what felt like days but was little over twenty-four hours he felt no pain or anguish, though bandages swathed his face, arms, and chest.

Was this Purgatory? Or an illusion from a giant hit of morphine?

He crawled out from the covers of his hospital bed—no aching shoulders, no sore muscles, no skin inflammation. He'd expected the worst—hell, he expected to be dead—but he felt refreshed, energized, even.

Was this heaven, or another form of hell?

The answer arrived when a mousey nursing assistant wearing a bronze beret tapped on the metal frame door and asked in Turkish, "Are you ready for lunch with the Shahanshah?"

"I'm alive?" Todd muttered in amazement.

His stomach growled. For the first time in days Todd felt hungry. He nodded at the petite girl. "Yes." And nodded again for emphasis.

"Suitable clothes are ready in the corner box," the girl replied with a shy smile. "In ten minutes, you must be at the command room."

Zarkisian was not summoning him to tender Hayastan's surrender, Todd mused. So then why? Agreement terms? Disposition of combatants' claims? Assuming Zarkisian now recognized Todd's official capacity, he needed to play the part to stay alive another day. After what he experienced, living is what he craved most of all.

He went to the sink, opened the medicine cabinet, and noted the pocket razor on the bottom shelf. Should he shave for the occasion? Did he dare? He closed the cabinet door and palpated the skin under the bandages on his right cheek and forehead. A dozen or more blisters remained swollen and tender.

Todd winced at the pain. His wounds were extensive, yes. Recoverable? Yes, with the aid of skin grafts and a plastic surgeon.

He stared at himself in the mirror. Why was he spared—again? Mercy was not Seraphina's strong suit. And it wasn't Zarkisian's. The fates of the Yazidi and the Turkish-American attack force would not be as favorable as his.

Anger welled in Todd's throat. Why must all those good men sacrifice their lives? For Ahriman's glory? For Zarkisian's ambition? If this was a taste of life after End Time—

Save your anger. Control it.

Todd gripped the sink with both hands and trembled.

Now do what you need to do.

With meticulous care, he shaved every uncovered part of his face with the pocket razor, then washed his face. Donning a set of the Anausavared's fatigues, he marched to the meeting room calm, refreshed, and determined to negotiate a settlement worthy of the sacrifice of the fallen soldiers.

Zarkisian and Seraphina awaited him in the New Immortals war room. Seraphina sat demure and professional at Zarkisian's right hand; the self-proclaimed Arteshbod lounged at the head of the table with the pomp of a Persian generalissimo, an aide-de-camp at each elbow. A magnificent golden-threaded image of a peacock emblazoned the front of Zarkisian's robe while a tall, glittering gold headpiece symbolizing his power tottered on top of his head.

Mission: Soul Sacrifice

Zarkisian nodded in acknowledgement at Todd's entrance, and the gilded adornment slipped down his forehead. Zarkisian removed the wayward crown and set it on the table in front of Seraphina. "Would you care to join us for lunch?"

"I wouldn't have thought there was time for such niceties," Todd replied, taking a seat across from his former lover, "when there's a war still to be won."

Still wearing her military fatigues, Seraphina tore off a morsel from the soft finger bread, matnakash, perched in one of the gold dishes arrayed on the table and chewed it in mute concentration on the plate in front of her.

Zarkisian, however, was more expansive. "We all must eat," he declared and nodded at Seraphina. "Arteshbod Abduri assures me that everything is proceeding according to our expectations."

"Arteshbod Abduri," Todd replied, raising his eyebrows in mock approval. "A full general."

He smiled at Seraphina. "Though Mr. Albrecht's recent demise couldn't have been what any of you expected." When his remark sparked no reaction, Todd turned toward Zarkisian, "Or did you foresee that, too?"

"Farmadar Albrecht will rejoin us soon," Zarkisian said with an airy wave of his hand. "Preceded by Ahriman, the Shahanshah-to-be of Hayastan."

"I thought you were the Shahanshah," Todd remarked.

"Until Ahriman assumes his rightful place in this world," Zarkisian replied.

"What role will you have then?" Todd responded.

"I will assume the title of Eran-spahbod," Zarkisian said. "General of generals."

"And Farmadar Albrecht?" Todd asked, bemused by Zarkisian's wanton bestowal of titles. The man's ego knew no bounds. "What does that mean?"

"Commander or ruler," Zarkisian explained. "That's its literal translation in English but appropriate as the chief of finance."

"Albeit presumptive, given the war going on and the fact he's dead," Todd observed, arranging his silverware around his gold plate. He peered up to see Zarkisian's reaction. "Don't you agree?"

"Not at all," Zarkisian grinned. "No doubt you noticed the rift in the sky over Mount Ararat?"

Todd did not reply. *Zarkisian's baiting me—why?*

"If you have," Zarkisian added, "you've also noted the progress of the gateway viaduct under the Farmadar's direction."

Albrecht alive? How?

"I've bounced around so much I haven't had time to notice," Todd replied, trying to sound detached. "It's going well?"

"Very," Zarkisian replied, "and due to him, despite your ridicule." Zarkisian's smile turned upside down. He pointed at the sweet bread on Todd's plate. "Is the meal not to your liking?"

Realizing any display of rudeness would sink his chances at the outset of such an important meeting, Todd sampled his meal of the sweet bread, olives, and string cheese. Never had such plain fare tasted so exquisite or been so satisfying. Ignoring the circumstances, he devoured everything on his plate and let out a hearty burp.

"Oops," he said, glancing about the table. "Please forgive my table manners."

"Your candor, Mr. Helsingford, is refreshing for a diplomat," Zarkisian said, dismissing Todd's remark with another wave of his hand. "And quite in keeping with the results we expected from our little experiment."

Experiment?

Mission: Soul Sacrifice

Todd reached for his napkin to disguise his apprehension. *Something else is going on—but what?*

Zarkisian turned toward Seraphina for confirmation, who returned his gaze but provided no verbal response. Nettled, but undeterred, Zarkisian turned back to Todd and pursed his lips. "How are you feeling, Mr. Helsingford?"

"Better." Todd smiled despite himself. He couldn't deny the truth. "Better than I have in some time."

Zarkisian's smile broadened. "Such an endorsement might convince people looking for an unusual and refreshing spa or getaway vacation, wouldn't you say?"

Is Zarkisian mad? Or just arrogant?

"You're serious?" Todd asked, and Zarkisian's brows furrowed with intensity. "You want my opinion whether this cave makes a satisfactory vacation hotel?"

"Not here," Zarkisian replied. "Hayastan. We must deliberate about our place among our fellow nations." He glanced at Seraphina who grunted her confirmation. He returned his gaze to Todd and grinned. "Where else have you felt so relaxed and refreshed?"

Todd shook his head in amazement. Despite all that had happened, he had to admit the truth of Zarkisian's assertion. He fingered the bandage covering his burned cheek and forehead. Even the best burn hospitals couldn't treat extensive injuries like his to where patients walked around and enjoyed dinner like regular healthy people. Still, Zarkisian's proposal was preposterous. "You think the countries you've been fighting will accept Hayastan as a vacation resort and health spa run by human parasites?"

"The benefits are obvious, are they not?" Zarkisian replied. "Faster psychological and physical benefits than recovery by conventional medicine."

"At the expense of their souls," Todd retorted.

"Please!" Zarkisian raised his hands in objection. "You, yourself, are experiencing the benefits of such an energy exchange. A simple quid pro quo—orgonic energy for us; health and well-being for humankind."

Todd's jaw dropped. "It's inconceivable that anybody would accept commerce based on an exchange of energy between human beings and psychic parasites."

"No more inconceivable than an inter-dimensional portal between the corporeal and Lower Worlds," Zarkisian replied. "Wouldn't you say?"

This is crazy! Isn't it?

"How could such trade be worked out?" Todd asked, overruling his instincts.

"Negotiating the first working treaty between our nation and the Allies would be quite a feather in a diplomat's cap," Zarkisian replied, putting the tips of his fingers together. "It would put that person a leg up in his consular career."

Todd squirmed with discomfort. There it was—the personal lure that made Zarkisian's offer tempting. Was he that easy to read? Or were the limits of his bargaining position so transparent?

Negotiating the treaty to a successful conclusion removed any lingering doubts Todd had over punishment for deserting his embassy post. Actions done in the field on the country's behalf, however, were not always appreciated or acknowledged during the State Department's formal review. He also knew somebody else would negotiate a similar deal, assuming the End Time arrived as Zarkisian planned. Preposterous as his proposal sounded, the parasites' recent successes and the renewed vigor of Todd's own body rendered Zarkisian's offer difficult to refuse.

"This is a tough decision," Todd said and blew the air from his cheeks. "But if you think I'd sacrifice Armenian, Azeri, and Turkish souls for some vague health benefits offered by mental parasites, you *are* crazy. No diplomat would cave to such extortion."

"Real politik, Mr. Helsingford," Zarkisian replied. "Successful diplomats and nations should weigh all the benefits and consequences in the political equation."

"Speaking as a professional diplomat and as an individual citizen," Todd replied. "That is my final response."

"Suit yourself," Zarkisian said and eyed Seraphina. "Disconnect from Mr. Helsingford's aura."

She peered up from her plate and frowned as she directed her concentration on Todd who doubled over from pain a hundred times stronger than he felt in the Ahora glacier field. He slumped in his chair, dropped to the floor, and writhed in agony.

Gentle hands lifted him to his feet, returned him to his chamber, and laid him on his bed. None of that eased his suffering, however. "Give me a narcotic."

"Did you mean what you said?" Seraphina asked.

"Yes," Todd replied. His cheek brushed the cool fabric of the pillow and his pain ebbed. "I keep my word."

"For all Armenians?" Seraphina asked.

Todd grunted. "Azeris, too."

The outline of Seraphina's face floated into view. How long before he became another casualty? Maybe he already was one and didn't know it.

His agony dwindled to acute pain, then discomfort. And disappeared.

How is this happening?

"You would accept us Hayastani for what we are?" Seraphina asked, interrupting Todd's thoughts. A smile flitted across her face. "Easers of pain and suffering instead of deliverers?"

Todd studied her face. The corners of her eyes crinkled with concern. Her earnestness seemed sincere.

What is she asking of me? Is this another of Zarkisian's ploys?

"As petitioners for status as a nation among equals, yes," Todd replied. He sat up on his bed, his pain and discomfort gone. "Not as conquerors or mental parasites."

"And if I were to grant this agreement to you?" Seraphina continued.

"As a new Arteshbod of Hayastan?" Todd asked with a doubtful twist of his mouth. "Is it something that is yours to give?"

"It is as a citizen and guardian of my country," Seraphina replied. "It is something many orgonics want."

Todd nodded. Zarkisian's authority appeared so absolute that dissension among his fellow psychic leeches seemed nonexistent. "You could be granted special territory status like some of the islands surrounding the E.U.," he said, considering her behavior. Seraphina's hesitancy seemed out of keeping with her customary decisiveness. Should he trust her? How extensive was this undercurrent of rebellion? "Can you do it without Zarkisian's approval?"

"Not all of us agree with the Eran-spahbod's vision. From a military standpoint our country cannot survive under his leadership, dominating everyone not like us." The corners of Seraphina's mouth twisted. "With Ahriman and the other Dakhanavars in our corporeal world, Hayastan's situation would become worse."

Her dusky eyes revealed something Todd never witnessed in them before—respect. "Your actions have shown me there is more than one kind of courage. People show courage by finding other ways to live their lives among men," she said. "What must I do?"

It's happening all so fast!

Todd groped about him in surprise and astonishment. Had Victor contacted enough, or any, shamans to free the souls along the Lethe in

Mission: Soul Sacrifice

Hades? Who knew? Learning whether Victor had succeeded would take too much time—he needed an alternative. "Could you close the sky portal?"

"That is not an option," Seraphina replied. "Once opened, the only power to close it lies in the spiritual dimension that is Ahriman's."

"You're orgonic," Todd said. "Could you take on Zarkisian?"

"As the titular ruler of Hayastan the Shahanshah's power dates back centuries, millennia," Seraphina explained. "Ahriman alone has the power to defeat him."

Todd grimaced. Was there another way? "Are there others who'd be willing to help you?"

"None as strong." Seraphina cast her eyes downward. "Rupert could have, but—"

"Albrecht's unavailable." Todd repressed a smile at the finality of that statement. Or was he? "If he gets through the portal somehow—"

"Rupert abdicated his position," Seraphina declared. "As royal consort, he was the second most powerful man in Hayastan, but he never wanted the responsibility—I could tell."

"Hmmm." Todd contemplated everything he knew about Albrecht. Though powerful enough, Albrecht's actions in the canyon revealed his unreliability. His supervising a Lower World bridge built to the portal also showed Albrecht's opportunism.

Todd frowned. Despite his weaknesses, however, Seraphina's dejection showed Albrecht had been the focus of her affections all along. "Consort implies marriage to the royal blood line. Who was that going to be?"

"Zarkisian's daughter," Seraphina replied. "Miriam Gorovic."

Todd's jaw dropped. His advice to Miriam to not get involved was sound but for the wrong reasons.

None of that mattered. "Would Albrecht help us once Ahriman and the others crossed into our world?" Todd asked.

"I'm sure of it." Seraphina's eyes flashed and clouded again. "But there's no way to contact him before then."

Todd groaned. Holbrook told him once that real diplomacy involved working with questionable allies. The truth of that statement was about to be tested first-hand. If Albrecht aided the rebel Anausavareds, fine. If he got killed, that was fine, too. "Albrecht's a quick study," Todd said. "If we get the chance, I'm sure he'll recognize our intentions when the time comes."

{26}

Miriam wrapped her arms around Evelyn who steered Altaira through the intense hand-to-hand fighting between the Kurgan warriors and Ahriman's demons at the top of the gorge. The mare ambled through the carnage as if she were another war horse whose rider had fallen in battle.

Her emotions felt out of control. Awed by the strength and precision with which Wodenaz hurled his thunder bolts and Thunraz hammered his enemies, she admired the endurance and resourcefulness that Ahriman and Akvan used in their counterattacks. Though decimated by the lightning bolts and outnumbered at first, each of Ahriman's remaining blue demons continued their attacks with a strength and ferocity equal to three of Wodenaz's warriors.

Freya and Wodenaz's troops broke through Ahriman's left flank and joined Tisiphone, her sisters, and the rest of the Erinyes along the top of the bluffs overlooking the river. A wave of Ahriman's replacement troops sealed off any chance of escape further east along the bluffs. Trapped between the lava advancing from the west and Ahriman's forces to the north and east, the combined Kurgan forces retreated little by little toward the ravine where Cerberus struggled with his chain.

Evacuees from Tartarus and Elysium shoved Altaira, Miriam, and Evelyn to the rear of the fighting. The flood of heroes and unjudged refugees from Asphodel Meadows overpowered the ravenous guard dog and descended into the ravine. Discovering their only means of escape, Charon's ferry, sunk a quarter mile downriver deepened their general misery.

Freya's cat-drawn chariot plowed through the tide of refugees toward the head of the ravine. Victor panted in chains behind it.

Evelyn turned Altaira sideways and blocked Freya's path. When Freya reined her cats to a halt, she and Miriam slid off Altaira's back and ran to Freya's hapless prisoner. Evelyn tended to Victor's scrapes and cuts while Miriam surged to the side of Freya's chariot. "This is the courtesy you grant my father after he alerted you of the danger?"

"Hold your tongue or join your father at the rear of my chariot," Freya replied. She uncoupled Victor's chains from the base of her chariot's handrail and deposited the lock into the hands of two Valkyries who assisted Tisiphone in restraining her prisoners.

The haughty goddess attempted to transfer the key to Tisiphone, but Miriam stayed Freya's hand. "What offense has this man committed for you to treat him this way?"

"You know his crime," Freya spat, her eyes blazing. She displayed the falcon-feathered cloak to everyone gathered around her chariot. "Victor Furst stole this."

"He borrowed it to find shamans," Evelyn protested.

"Without my permission," Freya replied.

"I took it," Miriam declared, finding Freya's arrogance beyond endurance over such a trivial offense. "Victor is innocent."

Evelyn glared at her daughter. "You saw Hermes give—"

Miriam pinched Evelyn's arm. "It doesn't matter who took it," Miriam said and whirled toward Freya. "You know Victor had no other way to reach Lethe's shore in time."

"Then you shall join him in Tisiphone's custody," Freya replied.

Who is this bitch to order me around?

"I will not," Miriam said. "Look around you. The Kurgans are losing the battle for the Lower World. You need every soul you can get to defeat Ahriman."

"Yes," Freya agreed. Her eyes gleamed and her fingers tightened around her sword handle. "But yours won't be one of them."

Mission: Soul Sacrifice

Miriam concentrated on Freya's pituitary gland that controlled her energy. All of Freya's movements slowed to a crawl as she raised her sword and lunged forward. Miriam side-stepped the glistening blade, hopped into Freya's chariot, pinned her sword arm behind her back, and shoved her torso over the chariot side guard. Wriggling and screaming vengeance despite her vulnerability, Freya scratched and clawed Miriam's face with her free hand.

"Stop! Stop!" Evelyn cried. The crowd pressed closer around the battling women. Victor slipped two fingers under the links of Tisiphone's choke chain. "Cease your fighting," he cried. "If staying in Tisiphone's custody will help save the Lower World, I'll do it."

Freya reached for her whip lashed against the handrail, but Miriam pinioned the goddess' flailing wrist against the chariot's side guard. The taller, larger goddess heaved right and left, flinging Miriam from one side of the chariot to the other.

But Freya's struggles were fruitless. Miriam matched the goddess's power surge and held her fast against the chariot wall.

Why stay on the defensive?

She focused on Freya's solar plexus. The goddess' energy reserves frothed in the organ's energy streams like water around the power rods of a nuclear reactor. Miriam drained Freya's psychic reserves like a thirsty child sucking a slushie on a ninety-degree day. Freya staggered and fell to one knee.

Ha! Now you know how it is to feel mortal.

Miriam tightened her grip until the goddess ceased to struggle.

Lightning glinted in the corner of her eye. Wodenaz and Thunraz scorched the top of the cliffs with thunderbolts. Despite Thunraz's additional firepower, Ahriman's rabid blue demons closed upon the Kurgan vanguard from three directions.

Miriam's opponent was helpless, spent. "If I let go," she asked, "will you assist them?"

251

"Gods do not bargain with mortals!" Freya replied, wriggling her wrists and fingers. "You are not of a rank to offer me anything!"

I'm immortal, too!

"I am the daughter of the most powerful person in Hayastan," Miriam proclaimed as she drained the goddess of her last erg of energy. "I will break your wrists and then your arrogant back unless you change your mind."

"Aggh!" Freya groaned as her left wrist bowed backward. If she didn't capitulate soon, her wrist would snap under Miriam's grasp.

"Freya!" Victor shouted and pointed toward the blobs of lava oozing down the cliff face toward the river. "All we ask is the chance to summon my fellow shamans before the lava reaches the river."

"What good will that do?" Freya snorted. "The water will cool the lava."

"Ahriman is counting on that," Victor replied and explained how lowering the lava's temperature would allow Ahriman and his demons to pass through it unharmed.

"Purified by this ritual, Ahriman and his demons become omnipotent," Victor added and pointed toward the bridge on the other side of the river. "As rulers of the Lower World, they will extend their dominion by mounting that bridge and entering the portal into the corporeal world."

Freya's sword clattered on the chariot floor. Miriam relaxed the pressure on Freya's wrist but maintained her grip around it. Had Victor gotten through to her? Or was Freya's gesture a feint to reassert control once freed?

Miriam released Freya's left wrist as a calculated display of trust. The disgraced goddess rose to her feet and rubbed her sore left wrist against her thigh. Miriam released Freya's other wrist, and the goddess massaged her injury. She turned toward the rear of her chariot without looking at Miriam. "How can you stop the lava's advance?"

Mission: Soul Sacrifice

"I can prevent the water from cooling it," Victor replied.

"You would stop the Lethe from flowing?" Freya asked in amazement. "How?"

"I would lower the water level," Victor replied. "To accomplish this task, however, more shamans must be summoned to retrieve those souls whose energy Zarkisian drained to swell the River of Forgetfulness to overflowing."

Freya looked about. Noting the Valkyrie standing beside her chariot, she jerked her head in Evelyn's direction. In a heartbeat, Brunhilda grabbed Evelyn around the waist and pinned her arms behind her.

"Evelyn has done nothing!" Victor cried.

"Insurance," Freya replied.

So much for trusting the gods.

Miriam clasped and unclasped her fists. "You trusted Victor before, why not now?"

"Him, I trust," Freya replied, her eyes flashing with vengeance at Miriam. "You, I do not."

Miriam gritted her teeth and watched Brunhilda pull Evelyn away with a knife at her throat. *Beings who put petty squabbles before their own destruction aren't worth saving. But what other options do I have?*

She turned toward Victor. "Aren't you going to do something?"

Victor smiled, closed his eyes, and summoned his horse spirits. Altaira reared and struck Brunhilda beside the head. Plunging and snorting, the mare prevented the other Valkyries from rescuing their sister despite repeated strikes from Freya's whip. Shalah and four more horses charged up the beach toward Freya's chariot. Three of them feinted and parried with the black cats that pulled it; the other two kicked out the axle and chased the cats away.

Several nearby Wailers stood up and pummeled Freya's Valkyries who tried to restore order. More Wailers descended upon them. The open area surrounding Charon's pier became a dusty scrum of desperate Wailers, vengeful goddesses, plunging horses, and retreating Kurgan soldiers.

Tisiphone wrapped Victor's shackles around a dock post and charged into the melee. The Wailers fell back under the relentless sting of her whip. She forged a path for Freya's retreat, but Victor's horses sealed off that escape route. The Wailers surrounded the goddesses again and renewed their attacks. A score of disgruntled soldiers joined their efforts. Realizing escape was impossible, Tisiphone and Freya surrendered their weapons.

Evelyn grabbed Tisiphone's keys, freed Victor from the shackles and choke chain, and guided him toward the pier. Miriam followed them, tortured with indecision. If they swam, they would have time to escape to the other side of the river before Ahriman's army overwhelmed Wodenaz's warriors. But how could she abandon the Wailers and the Kurgans to their fates after ridiculing Freya's behavior? The Kurgans needed every good warrior they could get. Forsaking them now wouldn't be hypocritical but cowardly as well.

Like Victor abandoning me and Evelyn. How can I act like him?

"See that?" Victor exclaimed and pointed toward the blobs of lava engulfing Charon's pier. One support post caught fire and toppled into the river. "Our stand must be made here."

"Don't you need more shamans?" Miriam asked.

"Our power animals must help," Victor replied. "You must assist them."

Miriam's fingertips tingled with energy. "What good can I do with the power animals? I'm neither a nurse nor a healer." She shook her head, picked up a discarded sword, and eyed the fighting around her. "Why help shamans when I can bring goddesses to their knees? Why must I be on the losing side?"

Mission: Soul Sacrifice

"Miriam!" Victor grabbed her arm. "Don't be taken in by the might of the violence that surrounds us."

"Why not?" Miriam replied, tired of weighing chances and choosing sides. "Ahriman's forces have almost driven us into the river."

"Demons can't help doing what they do," Victor said, "but you have a choice."

"What choice?" Miriam retorted. "Being a handmaid in some ritual I don't even understand?"

"At least it would direct your efforts toward something that helps rather than hurts," Victor countered.

"That might work for someone like you," Miriam replied. "But shamans can't stop Ahriman!"

"Maybe not," Victor agreed. "But they can reduce the number of eel demons draining energy from the Wailers' solar plexuses and dumping it in the Lethe. If our shamans remove enough of those eel demons, it will lower the river enough so the lava won't cool, and Ahriman can't be purified. Reducing the number of Ahriman's eel demons also might weaken Ahriman's strength for the Kurgans to destroy him and his blue attack legions."

"You expect me to wait to see if that works?" Miriam scanned the top of the ridge. Inch by inch, Ahriman's army forced the Kurgan retreat down the ravine toward the river. "Hoping for a miracle isn't a workable solution."

"Hope is all we have left," Victor replied and squeezed her hand. "What we place our hopes on determines what saves us."

The strength of his grip penetrated Miriam to the core. *He believes that?* She pulled her hand away. His statement applied to her, but she did not understand how. How can hope help them when power could not?

The ground shook under her feet. And shook again. Thunraz and Wodenaz retargeted their lightning strikes to the base of the cliffs. The Kurgans would make their final stand along the banks of the Lethe.

{27}

"I realize you don't understand," Victor said with a pat on Miriam's shoulder. "But my shaman skills are what we need at this moment."

He sank to his knees, crossed his legs, and chanted in his bass-baritone voice, "This little song is for all humanity with all the love flowing through me . . ."

Miriam balled her fists. Had Victor lost his mind? The Kurgans needed warriors, not troubadours singing children's songs.

Evelyn joined Victor's melody on the second verse. Its low register, slow tempo, and simple words made singing it easy. Her vibrant soprano rang against the nearby bluffs and back again. Nearby Wailers swiveled their heads toward her. Those further away picked up the refrain, others less musically inclined shielded Victor and Evelyn from the fighting. More, including the Wailers guarding the goddesses, joined in until the volume of their combined chorus rivaled the clash of swords and explosion of bombs.

A gray, wrinkled man rode up the beach mounted on a giant peacock. Dressed in a robe as colorful as the fowl he rode, he dismounted at the chanters' perimeter, greeted his fellow Yazidis, and joined the chorus. Gladdened by Eylo's return, the Yazidi souls sang along.

A muscular young shaman dressed like a surfer bum dismounted his dolphin and waded through the shallows. More shamans approached the cluster of chanters from several directions, some alone, some on their power animals until their number was more than Miriam could count.

Victor rose to his feet and dropped his thumb on top of his index finger to signal a decrescendo. Evelyn and the other singers lowered their volume to a hum while he addressed his fellow shamans. "Thank you and your power animals for your courage and speed in coming."

He pointed toward the ravine. Lava oozed down the fissure and headed toward Charon's pier. "Direct your power animals to bring us all the souls with like power animals.

"Regardless of race or ethnicity, many of us share the same types of power animals as those afflicted. Use them to help probe the souls they bring you. Most, if not all of those souls, were attacked by Ahriman's eel demons which feed on the orgonic energy generated by the victims' solar plexuses. Stripping those creatures from their power sources frees the souls stranded in Hades to return to their corporeal bodies."

"That saves them from their ailments," Miriam protested. "What about Ahriman's army?"

"They're connected to each other," Victor replied. "The energy Ahriman's eel demons drain from their victims they empty into Lethe which increases its volume and water level. If we prevent them from ingesting the Wailers energies, we stop them from dumping the excess they ingest into the Lethe."

Miriam's eyes lit up. "Which reduces its water flow and its ability to cool the lava which would enable Ahriman to walk through the fire of the purification ritual and enter ordinary reality," she said, glowering. "I see the cause and effect," she added. "But how does river water connect to mental energy?"

"Hades exists in both our respective unconscious psyches, remember," Victor replied. "As part of Hades, the Lethe's water and the Wailers' emotional energy are manifestations of the same psychic energy in all of us."

"If you say so," Miriam acknowledged with a slow shake of her head. "But if that's so, how does the reduced water level help fight Ahriman's army?"

"It doesn't directly," Victor admitted. "But Ahriman's strength comes from the energy his power eels consume and pass along to him.

Mission: Soul Sacrifice

If we put enough of his power eels out of commission, we weaken Ahriman's ability to continue the fight with the Kurgans."

None of this makes sense! Miriam shook her head in disbelief. "I'm here, I see it, but I still don't believe it."

"You'll see the effect on his army after the shamans dispatch the eels," Victor assured her with a rueful smile. "I hope."

Several of the Wailers hiding under the wrecked pier emerged and joined the shamans huddled in the center of the protective cordon. More filtered through the fighting to join the throng in song.

Miriam cowered from the flash of an errant fireball striking the water. Victor's proposal was madness in the midst of combat. "There's no time for that!"

"Then buy us some," Evelyn said and pulled Miriam aside. "Victor's solution is our only alternative. Make nice with Freya, Tisiphone, and her sisters so they'll help us."

Miriam hesitated. Her mother's conviction was genuine; what about Victor's? He seemed sincere, but he'd deserted them before. His motives were different this time, but if their souls survived, what would stop him from leaving Evelyn again?

Does that really matter at this moment?

Miriam took a deep breath and plunged into the fray surrounding the Wailers, slashing right, then left through the warring factions until she reached the sequestered goddesses. One blow from her sword severed their restraints. She returned Tisiphone's whip and Freya's sword. "Protect Victor's shamans from Ahriman's warriors."

The goddesses did not move.

"Well?" Miriam asked. "Are you going to join Wodanaz and the Kurgans or not?"

"We do not take orders from mortals," Freya replied and raised her sword. "Stand away."

"Haven't you learned anything?" Miriam said, losing patience. "As you well know, I could make you do it, but *I'd* rather use my powers against Ahriman."

"You may have the power, but you are not one of us," Tisiphone said. "Wodanaz or Thunraz alone have the divine authority to tell us what we must do."

"Hades is crumbling around you!" Miriam cried in frustration. "Can't you see that? Ahriman has set forces in motion to destroy both the Lower World and the corporeal, yet you worry about who gives orders?"

"You have much to learn about approaching the gods with proper respect." Freya's ringlets danced with an angry shake of her head. "Especially for a being who claims to be one."

"Maybe so," Miriam agreed and beat her sword hilt against her chest. "But you fools would have all the spirits in your kingdom killed just to prove your point. That's why so few in the corporeal world believe in you anymore."

She wheeled toward the Wailers surrounding them. Few of them appeared to be of western heritage. One male concealed behind the pier post followed her actions with curiosity. She grabbed his arm and spun him into the open for everyone to see. "Your goddesses haven't the courage to fight for their world. Have you?"

Brought into the open, the man's focus disappeared. He rubbed his hands and peered about the throng. "I d-don't kn—"

Miriam penetrated the hesitant man's soul, tightened her grip, and released some of her orgonic energy into the guttering flame that marked his solar plexus.

"I-I guess so," the man spluttered.

"Here's one!" Miriam cried and raised their conjoined hands above their heads. "Who else has the courage to join us and change their fate?"

Two, three, then a score or more declared their willingness to fight Ahriman's demons. Miriam spun toward Freya and her sisters. "People who once or never believed in you have the courage to fight for your world. Have you the courage now to lead them?"

Freya, Tisiphone, and her sisters exchanged glances. The wrathful Freya raised her sword into the air and declared, "It is time to show the Dakhanavars what divine warriors can do."

She turned back to Miriam and hissed, "This changes nothing between us."

Freya and the goddesses charged toward the ravine and attacked Ahriman's devils. Scores of demons succumbed to the lashes from the Furies' whips and Freya's flashing sword. The bodies of mutilated demons soon littered the ravine, their cries of pain rivaling the Wailers' in volume.

The ferocity of the goddesses' counterattack enabled Miriam to recruit a squadron of Valkyries along with the strongest of the abandoned souls. Their protective cordon stretched in an arc from the ruined pier along the river's edge to the marsh north of the pier. Armed with swords, knives, and small arms scavenged from the fighting, three ranks of defensive fighters fought off wave after wave of Akvan's blue demons while the shamans and their power animals inside healed the souls along the Lethe.

Akvan and his blue demons responded with the fury of soldiers who had everything to gain and nothing to lose. His infantry squads hurtled into the center of Miriam's phalanx to be blown apart by Wodenaz's thunderbolts or hacked to pieces by her recruits. Again and again, Akvan drove what seemed like an infinite number of replacements into the teeth of her protective barrier.

The demons' numbers and ferocity diminished. Where three or more once had attacked the protective cordon, just one repeated its same headlong charge. Repulsed after a fourth attack, Akvan's troops retreated toward the foot of the ravine.

Miriam redeployed her troops in front of the pier and totaled their respective forces. Akvan's infantry forces now matched the numbers of the Kurgan and contemporary military forces.

The demons halted halfway up the ravine and spread along the ridge. Miriam wondered if they were regrouping for another charge or if Ahriman had changed his strategy.

She paced back and forth in front of Freya's Valkyries like a football coach, berating some and encouraging others. The Valkyries at the head the cordon broke ranks. A dazed Brunhilda staggered through the lines.

"Welcome, mighty goddess." Miriam grasped Brunhilda's forearm in a show of support. "Enter our ranks and receive treatment."

"I need to be out there," the disheveled deity replied.

"Rest and be treated," Miriam said and escorted her toward the shamans. "The battle will last long enough for you to return to the fight."

At the center of the spiritual barricade dozens of Wailers radiated with restored psychic energy. Once the shamans and their assistants were certain the eel demons were gone, the restored souls disappeared—like flashbulb bursts at a Hollywood premiere.

Miriam whirled, scanned the river's surface, and shouted to her mother over the crowd, "The water level looks the same!"

"No," Evelyn shouted back and pointed at a powdery ring around the one undamaged pier post. "The water level's more than a foot below that mark."

"Our efforts are succeeding!" Miriam turned toward the Kurgan forces, cupped her hand around her mouth, and cried to Wodenaz, "You have brought Ahriman's forces to a standstill."

Mission: Soul Sacrifice

As if on cue, Akvan's fiercest demons charged down the ravine. Wodenaz's thunderbolts destroyed as many of Kurgan warriors as Ahriman's at such close quarters. When the gods stopped their lightning barrage, Ahriman's determined demons sliced through Thunraz's forces and split the phalanx around the pier.

Thunraz's troops retaliated, but Akvan's demons held off their counter-attack. A score of them raced onto the rock jetty formed by the lava emptying into the river, jumped into the boiling water, and disappeared. Minutes later, a half dozen demon heads encased in golden aureoles bobbed upon the surface. The transformed demons swam across the river to the opposite bank and mounted Albrecht's bridge toward the sky portal.

Miriam raced back to the shamans. On her arrival, the first thing she noticed was the number of rescued souls had dwindled to a trickle. Victor returned to his full stature after leaving the soul of a noxious wailer, stumbled, and caught himself.

"What happened?" Miriam asked. "A dozen demons penetrated our defenses and passed through the lava unscathed."

She pointed toward the construction on the other side of the Lethe. "If they survive the purification process, Ahriman will send more to follow them."

"Ahriman has counteracted the shamans' interventions," Victor replied with a doleful nod of agreement. "The eels have grown stronger than our shamans' powers to remove them."

{28}

Victor sank to his knees and rubbed the back of his neck. His subtle body ached all over, every atom of his soul screamed in pain. Removing demons from souls in the Lower World proved far more grueling than returning his soul to the corporeal world had ever been.

McDougal, a craggy Irish shaman wearing a Druid's cone hat and gown, approached him. "Dr. Furst, four shamans have tried to restore the souls of their patients," he reported. "And all of them have experienced the same inability to dislodge the eel demons from the energy furnaces of their hosts."

Victor frowned and scanned the river. The river water lapping the pier post corroborated McDougal's report, its level rising by more than half a foot. Bursts of indigo flashed within Lethe's murky depths.

Eel demons!

Gorged with energy, Zarkisian's eels discharged wave after wave of psychic energy into the water before returning to the psychic furnaces of the Wailers' souls.

"How is that happening?" McDougal asked.

"More important," Evelyn added. "How do we stop it?"

How do I know?

"Ahriman must direct his energy reserves to his power eels," Victor replied, rubbing his hand across his chin to disguise his uncertainty. "With that extra power Zarkisian's spirit eels now clench the Wailers' solar plexuses so tightly we can't remove them without destroying the souls they feed upon."

Miriam's brows knitted with determination. "If Akvan's forces are on the defensive, now is the time for a counterattack," she declared. "We're outnumbered and vulnerable here along the river, so Akvan wouldn't expect us to attack. We could break through to Wodenaz's forces on the other side of the pier."

So impetuous. She didn't get that from me.

Victor checked Wodenaz' troops fighting Akvan's blue demons on the other side of the lava flow plunging into the river. Pinned down on the beach with the lava at their backs, the Kurgan gods and the souls of their modern military counterparts held their own against wave after wave of Akvan's blue demon infantry. If the Lethe continued to rise, their repeated wave attacks would run over the Kurgan forces.

"Aside from the problem of crossing the lava stream, your suggestion is what Akvan wants us to do," Victor countered. "Concentrate our forces and waste our energies attacking Akvan's troops while Ahriman and his demons purify themselves and cross to the other side of the Lethe."

Victor turned and scanned the river. Out in the middle, the first detachment of Ahriman's purified demons danced and stomped on the jetty while waiting for the cooling lava to reach the other side of the river. On the opposite bank, Albrecht's crew lowered the first support girder into place on the viaduct that rose toward to the portal.

"I must summon Pizca," Victor declared. "He and his water spirits can help prevent Ahriman's eel demons from raising the water level."

He focused on the depths further offshore where his water spirit animals resided. "Help us, Pizca. Bring all your friends to Charon's dock."

In moments, a dozen silver salmon splashed their fins at Victor's feet with Pizca leading the way.

"Welcome, my friends," Victor greeted them and pointed toward the frothing water. "You saw what we're up against?"

"Thank you," Pizca replied and turned toward the maelstrom. "Yes, the eels are voracious energy engines," the spirit fish agreed. "The more they consume, the more they want. We could distract them long enough for your shamans to implant a command to cease feeding."

Victor shrugged his rejection. "Their energy organs recharge so fast they're too strong to try that again. You'd be sacrificing yourselves to no purpose."

"Could they consume too much?" Pizca asked. "And burst like overinflated balloons?"

"That worked the first time I met them when I rescued Evelyn," Victor replied and shook his head. "No. The eels seem to have learned since then to purge themselves every time they feed before they get too full."

His mind raced, searching for answers. "Unlike Zarkisian and his corporeal parasites, however," he mused out loud, "Ahriman's eel demons don't drain their victims' energies as needed. They never stop feeding so their hosts' energy furnaces can recharge and don't realize their gluttony could destroy their hosts' souls and obliterate their spirits."

Or don't care. The demons don't need to be cautious!

Victor trembled at the realization. Ahriman was close to achieving his goal. They must act now.

He signaled the salmon to join him at the base of the solar plexus of the last Wailer he had examined. Across the river Albrecht's demons lowered the second girder of the viaduct into place. He squeezed Evelyn's arm and turned to Miriam. "If Ahriman fords the river before I get back, attack him with everything you've got."

Miriam grabbed his shoulder. Her emerald eyes blazed like laser beams. Orgonic energy surged through him like electric current from a car battery. If her energy was a sample of the eels' power, he and his salmon helpers could not stop them. He removed her hand and squeezed it. "Save your energy in case this doesn't work."

Miriam frowned. Evelyn's brows knitted with anxiety. "What are you going to do?" she asked.

"Learn how the eels transfer the energy they absorb into the Lethe," Victor answered, prioritizing their next steps. "Evelyn, keep the shamans removing the eel demons. Miriam, hold off Akvan's ground troops as long as possible. Be ready if I need help returning to ordinary size."

He kneeled beside a mourning Wailer woman, gazed into her sorrowful face, and smiled, knowing Miriam would take action whatever the outcome of his attempt. If the eels could not be prevented from feeding, her counterattack would be humanity's final battle in the Lower World.

He encircled the crown of the woman's head between the palms of his hands and chanted, "Let us bring our souls together, let our spirits become as one. . ."

After a moment, the sound waves from his throat resonated throughout his body. Launched into a state of euphoria, his soul coursed through the woman's energy system. He directed his accompanying salmon power animals to a point above the buttery locus that corresponded with the woman's solar plexus.

Concealed in the turbulence of the woman's energy stream, Victor watched a clump of black eels slurping up energy like lapsed bulimics at an all-you-can-eat buffet. When their wriggling bodies stiffened into glowing, black-light sausages, the eels detached their suckers and formed two flotillas of six demons each. Flanked by escort eels on either side, the twelve engorged eel demons edged out into the energy channel where its current whisked them away.

Victor scratched his chin. Why the escorts? Before, when the bloated eel demons detached from their host's energy source, they floated down the host's energy stream. Where were these new groups going?

Mission: Soul Sacrifice

He signaled his salmon spirits to fall in behind him and followed the eels down their host's main energy channel until the eels reached the point above her kidneys that coincided with her physical body's adrenal glands. Rather than ride the current that fed the soul's higher functions, the two flotillas separated. Each swam down an energy channel that coursed through one of the host woman's legs.

Victor paused. The eels' behavior was unlike anything he had witnessed during his psychology studies. Or his shamanic training. He signaled Pizca to come forward and pointed at the departing eels. "Do you have any idea where they're headed? Or what their purpose might be?"

"I do not," Pizca replied. "But it must have something to do with the transference of energy or the eels would have purged themselves by now."

"That seems reasonable," Victor agreed, pondering. Did he dare split up his forces? What if the eels destroyed one or both sets of his salmon agents?

Ahriman wins for sure if I don't.

"Take six of your companions, Pizca, and follow the eels down the left leg," Victor said. "See where they go and what they do with the energy they've accumulated. I'll take the remaining salmon and follow the eels taking the right."

Victor headed toward the right leg and stopped. What if the eels escaped or if either of Victor's squads got lost? Time was meaningless in the spirit realm. Ahriman's activities, however, had disturbed the unending uniformity of events in the Lower World. He had to take that chance. Time, causality, life itself promised to change if he did not.

He turned and called out to Pizca. "Count to thirty by one thousand ones while following them; then return to this spot. We'll do the same and figure out what to do from there."

They parted, and Victor and his six salmon headed down the right channel. The channel grew dank, dark, and more forbidding with every count: *One thousand one...One thousand two... One thousand three...*

They reached the sole of the woman's foot by the time Victor reached five. The woman's flagging energy system chugged far above them. In front of them the protector eels guided their overstuffed companions to a point where the arch of her foot touched the ground, and her spiritual skin was paper-thin. The engorged eels squeezed through the pores and wriggled into the dirt beneath her feet.

...One thousand seven...One thousand eight... One thousand nine...

The guardian eels concentrated upon the energy-carriers squirming through the pores. Victor paddled into the middle of the channel for a better view. Two more eels squirmed through her pores and wormed their way through the sand to the shallows of the River Lethe. Twin purple phosphorescent bursts punctuated the dark water. The eels crawled out of the water, wriggled back through the sand, and emerged back through the pores thin, dark, and snappish, eager to ingest more orgonic energy.

...One thousand twelve...One thousand thirteen...One thousand fourteen...

The third duo returned from the shallows, and the eels reformed their convoy. Victor swam back to his salmon spirits hidden behind a bend in the energy stream. "Head back to the fork in the main channel," he ordered and grabbed the dorsal fins of the two nearest salmon. "Hurry, before they spot us!"

...One thousand eighteen...One thousand nineteen...One thousand twenty...

Victor and the salmon struggled against the energy current. Behind them, the escort eels goaded their energy-depleted cohorts with

Mission: Soul Sacrifice

discharges of energy on their tail fins. Despite those shocks, the carrier eels paddled in slow motion, too drained to retaliate or swim faster. At last, Victor and his salmon companions reached the point where the channel returned to the root of the woman's energy system.

Pizca and his six companions were nowhere in sight. Victor counted off five more one-thousands. Where were they? Had they been captured?

One thousand twenty-six. . .One thousand twenty-seven. . . One thousand twenty-eight. . .

Victor paddled toward the stream coursing down the woman's left leg and peered down the maelstrom.

One thousand twenty-nine . . .

Pizca and his salmon companions appeared in the opening equivalent to the woman's knee, struggling as Victor had with the strength of her energy current.

"They swim through the skin of the Wailers' feet into the river," Pizca gasped when he and his troop reached Victor.

"We witnessed the same thing," Victor replied. "The psychic patalas. Let's hurry and return to the others before the eel demons spot us."

Victor signaled his six salmon to join him, Pizca, and his squadron in the middle of the upward energy stream that whisked them up to the woman's lacrimal glands. Embedded in the wailing woman's tears, they emerged out of her tear ducts, fell to the dusty ground, and swelled to normal size.

Victor slumped onto the sand in pained exhaustion and gazed at the battle raging beyond the confines of Miriam's cordon. Thunraz and Wodenaz hurled thunderbolts at Ahriman's archers; Miriam, Freya and the Erinyes battled Akvan's ground troops in hand-to-hand combat. The fight remained a stalemate, as far as he could tell, but the lava continued to pour into the river. To his horror, he saw that it already extended halfway across the swollen river, forming a delta as it cooled.

Ahriman's purified warriors soon would cross to the other side and climb the awaiting viaduct.

"Shalah," Victor said. "Summon all available shamans for an emergency meeting here. Hurry."

In moments, twenty shamans gathered in a ragged circle around him. He explained what he and the salmon had witnessed. "Does anyone know why the eels changed their strategy?"

"Aye, it reveals how important Ahriman's eels are as energy sources for his attacks," McDougal said. "Without them, his forces couldn't maintain the ferocity of their frontal assaults on our Kurgan forces."

"But why discharge their energy into the river?" Victor asked. "Why take the extra precaution with escort eels? Why not escape through the soul's higher portals?"

"Do we even know how they transfer their ingested energy?" Evelyn asked.

"They discharged it into the air before," Victor replied.

"For attack or for their own protection?" Evelyn asked, her brows furrowed in thought. "We never investigated how the eels transferred the energy; just that they did it."

"There hasn't been time for scientific analysis," Victor snorted. *Evelyn can be so annoying. Why bring this up now?* "There'll be time enough for that later, assuming there is a later for any of us."

"Dr. Furst," called a deep voice tinged with a British accent. A dusky, knobby-kneed man wearing horn-rimmed glasses and a wine-colored loin cloth stepped in front of McDougal. "May I say something?"

"Who are you?" Victor asked.

"Depak Sapandra, shaman from Kashmir province."

"Why not?" Victor replied, waving his hand at the man. "You have the floor."

"In the Hindu and Buddhist spirit worlds, the holes in the soles of the psychic feet, the patalas, are transfer points for hate, vengeance, and murder—all the negative forces that enter the spiritual body and tie it to the physical realm," Sapandra said. "Could this mechanism not work also in the spiritual realm as well?"

"Sure!" McDougal said. His square face grew florid. "Crawling through that filthy marsh dirt would lend extra negative energy to anything those eels might discharge into the river."

"The negative energy would explain how the river wipes away the memories of those who drink it," Evelyn said. "It would erase the positive charge of the memories stored within the soul."

"And neutralize the positive forces from the heat and fire of the lava flowing into the river," Victor added while scratching his beard, unconsciously trying to tame the sticky mess his swimming in the energy currents had created. "In Freudian theory, the destructive forces of the mortido, the negative opposite of the libido, originated from the lower portions of the subconscious." He nodded at Sapandra. "Feet, in Hindu cosmology."

Of course!

"That's how Ahriman and his demons are purified—at the point where the river water neutralizes and cools the lava pouring into it."

"But how do we prevent that from happening?" Shalah asked. "Ahriman has placed guard eels to protect them?"

"We don't," Victor replied. "At least not head-on. But if we destroy or divert at least half of them—"

"We give Miriam and the others the chance to defeat Ahriman!" Evelyn hugged Victor's neck. "Before he and his demons can be purified."

"Yes," he agreed. Evelyn's eyes glowed. Her breath blew hot against his cheek and sparked something inside him.

No. No time for personal drama.

He undid her arms and placed them at her sides. "There's a lot to do."

Evelyn spun away. Victor reached for her shoulder, but she brushed his hand aside and ministered to the wailer from which he'd emerged.

Dammit—my fault, this time. No apologies.

He turned toward Shalah. "You and the mares maintain the cordon around the shamans as long as possible." He stepped to the river's edge and addressed the salmon. "All of you follow Pizca into the soul of the female wailer from which we emerged and meet me where the eels ingest her energy. It will be an ordeal for her, but her spirit will disintegrate if we fail."

He knelt beside Evelyn, enfolded his hands around the wailer's head, and repeated the procedure to reenter her soul's psychic energy stream. Gliding down the current, he met the salmon already assembled outside the woman's guttering psychic power source.

Ahriman's eel demons devoured the last of the woman's psychic energies. Several foraged upon the morsels left by the more rapacious eels. Twelve fat indigo eels maneuvered into formation, ready to depart.

"Pizca," Victor said. "Take six of your eels and wait at the left passage of the energy divergence point. I'll take the other six and wait for eels on the right fork."

"What then?" Pizca asked. "Do we attack? The bolts from protector eels looked strong enough to destroy us."

"No. Harass them as you did before with Evelyn," Victor replied. "Have the eels use up as much of their energy as you can but divert their convoys from heading toward the soles of this Wailer's feet."

"What will diverting them do?" Pizca asked.

"If we disorient them enough, the energy-carriers may get swept into the woman's upward energy stream," Victor replied. "Gorged as

Mission: Soul Sacrifice

they are, swimming against the energy current may tire them enough so it sweeps them into the soul's higher realms. There their stored energy can be used as positive energy for their host."

"Sounds dubious," Pizca replied. "But we will do our best to make it happen."

"Even if half of them are swept upward, that will reduce the negative flow into the river overall," Victor said. "And give the host soul a chance to heal for her return to corporeal consciousness."

Pizca culled six salmon from the ranks and swam toward their destination. Victor directed the other six toward the opposite fork in the Wailer's downward energy stream. Two eel flotillas appeared at the channel entrance not long after. When they divided into separate squads, Victor signaled Pizca to attack. He and the other salmon darted toward the eels headed to the right leg channel.

The swifter salmon singed the whiskers of the ponderous, energy-carrying eels. They snapped and snipped the engorged eels' tendrils, then darted out of reach when their protector eels retaliated. The guard eels fired energy bolts at the marauders, but Pizca and his salmon comrades kept the energy carriers between themselves and their guards. One, two and then three of the energy-carriers floated upwards along the energy current, too exhausted by the salmon's hit-and-run attacks to retaliate or elude them. Two more carrier eels floated upward, but with the attack salmon's cover reduced, the protector eels' energy bolts slammed several salmon head-on. The wounded fish swam away in agony. Three exploded and disappeared.

"Retreat and regroup," Victor shouted, pointing toward the main energy channel. Pizca and his three salmon joined Victor and his four survivors. The eel demons regrouped and headed down the right leg. "I counted four remaining storage eels out of the original twelve."

"You said eliminating six would be enough," Pizca replied. "Eliminating eight should be much better."

"Yes," Victor agreed with a smile. "It's a very good start if the majority of the eels' energy converts into positive power through the soul's higher energy distributors." Victor grabbed two of the salmon's dorsal fins. "Let's report our results to the others."

They swam toward the woman's lacrimal glands and emerged with her tears. After swelling back to his normal physical size, Victor's female patient wrapped her arms around his neck and kissed his cheek. Shaky, yet revitalized, her soul disappeared in a blinding flash.

"Recruit more salmon," Victor said to Pizca and his salmon companions. He turned toward the surrounding circle of shamans. "Each of you will have six salmon power animals to harass and disorient the eels in each of the Wailers in which the eel feeders are not yet removed."

Pizca returned followed by a school of silver salmon. Following Victor's instructions, they divided into five squadrons and descended into the Wailers' souls. Upon their return to the riverbanks, the team reported varying degrees of success in disrupting the eel demons' energy convoys. Four of the five host Wailers disappeared in blinding flashes. The fifth collapsed on the ground, too enfeebled for her soul to return to ordinary reality.

The successful shamans instructed the others in the technique, paired them with their own aqueous power animals, and scattered them throughout the cordon. Scores of restored souls soon embraced their benefactors and disappeared in flashes of light.

The Lethe's waters receded to reveal the puffy pillow lava extending halfway across the river. The lava from Dakhanavar's mountains, however, flowed down the delta without letup. Stranded in the middle of the river, scores of Ahriman's blue demons attempted to wade back to shore, but sank and burned in agony, imprisoned in the hardening lava. Others drowned trying to swim to the opposite shore. Victor's salmon feasted upon the rest.

Evelyn hugged and kissed him. The shamans hoisted him on their shoulders. "Time for this later," Victor said and slipped off their shoulders to the ground. "We must cure all the Wailers still stranded on the riverbank."

"Attack!" Two perimeter guards shouted. "Attack on the northeast—"

Two pale blue demons slashed Miriam's sentinels to pieces, but Tisiphone and her sisters headed them off. Hacking off limbs in every direction, they slowed, then stopped the demons' advance.

"Recall the shamans, Victor!" Miriam cried. She parried sword thrusts with two demons. "We need every spirit to hold off Akvan's attackers."

"No! Hold it," Victor ordered as he fended off a demon and chased it away. "It's another of Ahriman's deceptions."

Was it an attempt to divert them from continuing their soul retrieval strategy? Or was it what it appeared—an overwhelming frontal assault?

He skewered a shrieking demon and scanned the battlefield. More demons joined Akvan's assault. The light flashes of wailer souls returning to consciousness also increased in number. Wodenaz hurled thunderbolts at Ahriman's archers who responded with a rain of fire arrows from the top of the bluffs. Behind them Victor spotted a familiar, giant pyramid lumbering into view. A squad of Ahriman's archers disappeared inside.

Victor turned toward his comrades. "They're setting up some kind of diver—"

{29}

Miriam chopped off the arm of one demon and skewered another against a dock post. When his chest no longer moved, she withdrew her dripping blade and searched for more foes for it to feast upon. Engaged in fierce hand-to-hand combat in the tight-knit semi-circle around the dock entrance, the Valkyries and Wailers more than held their own, sending their blue-skinned opponents up the gorge in tattered disarray.

She turned her gaze toward the shamans and their assistants in the protected center of their cordon. The flashbulb flashes of souls returning to ordinary reality had abated. Off to one side, she spotted Evelyn huddled against a pier support, her mouth set in a frozen O.

"What's the matter, Mother?" Miriam called, grinning as she wiped her blade on the furze. "It's only demon blood."

When Evelyn did not respond, Miriam scanned the shamans nearby.

Where's Victor?

Her eyes swept the battlefield and didn't spot him. "Where's Victor?"

No response.

"Is he ridding another soul of eel demons?" Miriam asked and Evelyn shook her head. "Then where is he?"

"Gone." Evelyn stared at the river. "He disappeared."

"Where is he?" Miriam repeated, shaking her mother's shoulders with suppressed rage. "Where is he, Evelyn?"

"I don't know, I don't know," Evelyn whimpered. She hunched her chin against her chest and slumped to the ground. "I don't know."

Gone again. As I expected.

Miriam kneeled beside her mother. "It's all right, Mom. He'll be back," she said without enthusiasm. Her chest knotted. For a moment before he went inside the Wailer, Victor had seemed almost caring. Now he disappeared again. Why? Where had he gone?

Why ask? Abandonment always feels the same.

A sword tip clipped Miriam's shoulder. She pivoted and plunged her sword to the hilt into the back of a four-armed demon that attacked Brunhilda. The demon writhed on the ground in unending pain.

If that demon had been Victor—

She pulled her sword out of the four-armed demon and slashed all of the fiends around her. If Ahriman wanted control of Hades, many of his demons would perish before she surrendered her portion of it.

She peered inside the writhing demon's chest. Its internal physiology was simple and chaotic, the chemistry easy for siphoning off its power reserves. Miriam whirled and siphoned energy from six nearby demons. Too weak to defend themselves, the six demons lost an arm or a leg to her slashing sword. She left them on the ground to writhe in pain, exultant in knowing no one would retrieve them or ease their suffering.

*This is what I'm made fo*r! *No evasions, no apologies as with Freya—simple cutting and hacking—like a surgeon removing abscess from a limb.*

The more demons she destroyed or crippled, the more powerful she felt. She wondered why she hadn't been doing this from the start. Miriam broadened her focus beyond the devils attacking Brunhilda's forces to the Valkyries' opponents. The arc beyond the shamans' treatment area became littered with bodies of feeble, broken demons clamoring for relief.

She, along with Brunhilda, and her sister Valkyries, beat back Ahriman's demoralized demons and joined forces with Freya and Tisiphone in front of the pier. Their attack slowed and stalled, Akvan's dispirited demons retreated toward the ravine.

The male Kurgan warriors doubled their attacks against Ahriman's main force. The god and his demons scrambled up either side of the lava stream coursing down the center of the ravine and regrouped with Akvan's forces on top of the bluff.

"Attack while we have them on the defensive!" Miriam cried.

Wodenaz grabbed her arm and restrained her. "Give Freya a chance to tend to our wounded."

"And allow Ahriman's forces to regroup?" Miriam asked.

"Ahriman retains the high ground," Thunraz replied. "Chasing them headlong could lead to another trap that would separate our forces again and sap our strength further."

Slapping Freya and Miriam on the back, Wodenaz lauded the warriors. "Your efforts shall not go unrewarded," he said, squinting at Miriam through his good eye. He thrust one of his favorite lances in her hands. "Accept this for your wisdom and fortitude in the face of adversity."

"Thank you." Miriam hefted the weighted shaft, thrust its metal tip skyward, and the Kurgan warriors cheered. Never had she felt such adulation, such respect, such warmth. Never did she want it to end. "Thank you. With all my heart."

A blue-nosed emissary waved a white flag using both sets of arms as he stole down the escarpment. Bowing from one side to the other in answer to the Kurgan warriors' catcalls, Akvan halted before Wodenaz and Miriam and knelt at their feet.

"On behalf of Lord Ahriman, I am here to negotiate for peace and an end to this quarrel," Akvan said. After the jeers and insults died down, he added, "Ahriman wishes to know your terms so that the Lower World can be ruled and inhabited in peace and safety for all."

"We did not start this war," Wodenaz replied with a fierce squint. "Nor will it end until the ruler of Dakhanavar and its denizens withdraw to their original borders and sign an agreement never to transgress Hades and its ruler's authority."

"You don't expect Lord Ahriman to renounce his gains for the sake of peace," Akvan said, pulling on his bulbous nose in indignation. "We still hold the high ground of the Asphodel Meadows," he added with a grin. "Some of you must have noticed that."

Thunraz and his warriors howled in protest. Freya, Tisiphone, and the other guardians of Hades said nothing.

"Yes," Wodenaz said, nodding to acknowledge his followers' conflicting feelings before raising his hands for quiet. "What does Lord Ahriman consider equal terms to stop hostilities?"

"In exchange for peace on all sides," Akvan replied, "Ahriman requests access to the shores of the River Lethe."

"That would grant them access to the portal," Miriam said and raised her lance into an attack position. "That's what all this fighting was about to begin with."

"Our land-locked kingdom has no access to what you call Tethys, the mother of rivers," Akvan replied. "Let alone to the great ocean you know as Thalassa."

"This battle was never about water access," Evelyn said. "It was about control of the Lower World, and you know it."

"Must our kingdom remain a small, impoverished domain for all eternity?" Akvan asked. "Is that what your counterparts in corporeal reality consider equality?"

"You expect your aggression to be rewarded?" Miriam replied, quivering in anger.

"Is this not the Lower World?" Akvan responded. "Peace and harmony do not reign here as they do in the higher realms." He rubbed his nose. "But what divine prophecy promises applies to all dominions. Lord Ahriman expects to receive what Fate has foretold."

"What is that?" Wodenaz asked.

"The End Time—where Ahriman assumes his rightful place in the universe."

"We should just grant that to you?" Miriam said.

"You should acknowledge what is foreseen as inevitable. Whether through negotiation or force of arms, the legitimacy of our claims shall be honored." He looked down his long nose at her. "Given your heritage, you of all the spirits inhabiting the Lower World should be least likely to oppose Ahriman's entitlements."

Wodenaz, Freya, and the other Kurgan warriors denounced Akvan's message, but Miriam grew thoughtful. Akvan had wheedled into her mind and questioned her actions. Was she fighting on the wrong side against her true psychic brothers?

Grappling anew with her conflicting thoughts, she knelt and beat the ground with her fists. Her new-found powers gave her recognition she had never felt before. But she was part parasite, too. Could she accept the Kurgans' praises if what Akvan said was true? Was everything from his lips a lie?

Oblivious to the turmoil inside Miriam, Freya pointed toward the ravine and called out, "Look! The lava's moving again!"

Molten globs the size of Volkswagens spilled down the ravine, splashed across the jetty, and plopped into the river, causing the melding point to fizz with a noxious haze that obscured the opposite bank.

Chortling with glee, Akvan flung his truce flag at Wodenaz and dashed toward the safety of Ahriman's forces. During Akvan's distraction, Ahriman's demons assumed defensive positions high on the ravine to the river's edge. Behind his fiercest demons' protective phalanx, a sixty-foot, pyramid-shaped war wagon lumbered into view.

Lugged by a dozen bull elephants draped in bronze battle plate, the wood and iron monstrosity, crammed with a dozen of Ahriman's finest archers, made its way down the dry lava bed towards the jetty.

Wodenaz and Thunraz released a withering barrage of thunderbolts toward the cart. When the cart reached the riverbank, Freya, Tisiphone, and the Kurgan warriors charged up the ravine. Wailers and shamans hid in the marsh reeds or under the ruined pier.

Miriam despised Ahriman and his demons. Yet, she admired the cleverness of Akvan's deception and the depth of Ahriman's determination. His first attack had sapped her allies of both qualities and transformed the Lower World from everlasting gloom to an abiding struggle for supremacy. She realized if Ahriman and his forces failed this time, they would attack again and again until they succeeded.

Evelyn grabbed Miriam's arm. "Aren't you going to stop them?"

"How can we?" Miriam replied, shading her eyes to gaze at the top of the bluffs. "Ahriman's too protected."

"We have to do something," Evelyn replied as she skimmed her hand across the water lapping their feet. "The river's rising again."

On the opposite bank, Albrecht's demon laborers riveted the final support girder into place. With his war wagon and demon forces in place, Ahriman would soon purify himself and cross the bridge into the corporeal world.

{30}

"Dammit!" Miriam cursed, ducking as a fiery arrow whizzed past. Wodenaz's thunderbolts and Freya's Valkyries might hamper Ahriman from crossing the river, but protected by his war wagon, their attacks could not deter Ahriman and his minions from reaching the other side. "Double damn!"

Ahriman's massive battle carriage lumbered onto the steaming jetty. Without the downward slope of the ravine to assist them, the elephants struggled across the lava's hot, soupy, uncertain crust. The battle tower foundered halfway to the river's midpoint where the lava plunged beneath the water's surface. Lashed by their handlers amid the Kurgans' unrelenting torrent of arrows, several elephants collapsed in their harnesses and stalled the fortress' advance.

"Wodenaz and Freya's forces stopped them," Evelyn said.

"Yes," Shalah agreed. "The shamans' efforts have weakened Ahriman's powers."

"They can increase their bombardment, but they can't prevent Ahriman from reaching the purification point," Miriam said. "Ahriman's Keres and demon archers protect his battle wagon too well."

She stretched her neck upward as much as she could and surveyed Ahriman's forces with an eye tempered by the experience of their recent battles. The bulk of Ahriman's forces guarded the ravine all the way to the river's edge; his elite troops protected his twelve-wheeled carriage. "Ahriman must be convinced we can't stop him." She squatted beside Evelyn and pointed at the handful of sentinels guarding the ridge. "He's overextended his forces. A flank attack could separate him from his troops occupying the ridge."

"Why don't you attack him there?" Evelyn asked.

"It would be a waste of time," Miriam replied. "Once Ahriman and his demons pass through the lava and achieve purification, they become the supreme powers in both worlds."

"Why would Ahriman take such a risk now?" Evelyn wondered. "If he has the high ground and numerical advantage, why didn't he unite his forces before making his final assault?"

"Because . . ." Miriam stopped in confusion.

Why doesn't he?

"Perhaps Ahriman no longer enjoys numerical superiority," Miriam said. "Rather than a tactical gambit, his deception might be born of desperation."

"That may be right," Evelyn said. "No new recruits have replaced the fallen demons in Akvan's infantry for some time now. Uniting his forces makes sense if Ahriman planned another attack. That he hasn't suggests that he has decided achieving purification trumps any counterattack Wodenaz's forces could wage."

"The time factor still gives him the advantage," Freya pointed out. "We can't stop him before he reaches the purification point."

Shalah shook his head. "One possibility remains," the stallion said, "though no one has tried it on this scale before—sound healing."

Crazier and crazier.

"Sound healing?" Miriam asked.

Evelyn's eyes lit up in recognition. "It's a therapy where a specialist uses music to improve a patient's mental and physical health. Aesculapius used it."

"You're kidding, right?" Miriam said.

"Not at all." Depak Sapandra crawled out from under the dock "It is the Tibetan Buddhist philosophy that all objects can be brought into harmony by finding the right harmonic frequency. In Western terms, frequency plus intent equals healing."

"You can't be serious," Miriam replied.

"Serious as can be," Sapandra replied. "We've never met in person, but your father and I exchanged emails about it several times."

He's NOT my father!

Miriam edged away, certain their plan wouldn't work. Shalah, however, nudged her toward the shamans rescuing souls in the shadow of Charon's pier. When Miriam ducked away in the opposite direction, Shalah cut her off again.

"What do you think you're doing?" Miriam asked.

"What your fa—," Shalah paused. "Keeping you here so we can try what Victor already showed us."

"To fall on our knees and sing?" Miriam replied, twisting her mouth in disdain. "That traitor disappeared when we needed him most—again. I'd rather be shoved into that lava flow before trying something else he proposed."

"So be it," Shalah snorted. "Other souls may be more receptive to Victor's idea."

The stallion whirled toward Evelyn and lowered his muzzle onto Evelyn's shoulder. Evelyn stroked the hairs on the underside of the stallion's chin while Shalah nickered in her ear.

How can Mother fall for such nonsense?

Miriam scowled and crossed her arms. "You're listening to—"

"Shush," Evelyn said while stroking the top of Shalah's mane and whispering to him. "Despite your powers, some forces remain outside your understanding."

Miriam grabbed her mother's elbow. "How can this help us now?"

"Nothing else has worked," Evelyn replied, removing Miriam's hand. "So, hope is all we have, like Victor said."

Miriam's skeptical expression did not change, and Evelyn said, "Healing chords are powerful forces in music therapy." She squeezed Miriam's shoulder. "Google sympathetic resonance when your soul returns to its body."

One of the blue demon's arrows whizzed past Evelyn's face. It splashed into the Lethe behind them and fizzled out.

"I can't let you do this!" Miriam cried, gazing across the river. "There's still time for us to escape."

"Even if there is, I have to," Evelyn replied. "Victory never comes without sacrifice."

"But sound resonance!" Miriam protested. "Ahriman's demons are all around us, and you think such a passive, pitiful response will help?"

"You witnessed how our chanting helped remove the eel demons from the Wailers' bodies," Evelyn countered. "Why won't you believe in it now?"

She cocked an eyebrow and eyed her daughter. "Is it because Victor used it as part of his healing treatment?"

Of course not!

When Miriam did not respond, Evelyn sighed and squared her shoulders. "I hope I can find the right chord to make this work."

Make what work?

Miriam gaped in astonishment as her mother marched into the crowd of shamans and Wailers waiting to have their souls cleansed. Standing on a mound of dirt, she ducked another of Ahriman's fire arrows and raised her arms above her head.

"Gather round," she said, beckoning with her fingers to encourage those surrounding her to come closer.

Glancing back at Shalah who shook his head in a gesture of encouragement, Evelyn scanned the throng and declared, "Let everyone within hearing distance join me in chanting Victor's shamanic tune."

"What good is singing going to do?" one Wailer shouted.

"We can still escape before Ahriman reaches the end of the lava jetty," cried another.

"It sounds silly in the face of arrows and war wagons," Evelyn agreed, "but singing is our only chance."

Mission: Soul Sacrifice

She surveyed the skeptical faces surrounding her. "What my hus— what Victor did before on an individual basis to restore psychic energy removed the demons draining your soul's organs of their psychic energy."

"Yeah, but he disappeared," hooted one Wailer. "Big help there. Now things are much worse."

"Amen to that," Miriam said, nodding her agreement.

"I agree but hear me out!" Evelyn said, extending her arms. "We can't remove the demons from your bodies anymore, but we can change the energy they feed on from negative to positive."

"So what?" several Wailers asked in unison. Others grumbled or moaned their disagreement.

"See the mayhem out there trying to crush us?" Evelyn asked, extending her arm toward the jetty. "That's the negative result of Ahriman's eel demons feeding off the energy of your spiritual bodies. If we feed them positive emotional energy by singing in unison, the combined harmonic energy in our voices will neutralize the negative energy Ahriman uses to fight against us."

Miriam noted several Wailers expressing their skepticism by retreating from Evelyn toward the shelter of Charon's broken pier. "Even if I thought your scheme might work," she said, grimacing, "are there enough of us to offset Ahriman's negative energy?"

"If I'm half the empath Victor thinks I am," Evelyn replied with a tight smile, "and all the choral professor I've been for twenty years, we'll have more than enough energy."

Evelyn peered at the faces around her. "You know the lyrics, but we need to sing it as loud as we can with everyone joining in."

"Singing on steroids won't stop Ahriman's arrows!" Miriam said.

"Or Akvan's demons!" a Wailer cried.

Shalah stepped in front of Evelyn and addressed the crowd. "It won't save you if Ahriman achieves purification, but we can prevent that if our singing stops the lava from flowing."

"Singing stop molten rock?" Miriam retorted. "I'd love to see that."

Shalah's withering gaze silenced her. "You've been in the Lower World for sufficient time to discover and use many powers you did not realize you had. Yet you fail to comprehend the link between outlook and occurrence that rules within the spiritual realm."

Miriam's jaw hardened. *What link does Shalah mean?*

Evelyn raised her arms like a conductor cueing her orchestra. Focusing on the half dozen shamans standing in front of her, she led them through a chorus of "For All Humanity" in such a low register that their voices rumbled like boulders tumbling downhill. One by one the Wailers and shamans joined in, and by the third repetition all the souls within Miriam's cordon of protection and some of Wodenaz's surrounding soldiers sang with them.

At the onset of the fourth verse, Evelyn modulated the tune half an octave higher. When the multitude completed the chorus, she raised the pitch another half octave on the repeat. And another half step higher for the verse after that.

On the seventh repetition, Evelyn raised her voice another half octave above what the men were singing and pointed at the female Wailers to follow her lead. A few did at first, then more joined in at this more comfortable register.

Evelyn scanned the crowd and pointed out the men and women who weren't singing. Shalah and the other horses singled out these people and nudged their backs until their voices joined the others.

Satisfied every Wailer and soldier was contributing, Evelyn elevated the pitch of the soprano voices another half octave. On the far horizon beyond Hades' bluffs, Dakhanavar's volcanic silhouette paled to fiery salmon. Noting the correlation, Evelyn spread her arms to increase the volume of the Wailers' chants and elevated the tune another half octave. The brimstone flecks in the lava winked out, and Dakhanavar's angry skyline disappeared.

A warm glow suffused Miriam's being. Anger and revenge melted away. She joined in the eighth repeat of the simple melody. Its otherworldly tones echoed within the deepest recesses of her body.

They COULD win.

Ahriman's archers directed more of their arrows in Evelyn's direction. Miriam retrieved the shield from one of Wodenaz's injured soldiers and stationed it above her mother's head to deflect Ahriman's redirected aerial barrage.

Certainty pounded in Miriam's chest and bubbled out her lips with every deflected blow. Around her everyone shared in the ecstasy of Evelyn's orchestrated communion.

Evelyn directed Miriam's gaze toward the crest of the ravine. A giant glob of lava plunged down the embankment, skidded across the jetty, and plopped into the river. No more fiery blobs followed. She launched into the tenth chorus a half octave higher than the previous pitch but directed the nearby female voices to maintain the pitch they had been singing.

Through the dissipating cloud of sulfur gas and steam on the opposite bank Miriam spotted Albrecht's headless torso roaming back and forth like a caged tiger upon the viaduct's highest girder. His severed head badgered his demon builders to complete their tasks. Behind him the aperture walls to the corporeal world shuddered and moved toward each other.

Akvan repositioned the bulk of his forces halfway up the ravine. Wodenaz and Freya's troops split in two along either side of the lava flow. Half the Kurgan forces joined the chorus with the Wailers while the other half charged onto the jetty to join Freya's attack on Ahriman's war carriage.

Despite thunderbolts, Kurgan arrows, treacherous footing, and five dead elephants, Ahriman's war carriage rumbled within one hundred yards of the purification point, veered ninety degrees, and collapsed on its side. Two of its three right rear wheels lay cracked and burning in the steaming lava. A squad of demons jumped out of the tower and dashed toward the purification point. Kurgan arrows cut down all of them.

Ahriman's archers counterattacked with a barrage of flaming arrows while a dozen of his infantry rolled a steaming rock beside the tower and jacked it up with a spare cross beam. In moments two of Ahriman's demon engineers attached three new wheels, and Ahriman's archers retreated inside their war wagon.

The driver lashed the seven remaining elephants until their torn ears bled. The wagon lurched forward fifty yards before two wheels on the opposite side cracked in half. Their upper parts immobilized the axle; the lower halves sank into the fiery ooze.

Evelyn's choir of Wailers and soldiers launched into another chorus of Victor's song, the highest voices six octaves above the song's original register. The simple soaring melody resonated off the cliff walls and echoed against the cliffs on the river's opposite side.

Inside Miriam's head the rise and fall of the notes plucked and strummed her senses like fingers on strings of a banjo.

How is this happening? I'm a spirit, a ghost.

Miriam sang as loud as she could despite her mind sloshing like psychic jelly. Craning her neck above the huddled shamans and Wailers chanting with all their might, she surveyed the lava jutting into the river. The lava slowed and halted; the sky aperture shrank.

Mission: Soul Sacrifice

At midstream, the steam clouds hovering over the purification point evaporated, and the hammering of Albrecht's workers ceased. Ahriman's war carriage lay stranded meters away from its destination. She felt like rejoicing. Then she spotted Albrecht grabbing his head and plunging into the river. Side-stroking like an Olympic swimmer, he crossed the Acheron with his grisly head skimming high above the waves.

Gas pockets spumed around the edges of the maelstrom where the lava entered the river. Treading water, Albrecht held his head high above the water's surface, clamped it onto the stump of his neck, and plunged into the vortex.

Miriam scowled in doubt and fear.

Albrecht is no fool. Why risk certain annihilation?

She sighed with relief when his sinister head didn't reappear. *Even financial wizards make errors in calculation.* She adjusted the tilt of the shield and focused on protecting her mother from the rain of Ahriman's fiery arrows.

The loud fizz, like thousands of champagne bubbles popping, pierced the vocal clamor. Miriam glanced back toward the river and spotted a pale, transparent globe rising out of the bubbling water. Inside the globe, Albrecht's head bobbed on the river's surface encircled by a shining gold crown.

The globe headed toward the opposite shore. When the head inside neared the riverbank, Albrecht's body emerged from the water. Neck and head reattached, he crawled onto the bottom of the viaduct's superstructure, got to his feet, and, radiant as a comet, dashed up the viaduct toward the contracting aperture.

"Sing!" Evelyn urged behind Miriam. "Sing at the top of your lungs!"

The Wailers and Kurgans launched into another chorus with an ear-shattering roar of blended harmonics. All Hades reverberated with the joy in Victor's anthem.

Albrecht climbed to the top of the viaduct, teetered on the support beam, caught his balance, and leaped between the portal's collapsing walls.

POOF!

The portal disappeared.

{31}

"Ahmfff!"

A clot of fuzz (cotton balls?) muffled Victor's groan; a bound cotton sheet (pillowcase?) covered his head and shoulders. A long, strong, rubbery string (electric cord?) bound his wrists and ankles.

Keep still. Whoever tied you up may be in the room.

Victor wondered if the women were all right. Were the three of them still in custody? Or someplace else?

He continued to take stock of his environment. He felt heat on his right cheek through the cloth and cold on his left from the hard surface he was laying on. He sniffed through his cloth and smelled an odor of gas penetrating through the scent of dust and detergent the cloth gave off. He determined he must still be in his hotel room, but somehow, he'd been moved in front of the fireplace.

What happened? The last Victor remembered was Ahriman's war wagon rolling to the top of the gorge. He couldn't have been able to be pulled back to ordinary reality like that without interference from Desdemona.

He checked his bonds—no give there. He made a mental inventory of his body: nerves incandescent, pain coursing through him in waves—typical symptoms of emerging to consciousness too fast.

Restored consciousness always provoked discomfort, but this was beyond endurance. How long were his body and soul disconnected? Hours? Days? It felt like weeks.

"Ooohmmm!" Evelyn whimpered above his head.

Her voice sounded distant as if leaking out of a mineshaft. She must still be in the Lower World. Was Miriam there, too? Victor resisted the urge to turn his head in Evelyn's direction and disclose he'd returned to ordinary world consciousness.

Where the hell was Desdemona?

Victor heard a scrunch on the tile beside his head and the rasp of metal against stone. A moment later the crash of glass exploded next to his head. He flinched at the shards showering his head cover.

"Ah, you *are* awake," Desdemona hissed in a guttural voice unlike its usual timbre. "So much the better."

What's going on? Her voice sounds deep as a man's.

A second piece of glass shattered against the fireplace followed by the scraping of a shoe on the hearth and the tinkle of glass pieces against metal.

The hallway door slammed against the wall. "What's going on here?" Cavanaugh bellowed.

The officer's thick-soled shoes thumped across the room and stopped beside Victor's head. "Did you do this, Ms. Gorovic?"

"I had to," Desdemona replied in her customary contralto, brushing the shards into the fireplace. "To protect ourselves. He's been holding us against our will before we got on the plane from Romania."

"The lady on the bed," Cavanaugh replied. "Who did that?"

"He did," Desdemona replied. "He put her in a trance—to rescue her daughter from the Lower World, he said."

"Mm—hmm," Cavanaugh grunted, stepping around Victor who squirmed and shook his head. The pillowcase and cord stayed fast.

"And this?" Cavanaugh asked.

"Broken mirrors," Desdemona replied. "Victor used them to help put his daughter under the same trance."

"I see," Cavanaugh replied. "Don't move."

"Can't you at least move him out of here?" Desdemona asked.

"He's not going anywhere," Cavanaugh replied.

"He's dangerous," Desdemona rasped. "Who knows how long that cord will hold him?"

"Long enough for me to notify my superiors," Cavanaugh said.

"But—"

Victor smiled insider his head sack. Cavanaugh's adherence to procedure upset her. Why was she so eager to get rid of him?

Had something gone wrong in the Lower World?

His heart leapt. Before Desdemona pulled his soul back to ordinary reality, the shamans, Wailers and Kurgan warriors had held their own despite being outnumbered by Ahriman's blue demons. Perhaps they'd driven them back to Dakhanavar. Hell, Ahriman could have dived into the Lethe and burned to a crisp for all he knew.

Victor suppressed his giddiness and retested his bonds. Tight as ever. *Give Desdemona credit—she knows how to tie a knot.*

Might as well wait until Connery arrived. He took as deep a breath as his gag allowed and assessed his situation. Desdemona's claim he was insane was an act of desperation. It wouldn't hold up once he told Connery his side of the story.

Her lie reinforced the notion that Ahriman's plan to enter ordinary reality somehow went wrong. The tone of her voice when she discovered Victor had returned to consciousness sounded unearthly—like Ahriman's voice.

Or Zarkisian's.

That must be it, Victor reasoned. Tying him up removed whatever doubt he had about Desdemona's allegiance to him. She kept him in the Lower World as long as his being there served Zarkisian's purpose. Victor's existence in the corporeal world didn't serve Zarkisian's plans either, so restraining him in this hotel room was an expedient until he found a permanent solution.

Is Evelyn next?

Victor shivered. This wouldn't be the first time Desdemona betrayed her sister. Is she so jealous of Evelyn's role in Zarkisian's life that she'd sacrifice her sister's soul to this psychic parasite? Would she do the same to her niece as well?

That possibility prompted him to refocus on the cord that bound his hands behind his back. The rubber coating surrounding the wire felt slippery from his sweat. He pushed and pulled his wrists in opposite directions, searching for a weak spot.

More shoes thudded the floor under Victor's cheek. A half dozen or more stepped into the room and surrounded the bed.

"Get that man to his feet," Connery ordered. "And remove that pillowcase from his head."

The hem caught under Victor's chin before the pillowcase popped off his head. He blinked and turned away from the rush of light. Squinting, he identified Cavanaugh as the man holding the pillowcase.

"Great Scot, Cavanaugh," Connery bellowed next to him. "Untie the man and remove the toilet paper from his mouth." He turned toward the stout man in the rumpled suit and overcoat standing next to him. "Poor Mr. Furst could've suffocated, and then where would we be?"

"Where would *you* be with three criminals wanted by our Homeland Security," Kincaid replied with a nod toward the two men in pressed suits standing behind him, "and them lounging in a Liverpool airport hotel under your direction?"

"That's after your state department demanded we treat them with kid gloves," Connery retorted.

"Ch-Charles," Victor spluttered, spitting out the rest of the toilet paper wad in his mouth. "What are you doing here?"

"Pulling your chestnuts out of the fire," Kincaid replied, stifling a yawn. "And bringing clarity and common sense to this tomfoolery, I hope."

He peered at Cavanaugh. "Could your man untie him?"

"One of the women," Cavanaugh said, nodding toward Desdemona, "claims Furst abducted her and her sister and held them against their will. He's deranged and could be violent, she said."

Mission: Soul Sacrifice

"I'll take that chance," Kincaid said, grimacing. "For now."

"You're rescuing us?" Victor asked as Cavanaugh untied the double-knotted cord around his wrists. "I thought the State Department was sending over emergency passports for our flight back to the States."

"We have the passports," Kincaid replied. "But it's not a rescue. More of an intervention, to my mind."

"That's why you're here?" Victor replied in astonishment. "To disprove shamanic therapy?"

"I've witnessed its effects," Kincaid replied with a sour look at Evelyn lying on the bed. "And felt I had to save a psychiatric patient once under my care."

Incredible.

"Thanks a bunch," Victor replied, curling, and uncurling his fingers. "In that case, I wish you hadn't come at all."

"I might not have," Kincaid retorted. "But Ambassador Gifford appealed to my sense of duty as a military officer and a citizen."

"See that!" Desdemona cried, pointing at Victor's fists from the safety of the sofa. "The suppressed rage? He's capable of violence."

"Mmmpf," Evelyn groaned and sat up. "Ye-ess-s."

"We all are at this point," Connery said dismissively and turned toward the FBI officers Rouse and Morris. "Are these their custody transfer requests?"

Connery grabbed the sheaf of papers from Rouse and scanned them. "Everything looks OK," he said and pulled a pen from his vest pocket. "Where do I sign?"

"Custody transfer?" Victor asked as Rouse identified three places for Connery to initial. "I thought you said we got temporary passports."

"They *are* temporary," Morris replied. "Enough to return you to the States where a formal hearing can be held regarding the charges against you. Did you think you'd be getting a souvenir booklet?"

"Charges!" Desdemona cried. "I've done nothing wrong."

"That's for our American authorities to decide," Morris said. "We're here to take you back so they can do their job."

"That is not acceptable," Desdemona replied in the unnatural voice she used earlier. Her face contorted to a venomous mask. "Our plans have changed due to recent events in the Middle East. We seek asylum in this country as war refugees."

"From what country?" Rouse asked.

"Hayastan," Desdemona replied.

"I'm not aware that such a country exists," Rouse said. "Nor persecution of its citizens."

Ahriman was defeated?

Victor's heart soared. Todd must have survived Ahriman's attacks and gotten through to Kincaid. Or did he?

Victor checked his watch—almost ten a.m., British time; one p.m. in Turkey.

"What about the fighting around Mt. Ararat?" Victor asked. "Did our air force bomb the mountain? Were Zarkisian and the Anausavareds defeated?"

"We were on a red eye flight over the Atlantic the last six hours," Rouse replied. "We know nothing about it, do we?" He asked Morris.

Morris affirmed Rouse's statement with a curt nod. "The news blackout's still in place in Turkey last I heard."

Great. No help there. Victor turned to Kincaid. "What about Miriam?"

"Still under her doctor's care, I assume," Kincaid replied.

"You assume?" Victor asked in a scathing voice. "After you told me her doctor said she felt trapped in Tartarus?"

"Patients often project their feelings onto their surroundings," Kincaid replied with a sweeping glance of the people around him. "Persecution is just one of them. Dr. Furst knows that."

"Our people have been persecuted for centuries," Desdemona declared, turning to face Connery. "And our lands taken from us illegally."

What people is she talking about?

"You do not qualify as war refugees," Connery said, glancing up from signing the transfer papers. "You're American citizens."

"We claim dual citizenship," Desdemona replied. "My sister as the wife or zan of the Shahanshah of Hayastan and for myself as her closest relative and sister."

"Your status will have to be decided in an American court," Connery said, signing his name with a flourish. "There!

"They're all yours now." He turned, handed the papers back to Rouse, and said under his breath, "Heaven help you."

With a curt nod to Cavanaugh, Connery turned to leave the room.

"Wait!" Desdemona called, grabbed Evelyn's arm, and pulled her lethargic sister to her feet. "Get up, Evelyn!" she said and followed Connery to the door. "Detain us as illegal aliens then!"

Connery passed through the doorway with Cavanaugh in his wake. Morris closed the door behind them while Rouse stuck the transfer papers inside his suit coat.

"Better yet," Desdemona said through the closed door, her jaw jutting into Rouse's chest. "Deport us to our country of origin."

"In due course after the immigration court examines the facts of your case," Rouse replied and shepherded the two women back to the center of the room. "If it decides you're telling the truth, you'll be free to go wherever you like."

"You don't believe me?" Desdemona groaned.

"It's not our role to pass judgment," Rouse replied. "We're here to insure your safe return to the United States."

"That includes me, too?" Victor asked.

"Of course, it does," Rouse said. "Equal and impartial treatment for all," he added with a nod at his partner for support. "Right?"

When Morris nodded agreement, Victor turned to Kincaid. "And you, Charles?"

"Sure," he replied, rubbing the back of his neck. "Though I'll testify before any court of law that your unprofessional behavior in this matter is the primary reason these women face flight, aiding and abetting, and other charges."

"That's your professional opinion?" Victor replied.

"It is," Kincaid retorted.

"And Cavanaugh finding me tied up like a steer for branding has nothing to do with it?" Victor asked.

"No," Kincaid replied. "Though it must have looked ridiculous, it's something a hostage terrified for her life might do if she were brave enough."

"Terrified *and* resourceful, wouldn't you say?" Victor asked, convinced this was his last chance to exonerate himself in his friend's mind. "Did she ever explain how she managed to tie me up?"

"No," Kincaid replied.

"Or why she shattered two of our improvised psychomanteum mirrors and swept them into the fireplace?" Victor continued.

"No," Kincaid admitted and turned toward Desdemona with an upraised brow. "Well? Care to explain?"

"I didn't want Evelyn to go to what he called the Lower World again," Desdemona replied in the guttural tone that copied Zarkisian's voice. She coughed and cleared her throat, her eyes searching Kincaid's face for support. "You can see she's unhealthy from all the times he put her in a trance," she added in her normal voice. "It was my only way to prevent it happening again."

Kincaid turned back to Victor. "Pretty convincing."

What about Miriam?

"Evelyn's daughter, Miriam, told us in the Lower World that Desdemona sent her to retrieve us," Victor said. "Ask her about the cell phone Connery gave us to communicate with the State Department."

"What about it?" Kincaid asked.

"Desdemona used it to send her to the Lower World," Victor replied.

Kincaid turned toward Desdemona.

"I don't have it," Desdemona replied. "Why should I?"

"Well, I don't," Victor declared. "And I didn't see him take it with him."

"That doesn't mean he doesn't have it," Desdemona retorted.

"Easy enough to check," Rouse suggested. He phoned Connery's office, nodded a few times, and shut off his phone. "He doesn't have it."

"I don't have it either," Desdemona declared.

"The case of the missing cell phone," Kincaid scoffed. "We have a plane to catch. Connery'll have to tell us if he finds it."

The two crashes on the hearth!

"Wait a minute!" Victor said, squatting before the fireplace. He peered under the twin rows of fluted pipes that held the plastic log. A five-inch beveled edge of rubber stuck out against a large glass shard under the log. "What's this doing here?"

He pulled out the phone, wiped the monitor clean with his thumb, and pressed the 'on' button. "SIM error" appeared on the screen.

"What does that prove?" Desdemona said, leaning over Victor's shoulder. "If it doesn't work, why keep it?"

"Not many people throw a cell phone into a fireplace," Rouse said over Kincaid's shoulder. "Too dangerous even if it doesn't work."

Victor rummaged through the shards under the ceramic log. Near the back he found a dusty one-inch metal square. "Here's why," he said, showing the square to Kincaid. "I bet it's the phone's SIM card."

Kincaid handed the square to Rouse who removed the back of the phone and inserted the square inside. The phone's face lit up.

"Check the listing of recent calls," Victor said.

Rouse pressed the heading and scanned the list. "A couple to the U.S. State Department," Rouse said, scrolling with his thumb. "The one on top is to a civilian number." He showed the listing to Victor and Kincaid. "Recognize it?"

"See—that's my apartment number," Victor replied and whirled toward Desdemona. "Where's Miriam?"

"She's safe—somewhere," Desdemona replied, squatting beside the fireplace. She picked up the jagged shard between her fingers, and chuckled. "We will make sure of that."

She sprang to her feet and jabbed the pointy end under Evelyn's chin, drawing blood. "Evelyn and I will be too, once we're out of here."

Desdemona side-stepped toward the door, keeping the point under Evelyn's jawline, and threatening her carotid artery. Using her sister as a human shield, she steered Evelyn toward the hallway door.

Morris and Rouse cut off their advance.

"Let us through," Desdemona demanded. "Or I'll plunge this all the way into my sister's tongue."

The two agents didn't budge.

"I MEAN IT!" Desdemona screamed.

"This won't work, Desdemona," Kincaid said. "Using your sister to escape just makes matters worse for you."

"Sure, it does," Desdemona agreed. "But it's the only move I have left because she's the only thing any of you care about."

Her eyes blazed at Kincaid. "Now tell the Homeland agents to let us pass."

"I can—"

"He hasn't that authority," Rouse replied, creeping closer.

"We can wait you out," Morris added, inching forward alongside his partner.

Desdemona nudged the shard deeper into Evelyn's throat. Thick blood droplets began to trickle down Evelyn's neck.

"Victor?" she growled, her guttural voice resurfacing. "You know I'll do it. You don't want anything like that to happen to her, do you?"

Is her hatred that strong?

"Of course not," Victor replied, shielding his eyes from a sudden flash of blue light. Squinting, he spotted a seething blue/black aura around the two women. Combined with the voice change, he knew the woman holding Evelyn hostage wasn't Evelyn's sister. "But we can't let you leave with her, either."

"So be it," Desdemona replied in Zarkisian's voice. "But you are responsible for what happens here to her and the others."

She pivoted toward Rouse. He reached for her right hand, then touched his right temple, staggering as if he was about to faint. He caught himself, grabbed her wrist, causing the shard to fall, and pinned her arm behind her back.

Morris hesitated too, then recovered. He grabbed Evelyn's shoulder and pulled her from Desdemona's grasp.

Desdemona spun Rouse around, clawing the air with her free hand, and collided against the wall. Rouse pinned that hand behind her too, but wriggling within the agent's grasp, she leveled a laser-like stare on her groggy sister.

"ANGRA MAINYU!" Evelyn shouted, tossing Morris aside like a stuffed toy. Grabbing the shard from the floor, Evelyn slashed Morris's shoulder and arm before he dived over the bed.

Evelyn shoved Desdemona toward the door with one arm and scythed at Rouse with the other. Backing him against the fireplace, she slashed both his arms he used to protect his face.

Rouse feinted left, rolled under Evelyn's outstretched arm, and sprang to his feet behind her. When she turned to face him, Morris tackled her, and they fell to the floor. Grappling each other, they rolled over and back, he holding her wrist outstretched to keep the shard away and she seeking a vulnerable spot for the kill.

Rouse danced around the grapplers, scrabbling at Evelyn's fingers to pry the shard loose, but the fury of their struggle thwarted his efforts.

"Call Connery!" Kincaid cried in horror beside the fireplace. "Have him send more men!"

Rouse pulled the phone from his pocket, but Evelyn kicked it under the bed. When Rouse dove to retrieve it, she grabbed his ankle and held him in place.

If Zarkisian possesses her, she funnels his strength too.

Victor turned and spotted Desdemona in front of the hallway door, focusing on Evelyn with frog-eyed concentration.

Evelyn slid her knees under Morris' arms, kicked both her legs into his chest, and sent him flying across the room where he crashed against the wall and slumped to the floor.

A pleased grin flitted across Desdemona's face.

One down, three to go.

Victor edged along the wall, staying out of Desdemona's line of sight. If she escaped, any chance of finding Miriam and thwarting Zarkisian went with her.

Inch by inch, Evelyn pulled Rouse out from under the bed. Kincaid darted from the fireplace and jumped onto Desdemona's back.

"Victor!" Kincaid cried, struggling to pry her fingers from the shard. "Help me!"

Victor froze. If he aided Kincaid, Desdemona escaped. If he caught Desdemona, Evelyn would pummel his friend.

Wrapping one arm around Rouse's ankles, Desdemona got to her knees and rolled sideways, loosening Kincaid's grip on her. With her free arm, she elbowed him in the solar plexus.

Gasping for air, Kincaid staggered back. Evelyn's next attack, a swift kick into his stomach, sent him reeling into the fireplace.

That makes two.

Rouse shook one leg free of Evelyn's grip, kicked her in the face, and scrambled toward the hallway door. Unfazed by the blow, Evelyn grabbed the agent as he opened the door, put him in a headlock, and pulled him back into the room.

Rousing himself, Kincaid leaped from the fireplace and hugged Evelyn around her waist. Freeing her right hand, Evelyn punched the top of Kincaid's head twice.

Kincaid slid down her leg and entwined his arms around her ankles like a distraught toddler. Evelyn kicked him in the stomach until he fell away, then redoubled her lock around Rouse's head.

Two out and three on his way. It's up to me.

Victor scooped a smaller shard out of the fireplace, skirted the Greek wrestling match in the center of the room, and crept behind the rapt Desdemona. Seizing her by the collar, he stuck the pointy end between her carotid artery and Adam's apple. "Order Evelyn to stop fighting."

"No!" Desdemona cried, struggling in Victor's arms. "I can't."

"Why not?"

"I'm Basil's familiar!"

Evelyn tightened her bearhug around Rouse's neck, shook him like a dirty dust mop, and hurled his body onto the bed. She crossed the room toward Victor, her face seething with blood lust.

"Free yourself," Victor said and pressed the shard tip into Desdemona's skin. "Make Evelyn stop!"

He backed away, holding Desdemona in front of him as a shield. The bathroom door was the only interior door that locked. Could he reach it?

"Stop her, Dez," Victor cried. "Try!"

"He's too strong," Desdemona grunted through parted lips. "Even at this distance."

Victor pressed the shard against Desdemona's neck. If Evelyn's soul remained in the Lower World, Desdemona channeled psychic energy from somewhere else.

"Break the link, Dez!" Victor cried and pressed until the tip drew blood. "Now!"

Desdemona closed her eyes and fell limp in Victor's arms. Rouse staggered to his feet and jumped on Evelyn's back, but she flung him aside like a discarded knapsack.

"Don't make me kill your sister," Victor warned as Evelyn edged closer.

"You-you won't do that," Desdemona gasped.

"You don't give me much choice," Victor replied, feeling the wall against his back. Desdemona would channel all of Zarkisian's power into Evelyn until she accomplished his bloody task. "Zarkisian isn't worth it."

"I know," Desdemona replied. "But I'm not controlling her anymore."

She pointed at Evelyn. "YOU stole him from me."

She resents Evelyn that much.

Evelyn gripped Victor's arm around Desdemona's neck and squeezed. HARD.

Victor writhed with pain.

No pain, no gain!

He rammed the shard deep into Desdemona's skin.

Blood spurted.

Evelyn's face contorted.

In agony? Or release?

Victor dragged the point across the artery, making a furrow in Desdemona's skin.

Blood spurted everywhere.

Evelyn collapsed at Victor's feet. The blood from Desdemona's neck gurgled, then ebbed. Victor laid her body on the floor and checked Evelyn's pulse—weak but steady. Her eyes focused on the ceiling; Evelyn didn't respond when he squeezed her hand.

Victor crossed the room and raised his friend upright against the foot of the bed. Kincaid flashed a weak smile. "I'm sore everywhere, but nothing seems broken."

Rouse staggered into the bathroom and reemerged wiping his face with a hand towel. He tossed a bath towel to Morris and draped another around Kincaid's neck.

"I'm all right," Kincaid said, wiping the towel across his face. He handed it to Victor. "You could use this yourself."

Victor stood up, lurched into the bathroom, and stared into the mirror. His face resembled a steer's hindquarter at butchering time. He vomited into the sink, raised his head, and puked again.

After his stomach spasms subsided, Victor dampened a towel, wiped the spittle from his mouth, and stared at his image again. What did he feel? Remorse—yes. Shame—yes. But no regret. He had to kill Desdemona. It was the only way to sever the psychic link between her and Zarkisian.

William Fietzer

He studied his blood-stained hands, claw-like and quivering like a child's after holding the safety bar during a roller-coaster ride. The dirtiest insight of all? Never had he felt more alive.

{32}

What's happened to me?

Victor covered his face in horror and shame. He never felt so vengeful and bloodthirsty before. Never to the point he wanted to kill someone, let alone enjoy it.

You reveled in it. The power, the lust, the . . . abandon.

He scrubbed his hands until they were pink, rinsed the blood-flecked foam out of the sink, and rejoined the men in the bedroom. Evelyn groaned on the sofa bed; her sister lay dead beside the door.

"Just lie still," Kincaid said as he stretched the dampened handkerchief across Evelyn's forehead. "Close your eyes and breathe deep."

He turned toward Victor. "I never saw anything like it. Evelyn's breathing and pulse rate are as steady as if she'd just taken a walk in the garden. How she fought us like that is astounding."

His face clouded. "She is, however, unaware of her surroundings. Why is that d'you suppose?"

Victor scratched his beard and sat on the edge of the cot. He doubted they'd believe his explanation, but knew it was his last chance to make them understand. Kincaid and the agents gathered into a semicircle in front of him.

"First of all, Evelyn has superhuman powers," Victor said, scanning the faces of the three men surrounding him. All three regarded him with cynical detachment. "Can we agree on that?"

The men's faces remained impassive.

"You know what she did to three experienced officers," Victor said, glancing at each of them in turn and ending with Kincaid. "You feel it in your bones."

Morris grimaced and nodded. Rouse followed Morris' lead. Kincaid's expression did not change. "Where does this power come from?" he asked.

"Orgonic energy," Victor replied.

All three men shook their heads in disbelief. "There's none of that here," Rouse said.

"It's in everyone," Victor retorted. "Psychic parasites like Basil Zarkisian drain it from their victims."

"Here we go again," Kincaid muttered.

"I don't see anyone with that name here," Rouse said, glancing around the room.

"That's because Desdemona channeled Zarkisian's parasitic energy to Evelyn," Victor replied.

"How?" Morris asked.

"Desdemona is, well, was Zarkisian's familiar," Victor replied. Noting the perplexity on Rouse's face, he added, "Like a black cat was for witches during the Middle Ages."

"That's why you killed her?" Kincaid said aghast.

"No," Victor replied before continuing with his explanation. "She enabled him to vent his strength through Evelyn."

They're not buying this. Make them understand.

"Killing Desdemona should have broken the link between Zarkisian and Evelyn," Victor said with a glance to the inert figure lying on the bed. "Evelyn's catatonic state shows some powerful force or circumstance still prevents her soul's return. If Zarkisian can now project his power over a distance without the help of an empath or a familiar, Ahriman may have taken command of Mt. Ararat."

Kincaid rolled his eyes in disbelief. "You're certain of that?"

You've gone this far. Explain it all. Make them understand.

Victor recapped the current situation in the Lower World, its relationship to the New Immortals in Turkey, and his efforts to thwart their takeover of Mt. Ararat. "Our attempts weren't as successful as we had hoped."

He cupped Evelyn's hands in his and directed his next words to her. "We need your help now," he urged. "Before Zarkisian becomes too powerful to stop."

Morris and Rouse exchanged uncertain glances. Kincaid wrapped his arm around Victor's shoulders. "She should be taken to a hospital. She's dehydrated. Nourishment would be good for you, too."

"I'm fine," Victor replied and shrugged Kincaid's arm from his shoulder. His display of concern did not conceal his skepticism. "If we don't stop Zarkisian now," Victor added, "her lack of nourishment will be the least of our worries."

None of their expressions changed. "Give me a moment and I'll show you," Victor said, spotting the shard Evelyn wielded. "You know how strong Evelyn was. I can show you how and why."

Morris rubbed the back of his neck. "I dunno, Dr. Furst. What you're saying is so unbelievable."

"I'm not making this up!" Victor replied.

"Psychic vampires?" Rouse blew air between his lips. "From the spirit world?"

"'Parasites' is more correct," Victor said. "They feed on the orgone energy inside us."

"We better inform Connery about the body," Rouse said, turning toward Kincaid. "But I'm not putting any of what Furst just said into our murder report."

"Murder?" Victor cried. "You saw it. I had no choice!" He turned toward Kincaid. "Charles?"

"Well. . ." Kincaid cocked a doubting eyebrow.

"Just let me show you," Victor begged. "Please?"

"OK. We've gone this far," Kincaid said. "Anything more you want from us?"

My last chance.

Victor sighed. "I want you to monitor Evelyn's vital signs. Rouse, contact Ambassador Gifford. Morris, get hold of vice-consul Helsingford."

He scanned the floor, picked up Evelyn's shard and two more from the fireplace, and placed them in a line against the log.

"No response from the ambassador or his diplomat," Rouse reported. "Communication's still out in the Caucasus and Eastern Anatolia."

"Distressing, but not surprising," Victor replied, wondering if they were too late. "Turkey's continued blackout shows Zarkisian remains in control of Mount Ararat and his followers. All the more important we know what's going on."

He explained how Zarkisian, and his parasites fed on human anxiety. "It's not conventional medicine, Charles, but it *is* the only way to diagnose Evelyn's current condition."

Victor directed the two agents to turn off the lights and concentrate upon the shards. After the agents carried out his instructions, he turned on the light in the bathroom to backlight the mirror pieces, then crossed to the bed, sat beside Evelyn, and clasped her right hand.

Evelyn did not respond.

I'll bring you back. I promise.

Victor patted the top of Evelyn's hand for reassurance, turned, and glanced down at Desdemona's body.

I'm doing this for you, too. And Miriam if I can find where she is.

He focused on his reflection in the center shard. This demonstration better work, he thought. It had to. If Kincaid and the Homeland Security agents witnessed the Lower World, the experience would force them to advocate whatever was necessary to prevent Ahriman's dominion over it and their own reality.

His journey into the Lower World was not as pleasant or rapid as his previous descents. No euphoria marked his transition into the

Mission: Soul Sacrifice

Lower World. Instead of a warm glowing sensation, his reentry recalled sliding into a tub filled with tepid bath water. After several minutes of humming and staring into the mirror, his reflection clouded, the black diamonds materialized, and he landed on the Hades side of the Lethe.

Ahriman's mobile battle fortress lay on its side, a flaming hulk at the end of the lava delta upon which Wodenaz and Thunraz rained a barrage of thunderbolts. Now and then a squad of blue demons scurried from the fortress to the fizzing water, but Freya's archers on the riverbank cut them down. The lava beneath the water's surface incinerated the one or two that reached their goal.

Akvan's infantry roiled in confusion on the ridge overlooking the river. Ahriman's archers rained volley after volley upon Freya, Tisiphone, her sisters, and the Valkyries. Protected by the Valkyries' shields, however, the shamans purged scores of Wailers' souls of eel demons at factory speed. Flashes of retrieved souls returning to the corporeal world matched the explosions from the gods' aerial bombardments.

The opposite side of the river, however, remained quiet. The devils formerly under Albrecht's command sat upon the truncheons of the viaduct entrance and gazed at the Lethe's turbid waters. A few scavenged what was valuable among the scraps of building materials littered about the deserted spans.

Victor squinted toward the top of the viaduct.

The sky portal is gone! They won. Ahriman's quest to for the corporeal world failed.

But where was Albrecht? Victor scanned the length of the opposite shore before a chill coursed down his spine.

Had Albrecht succeeded where Ahriman had not?

He ducked between two Kurgan guards, dodged a stray arrow, and approached the Wailers' protective cordon. Freya parted the bevy of shamans standing in the center. Evelyn's body lay upon an improvised stretcher at the center of the safe zone.

"Give me an update on Evelyn's condition," Freya said.

"Despite our efforts we haven't pinpointed the cause of her illness," Eylo answered with a sympathetic shake of his head. "If Miriam had not disappeared—"

"But she did." Freya hoisted her sword point under the Mir's chin. Her blazing eyes scanned the shamans. "Find the cause or I will allow Ahriman's forces to seal your fate."

"She's caught between worlds!" Victor said, wondering why Freya didn't recognize him. "Zarkisian—"

Shouts came from the jetty. Akvan's troops poured down the ravine. A giant frog burst from the wreckage of the battle wagon. In two giant leaps, the frog reached shore. Before Wodenaz's archers could redirect their fire, it leaped into the middle of Freya's cordon.

"You fought well," the frog said in Ahriman's booming voice. "Shoot if you will but know this." It gestured toward Evelyn's inert body. "My agent has her under his control. If I am fated to remain in the Lower World, so must her soul. Evelyn's powers shall be turned upon herself for as long as I am exiled in Dakhanavar."

Ahriman bounded into the midst of Akvan's troops. Assured that his master was safe, Akvan withdrew the remnants of his army up the ravine.

Freya parted the scores of souls still seeking treatment with an angry sweep of her battle shield. "Hold your fire! Shoot them if they try anything."

"Freya!" Victor clutched her mantle, but her Valkyrie bodyguards grabbed his arms and pulled him away. The goddess turned and eyed Victor with disdain. "Should I know you?"

"Doctor Victor Furst." He struggled to free himself, but the Valkyries' grips were strong. "The shaman who freed all the souls along the Lethe?"

"Ah, yes!" Freya glowered in recognition. "The man who abandoned them and the rest of the Kurgans at the height of battle *after* he stole my cape."

"That was a mistake," Victor replied. "Miriam never should—"

"That one!" Freya growled. She turned with a sweep of her cloak and marched toward the battle lines. "We have had enough of the house of Furst."

What did she mean about Miriam? Why isn't she safe?

"Freya," Victor called. The guards' grips remained locked around his arms. "Freya!"

"Victor!" a voice called him.

The ground rumbled beneath his feet. Who called him?

"Victor!' the voice repeated.

This second call was more a summons than one of recognition. The Valkyries' grip dissolved. His body soared into the sky. The bridge, the bombardment, and Ahriman's retreat faded.

"Victor." Kincaid shook his shoulder. "Wake up!"

"You s-saw th-them?" Ugh! His mouth felt full of cobwebs. His body ached like hell. The twist of Kincaid's mouth and Rouse's frown revealed they had not. "Evelyn's still trapped in the Lower World. Maybe Miriam, too."

"We have to get Evelyn to a hospital," Kincaid said and patted his friend's shoulder. "Miriam too, when we find her. They need Lorazepam before their paralysis becomes permanent."

"Drugs will worsen her condition," Victor replied.

"What alternative would you propose?" Kincaid's voice dripped sarcasm. "Doctor?"

"Limbic resonance," Victor replied.

"Empathic resonance?" Kincaid rubbed the back of his neck. "I don't think—"

"Evelyn's an empath," Victor said. "Her soul mirrors and amplifies the feelings of those around her."

"But that's all speculation," Kincaid replied. "None of it's proven."

"Look, Charles." Victor grabbed Kincaid's elbow. "The abilities you've seen here in this room I witnessed first-hand in the Lower World."

Kincaid removed Victor's fingers from his coat. "Even if what you say is true, what would those abilities accomplish here?"

"Her soul is in the Lower World for over a day in terms of corporeal world time," Victor replied. "Our only hope is if we put her body in motion here, her subconscious mind will synchronize with her corporeal world experience."

Victor grabbed Evelyn's ankles. He bent one leg, then the other to simulate a jogging motion. "Do the same with her arms."

Kincaid's lips curled in derision, but he did as Victor requested. Evelyn did not respond at first. Then her eyes flickered and opened.

"Angra Mainyu!" she cried. Her arms and legs broke free and pumped on their own. "Angra Mainyu."

"See!" Victor exclaimed.

"No!" Evelyn said and cowered into a fetal position. "Basil, no." She raised her arms and kicked the air. "Don't!"

Her eyes fluttered open, and spotting Victor, she squeezed his hand, smiled, and vomited.

Evelyn loved him all along.

"You heard her," Victor exulted, giddy with this new evidence. "I knew Zarkisian attacked her. She never submitted to him. That's the reason behind her body's rigidity and unresponsiveness."

"Victor. That sorry display proves nothing," Kincaid said. "Your treatment provoked the negative response you wanted, and you tied it to a professional rival you've been at odds with for years."

Victor's jaw dropped. "Are you so steeped in conventional medicine you can't acknowledge the catharsis you just witnessed with your own eyes?"

"I know jealousy plain enough," Kincaid declared. He pulled out a handkerchief and wiped the spittle from the corner of Evelyn's mouth. "Evelyn needs proper hospital care." He glanced at Desdemona's body, then at Morris, and jerked his head toward the door. Taking care to screen Evelyn from seeing her sister's body, Morris and Rouse raised and carried it into the hallway.

Upon hearing Connery's voice over Rouse's cell phone, Kincaid turned toward Victor, eying him like a father with a wayward son. "Hospital would do you good, too."

Evelyn groped for Victor's hand and seized it, her grip weak yet firm. She was months away from good health, Victor knew, but they had broken through the armoring response that Zarkisian used to control her psyche.

Kincaid was right about one thing—Evelyn needed hospital care. He turned to Rouse who had reentered the room. "Have you contacted Ambassador Gifford?"

"Communication with eastern Turkey is still out," Rouse replied.

"Do a workaround," Victor said. "Contact Helsingford on his personal cell phone number."

Rouse shrugged. "I'll do what I can."

"Tell Connery to send an ambulance to meet us in the lobby," Kincaid said as he helped Evelyn to her feet. "Morris can take care of matters here."

"Miriam? My sister?" Evelyn asked in a daze. "Where are they?"

"They're fine for the moment," Kincaid replied, patting her wrist. "Right now, it's you I'm concerned about.'

"What about Miriam?" Victor whispered in Kincaid's ear. "We need to find her!"

"Give your family a rest," Kincaid advised, guiding Evelyn through the door. "I'm sure Miriam will turn up."

"Evelyn's autonomic nervous system needs to reset," Victor said as he followed them down the hallway. "As long as Zarkisian is alive, Evelyn and Miriam will always remain dissociated from their own bodies."

As long as he's alive.

Victor's knees buckled. *Is that my only recourse?*

"Charles, listen," Victor said as they entered the elevator. "I'm begging you. Reset Evelyn's limbic system now. It's the only chance we'll have."

Kincaid ignored Victor's pleas as the quartet entered the lobby. Victor spotted an EMT waiting beside an ambulance outside the lobby door. Its side panel read: Property of the Educational Development and Information Center, UK Div.

EDIC! Zarkisian's treatment center!

Connery and Cavanaugh grabbed Victor's arms and steered him outside.

"Why, Charles?" Victor cried over his shoulder.

"You need help," Kincaid replied. "I was advised it's the best they have over here."

"Charles, I'm begging you," Victor said as the medical technician plunged a syringe into his shoulder. Victor staggered and slumped to his knees between the two Homeland agents.

Todd's my last ho— . . .

{33}

A low rumble shook the antechamber where Todd awaited Seraphina's return. The basalt walls quivered, and the ceiling cracked, black dust and sand filtering down and forming a small mound on the slate floor. Are the tremors from an earthquake, Todd wondered. A counteroffensive from Zarkisian's defenders? Or the Allies detonating their bomb cache? He couldn't tell.

Todd tried the door—unlocked. Zarkisian's support staff milled about in the hallway rubbing their knuckles together and murmuring "Angra Mainyu" over and over. Threats and bayonets from Zarkisian's security staff failed to force his drones to complete their work assignments. And why not? The next vibration might collapse the mountain.

The Shahanshah's non-appearance was worrisome. All leaders, Gifford once told him, no matter how arrogant, inadequate, or despotic, needed to reassure their followers they were in charge and bringing the situation under control. That neither Zarkisian nor his military chiefs, or spahbeds, had appeared to reassure their forces showed something was wrong.

Todd's heart leapt. *Has Ahriman failed to make it through the portal?* If that were true, what happened to Miriam and her parents? He hadn't heard a thing from them since his phone call to Dr. Furst.

Maybe Seraphina and like-minded commanders had staged an in-house coup. That could be why the soulless compliance of Zarkisian's drones was fraying.

No way.

Todd frowned. Seraphina hadn't the time. And if she had secured the like-minded marzbans at her rank, nothing guaranteed that Zarkisian would acknowledge their viewpoint or adopt a more conciliatory approach toward the Allies.

Just the opposite, he concluded. Their actions and his speculations amounted to nothing if Ahriman had passed through the portal.

He glimpsed his reflection in the window panel of the communication center and fingered the right side of his face. The mottled skin on his cheek and around his eye shone pink under the chamber's recessed lighting. He lifted the corner of the bandage covering the left side of his face. Rosy skin showed where the worst charring had occurred.

Thank you, Seraphina.

Her orgonic powers applied to his internal chemistry quickened his healing process. The zalim's powers were as potent as Zarkisian advertised—and as beneficial.

Todd's stomach tightened as he weighed the possibilities—pain-free skin grafts, accelerated recovery times, who knows what. The notion had seemed incredible when Seraphina proposed it, but if coexistence was a possibility . . .

Zarkisian's drones roused to ragged attention. Their master, garbed in martial splendor, marched through the corridor accompanied by a half dozen of his chief spahbeds. Seraphina marched past with the contingent of Hayastani officials and flashed Todd the faintest nod of recognition.

Hayastan's rebel leader halted at the intersection of the two hallways. "Resume your posts," Zarkisian ordered. When his subordinates cleared the area, he said, "Let us proceed."

He and his entourage marched into the conference room. Two lesser-ranking officers split from Zarkisian's retinue, marched up to Todd, and saluted. The one on the left addressed him. "Your presence is requested in the conference room."

They flanked him shoulder-to-shoulder as they marched into the room where Zarkisian and the rest of Hayastan's leadership awaited him seated at the oblong table. Surrounded by a shimmering nimbus of

Mission: Soul Sacrifice

gold, Albrecht sat at the head of the table in the chair saved for Ahriman. His head and body showed no scars or disfigurement.

Todd's two escorts deposited him in the remaining seat at the table's opposite end. Zarkisian rose to his feet beside Albrecht and murmured an incantation in ancient Armenian. Clutching the Shahanshah's tall, gilded helmet in both hands, Zarkisian raised it skyward, edged behind Albrecht's chair, and lowered it. Sparks flew from Albrecht's halo as the helmet settled onto Albrecht's forehead.

Zarkisian turned toward Todd and flashed a cunning smile. "With all of the tributes, levies, affiliations, and responsibilities past, present, and future that are conferred upon this office," he concluded in English, "I, your loyal Arteshbod, name you the first Shahanshah of the restored state of Hayastan."

What's happened here? Albrecht's the new Shahanshah?

Todd applauded with mute courtesy, stunned by the enthusiasm of the spahbeds seated around the table who clapped and cheered their support. When one spahbed standing along the wall whistled his appreciation, however, his comrades plucked his fingers from his mouth and hustled him out of the room.

He noted Seraphina's glistening cheeks as Albrecht rose to his feet and addressed his new subjects. "Many difficulties and struggles lie ahead for our new-formed state . . ."

Todd smiled to conceal his bewilderment. How was it possible that Albrecht had replaced Ahriman? Unless Ahriman didn't get through the portal—

Did that mean Albrecht has divine powers? That would explain his halo and why Zarkisian ceded authority to Albrecht.

Preposterous! Zarkisian would never agree to such a power exchange. Yet presenting the last part of his speech in English seemed for Todd's benefit—which made sense as a diplomatic gesture if

Zarkisian was reaching out to an American envoy in the new regime's behalf.

Todd shivered at the thought. If Albrecht occupied Ahriman's chair, a new, less trustworthy force controlled the reins of power of this fledgling state.

". . . and extend an olive branch to our neighbors and those in a position to help us become full-fledged citizens of the world," Albrecht said with a sweep of his hand in Todd's direction. "Thus, we have included the representative from the United States as witness to our ceremony."

Enough pomp and circumstance.

"Where's Ahriman?" Todd asked.

"Where I left him," Albrecht replied with a grin.

"He didn't make it through the portal?" Todd continued.

"No." Albrecht's face sobered.

"Just you?" Todd replied, steeling himself for the critical question. "What's to prevent Ahriman from coming through, too?"

"The portal is closed," Albrecht declared. "That's what all the shaking earlier was about."

"How?"

"Does it matter?" Albrecht replied and grinned at his colleagues and subjects. "You're dealing now with the azatan, Hayastan's aristocrat class—a much more reasonable group, believe me."

"Reasonable?" Todd replied and glanced at Seraphina. Her rapt attention on Albrecht's every word suggested that policy matters weren't much different than before Albrecht's ascendancy to the throne. "In what way?"

"We're willing to cease all hostilities for recognition as a new state," Albrecht said, laying his hand over Seraphina's in a show of unity and affection. "We feel certain the regional powers and the U.N.

will recognize the legitimacy of our claim once they see the peacefulness of our intent."

Todd sat back in his chair, mute but seething inside. Had Seraphina saved his life to give him witness to Albrecht's ascension to the throne? She couldn't be more heartless.

He studied Zarkisian whose face was a mask of concentration and glanced about the table. One quarter of his allies from their previous meeting were not present at Albrecht's coronation.

Were they purged?

"What about him?" Todd pointed at Zarkisian. "If he and his adherents are still—"

"The views of the Arteshbod and his followers do not represent the viewpoints of this council as it is now," Albrecht replied. "The outbreak of hostilities was seen as ill-advised by many of its members."

"But you took part in its inception," Todd replied.

"As a financial adviser," Albrecht said, his halo glimmering. "I took my leave from that position as soon as Dr. Zarkisian expressed his belligerent intent—with fatal consequences, as you know."

Huh?

"Do you expect everyone to believe you and Zarkisian have reached some kind of agreement?" Todd retorted. Their rapprochement did not represent another example of Zarkisian's Realpolitik. "At the risk of laboring over the obvious, if Arteshbod Zarkisian is still here, the legitimacy of your government remains in question."

"That is why this body is applying for recognition under a U.N. mandate," Albrecht said, removing his hand from Seraphina's. "Under its protection," he said, leaning forward to insure everyone at the table heard his words, "Hayastan can pursue the legitimacy of its claims to be accepted as an equal among nations."

"And Zarkisian and his followers?" Todd asked.

"His previous actions speak in no way for this new governing body of Hayastan," Albrecht said. "He has accepted his role as Arteshbod in exchange for our clemency as a war criminal."

Albrecht scanned each of his followers, smiling with benevolence before his luminous eyes rested upon Seraphina's. "We beseech you as a representative of America and its allies," he said, turning back to Todd, "to cease hostilities and present the case on our behalf before the United Nations for admission as a peaceful nation."

There it was. Todd rested his elbows on the table and covered his head in his hands. Everything Albrecht said had a ring of authority that would resonate in the diplomatic halls of his own country and in the League of Arab States. Regardless of the accord proffered by Albrecht's glowing words, Todd trusted Zarkisian's actions more. He brutalized his enemies, yet he did it on behalf of something he believed in, even if that something was misguided and evil.

Unlike Zarkisian, Albrecht was mercurial, with no other moral conviction beyond seizing the most lucrative option in front of him at any given moment. Believing in nothing other than seizing the main chance, he remained as likely to change sides as ever despite his divine appearance.

Gifford had directed Todd to gain a ceasefire at any price. The one offered here was under the quid pro quo of national recognition. Zarkisian was by no means a sympathetic character, but he deserved better than to be sold out for serving his god and his religion. He also must realize the clemency Albrecht offered him held little weight in an international court of law.

"Well, Mr. Helsingford?" Albrecht asked. "What do you say to our proposal?"

"What about Ahriman?" Todd asked. "What's to prevent him trying again to enter this world? Perhaps through you?"

"He had his chance," Albrecht replied. "The portal closed without him passing through it. It will not open again."

"How can you be sure?" Todd asked.

"Zurvan's prophecy decreed it," Albrecht said. "Fate determined Ahriman would not succeed in his efforts. And now that it is fulfilled, he shall remain exiled in Dakhanavar forever."

"And you, Arteshbod?" Todd lowered his hands to gauge Zarkisian's reaction. "The Shahanshah's terms are acceptable?"

"One cannot fight Destiny," Zarkisian replied, bitterness flickering in the pupils of his eyes. "Nor the realities of a new political dynamic."

He nodded toward Albrecht. "Personal well-being must comply with the welfare of our new nation and its citizens."

Albrecht smiled and scanned the other spahbeds. Their non-reaction was as good as compliance, he decided and wrapped his arm around Seraphina's shoulders. "To show the world that our new nation seeks stability and peace, we announce the joining of two great and powerful families of old Hayastan."

Seraphina beamed. Todd gritted his teeth. *How can she love that guy?*

"May our impending nuptials end hostilities among nations," Albrecht said, nodding at Todd. Seraphina blew him a kiss. "And with Mr. Helsingford's help, pave the way for our nation's future."

{34}

Todd approached the cave's blast door with misgiving. Despite the New Immortals' jubilance at the Allies' acceptance of Albrecht's peace terms, the new Shahanshah was taking no chances. Albrecht surrounded himself and the other New Immortals with their most trusted lieutenants before they marched out of the cave. Flanking them three deep on either side, the Anausavareds' devoted soldiers wielded machine guns, rocket launchers, and small arms in case of ambush.

Gifford's response to Albrecht's terms had been terse. Requesting that he needed an hour to notify all the Allied troops around Mt. Ararat to stand down, he reported the Allies' representatives would be ready to sign an end-to-hostilities agreement in the Ahora gorge. He also approved Todd as the American representative until Gifford arrived. The New Immortals' TV cameras confirmed the three generals who coordinated the attack on Zarkisian's stronghold awaited them a hundred yards beyond the cave entrance.

Todd's immediate concern was Seraphina's decision to marry Albrecht. Had she sold herself to stabilize the nation? Marrying one of her own kind and becoming a queen in the process made sense. Offering herself to him in the cave may have been the best opportunity she could get at the time, but the kiss she blew to him suggested that her offer arose from an impulse deeper than affection.

Can you handle another rejection?

Todd slapped the side of his head. He had loved Miriam once; he didn't love Seraphina now. She had made her choice; he was a fool not to accept her decision.

A train of New Immortals and Hayastani dignitaries filtered through the cave opening onto the Gorge's debris field. The early afternoon sun etched the canyon walls in moonscape relief and revealed the outcropping at the head of the gorge destroyed. Abich glacier was now a soup of ice and boulders gushing water down the mountainside hours after the attack.

Allied generals waited for the New Immortals in the lee side of one of those boulders a hundred yards down the valley. Wood planks nailed together lay across the hoods of two transport carriers parked side by side to create an improvised review stand. As he approached the stand, Todd overheard Captain Johnson conferring with a slight, wiry man with rimless glasses who looked more like a desk clerk than a brigadier general.

"We're waiting for Ambassador Gifford's helicopter to arrive," General Pierce said after exchanging greetings with Albrecht and the other dignitaries. "He told us to start the proceedings and that he'd arrive in a few minutes to fulfill our part in the ceremony."

Albrecht's nimbus darkened. "Take your defensive positions," he ordered. Following his hand gestures, his retinue fanned out and surrounded the review stand. Outnumbering the Allies' forces two to one, they formed a formidable cordon to prevent physical access to Albrecht, his fiancée, or the rest of the New Immortals delegation.

Albrecht stationed two protector drones at each end of the stand, donned the ceremonial spangenhelm, and waited for the other New Immortals to file onto the dais.

Seraphina paused at the foot of the stand and whispered to Todd, "I thought Gifford had given you full power to represent American interests."

"Must have changed his mind," Todd replied with a wry smile. "The State Department must have decided that the event was too important for a junior member of its diplomatic corps to handle."

Seraphina pursed her mouth and refused to mount the steps. Zarkisian, the other New Immortal who had yet to mount the platform, noted her hesitation. "Is this any way for the royal consort to act before our allies?" he asked, nodding toward Todd. "Are you afraid to sign a piece of paper?"

"Not at all," Seraphina replied with a shake of her head. "I don't like the seating arrangement, though. Why are the New Immortals' seats so high and prominent?"

"We're the feature attraction," Zarkisian replied.

Seraphina peered toward Albrecht seated in the middle chair of five chairs on the improvised dais. "Are you satisfied with these seating arrangements, Shahanshah?"

"We are the stars of this event as the Arteshbod said," Albrecht replied with a smile. "Shouldn't everyone witness our moment of triumph?"

"But I feel so exposed up there," Seraphina said, shielding her eyes from the glare of Albrecht's nimbus. "What if we're attacked?"

"From where?" Albrecht replied, raising his arms, and gazing around the area. "Our security people outnumber the Allies two to one." He beckoned her to the platform. "Come up and join me."

Seraphina hesitated.

"If you're dissatisfied with your seating location, take mine," Zarkisian said and pointed to the seat at the Shahanshah's right hand. "It's the next best seat in the house."

"Fine!" Seraphina retorted and mounted the steps. "I'll take it."

She paused at the top of the platform and turned toward Zarkisian. "You're not joining us?"

"In a moment," Zarkisian replied and gazed toward the bottom of the pass. "I'm expecting the helicopter DOD told me would come."

Helicopter? Nobody told me!

Captain Johnson nudged Todd's shoulder and pointed toward the Blackhawk helicopter flying over the ridge. "There it is."

The American and Turkish infantry forces parted in front of the dais. A utility helicopter painted with the State Department insignia descended to a height Todd estimated as fifty feet above their heads when all the Allied soldiers fell flat against the ground. Johnson clapped a gas mask over Todd's face and pushed his head into the dirt as the helicopter enveloped the platform in a pale yellow mist. Despite the mask, Todd smelled a pungent odor like a strong cough drop.

The New Immortals' guards retched green vomit. A few sprayed the airship with gun fire. Lethargy dominated the few who remained conscious. Some focused their fading energies on disabling the pilot; others focused on the Allied troops surrounding the platform. The helicopter sprayed a second cloud and everyone on the dais fell onto the floor.

Many Allied soldiers retched and vomited. Some convulsed, blood spurted from the mouths of the few who severed their tongues during their spasms. Others got to their feet and rushed the podium.

"Stay back!" General Pierce ordered.

Grumbling their reluctance, the Allied soldiers retreated while Captain Johnson accompanied by two medics mounted the stage. The medics inserted syringes into the shoulders of the half dozen New Immortals still quivering with life.

This is an outrage!

"Stop this atrocity!" Todd cried and ripped of his mask. "I wanted them stopped not poisoned."

He spun and confronted the General. "This is how we honor our agreements—by killing our enemies?"

"We killed nobody," Pierce replied and motioned for the medics to lower the bodies into lead-lined body bags. "What d'ya think the medics are for? DOD wants to study these creatures first."

"Study them?" Todd asked in horror.

"First lesson in warfare, son," Pierce said. "Know your enemy."

"Those 'creatures' had a peace agreement," Todd said.

"Nobody signed nothin'," Pierce replied. "Good gracious, son. What do you care?" He pointed at Albrecht. "That one's not even human."

"How can you say that?" Todd cried, his indignation erupting from his chest.

"Nothing human could take a double dose of GD and survive," Pierce replied as he signaled the soldiers carrying Albrecht down the steps to halt beside the helicopter.

"GD?" Todd asked, pulling on Pierce's arm. "What's that?"

"Soman gas, son," Pierce replied, cracking a smile. "A milder version of sarin but plenty effective at close range." He turned toward the soldiers hauling black body bags. "Make sure the one with the halo is sealed in an escape-proof container," he ordered. "DOD wants him studied first."

Two soldiers sheathed Albrecht's inert body inside a bag and tossed it into the helicopter bay. Another picked up Albrecht's spangled helmet from the floor of the dais and stuck it next to the Shahanshah's body.

Couldn't happen to a nicer guy.

Todd smirked despite himself. The soul of the new leader of the New Immortals had escaped from Hell. Now his restored corporeal self would subsist in diagnostic hell. Who would have foretold that fate?

His grin turned upside down when two medics deposited an unclosed body bag besides Albrecht's. Seraphina's open eyes stared upward and vacant beside her betrothed. With her full red lips and raven hair, she resembled a slumbering Snow White waiting for a wakening kiss.

A lump rose in Todd's throat. Beautiful, smart, sexy, and ruthless—he'd never felt this way about a woman before. True, she was treacherous, but wasn't she also the one who healed his burns? Hadn't she offered a cooperative solution to deal with the Hayastan parasites?

"Where are you taking her?" Todd asked.

"A place safe," Captain Johnson replied and climbed into the copter bay. "Where they can be studied."

"Where's that?" Todd asked, fearing the worst.

"What d'you care?" Johnson replied.

Todd's chin quivered. "Where *are* you taking her?"

"Never you mind where," General Pierce answered.

The medics loaded more New Immortals into the helicopter bay. Todd stepped aside. It appeared all the Hayastani survivors were destined to receive drug-induced arousals from lab-coated bureaucrats at remote testing facilities where their organic powers could be studied with minimal risk.

Such treatment is neither fair nor ethical.

Todd's chest tightened. Of all the outcomes, he'd never expected this one. Why hadn't Seraphina or another New Immortal incapacitated the pilot before he sprayed the poison gas? He stepped around the fuselage and peered inside the cockpit. A bundle of wires and hydraulic tubes occupied the pilot's seat—a drone helicopter.

The body of the last New Immortal entered into the helicopter, and Captain Johnson slapped the side of the hatch twice. "Let's go!"

"Is that all of them?" Todd shouted above the whirr of the rotor blades. When Johnson nodded in confirmation, Todd scanned the bodies inside the bay, counting five. "Is Zarkisian's body in there?"

"Five's the number we were told to take," Johnson replied. "And that's what we got."

Johnson grinned and closed the hatch door. Todd watched the copter rise into the air and clear the ridge.

Military efficiency.

Mission: Soul Sacrifice

Todd shook his head and ran to General Pierce's Humvee. "Where's Zarkisian's body?"

"His ain't in there?" Pierce asked while adjusting his seatbelt. "What did Captain Johnson say?"

"He said all five were there and accounted for," Todd replied.

"Well, then," Pierce said.

"But there were six chairs on the dais, one for every Anausavared dignitary," Todd replied. "But only five body bags were put in the helicopter."

"Maybe you miscounted the number of chairs," Pierce suggested. "Did you check the identity of the body in each of the bags?"

Of course not. Why should I? I wasn't part of your plan.

"We have to find him," Todd cried, fearing Zarkisian had escaped. "He's the most dangerous one."

"Worse than Albrecht?" Pierce chuckled and patted Todd's shoulder. "Don't worry, son; you did your job."

What have I done?

"You never told me this would happen," Todd said as Pierce's driver started the engine. "Why didn't you tell me?"

"And witness your hissy-fit over it?" Pierce replied. "No thanks."

Todd flushed with shame and anger. They'd never met before yet the General somehow expected Todd's reaction. "Can you tell me who gave you the order for this operation?"

"Office of the Deputy Director at the Department of Defense," Pierce replied, putting on his sunglasses. "That's all I know."

I know nobody there. Who would do this?

"I don't care who ordered it," Todd declared. "The outcome is unethical and unacceptable."

"A well-executed operation with no loose ends?" Pierce replied, taking the passenger seat. He grinned back at Todd. "Five enemy combatants sought, five captured. I'll take that result every time."

Zarkisian makes a bargain; DOD keeps its end.

"That's hideous," Todd said.

"Not my problem," Pierce said, shrugged, and nodded towards his driver. "They're under DOD authority now."

Stones and gravel spurted from under the Humvee's tires and sprayed Todd before the giant vehicle gained traction and rumbled away.

{35}

Two backfires wakened Victor from his stupor. The rough stitching underneath the canvas straps rubbing against his wrists and legs pinned him against his seat. A foot beyond his knees ran a line of Humvees down the center of what appeared to be a plane's cargo hold. His stomach flipped as the plane dipped and shimmied through the buffeting storm clouds.

Next to him Miriam clutched her arm rests in a death grip, a cross-strap harness locking her to her seat. On her other side, Evelyn lay splayed out and locked in her seat, unconscious.

How did Miriam get here?

An EDIC guard with a neck as wide as his shaven head eyed him from his vantage point at the head of the Humvee line. The plane hit another air pocket and dropped several hundred feet. Victor's stomach flopped and turned over.

Despite nausea and post-narcotic haze, Victor turned as far toward Miriam as his straps would allow and whispered, "How did you get here?"

"I don't know," Miriam replied, reaching around the straps crossing her chest and touching her forehead. "The last thing I remember was seeing the portal close in the Lower World before waking up in this plane."

Victor's heart skipped with joy. "Then Ahriman *is* defeated."

"I guess so," Miriam replied, squirming against her seat straps. They held tight. "But Albrecht slipped through."

The divine wild card. What powers will he have in ordinary reality?

"Let Todd handle him," Victor said with more conviction than he felt. They had more immediate problems. He glanced at Evelyn, stretched unconscious in her seat. "What about your mother?"

"I don't know," Miriam replied, her brows squinching with concern. "Mother, wake up!"

Evelyn didn't move. Miriam nudged Evelyn's shoulder. "Wake up!"

"Uhhh!" Evelyn moaned, raising a quivering hand to the side of her head. She peered at Miriam, then at Victor. "Where are we?"

"Quiet back there!" the bullet-headed guard growled. He turned and barked something in Slavic at the pilot and co-pilot inside the cockpit. After more turbulence and the plane dropped again, he stormed to the doorway and ordered the pilot to radio the landing tower.

"Now's our chance," Victor whispered to Evelyn who sat beside the cockpit door. "Lift the gun out of the guard's holster."

"I can't," Evelyn whispered in groggy voice. Her eyes glistened with pain and fear. "It's too dangerous."

"Are you crazy?" Miriam leaned toward Victor. "Risking a struggle when we could crash any minute?"

Victor scanned Evelyn. Her body retained the blue/black aura that had enveloped her at their airport hotel room. He closed his eyes and probed Evelyn's mind. Calm now, the aura shielded him from penetrating further into her subconsciousness. Did Zarkisian still control her actions?

"If you could undo the straps around my wrists, I'd do it," Victor said and retested the straps pinning his wrists. No give in them anywhere. He sat back and blew the air from his cheeks in exasperation. "We won't get another chance."

"Shut up back there!" the guard said. "Or I'll shut you up."

Victor balled his hands. A plane crash might be a better fate than what lay in store for him. "Look, Zarkisian won't welcome us with open arms when we land."

"How do you know that?" Miriam whispered. "We don't even know where we're headed."

"Look around you," Victor replied. "Do you know any other airline that uses EDIC guards as flight attendants?"

"At least he wants us," Miriam replied. "Unlike some mortals I could mention."

Miriam can't see the truth. Or won't?

"Zarkisian as a welcoming father figure," Victor chided. "You think everything's forgiven now he's gained control of Hayastan?"

"You don't know that," Miriam retorted. "There's been no confirmation one way or the other."

"I feel it in my bones," Victor replied and scanned Evelyn again. Her dark aura stirred and rippled around her body. "You would too since you inherited his powers."

"Be quiet," Evelyn said, slumping in her seat. "Both of you."

"See what you've done," Miriam said, wiping her mother's brow. "You've upset her. You know how she reacts to negative emotion."

"What *I've* done?" Victor said. "What about all the people Zarkisian sucked dry through her and Desdemona and other empaths like them?"

"Aunt Dezzie's an empath?" Miriam replied, surprised.

"A familiar, actually," Victor said, correcting himself.

"I had no idea," Miriam replied, frowning in chagrin.

"That's how she enabled you to return to the Lower World," Victor added. "Under Zarkisian's direction."

"It's so unbelievable to me—still," Miriam replied, and her eyes cast about the cargo hold. "Desdemona was returning with you. Where is she?"

Why lie about it?

"Dead," Victor replied.

Miriam's face crumpled. "How?"

"There was a struggle in our hotel room," Victor replied. "Your mother attacked two Homeland Security agents . . ."

Evelyn stirred beside her daughter.

"Were they hurt?" Miriam asked.

"No." Victor shook his head for emphasis. "Not seriously."

"But Desdemona died in the struggle?" Miriam asked.

"Yes," Victor nodded, hoping this story satisfied Miriam's curiosity. "Yes."

"At their hands," Miriam said.

Tell the truth, Victor. All of it.

"Well?" Miriam asked.

"She nee-needs to kn-know, Victor," Evelyn croaked, sitting up. Her voice quavered as if emerging from a pit. "Te-tell her what happened."

"I did it," Victor said. "Your mother attacked the agents and me under Zarkisian's direction, through Desdemona, and I had to stop him."

"By killing my aunt," Miriam said, horrified.

"It was her or us," Victor replied, watching Evelyn slide back against her seat. "I had to break the connection. It was the only way."

"You *had* to kill her," Miriam declared.

"She gave me no choice!" Victor replied. "Zarkisian put me in that predicament, knowing you'd react this way if I told you. Why can't you believe this?"

"Because he's my real father, maybe, I don't know," Miriam replied as she massaged her mother's wrists. Evelyn's face and hands adopted a healthier pallor. "Just as you ignore the obvious about my mother's health."

"Because I saved her," Victor replied and rattled his straps in frustration. "I was the one who retrieved her soul from the Lower World. Twice."

Why doesn't she believe me? Why does she resist the truth?

Victor watched Miriam's rubbing restore the color in her mother's cheeks. "You know what I told you is true. Why are you angry with me?"

"It's called resentment," Miriam replied. "Ever hear of it?"

After more rubbing, Evelyn opened her eyes and smiled. The plane dipped again. The guard scuttled back to his seat, and Evelyn clutched Miriam's hand.

"It's OK, Mother." Miriam wadded up her sweater as the plane leveled out and set it in the corner of Evelyn's seat as a pillow. "Try to relax. We're almost through this."

Evelyn settled back and closed her eyes.

Miriam leaned toward Victor, continuing where she left off. "You're the shaman. Figure it out. Where did Zarkisian get all his energy after you abandoned us?"

"You think it occurred after our divorce?" Victor replied. "Zarkisian's been after me for years!"

"After us," Miriam replied. "What better source of psychic energy could he have than a frightened woman who was the mother of his offspring?" She eyed Victor up and down. "And abandoned by the husband who's supposed to protect her."

I'm no martyr.

"What would you have had me do, Miriam?" Victor asked. "Should I have sacrificed myself for her? How? Becoming a shaman was the only way I knew to stop Zarkisian short of killing him."

"Did that not apply to how you dealt with Aunt Desdemona?" Miriam asked. "Or do you save your scruples for Zarkisian?"

Victor hung his head. "Killing Desdemona violates every principle a good shaman stands for. I'm sorry it came to that."

"Another in a long list," Miriam murmured.

"Yes, I have to live with it," Victor admitted and recalled his blood lust. "Yet I'm not sorry I did it."

A thunderbolt rattled the wings. Victor hunkered down in his seat while the plane shimmied fore and aft and back again. He realized now that instead of leading Zarkisian away from Evelyn, leaving her played right into Zarkisian's hands. Was all his pain and suffering to learn the shaman's secrets another self-deception? His stomach knotted. It couldn't be. "If you want to protect your mother," he whispered, "grab the guard's pistol next time!"

Another thunderbolt hit the wings, and the plane rattled violently. The guard removed his seat straps, hunkered down, and stole over to Victor.

"I told you to shut up!" He pulled the Grach pistol from his shoulder holster and slammed it across Victor's face, then poised the butt above the women. "That goes for the rest of you."

The guard retreated to the safety of the doorway. Victor smiled. Blood dribbled down his chin. "Still think we'll get a family welcome?" His iron spittle tasted delightful. His stomach growled. "Or do you welcome being a parasite, although a psychic one?"

Tears welled in Miriam's eyes. Her jaw hardened. "I want to slap you myself." She sat back in her seat and folded her arms. "I see now why Mother let you go."

"What do you mean?" Victor asked.

"It's more than just ego with you," Miriam said. "You can be cruel, too."

Lightning hit the tail, and the plane lurched upward at a forty-five-degree angle. The guard slammed into the first parked Humvee and stumbled against Evelyn's knees.

"Grab his gun!" Victor said.

Reaching around the cross-straps locking her into her seat, Miriam steadied the man after he propped his left elbow against his knee and lunged onto his feet. The plane leveled out.

"Thank you," the guard muttered in English. He whirled toward Victor and brandished his pistol. "As for you—"

"Please don't." Evelyn grabbed the guard's sleeve. "Don't we have enough mayhem already?"

The guard blinked, holstered his pistol, and returned to the cockpit doorway. "Land at the nearest airport," he ordered the pilot. "Now."

"Orsova is the nearest airport," the pilot replied.

The guard cocked his head toward Evelyn. "Hear that?" He glowered at Victor. "Lucky for you."

The plane's landing gear hummed, and the plane dipped forward. The guard scurried to his seat on the other side of the line of Humvees.

"Thanks," Victor whispered after the guard strapped himself in. "How'd you do that?"

"You wished it." Evelyn's brow curled upward. "Don't look so surprised, Victor. You know empaths channel emotions. Yours was the strongest at that moment. I strengthened your wish into his action."

She sighed and hunkered into her seat as the plane descended. "Did you want me to let him smack you again?"

Victor scowled. "Why didn't you have him give you his gun?"

"He wouldn't do *that*," Evelyn replied. "And Miriam wouldn't have allowed it."

"Why not?" Victor asked.

"She wants to meet her father." Evelyn closed her eyes. "And nothing will stop her."

Victor bristled. "You might have picked a better time for a family reunion. Like ten years ago."

"After you left us, you mean?" Miriam asked.

"I was keeping Zarkisian away until I learned how to defeat him," Victor replied.

"Are you certain of that, Victor?" Evelyn asked. "Or was that your rationalization for staying away?"

"What was there to come home to?" Victor asked, repressing his urge to turn away.

"Your family?" Evelyn replied.

"Quiet over there," the guard growled. "Just because we're landing doesn't mean I won't slug you one if you don't behave."

"A person doesn't become a shaman overnight," Victor said. "It took years of effort to gain the Ayumi's trust."

"A husband doesn't lose a family overnight either," Evelyn replied. "It takes time to neglect people so much that you don't matter to them anymore."

"You sought *me* out!" Victor retorted and saw the guard unhook his seatbelt. He didn't care. "You had to realize even subconsciously Kincaid would call me in on your consult because of our professional relationship."

"Did I?" Evelyn said, eying the guard as he rounded the Humvee. "Despite being there against my will? Or is that the narrative you want to believe? Some might say it was jealousy."

"Desdemona—"

"I said shut up!" The guard slammed his gun butt across Victor's forehead.

"—said so," Victor groaned.

"And keep it shut!" the guard said, pistol-whipping Victor again. Victor slumped forward and said nothing more.

{36}

Victor opened his eyelids and winced. Oddly, his forehead throbbed where the guard slugged him, yet he felt all right otherwise. Leather belts strapped his wrists and bare feet to a metal-frame chair inside a wood box.

His naked feet gave him pause. Why strip off his shoes and socks? For torture? Or to insure a smooth connection to the Lower World and its demons?

He studied the joints running up the walls. The gaps in the glue revealed an exterior metal sheathing—an orgone box. Its quality of workmanship resembled the window caulking he saw at Zarkisian's health spa.

I must be in Orsova.

How long had he been out? Were Evelyn and Miriam in the same location, or even the same country? If they were in Romania, years might pass before anyone learned of their confinement—or cared.

Control yourself.

To deal with Zarkisian and Ahriman's demons he had to maintain his optimism. Escape would require every ounce of positive energy he could muster. As long as he remained hopeful, regaining his freedom was still possible.

Victor wriggled his wrists and feet. The leather security bands held them fast. Since the End Time had not come as foretold, he somehow must figure in Zarkisian's alternative plan.

Stop speculating.

Letting his anxieties run rampant played into Zarkisian's hands. Zarkisian was a foe to be defeated. He dreaded this emotional parasite's powers so much he'd ruptured his own family to protect them—what Zarkisian had wanted all along.

If Zarkisian had been Victor's patient, he would have removed the demons that caused Zarkisian's fixation on him much as he had removed the eels controlling Evelyn. Treating the demons that fueled Zarkisian's psychic energy might work the same way.

Victor frowned. He could never penetrate Zarkisian's psyche to find out what those demons might be.

His skin tingled. *The New Immortals require human hosts so they can feed upon the energy that humans' psyches create.*

The latch clicked on his orgone box, the door opened, and Zarkisian stepped inside with the same pair of Romanian medics from Victor's previous confinement.

"The straps are not too tight?" Zarkisian asked, checking Victor's bonds.

"I'm comfortable, given the circumstances," Victor replied, scanning Zarkisian's mind. Zarkisian's psyche was impenetrable, as always. "But it's not the Hilton," he added and glanced about the interior. "What is this thing, anyway?"

"An orgone accumulator," Zarkisian replied. "It concentrates psychic energy to spark the libido."

Keep him talking. He loves to talk about himself.

"Would it be too much for a former colleague to ask what you intend to do with it?" Victor asked, hoping Zarkisian might reveal something Victor could use. "Or with me?"

"We intend to keep you here until a fair exchange can be made," Zarkisian said.

"I place a high value on life, including my own," Victor replied. "What do you consider fair?"

Zarkisian's eyes glimmered like candle flames inside a jack-o-lantern. "Your life and those of your family for Hayastan."

"You're kid—" Zarkisian's ploy must not have turned out as expected if he still didn't control Hayastan. "You think that the United States and her allies value our lives so much?"

"The leaders of the United States and its allies value the rule of law. Part of the law is the honoring of contracts as you and I know." Zarkisian's nostrils flared. "Their contract with me was a simple quid pro quo—the lives of Ahriman's followers for the Kingdom of Hayastan."

Surprise! How can I use it?

"But you're Ahriman's agent," Victor retorted in disbelief. "You acted on his behalf in the corporeal world."

"As a follower of Zurvan I followed the destiny of Lord Ahriman," Zarkisian answered. "But Zurvan's prophecy foretold that Ahriman's attempt at everlasting power would fail. And it has."

Victor pondered this new bit of information. Could Zarkisian's occupation of Mt. Ararat have been a ruse? Bombing the Ark outcropping and destroying the gorge could have been gambits in a chess game leading to Zarkisian's seizure of the New Immortals' throne.

Maybe Zarkisian took advantage of an opportunity—like Albrecht would. "Not all of the New Immortals could have agreed to the outcome that now exists," Victor said. "Albrecht in particular would have opposed it."

"He did." Zarkisian smiled like a boy savoring the candy stolen from an Easter basket. "He even wore the gold spangenhelm of imperial power for a while—before the American Air Force fulfilled its end of our bargain."

Victor grimaced. So Zarkisian *had* manipulated the Allies into eliminating his two primary competitors for the leadership of his ancient country. Even Ahriman was not so devious. "What's your end?"

"No attacks, either physical or spiritual, upon the representatives and citizens of the United States and its allies until my ascension to the throne and consolidation of power is complete," Zarkisian replied. "Terms and agreements that maintain and embellish our nations' mutual understandings to be worked out at some future point."

Geopolitics is Todd's realm, not mine.

Victor shook his head to clear it. "And my role in all of this?"

"Collater-r-ral." Zarkisian trilled and savored the word. "As the one person left capable of impeding my aspirations for our homeland, your fate represents the potential outcome for other nations should my demands not be met."

Victor shuddered. As a cat's paw among nations, the rest of his life would be spent as Zarkisian's hostage in an orgone booth like this one, alive long enough to secure Zarkisian's ambitions. "And my family?"

"What family?" Zarkisian replied. "My daughter and the empath who bore her?"

As vain as ever. And more heartless than I remember.

"They have names, Basil," Victor said. "Are you afraid to use them?"

Zarkisian raised an eyebrow in irritation. "They shall be recognized when the time comes."

"They are *your* family," Victor goaded. "Have you no feelings for them at all?"

"Have you?"

Miriam's argument thrown back at me.

"Everything I do—" Victor replied, quivering with indignation. "Everything I've done—stems from my love for them."

"Is that so?" Zarkisian leaned closer. Twin voids swirled in the pupils of his eyes. "Would a loving father abandon his family if he knew a fiend was after them?"

Mission: Soul Sacrifice

"I-I d-didn't have the tools then," Victor stammered. "I didn't have the knowledge."

"You spoke of love," Zarkisian added. "That arises out of feelings not knowledge."

"I needed to learn how to defeat you," Victor replied.

"Did you?" Zarkisian asked. "Or is that the excuse you used to escape your responsibilities?"

"What love have you shown?" Victor retorted, stung by an argument Miriam had used. "Other than using it to survive off humans."

Zarkisian pulled his head away and stood erect. "I have survived for over two thousand years committed to restoring the state of my ancestors."

"To an idea," Victor replied. "Not an individual."

Zarkisian scowled. "What commitment have you ever shown to Miriam and Evelyn other than to defeat me?"

"To protect them," Victor replied, but his chest burned inside. His answer rang hollow. Evelyn and Miriam thrived while he stayed away.

Had Zarkisian helped them while I was gone?

Victor shuddered.

"I was Vahagn," he protested. "The one chosen to defeat Ahriman. Akvan said so."

"And what has that gotten you?" Zarkisian pointed at the door. "Miriam and Evelyn are outside. Ask them how much your being Armenia's chosen one comforts them."

Victor's chin dropped to his chest. He had done everything in his power to prevent Ahriman's takeover, but for what—his own glorification? Jealousy? That made him no different than Zarkisian.

Zarkisian's viewpoint is self-serving. It must be.

Victor drew himself up and threw out his chest. "Do you have any personal feelings for them?"

349

"The Anausavreds have none of the sentimentality that passes for feelings among humans," Zarkisian replied. "Miriam and Evelyn Gorovic are important to the future of Hayastan and shall be venerated in that regard."

Victor weighed the options. Gifford and Helsingford may have believed they could control Zarkisian, but his ambitions would not stop with the fulfillment of their proposed agreement. "When would your consolidation of power be complete?"

"What's the customary determinant in matters of royal succession?" Zarkisian's twisted smile betrayed how much he relished Victor's misery. "Production of an heir."

"With what available candidates?" Victor asked. A horrifying possibility emerged. His heart pounded. "You can't mean Evelyn."

"Not likely," Zarkisian replied. "Royal blood must course through both sides of one's parentage for the heir to become legitimate."

Victor groaned. One person met that standard—Miriam.

I have to kill him.

It was the only solution. He killed Desdemona to protect Evelyn and Miriam, but he never directed the dark side of his shamanic powers on any being. But with the murders of Desdemona and the Walter Reade Security guard already on his hands, his scruples, as Miriam pointed out, seemed insignificant in light of everything that happened.

Zarkisian smiled with amusement. "You're thinking I need to be eradicated and wondering how to do it. Anyone who has lived as long as I have foresees all possibilities."

"On the contrary," Victor lied. "I was contemplating how to heal you."

"Heal *me*? I have lived two millennia," Zarkisian said. "What in the world makes you think I need anything to help me?"

I struck a nerve.

Victor's mind raced. Pride in his self-sufficiency might be Zarkisian's Achilles heel. "In all that time you needed no one? Never cared for anyone? Never wanted someone to hold you?"

"There have been plenty of human females," Zarkisian replied. "Hundreds."

"But none that aroused feelings of love in you," Victor countered. "Or produced a male heir."

"It's more than a matter of succession." Zarkisian frowned. His neck flushed. "Because I'm an Immortal, you think I'm incapable of attachment?".

Victor grimaced. Glimpsing Zarkisian's softer side didn't make his ambitions more tolerable.

If Zarkisian can feel love, he can feel mercy too.

"A loving father does not condemn his daughter to Hades while she is still alive," Victor retorted. "Nor procreate with her. If you care about Miriam at all, stop this. As one man to another."

"A gentleman's agreement?" Zarkisian chuckled and shook his head. "We New Immortals have greater concerns than to worry over human sexual taboos. Sympathy and pity are not options for us."

You haven't lost him yet.

"Just something to manipulate us poor humans with," Victor replied. "Is that it?"

"What do you mean?" Zarkisian asked with uneasiness.

Play the hook.

"Was it love or pity that drew Evelyn to you?" Victor asked.

The fire in Zarkisian's eyes dimmed. "What does it matter? The results are the same."

Keep the lure before him.

"Are they?" Victor licked his cracked lips. Let Zarkisian squirm for a change. "It can't be love because Anausavareds don't believe in it. With pity, you can never be sure whether their compliance is complete and certain."

"That's where you're wrong," Zarkisian declared.

Careful, don't lose him now.

"Am I?" Victor replied. This was the delicate and dangerous point in therapy where epiphanies occurred, and transference took place. "Think it through, Basil. Evelyn's an empath. What other human emotions could she feel toward you and your kind except pity and sorrow?"

"Ridiculous!" Zarkisian eyes and mouth curled downward. "If she wanted me by the nonsense you humans call love, so much the better."

Keep him dangling.

"Maybe so," Victor replied. "But love is a two-way emotion whose power is everlasting. Sympathy gives out because one tires of giving energy to the person who needs it."

"You're wrong!" Zarkisian said. "I need no one. I am immortal."

Don't lose him!

"Through the compassion of humans," Victor declared, ignoring his training and better judgment. "Or those you can deceive or manipulate. Without us, you and all your kind become extinct."

"That's a lie." Zarkisian crossed his arms in defiance. "The sole reason you've lived so long is because I willed it."

Got him!

"Ha!" Victor crowed in jubilation. He glanced around the wood interior and grinned. "I thought I owed it to your under-active sperm count."

Zarkisian's face contorted into a seething cauldron of menace and revenge. He snapped his fingers, and both orderlies sprang into action. One tightened Victor's straps; the other inserted a red ball-gag into his mouth.

Mission: Soul Sacrifice

"The exchange of psychic energies between host and master can be a pleasurable experience," Zarkisian said and unlatched the door which allowed Victor to glimpse Evelyn and Miriam sitting in the front row. "Or it can be quite the opposite, depending upon the mood of the master and the reserves of the host."

Now you did it!

Pain rippled through Victor's body like an orgasm without climax. The gag turned his screams into impotent snorts.

"No clever taunts? No lightning ripostes?" Zarkisian leaned beside Victor's right ear. "Do not despair. Your final role shall be most honorable."

He scanned the box's interior. "Through this device we shall focus your psychic energy to help propagate a new line of Hayastani royalty."

{37}

After Zarkisian closed the booth door, Victor's energy drain began. Hundreds of tendrils gnawed the edges of his consciousness and sapped his willpower.

Victor hummed his shaman's song for protection, his ball-gag reducing it to a gargle, but its vibrations rippled throughout his body. A warm, semi-conscious state opened a wormhole in his soul. He rode the ebb and flow of the energy emanating from his heart and glided down his autonomic nervous system to his solar plexus.

A sunny glow surrounded the autonomic ganglia that controlled his body's digestive and energy-producing systems. He homed in on the psychic furnace enveloping his solar plexus, and summoned his aqueous power animals, the silver salmon.

Pizca led three score of salmon up through the patalas or psychic portals in Victor's feet, swam up his energy streams, and met him at his spiritual furnace. "What would you have us do?"

"Form a protective cordon around my body's energy generator," Victor said.

The last power salmon assumed its position when Zarkisian's eel demons arrived. They deployed into eight squadrons of a dozen eels each. Each squad spread out into quadrants about his solar plexus until they surrounded the nerve nexus. Each squad divided into four groups. Two harassed the salmon while the other two strafed the outer layer of Victor's plexus like kamikaze bombers crashing into a battleship.

Victor's corporal body reeled from the impacts. His power salmon darted, nipped, and harassed the attacking demons, drawing them off course. Most of the eels' attacks missed, but their cumulative successful impacts reduced Victor's resolve.

Their sixth attack cracked open the myelin sheath that encased his solar plexus' splanchnic nerve. The demons' sharp-edged tendrils rasped and tore at the neural walls until they ripped a chunk of fiber from its casing. Three of the eels latched onto the sides of the opening and widened it, the other sucked out the nerve energy within. Shivers of pain cascaded up and down Victor's limbic system.

When one eel grew full, another eel demon replaced it. The sated demons discharged their absorbed energy at Victor's salmon and obliterated one, two, and then an entire squad of Pizca's cohorts. The eels zoomed through the gaps in Pizca's defenses and siphoned off more energy.

"We need reinforcements, Victor!" Pizca cried.

He tried. No response. The eels had drained enough of his psychic energy to inhibit his contacting the Lower World.

No reinforcements, apply defensive tactics.

"Have Pizca draw the cordon closer to the plexus," Victor ordered Sorel, chief among Pizca's subordinates. "That will give the remaining salmon smaller areas to defend."

The demons' attacks increased in intensity. For every eel Victor's salmon distracted or dislodged, two more demons hewed to his splanchnic nerve casing and gobbled up energy.

Victor's soul reeled from the attacks. Bouts of pain followed waves of euphoria. Clarity battled with nothingness. His psyche lurched between conscious control and spiritual defeat as his energy reserves neared zero.

He brought Pizca aside during one of his clear moments. "Scatter into my blood stream," he said. "I can't hold off my psychic enslavement much longer. Hide in my body recesses. Be ready for guerilla attacks to reclaim my soul later on."

Mission: Soul Sacrifice

Tendrils thrashing, the eel demons chased the fleeing salmon to Victor's aortic arch where the salmon dispersed into Victor's upper bloodstream.

Pizca limped back moments later with his tail fin in shreds and half his dorsal fin missing. Three salmon out of the dozen in his squadron followed behind him damaged in similar fashion.

"Where are the others?" Victor asked, weakened by the eel's onslaught.

"Destroyed, gone!" Pizca gasped. "Instead of haring off in a dozen directions to pursue us like they often do, the eels' pursuit is more systematic. They blockade the major arteries and veins extending out of your heart and higher organs. Then they fan out in groups of three and search every capillary until they find us."

Under Zarkisian's direction.

"Not their customary behavior," Victor said, fearing the worst. "And if they find you?"

"No mercy," Pizca replied. "Once they find us, they destroy us—everyone."

Three energy bolts scorched the tissue lining the aorta above Victor and Pizca's head. Victor peered toward the bottom of the aortic canal. Three more eels turned from black to indigo while charging for another barrage.

"Withdraw! Everybody Withdraw!" Victor ordered. "Head for the femoral artery. Regroup at the femoral junction!"

"That's what they want us to do!" Pizca replied. "Chase us to the bottom of your body, trap us, and exterminate us one by one."

"It'll buy us time," Victor replied. "Until I think of a workable alternative."

Victor and Pizca fled with their remaining two squadrons down the artery. Glancing behind them, he saw Zarkisian's eels deploying as

Pizca described. Using Victor's eviscerated solar plexus as a base, a battalion of demon eels headed down each of his femoral arteries.

At each contributory artery and vein, a company of twenty eel demons swam into the blood vessel that nourished each leg. Darting in and around the leucocytes, red blood cells, and other detritus floating in his bloodstream, the demons fired energy bolts at the fleeing salmon and blasted the limbic nerves embedded in the linings of Victor's blood vessels.

Rocked by the concussions, Victor's awareness of his physical surroundings ebbed from his consciousness. Images of Evelyn and Miriam conferring with Zarkisian alternated with the slaughter of his salmon power spirits alongside him, then faded away. When he no longer received stimuli from outside his body, Victor focused his remaining conscious resources on protecting the spirits that tried to protect him.

Region by region the demons completed their purge until just a handful of Victor's spirit salmon remained in hiding among the dorsal veins and arteries at the bottoms of his feet. Whenever he sent the salmon toward the escape portals under his arches, the waiting demons discharged their energy bolts and obliterated them.

"What now?" a despondent Pizca asked after his last report. "They cut off our escape."

What options do I have?

"A truce might buy us some time," Victor replied and pointed at Sorel. "Accompany Pizca to negotiate a truce."

"You haven't many spirit animals left." Pizca placed a fin on Victor's arm. "It's better I approach them alone."

Pizca swam forth to confer with the eels. Three eel demons changed color, discharged their energy beams, and disintegrated him.

Pitiless beings—like their master.

Mission: Soul Sacrifice

"How many spirits will you obliterate in my behalf?" Victor cried.

"What is it you want?"

"VICTORY!" the eels replied.

"If I surrender," Victor countered, expecting the worst, "will you and Zarkisian let my spirit animals return to the Lower World?"

"Complete annihilation is the sole acceptable result," the lead demon yelled back. He approached the hiding place of Victor's dwindling band, the tendrils of his sucking mandible writhing in voracious anticipation. "Zarkisian already has you. Unfettered access to your body is the prize we seek."

"On whose behalf?" Victor asked.

"All the demon forces of Dakhanavar," the demon replied.

Under Zarkisian's direction!

Victor evaded the energy beams the other two demons leveled at him and fled to a cavity in the artery wall formed by the demons' energy bursts.

They had little time. If Ahriman's eel demons obliterated all of Victor's salmon, they would have unfettered access through the patala openings. Zarkisian could then channel all the demons of lust, aggression, and murder from Dakhanavar through Victor. The only way to prevent such a power surge was to have his Lower World salmon close access on their side.

"Pair off," Victor said to his handful of remaining salmon as the eel demons surrounded their hiding place. "Head toward the patala across from this blood vessel."

"Don't do it!" the salmon warned. "You saw what they did to Pizca."

"It's our only chance," Victor replied. He emerged from their protective cover and waved the first pair of fish forward. "You must go back to the Lower World."

"Our duty is to remain here with you," the salmon declared.

"You and your brethren risk complete obliteration on my behalf," Victor said as he heard the agitated demon eels darting back and forth in the middle of his blood stream arguing which one should have the final blast. "I'm honored by your loyalty, but I can't let you sacrifice yourselves just to protect me. It is my obligation to return you to your existence in the Lower World."

He edged out into his corporal bloodstream and beckoned the first pair of salmon forward. "C'mon. Hurry!"

"You cannot trust them," Sorel declared. "They will destroy us as soon as we enter your blood stream."

"Use me as a shield," Victor said as he edged along the blood vessel wall. "These demons are not so foolhardy as to destroy the soul on which their master feeds."

Seeing the demons' turmoil increasing, the first wave of salmon edged out from their hiding place safeguarded behind Victor. When the first pair passed through the patala openings, the remaining duos lined up behind Victor.

He swam upstream to the midpoint in his peroneal artery that marked his patala threshold.

"Halt," the lead demon ordered. "You know we can stop you."

"I gave you your chance for a rational solution," Victor replied. "You want the salmon, but you cannot kill me."

"Can't or won't?" the demon said.

"It amounts to the same thing," Victor replied and edged further into the lukewarm current. His body temperature had plummeted. "Even demons cannot be so stupid."

His insult and the eels' gluttony destroyed their grasping the consequences inherent in Victor's argument. Their bodies charged from black to electric blue.

Victor dispatched the first salmon pair toward the blood vessel wall. Three energy bolts obliterated the fleeing fish spirits.

Mission: Soul Sacrifice

The remaining eels closed in for the final annihilation. Even if he shielded his four remaining spirit fish to the patala gateway, the demons would zap them out of existence before they crossed the threshold. His soul alone had a chance of surviving the eels' energy blasts. If their blasts destroyed it, nobody could stop Zarkisian. Miriam could thwart his plans if she was willing, but she'd be all alone.

Unless I let them.

He scanned the four openings of the nearest patala and frowned. They served as a gateway for spirits from the Lower World, good and bad, to enter this one. If he sacrificed his soul, the salmon could reenter spiritual reality. And all the vice and evil spirits from the Lower World could enter this one through his body.

Victor smirked while savoring a wicked thought. Kincaid never would have expected Freud's destructive urge, Victor's mortido energy, could be used for such a creative purpose. And Ahriman, now confined to the Lower World for all eternity, would never miss the chance to send his spirit demons to avenge the person who sent him there—Basil Zarkisian.

His choice was clear. If he stood aside, Miriam's human compassion from her mother's side alone stood between Zarkisian and a new nation of psychic parasites. If he gave up his soul, Ahriman would send all the demons of Dakhanavar and beyond into Victor's body, Zarkisian's personal reservoir of psychic energy.

My last chance—all I have to do is seize it.

Still, he hesitated. Besides the social and moral proscriptions against destroying one's life, he wondered if Miriam would take advantage of his sacrifice. His powers had dwindled too much for him to procure reinforcements from the Lower World, much less to inform her of this scheme. Even if she knew about it, would she cooperate knowing the ploy was his?

Am I asking too much from her?

He recalled that Miriam faced a similar choice before he entered the soul of the female Wailer. Their souls connected then. In their long history of mutual bitterness, would that shared moment be enough?

"Duck!" Sorel cried.

A dozen salvos of energy strafed the membranes of the cell tissues protecting him and his spirit salmon. Cellular fluid gushed everywhere.

It has to be!

"Go!" Victor shoved the four salmon toward the threshold. "As fast you can! Now!"

The eel demons surrounded them. Two eels discharged energy blasts at Victor. The others obliterated his spirit salmon.

Victor emitted a soundless scream. His deadened soul floated in the debris of his bloodstream, flushed out of his body, and bounced headlong down the caverns, outcroppings, and dead-ends to the Lower World.

"Ooof!" Victor cried, landing on his back. His spirit might now be in the Lower World, but the ground there felt rock hard as in corporeal reality. He rolled onto all fours, got to his feet, and peered about the gloom. No chants, lamentations, or explosions. No sounds anywhere except the Lethe's waters lapping against the shore beneath the bluffs of the Asphodel Meadows.

All the captive souls had returned to the corporeal world. Wodenaz, Freya, the Valkyries, and the shamans who aided them had vanished as well.

No bloody glow outlined the mountains of the northwest horizon. The river of lava descending into the Lethe was a delta of crusted pumice. The charred struts of Ahriman's war carriage lay buried in the rock, clawing the leaden sky. No fissure opened to a brighter world; what Wailers remained did not keen for their stolen souls. Nor did silver salmon or milk-white horses gallop up and pledge their loyalty.

Mission: Soul Sacrifice

Behind Victor three lines of dead souls snaked up the ravine toward the Plain of Asphodel for their final dispositions. Like them, Hades was his final destination, too.

"DAMMIT!" Victor cried. His expletive echoed among the cliffs, reverberated across the river, and faded among the reeds of the marsh on the opposite side. "Why here? Why me?"

Victor fell to his knees.

"Damn this place," he muttered, head clutched between his hands, another captive in a wasteland he helped create. "Damn me."

{38}

Miriam comforted her mother in the front row of the hospital amphitheater. The events of the past twenty-four hours paled in significance to her mother's fragile condition. Even in the Lower World, Evelyn had never looked so drawn and wan.

Zarkisian stepped down from the dais and sat in the chair next to Miriam's. "Welcome to Orsova Rehabilitation Hospital and Clinic."

"Why are we here?" Miriam asked. "Why not an American hospital?"

"Your legal circumstances do not permit it," Zarkisian replied. "Your mother's medical condition, however, made immediate hospital treatment imperative. Given my contacts with the Romanian government, the local medical authorities were most obliging."

Miriam scowled, wondering at the nature of her father's relationship with the Romanian government given his CIA background. "Then why is Evelyn in this theater instead of a hospital room?"

Zarkisian glanced at the nurses busy with cleaning the theater's medical equipment. "I have a proposal to make," he said, pursing his lips. "Custom requires that it be done in public before the intended's parents."

Intended? Miriam glanced at her mother and back at the eager Zarkisian. For whom? Albrecht was her betrothed before their descent into the Lower World. Something must have happened to him after he escaped from Hades.

Miriam eyed her father, careful to appear non-committal. She detected no energy emanating from this man but the tug of bottomless emptiness. "Where is Albrecht?"

Zarkisian placed his palms together. "Dead."

"How?" Miriam asked. If Albrecht was dead, it had not happened without bloodshed. "He was immortal."

"Soman gas, a nerve agent from the sarin family. Administered at the hands of the United States Air Force." In terse sentences, Zarkisian described the surprise gas attack that had leveled everyone who attended the treaty signing. "Albrecht and the other Hayastanis never had a chance."

What isn't Zarkisian telling me? What's he hiding?

"How do you know this?" Miriam replied. "Weren't you there, too?"

"Prior experience has taught me never to trust my opponents when they hold the upper hand," Zarkisian replied, peering at her over his fingertips. "Albrecht learned that lesson too late."

Trust no one.

Miriam mistrusted the messenger but had no reason to doubt Zarkisian's truthfulness on this topic. She felt little sympathy for Albrecht but calling the saturnine figure standing before her "Father" felt ridiculous. Outrageous. Yet the emotional pull was there, strong, insistent. Undeniable. "So, your hopes to establish a new nation of Hayastan have disappeared?"

An eerie leer crossed Zarkisian's face. "Not yet. My proposal depends on your cooperation."

Zarkisian's hiding something, something I don't want to hear.

"With Albrecht gone the Shahanshah's throne is vacant," Miriam said, crossing her arms over her chest. "What about Lord Ahriman?"

"He is still in Dakhanavar," Zarkisian replied.

Good. Keep him there.

"And Victor?"

Zarkisian opened the orgone box after Miriam asked this question. "Here receiving treatment," he replied. "With everything that's gone on, his physical and spiritual resources have grown quite depleted, I'm afraid."

An orgone box. This isn't treatment, it's torture.

Miriam stifled a gasp. Bound and gagged, Victor appeared near death like her mother. "Why is he gagged?"

"For his own protection," Zarkisian replied and closed the door. "Patients often bang their heads and bite their own tongues."

I doubt that.

"You said you had a proposal," Miriam said, gripping her chair arms in anticipation. Whatever this creature proposed, she would reject it regardless of her emotions or family ties. "What do you have in mind?"

"The nation of Hayastan is not dead," Zarkisian said. "A few of its sons remain to resurrect the country in all its former majesty." He scanned Miriam's face for a reaction. "They need a sign, a symbol that their dream of Ararat is not dead, that their struggle continues, that the nation goes on living."

"Aren't you enough?" Miriam chuckled. Envisioning Zarkisian as a patriot was laughable. "Wasn't Ahriman supposed to make the corporeal world a heaven on earth?"

"Ahriman failed. As Zurvan fated him to do," Zarkisian replied. His gaze softened. An expression resembling tenderness replaced his usual hauteur. He took Miriam's right hand and stroked the back of it. "Don't you see? We're free for the first time to do anything we want."

His caresses felt like eels slithering across her skin. Miriam withdrew her hand.

"Marry me." Zarkisian moved forward until their knees touched. "I'll get down on one knee, if you like."

He peered into her eyes. His aura intoxicated her. Miriam felt like a bubble rising in a glass of champagne—uplifted—as if nothing was beyond her power to see or do.

"Impossible." She shifted her hips to regain her freedom of movement, but Zarkisian's knee prevented it. "After everything that's happened, you expect me to marry you?"

"Why not?" Zarkisian asked. "We can make a new beginning—for ourselves and for our country."

Think. Think!

"But I'm not one of you," Miriam protested. "I'm not Hayastani."

"Yes, you are," Zarkisian replied. "More than any other you are fit to be the consort of the Shahanshah because of the blood coursing through your veins."

Miriam gasped. She rejected everything this creature stood for. Yet he also was her father, her biological sire, and she, his heir.

She glanced at her mother. Evelyn's face remained pallid, her features inert. Zarkisian was in total control. Could this possibility for Miriam's nuptials be the secret Evelyn kept all these years? Impossible. Not even Freya had such foresight. Miriam squared her shoulders. "Daughters don't marry the men who father them."

"Nonsense," Zarkisian replied with a sweep of his right arm. "The pharaohs of Egypt married their daughters all the time to perpetuate the royal line."

"This is not ancient Egypt," Miriam replied. "And I won't be matriarch for a new line of human parasites."

"You are Anausavared, like it or not," Zarkisian replied, thumping his fist on the chair arm. "A New Immortal. You feel it in your bones."

Can this be happening? Is Zarkisian right?

Miriam shook her head. Memories of withstanding Ahriman's demons and subduing Freya surged through her like a tonic. As queen she could pass on this power to a new race of immortal beings. The prospect was intoxicating.

"You'll do it?" Zarkisian asked.

Mission: Soul Sacrifice

Can a cub reporter from New York be queen of a race of psychic vampires?

Miriam bit her lower lip. The notion was preposterous, unbelievable. Yet, it was within her grasp. She had the power—the rapture in Zarkisian's amber eyes confirmed it.

"If I don't?" Miriam asked.

"You will die."

Miriam stared at Zarkisian's expressionless face. His ardor had dimmed. His statement did not seem like another scare tactic, yet his threat must be another trick.

Isn't it?

"It is the price of our immortality," Zarkisian said. "To remain immortal, we must mate with another Anausavared. It's why there are so few of our race, including females."

"But you've lived centuries—eons!"

"I know." Zarkisian folded his hands in his lap, his left knee lodged between hers. "Feeding on the misery of those around me, searching for another woman of my heritage—my frustration grew so great I had to create her myself." He glanced at Evelyn and returned his ardent gaze to Miriam. "You."

Miriam felt honor—outrage—revulsion. Even pity. But not love.

Zarkisian grasped her hands in his. "Even Anausavareds cannot escape the biological imperative. You must become my bride—your well-being, and that of our entire race, relies upon your acceptance."

Evelyn stirred in her seat; behind Zarkisian, Miriam saw Victor convulse once and lay still.

His death rattle?

Evelyn's eyes fluttered, focused, and narrowed upon Zarkisian's face like laser beams.

Miriam suddenly felt nothing but pity and contempt. Despite the prospect of centuries-long passion, the perpetuation of their race and the assurance her own well-being, she must refuse. Better to die than bear more parasites that fed off the anguish of the human race.

She shook her head no.

Zarkisian pried her knees apart, grabbed her wrists, and pinned them against the back of her chair. Miriam squirmed and struggled, helpless. She writhed back and forth under the ferocity of his attack, freed her left hand, and clawed his face.

Something gave way. Miriam's right hand jerked free.

"Yowwow!" Zarkisian jerked upright and clapped the left side of his head where blood gushed out.

"Bitch!" he cried and slapped her face hard. "Bitch!" And twice more. "Whore! Mortal!"

Miriam teetered on the edge of consciousness. Zarkisian pulled off her jeans, ripped away her panties, and pulled down his pants. His throbbing member penetrating the lips of her vagina snapped her back to consciousness.

Behind him, Miriam glimpsed Evelyn tottering to her feet. She lunged forward, grabbed Zarkisian's shoulders, and hurled him aside. Like twin harpies, mother and daughter pummeled the ancient parasite with their fists until he collapsed to the floor, blood still gushing from the left side of his head.

"Aargh!" Zarkisian cried, stumbled to his feet, and heaved the women aside. He headed for the stairs, but Evelyn cut him off. Miriam tackled him around the shoulders, but Zarkisian spun and hurled her away. The two women regrouped and pummeled him together, front and back, driving him against the stage.

Evelyn attacked first. Zarkisian sucker-punched her mid-section and dropped her to the floor. Miriam jumped on his back, but he threw her off, rolled her over, and pounced upon her like a cat after a mouse. Pinning her wrists above her head, he penetrated her again.

Mission: Soul Sacrifice

Miriam squirmed, struggled, scratched everything she could reach. Thrusting her hips upward, she focused all her energy on repulsing the thrust of his engorged male organ.

An enormous spasm rippled up the right side of Zarkisian's body and down the other. His eyes rolled back, he shuddered again, sat upright, and toppled sideways onto the floor.

Gasping and coughing, Miriam pushed him away and struggled to her feet. Zarkisian did not move. She knelt beside his body, alert to any movement, and checked his pulse.

Finding none, she unclenched her right fist. The pulp that was Zarkisian's left ear plopped onto the floor. She swatted the remnant away, placed two fingers against the left side of Zarkisian's neck, and rechecked.

Nothing.

{39}

Victor stood in line before the marble dais, waiting for Aeacus' final pronouncement. He still twitched from the attacks that had eviscerated his primal energy. Total annihilation of his spirit would be preferable to the lingering, agonizing hell to which the eel demons condemned him.

Zarkisian wins.

He tromped ahead in line, head down, seeing no one. Refusing the oblivion offered by the Lethe's soothing waters was Victor's final rebellion against the psychic parasite who ruled him.

The rugged peaks on the western horizon turned silver. The change in light prompted him to glance toward the skyline where a translucent disc bathed the strand in hoary radiance as it ascended toward the zenith.

Ignoring the press of petitioners around him, Victor followed the orb's march into the sky, his wasted spirit soaring free like a plane at take-off. Embracing his final annihilation with open arms, he rose to meet Destiny with a steadfast heart and a lover's desire for release.

Soft, smoldering clouds brushed his cheek and caressed his cracked lips, eyes, and mouth like twin fluffs of pink milkweed.

Oblivion isn't all bad.

Forgotten fires ignited inside him. Victor returned the caresses with feeble ardor and opened his eyes. A radiant oval loomed over the boundaries of his vision. Eyes, nose, primrose hair scent—a dozen scattered sensations coalesced into Evelyn's enchanting smile.

His lips, tongue, and palate felt cumbersome as boulders. "E— Eve— Evelyn."

Evelyn offered him a tumbler of water. "Don't drink it too fast."

This is Elysium?

The liquid quenched his tongue. Over her shoulder, he glimpsed the afternoon sunlight coursing like melted honey through the open window. His bare arms raked across a ragged plain of fresh cotton sheets. Was he back in the corporeal world? Or another form of hell?

Two more discs floated into view. One passed along the far end of his bed and uttered a language he did not understand. When it descended and lay at the other end of the pillow, its features coalesced—Miriam.

A hospital nurse packed the external defibrillator back into its case. After a brief consultation with the attending nurse, Amina Pahlavi left the room.

"Wh-where am I?" Victor asked.

"Orsova General Hospital," Evelyn replied. "At Ambassador Gifford's insistence."

He relaxed—for a moment. "Zarkisian?"

"Dead," Evelyn replied. "At least his body is."

"May his soul rot in the ninth level of Hades," Miriam added.

"Ahriman?" Victor asked.

"In Dakhanavar," Evelyn answered. "Forever."

"At last." Victor wept. A weight heavy as an elephant lifted from his chest. "You're alright?"

"Reborn!" Evelyn laughed and kissed his lips. "Like you."

It felt good to hear her laughter—joyous, in fact.

More perilous questions await me.

Victor wiped his eyes and turned to Miriam. "And you?"

"Zarkisian attacked me," Miriam replied. "I fought him off."

Good.

"Had to be done," Victor replied.

Miriam's brows knitted. "What did?"

"He had to kill himself," Victor said.

"How do you know?" Miriam retorted. "You were in the orgone box. Unconscious."

"My body was dead," Victor corrected her. "My spirit stood in Aeacus' line awaiting final judgment."

"Then how did—"

"It was him or us," Victor declared, his head rising from his pillow.

"There, Victor," Evelyn said. "It's all over."

"No," Victor replied, shaking his head. "She needs to understand." He tugged the pillow corner forward and propped himself up on one elbow. "With Ahriman trapped in Dakhanavar in fulfillment of Zurvan's prophecy and Albrecht eliminated by the U.S. government, Zarkisian became the Shahanshah of the New Immortals."

"I'm aware of that," Miriam replied.

Will she believe this? Do I?

"H-he needed to produce an heir to legitimize his claim to the throne and perpetuate his race of psychic parasites," Victor continued. "The only way to stop him was if he took his own life."

"With everything he wanted within his grasp?" Miriam replied. "Not likely. The doctors told us he died of massive cerebral hemorrhage."

"He did," Victor agreed. "But overcoming you and your mother's resistance without my psychic energy to sustain him strained his physical body's resources to the breaking point."

Miriam's eyes widened with skepticism. "You mean he exhausted his energy supply?"

"With me dead, and acting as a portal from the Lower World, there was nothing to stop all the demons of hatred and aggression in Hades from taking control of my body," Victor said. "And Zarkisian absorbed them."

"Demons killed him?" Miriam replied, shaking her head in disbelief.

"They took all his psychic energy until he had nothing left."

Miriam looked away, trying to absorb what Victor said.

"And you knew that would happen?" she retorted, turning back to him. "You planned that?"

"I-I hoped f-for it to h-happen," Victor croaked, fumbling for water. After a sip with Evelyn's help, he added, "I knew Zarkisian. And I trusted Evelyn. I hoped you would react like any human female would. With me dead, everybody would behave according to their primal urges, given the opportunity."

"With me as the staked goat," Miriam muttered, her upper lip quivering. "To cause my father's death."

She understands. Does she accept it?

"Our only chance was in your rejecting Zarkisian's proposal," Victor explained. "Your resistance amplified by your mother's empathic powers thwarted his ambitions to the point of releasing the death impulses which consumed his body."

Victor flashed a rueful smile. "His own demons sealed his fate when they destroyed my body and exiled my soul to Hades."

"I would have returned to Hades rather than become his bride," Miriam said.

"I know."

Miriam backed away from Victor's bed. "And you counted on that."

"To save you," Victor replied. "And every human on the planet."

What can I say to make things right?

"It was a necessary sacrifice," Victor declared. "On both our parts." He scanned Miriam's face. The hatred in her eyes seared his own. "There was no other way."

I've failed.

Mission: Soul Sacrifice

Victor fell back against his pillow, exhausted. *I sacrificed and I failed. Again.*

"There was no other way," he repeated in a tiny voice. "We did the only things we could."

"That's supposed to console me?" Miriam retorted. "Playing my part as bait to be raped?"

"You did the right thing," Victor murmured, staring at the ceiling. *I wanted—I expect too much.* "The only thing."

"It is," Miriam agreed in a sarcastic voice," if defeating your sworn enemy is the only thing that matters in life."

Huh?

"What do you mean?" Victor asked, indignant.

"What father—" Miriam spluttered with scathing contempt, "what person would ask what you did of any woman, much less his daughter?"

I'm her real father. She admits that, but—

"You're saying I'm to blame?" Victor asked in amazement.

"Who else?" Miriam replied. "Who else sacrifices his family in a single-minded quest for revenge?"

"Zark—"

Me, that's who. Victor flushed. *From her standpoint I AM wrong.* He fell back against the bed. *Wrong and self-centered.*

"I'm sorry I asked too much," Victor said in self-reflection. "I have far to go, I know." He extended his right hand toward both women. "But with all of us together again—"

Evelyn hesitated, cast an encouraging smile at her daughter, and clasped Victor's outstretched hand between hers; Miriam stormed out the doorway.

****

Todd Helsingford closed his laptop, rubbed his eyes with the heels of his hands, and stared out the window. His face remained puckered and tender over the skin graft along his hairline. A snowstorm on the Turkish side of Mt. Ararat gleamed above the peak like a visor on a burnished helmet in the afternoon sun.

His deputy vice-consul rapped on his office door and stepped inside the room. In the months after the explosion, Damon had been indispensable in keeping the registration section operable. With the rest of the staff killed or in the hospital, Gifford assigned Todd to manage the embassy in Yerevan until his relief arrived and Todd returned to the States for a formal hearing on his part in the Ararat rebellion.

"Sorry for the interruption, Sir," Damon said. "But do you have time to examine a passport application? The woman's passport shows American citizenship but claims her father's citizenship gives her the right to enter Turkey."

"What was his nationality?" Todd asked.

"Hayestani," Damon replied. "So she claims."

One person would be so bold as to claim that nationality.

"Send her in," Todd said, pursing his lips. His hand trembled as he flicked the switch of the tape recorder inside his desk. The State Department wanted transcripts of all applicants who wanted entry based on citizenship in the rogue state of Hayastan. "Wait outside."

A willowy woman dressed in a stylish black jilbab or outer coat and matching abaya strode into the room and took the seat in front of his desk.

The hijab or veil draped over her forehead prevented Todd from seeing her face. "Why do you wish a passport into Turkey?"

"I wish to return to the homeland of my ancestors," the woman replied.

"Why not go to the embassy in Istanbul?" Todd asked.

Mission: Soul Sacrifice

"They do not recognize Hayastani citizenship," she replied.

"Neither do we," Todd said. "What makes you think you have a better chance receiving a passport here in Armenia?"

"Because you are an honorable man, Todd Helsingford," Miriam replied, removed her shawl, and smiled. "Whatever our personal disagreements, I've always trusted your ability to do the right thing."

Miriam's formality pained him. Her characterization made his honesty seem like a personality flaw.

"All of our decisions are based within the guidelines agreed upon by embassies of both countries," Todd said. "Your request has neither the practical nor moral value to benefit either the United States or the countries of Turkey and Armenia."

Miriam's eyes widened. She slammed her fist on his desktop. "I must get back to the land of my ancestors."

"Why?"

"I feel it." Miriam rose from her chair and approached the office window. "My destiny calls me." She beckoned toward the horizon. "Out there."

"Due to the aftershocks, Turkey's eastern border remains closed to all foreigners," Todd said as he scanned her outline against the window. Her silhouette seemed thicker since the last time they met. "They wouldn't allow you in even if I signed the passport myself."

"You got in," Miriam said.

Todd grimaced. "And almost got killed in the process."

Miriam turned toward him with pleading eyes. "You won't help?"

"Can't," Todd said. "Even if I could."

"Why not?"

"You know why." Todd noted the bump beneath Miriam's stomach under her jilbab. "We can't take the chance."

Miriam's jawline hardened. "I'll sneak in as you did."

"Do what you must." Todd sighed. "But under the circumstances I cannot provide official sanction for your request."

Miriam pulled the jilbab over her head and strode to the door. The folds of her abaya swirled about her ankles like plumes of dust.

Todd rose from his chair. "If you stay in Armenia, you'll find the view of the mountain top spectacular from the monastery chapel at Khor Virap."

He cleared his throat. "Mr. Arkadian, the metropolitan there, knows the area's history very well."

Miriam retraced her steps, and Todd sat back in his chair. She bent down and kissed his forehead. "Thanks for the tip, Scout."

Todd squirmed. The moist imprint of her lips resurrected feelings long dormant. Even Seraphina with all her preternatural energy hadn't roused his affection as much. "Mir—"

Miriam turned and swept out the doorway. Todd approached his office window and scanned the petitioners entering and leaving the embassy's new security checkpoint. Beyond the automobile drop-off, a woman wearing a black abaya scurried up the sidewalk toward the outbound bus stop on Izakov Avenue.

THE END

Note from the Author:

Thank you for taking the time to read my book. Please consider leaving me an honest review (on Amazon, B&N, Goodreads, etc.). It is how I grow as an author and lets me know that I entertained you with a good story—no better compliment.

Warmly,
William 'Bill' Fietzer

About the Author

William 'Bill' Fietzer is an author, blogger, avid golfer, and YouTube addict. He moved with his wife and their Norwegian forest cat, Selene, to Poughkeepsie, NY from Minneapolis in 2019 to be closer to their sons' families on the East Coast.

He has published academic, newspaper, and online articles and stories about librarianship, the Twin Cities, the Hudson Valley, and national cultural scenes along with three novels. His first two novels, *Penal Fires* and *Metadata Murders*, examine America's underworld of class, crime, and technology. His third, *Mission: Soul Rescue*, adds the paranormal to that mix. His forthcoming novel, *Mission: Soul Sacrifice*, continues his investigations into our spiritual and cultural realities.

Mission: Soul Rescue

Book One of the *Escape the Immortals* Series

First book in the 'Escape the Immortals'; a series of novels that will explore the soul's power to nurture—or to destroy.

After many years of research in the Amazon, Psychologist Victor Furst finally acquired the shamanic ability to detect psychic vampires and retrieve the souls of their victims. As happens with endeavors driven by passion, his discoveries would not come without sacrifice—his wife, Evelyn, grew tired of his absence and left—taking his precious daughter, Miriam, with her.

As though commanded by fate, he finds Evelyn again when his old rival at the CIA, Basil Zarkisian, abducts her consciousness, leaving her body lying in limbo as though in a coma; diagnosis—Alzheimer's disease. But Victor knows Evelyn is in no coma and Alzheimer's is just for cover...

Victor is in a race against rebels and time. His hope for Evelyn lies with her eccentric sister and—Miriam. Miriam will be a tough sell when Victor reveals what he will need to help Evelyn...